The Nexis Secret

Barbara Hartzler

MORE TITLES BY BARBARA HARTZLER

The Nexis Series:
The Nexis Secret
Crossing Nexis (November 2015)
The Nexis Conspiracy (2016)
The Nexis Crusade (2016)

Waiting on the Lord: 30 Reflections
a 30-day devotional

The Nexis Secret

Barbara Hartzler

Printed in the United States of America

First Printing, 2015

ISBN: 1927154421

ISBN-13: 978-1-927154-42-7

Splashdown Books
Auckland, New Zealand

Editor: Grace Bridges

www.splashdownbooks.com

Cover Design by Jessica Martin / Indie Design Haus

Cover photographs © Vitaly Krivosheev, Fotoschlick, R.Babakin, Belphnaque, iko via Dollar Photo Club

For my Granna, who fought her own darkness and
found a way back to the light.

May I live up to the legacy you left behind,
carrying the light wherever I go.

PROLOGUE

A world of white blinded my eyes, but I couldn't blink. Too much effort. Vague outlines, then silhouettes of color emerged from the whiteness. The ivory outline of a man's face, his hair glowing like sunshine, his eyes full of light. "It's going to be okay, Lucy. You're going to be okay."

My eyelids sank shut. Too heavy.

The smell of antiseptic singed my nostrils. Faint voices wafted through the background. Mom's hushed whisper, "I don't know what to do with her. How can we just send her away after this?"

Dad's low growl, "We don't have a lot of options." His muted baritone faded into the darkness.

My eyes fluttered open.

A hospital room—finally something normal. So white, but not blinding anymore. The same bright-eyed man stared down with golden cat's eyes, a smile etched into his perfectly-sculpted face.

"Who are you?" I croaked through parched lips.

"Just here to help. You've been through a lot." With every syllable, warmth twinkled in his clear eyes, soothing my aching head.

"What happened?" I propped myself up on my elbows. Then the white world tilted on its axis. My head thudded back to the scratchy pillow.

"Easy there. You don't remember the accident?" His smile faded, but no frown lines creased his face. His finger hovered over my forehead. With a light touch, like the wings of a butterfly, it grazed my temple.

It all came back to me.

There they were, on the couch. My boyfriend with his arms wrapped around my best friend. His face smushed against hers, lips locked. I winced. How could they? Acid rose in the back of my throat as tears clawed at my eyes. I'd sprinted out of her house, then hopped into Mom's minivan and sped off. The tires of the family van hadn't peeled out like I wanted. Not even a squeal, how humiliating. Such a lame getaway car. So I revved the engine and ignored the speedometer. My hands had trembled so hard the steering wheel shook. When I wiped my eyes I veered off the road— straight into a tree. My head hit the dash, and it all went black.

Instinctively I reached for my forehead, brushing my fingers against the bandage over the incision at my temple. "Ouch." Back to reality.

"Major ouch." The man eased my hand down. "Better get some rest now."

"Good idea." I tried to smile, but my lids drooped again. His golden light drifted away.

Swoosh. I jerked awake.

A woman in scrubs drew back the curtain. "Doctor, she's waking up."

The sunshine man was gone and the day had darkened.

A light lasered into my eyes. A white-coated bald man flicked a flashlight at me, then withdrew it. "Pupils normal. Hello there, Miss McAllen."

"Where am I? Where's my family?" The words gurgled from the back of my throat, as if I hadn't spoken in days.

"They'll be along shortly." His beady eyes peered at me behind frameless glasses. He pulled out a pen and scribbled something on his clipboard. "Do you remember what happened?"

"Kind of, there was some kind of accident." I closed my eyes. The memory popped and crackled into focus like TV static. "I was upset, I swerved. Didn't see the tree until it was too late. How bad is it?"

The doctor flipped through the pages on the clipboard. Then a low whistle pierced my ears. "You were unconscious for a few days. There's a severe cut on your head, you lost some blood. Don't worry, we fixed you right up."

"What do you mean?" I clutched the side of the bed and pulled myself up. A shockwave pounded through my forehead, then the room wobbled and I slumped back down. "Like brain surgery or something?"

2

"Nothing like that." He dropped the clipboard at my feet and pointed to the IV bag full of clear liquid. "Just fluids to rehydrate you, and a transfusion. Head wounds can bleed a lot, especially if left untreated too long."

I raked my fingers through my long hair. Whew, it was all still there. I rubbed the dark ends against my lips. Soft, but greasy. "I need a shower."

"Your head injury required stitches. Eleven, to be precise." He handed the clipboard to the nurse and she disappeared down the hall. "You rest now. Nurse Sherry will check on you later."

"Okay, doctor." As he padded to the door, a chill crept through the empty room. I called out after the white coat. "What about that nice guy who was in here earlier? Is he a nurse?"

"I don't think you've had any male nurses in the three days you've been at Cedar Creek. Maybe a tech or something." He waved and dashed out the door.

Whoever the golden stranger was, his smile made me feel better. Somehow, he was the only one who did. Would anything ever be normal again?

1

Rough tree bark bumped against my fingertips, jagged as the scar at the edge of my hairline. The ridges blurred through my memory, then sharpened back into reality. It wasn't the same tree I'd plowed into to get myself shipped here, after catching my boyfriend frenching my best friend. Excuse me, ex-boyfriend and ex-best friend. This tree bore a different mark, unmarred by my mistakes. It marked the start of something fresh, something I needed so badly. A chance to put the past behind me—the first day of my new life.

I smoothed my fingers once more down the bumpy bark, as if I could simply wipe it all away. Then I turned to face my new reality at Montrose Academy.

So long Indianapolis, Lucy McAllen has moved on to bigger and better things. That's right, me, a sixteen-year-old, on my own in the Big Apple. The city of possibilities. Okay, just outside the city. More like Riverdale, New York to be precise. But still, what could be better?

The August heat suctioned my long hair to the back of my neck like a wet mop. Too many strangers jammed onto one sidewalk, it reeked like a cow in someone's smelly old gym sock. I wiped my moist palms on my plum tank top, but the stink hovered above the orientation-day crowd.

A guy squeezed next to me in the crowd. He flashed his piercing gray eyes at me, not to mention an adorable chin cleft, and waved a flyer in my face until I reached for it. "Welcome to Montrose. Hope to see you there." His cinnamon breath spiced the air.

I opened my mouth to respond, but nothing came out. Cute guys tended to have that affect on me. He tilted his chin up, like he knew it was his best feature. Or was he just trying to get me to read the flyer in my hands?

With a fire-like logo it announced the Nexis Society's new recruit drive. Odd way to put it, like it was some kind of fraternity. Must be as elite as my parents seemed to think, judging by the linen paper and gold emblem. Apparently becoming a Nexis member from Montrose Academy would be my ticket to a full ride at Yale. Not to mention back onto the parental honor roll. Enough plans to make my brain somersault into eternity.

The flyer fluttered in my hand. My brother, James, was Nexis president two years ago. Could this group help me find some connection to him? He hadn't spoken to me, or anyone else in the family, since he graduated. Bumming around Europe does that to people, I guess.

I scanned the crowd for my mystery man, but he'd already disappeared. No doubt the orientation dragon swallowed him up. Then someone ripped the flyer from my hand. The thick paper sliced through my flesh.

"Ouch." I pressed my fingertip to my tongue. "What'd you do that for?"

Another guy crumpled the paper against his polo and banked it off a tree trunk into the trashcan five feet away. Show-off. I glanced up to say as much, right into the most gorgeous eyes ever.

Hold the phone—smolder alert at the orientation fair. At least six foot with dark hair, aqua-blue eyes. Almost the exact negative of Nexis guy. Hello, hottie.

"Sorry, I didn't mean to hurt you. You should stay away from that guy, his group, too. You'll be a lot better off without them."

"Who made you king of the school?" I ground my teeth together, nicking the inside of my cheek. A metallic tasted filled my mouth. Yeah right, like it was his job to tell me what to do. "You don't know much about girls, do you?"

"Hold it. Why do you say that?" Those blue eyes seeped through my thoughts, muddling them into mush. I had to focus on something else. A gust of wind tousled the hint of curl in his dark hair, offset by pale skin that highlighted a dimple on his cheek. Okay, anything else. His mouth pressed into a hard scowl. That would do.

5

"Do you always answer a question with another question?"

"Touché." That scowl didn't last long. He held out his hand. "I'm Bryan Cooper. What's your name?"

My fingertips sparked at his touch. Probably just the paper cut. "Lucy McAllen."

His eyes widened like I'd just told him I came from the moon. He held my hand so long I almost pulled it back. Finally, he shook it. "Please, educate me on girls, since I have no clue."

"If I must." I wriggled my hand from his tight grip. Wouldn't want to give him any ideas. "Girls don't like to be told what to do. Next time ask or suggest something if you ever want it to happen."

He belted out a laugh so loud people stopped and stared. Then he doubled over. Seriously? One good jab to the ribs and he'd crumple to the sidewalk. He'd deserve it too, for laughing at me, but I wasn't that brave.

He propped his hands on his knees. "You're right, my mistake."

When he glanced up his blue eyes were hovering at my level now. Automatically, I backed up. "Don't let it happen again."

"Whatever you say, Lucy. See you around sometime." He stood up to his full height and waved, a laugh still lingering in his eyes.

I fought the urge to roll my eyes as he disappeared into the crowd. Like I really wanted to see him around. Hotties were always dangerous, especially ones with gorgeous eyes. The next time I saw him, I'd let him have it.

Teenagers packed the orientation fair. They surrounded me on all sides. I blinked at the clipboard shoved in my face. Can we say personal space, people?

The fabulous roommate I met this morning pushed her way through the snarled lines and snatched the orange Astronomy Club sign-up sheet from me. Her twelfth clipboard today. Shanda Jones needed an intervention.

"Let's take a walk." I slid my hands into the pockets of my frayed jean shorts.

"Okay, just a sec." With an ebony hand she flipped dark braids over her shoulder and grabbed another clipboard, scribbling her name on it.

I peeked over her shoulder. "Fall play tryouts? I say go for it." Memories of my stint in Alton High's drama club fought their way forward.

Shanda's eyes scanned my face like she didn't believe me. "Why don't you sign up, too?"

"Not me, I don't need that kind of pressure right now." The crowd caved in on us. Who could see anything in this maze of people? "I've been dying to explore the campus on my own."

On tiptoes, I gazed beyond the herd. Green lawn and freedom lay dead ahead.

"Sure. Let's get out of here." She carved a path through the pack of teens and parents. "I took the grand tour a few months ago. One of Dad's houses, the Central Park condo, is less than an hour away."

Wow, her dad must be loaded. Why wasn't he here? Probably the same reason my parents were AWOL—busy, busy, busy.

A light breeze blew across my face. "Much better." I inhaled the fresh air.

I had a feeling I'd love this school as much as James did. The Montrose campus sat on a hillside nestled above the Hudson River. Off to the west, green lawns leveled off into a quad of brick buildings that flanked a Gothic stone chapel on the far ridge. Those gorgeous arches and stained glass windows begged for a closer look.

"Eye candy at two o'clock." Her manicured nail pointed out a sandy-haired heart-breaker zipping down the cobblestone sidewalk across the quad. "He's got some potential."

"Not a bad pick." Tousled hair, but cute with the right amount of chisel, kind of like the mystery flyer guy. Why couldn't I go one day without thinking of boys? This was at least the second one today. *Get a grip, girl.* Like I could think about dating again after my last debacle. "So not happening."

"You wanna bet?" She raised a pencil-thin brow at me. "I can help you snag him."

"No way, I'm not into dating right now." I smacked my hand over my mouth, but the truth popped out before I could stop it. At least my brain won the battle of the hormones, probably because the nearest guy was fifty feet away.

"What?" She halted in the middle of the sidewalk, mouth wide as the sequined outline of Mick Jagger's lips on her rocker tee.

I plowed straight into her shoulder, and the horrible images rushed back. Clear as the cloudless sky.

7

Jake and Becca, kissing on the couch, tangled together. Their faces followed me anywhere, even a thousand miles away from home. I blinked hard and the scenery turned watery.

"Bad breakup?" Shanda's smile was soft.

"Yeah." I couldn't smile back, my lips just twitched.

She nodded with a familiar expression that said maybe she'd been there, too. "Wanna talk about it?"

"Not really." I shook my head. "I just want to start fresh. On my own terms."

"Understandable." She didn't say anything more, just resumed the pace like nothing ever happened. Now that was cool.

We marched on in silence, stopping at the stone steps of the chapel.

Like a mini Notre Dame Cathedral it towered above us, even more breathtaking up close. A kink formed in my neck from staring up at it. "Impressive, don't you think?"

"It's supposed to look that way, or no one would pay the huge tuition bills. Soon you won't even notice these cobblestone sidewalks or your so-called impressive buildings with too many steps. But if you start swooning over the benches dedicated to someone's dead grandmother, I'll have to kill you."

"Fine, I'll swoon in silence." I slapped my palm against my forehead and dropped to the nearest bench. "Bring me my smelling salts."

"Get up, girl, you're missing the true gem of Montrose." With her finger she outlined an enormous stone tower behind the chapel and the quad. Its white dome gleamed in the afternoon sun. "That's the observatory. It's huge. I can't wait to use the giant telescope."

"Now who's swooning?" I laughed as she helped me up. Overhead the sky sparkled bright blue, not a wisp of cloud. Yet a damp smell hung in the air, like the fragrance after a big rain.

Chiseled guy tackled the steps two at a time. A larger-than-life shadow trailed behind him, almost wraith-like. Weird, since the afternoon sun was nowhere near low enough to cast that kind of shape. At least I learned something in art class. Maybe another building refracted the light or something. He disappeared into the tower and so did the shadow.

I blinked and everything looked normal again. I must've stared at the sun too long.

Once classes started I wouldn't have time to worry about boys. As if I'd ever go for future Ivy League boys and senators' sons anyway. Dream on.

2

I had to make it to the top, or Mom would kill me. I jogged up the cement steps to the tower, my flats pounding louder than my heartbeat. The observatory rose from the top of the hill like a steeple. A domed pillar of brick watching over the whole campus. Night wind whipped my hair into my eyes, darkness closing in. I tossed the strands back, glimpsing moonlight once again.

Shanda's braids flapped in front of me as we booked it up the wide steps. "C'mon. We're missing all the fun."

My heart thundered, still two beats behind her. "We're never going to make it on time." The path dimmed with each step, even the moonglow faded. Only a glint of gold pricked through the darkness.

"I think it's in here." In the shadows she pointed out an engraved plaque etched with the words, *Stanton Observatory, established 1847*.

"Figures." Mom's voice danced in my head, cheering me on. Now I knew why she wanted me to "look up that nice Stanton boy." For once I actually listened, though not on purpose.

Something sank in the pit of my stomach and shot down to my knees. I wanted to run back into the moonlight, but I followed Shanda into a wood-paneled foyer. A familiar damp smell clawed my nose.

"Welcome, ladies." A brassy blonde ushered us toward a spiral staircase that snaked up the tower. She swept her hand over a tag on her shirt, Colleen. "I'll get you all set up."

She handed me a nametag and I plastered it below the sequins of my black t-shirt. Wouldn't want to trash Mom's expensive back-to-school gift.

"This better be good." I whispered to Shanda.

"You're telling me." Her stilettos clicked against the metal treads as she spiraled up the tower at a steady pace, like it didn't faze her one bit.

I gripped the sleek wrought-iron railing until my knuckles went white. Under my feet, the steps groaned and squeaked like an out-of-control carnival ride. Butterflies on caffeine flocked to my stomach. So I focused on Shanda's concert t-shirt. Phoenix, Denver, Shreveport. The name of each city numbed my swirling brain all the way up. At the top my feet found the hardwood floor and practically squealed their thanks.

Somehow the white-domed room felt airy and dark all at the same time. Moonlight slanted in from a giant panel propped open for the telescope. "What kind of club meets in an observatory?"

"The really cool kind, obviously." She pulled me over to a cluster of folding chairs.

"Obviously." My knees wobbled as I plunked down in the metal chair.

He stood at the center of the room. That so-messy-it's-cool sandy hair and those gunmetal grays flashing at me like they did this afternoon. "Welcome to the Nexis induction meeting. I'm Will Stanton, club president."

No, that couldn't be him. The whole room faded into darkness, refocusing around him. I curled my fingers under the cool metal seat until the world stilled back to normal. Mom's choice might be a tough one to turn down. Warning sirens blared in my head. *It's too soon. Remember what happened last time?* But Will's velvety voice lulled them into silence.

"We're an elite social club of gifted students. All of our graduating members have been able to attend the Ivy League college of their choice." The cleft in his chin waved at me as he looked around the room. "That's because we only recruit the best of the best. Each of you has been invited because of your academic or family status. If you decide to join, you'll meet the rest of the members during initiations."

He continued with his spiel, but I lost myself in those eyes. They sparked silver, right in my direction. Like he'd actually pick me over the Barbie dolls in the crowd. How could a girl concentrate on anything else? The patter of clapping jolted me back to reality.

How had I missed the whole speech? Wow, I must be losing it.

"You got it bad." A trademark cackle escaped Shanda's throat as the applause died down.

"Do not." But I couldn't help stalking him with my eyes across the room as the Barbies circled. Then I caught Shanda's expression, like she could probably read my mind. "Why, is it obvious?"

She snorted, yet somehow glided like a swan to the enormous telescope. I followed close on her heels. Anything to escape the strange feelings flocking around some guy I didn't even know.

Her fingers slid down the white cylinder, caressing the eye piece. She gazed up at the night sky, then moved the scope with a swift flick of her wrist. "Take a look at this."

I pressed the viewfinder against my eye socket. Three bright dots formed a glowing triangle. "Pretty. What stars are they?"

"One star, two planets." She counted it out on three fingers. "Saturn and Mars with a star called Spica. I'm calling this formation the August trifecta. They'll be in different orbits by next week when September comes. Enjoy it while you can."

"We aren't talking about stars here, are we?"

Her back arched over the telescope. "Don't get your hopes up about these guys. You've got to be loaded or a genius to get accepted with this crowd." She lowered her voice a notch. "And I don't think they're just trying to get into Ivy League schools."

"Don't tell Mom and Dad that." I shuffled toward the open slat in the dome to check out the night. So many stars dimpled the sky. They always made me feel small, but also kind of important. Like I might actually be on this planet to do something really cool. "My parents insist we have some inside family connection. If I joined Nexis they'd do a backflip. You have nothing to worry about. Your dad's loaded, right?"

"Yeah, but we're new money kind of people." She fiddled with the silver knobs on the side. "Sure, Dad wants me to be an Ivy Leaguer like your parents. It's the uppercrust breed of people that go there, that revolve around clubs like this. They're pretentious, not anything I want to be a part of."

Someone knew what they were doing when they paired us as roommates. I nudged my shoulder into hers. "Maybe that's why Nexis needs people like you. To burst their bubble."

"Good one." Her lips curved into the tiniest smile. It faded fast. "I still don't know."

"Honestly, this isn't really me, either. Just following in my family's footsteps." I chewed on my bottom lip. Could a posh prep school group be my only ticket to happiness? Probably not, but my parents would disagree. So let them. "I want to make my own mark."

Shanda's face lit up in the moonlight. "Maybe we're more alike than I thought."

Will and a blond guy muscled a path toward us in the dwindling crowd. "Hey, Lucy."

He said my name. The room wobbled like the rickety staircase all over again.

"How'd you know my name?" My voice came out froggy. How embarrassing.

"James was my mentor freshman year. You look a little like him, only much cuter." His white teeth were bright against the shadows.

Petals of heat crept of my neck, my cheeks. The darkness became my new best friend.

"You got a second? There's something I want to show you." His shining eyes made me wonder if I could ever be ready for what he had to offer. "Wait here. Kevin will entertain you." With that odd command he disappeared back into the shadows.

Kevin offered his hand to Shanda. "Where are you from?"

She shook his hand and angled toward him. "I'm from the city."

He crossed his biceps over his chest. "How cool. I'm from L.A."

She bobbed her head and moved to the scope. "Let's test the range on this baby. Wanna see Saturn's rings?"

"Sweet." He spiked up his hair and bent over the eyepiece.

I inched as close to the open slat as I dared and sat down, dangling my feet over the side. The moon bathed me in her silvery light. As the glow washed over me, the sky looked surprisingly normal. Almost like it did back home. What would my family be doing this Saturday night? Paige was probably out with her friends, Mom and Dad at some generic charity function.

Will's hand weighed on my shoulder. "Check this out."

His deep voice sent a shiver down my neck. I jerked back. With strong hands he steadied my shoulders.

"Careful now." He plopped down next to me and crossed his legs over the edge. Between us he opened a leather book with a symbol on it, an embossed circle of raised lines, like flames around a cross. "This is the history of our group. Since the beginning of Nexis, anyway."

I watched him turn the thin parchment pages, filled with strange words. "Is that Latin?"

"Very good." He flipped the pages, quicker and quicker each time, finally pausing on a picture of a woman with a halo around her face. Her eyes were dark and shadowed. The whole time he stared at me. "It's the founding tenets of our group."

I kicked the side of the tower. "She's a saint, right? Is she the founder of Nexis?"

He narrowed his eyes like I was under a magnifying glass. "Only members are supposed to see this book. Since you're practically one already, I'll give you an overview."

He would break the rules for me? I lifted my gaze from the ancient book and found him watching me again—his lips curled into a crescent, a slight dimple in his tan cheek. I could stare at this guy all day, especially with the way he studied me like he was actually interested. He angled closer, his voice low. "We have certain beliefs about the way things should be. There's so much potential out there for us, just waiting to tap into it."

Not another lecture on potential. I straightened my torso, putting some much-needed distance between us. "We're high schoolers, all we have is potential."

He dug his fingers into his short scruff of golden-brown hair. "If you join us, then we can help you realize your potential. Believe me, it's more than you think. You interested?"

I let my eyes wander from his face back to the book. The saint's picture seared into my brain, as if I'd seen it before. I tore my gaze from her hollow eyes to stare up at the moon, inhaling a much-needed breath. Everyone called it the man in the moon, but the face I saw in the sky was too pretty to be a man. So, I always called her the woman in the moon. She smiled down at me, like she wanted me to give this guy a chance.

"With so little to go on? Doubtful."

"Here's something you probably didn't know." He flipped to a black and white photo taped onto a back page. "As president, your brother oversaw my initiation. He made all the guys in our group drink a gallon of milk. The girls had to drink a half gallon." Sure enough, five guys and five girls were lined up, chugging on milk bottles, white liquid spilled over their clothes.

James stood behind the group, hands in the air. That familiar grin across his face. "Gross, bro."

Will turned from the photo and looked at me. "No one could drink it all. He said that was the point. We all needed to learn to fail at something before we'd ever really be good at anything."

Mist clouded my eyes. James always had a way of goofing off, and then turning serious when he needed to. All with his life-affirming spin on things. "I miss him."

Will's hand squeezed my shoulder. "I didn't mean to upset you. I thought you'd want to know how your brother loved this group."

"I do want to know." Pressure bubbled behind my eyes. I scrunched up my nose to keep the sting of tears back. "What do you remember about him?"

He slammed the book closed, with a grin on his face. "No more free info until you join."

"No fair. We'll see about that." I pushed myself up and reached for the book.

He stood just as quickly and hoisted it over his head. No way was dimples here gonna keep me from my brother. I jumped for the book, my fingertips grazing the brass emblem.

Butterflies dive-bombed the pit of my stomach as the bottom dropped out.

In a split-second I was transported to a dark field. Pillars of torchlight formed a semi-circle around James, his face contorted with fear. He reached for me. I stretched out my hand to him, but he faded away.

15

Then the ground buckled under my feet as stubby grass morphed into charcoal hardwood again.

The toe of my silver flat caught a nail in the floor. I lost my balance and teetered toward the edge of the platform.

Will's strong arm encircled my waist, pulling me toward him. Away from the tower's ledge.

Bang! The book thudded on the floor.

I flinched, and his other arm wrapped around my back.

"Are you okay?" His gray eyes sliced open the shadows.

The butterflies soared straight to my chest and clogged my lungs. I couldn't nod my head, I couldn't blink. Like a statue, the expression on my brother's face stamped in my mind.

Will's hand slid from my waist, the other steadied my back. "You're fine. I've got you."

Each breath brought more oxygen, more clarity. "I'm so glad you caught me."

"Me, too." His eyes softened around the edges. "I kinda want to keep you around."

I smoothed my hair down, my fingers bumping along the edge of my scar. It kicked off a drumbeat in my brain. Could I have some lingering head damage from the car accident six months? Or was I was losing it?

"I better get going now."

"You sure you're okay?" His eyebrows scrunched up like an upside-down V as he helped me to the stairs. "I hope that didn't scare you off."

I shook my head. It made the pounding worse. "You've given me a lot to think about."

His lips lifted into a smile. "Good. You've got a real shot if you want to go for it."

That charming face didn't scare away the fear rising in my throat as I descended the wobbly stairs into the darkness, my overworked heart thudding like crazy in my chest. Instead, James' scared expression, his hand outstretched, followed me into the depths. Did I just imagine the whole thing, because of this dark tower with its creepy haunted-house stairs? Or did something really happen to my brother because of this group?

"Wait." Shanda's voice rang out behind me. "I'll walk back with you."

She sped out the door and dragged me down the path, practically wrenching my arm out of its socket. She glanced around the empty quad— the strangest expression on her face. Bending down to tie her shoe, she motioned me to do the same. I crouched next to her.

She hissed in my ear, "This should do it. I didn't want to tell you before, because they might've heard. They're not using that telescope to watch the sky."

The air stilled around us. "What do you mean? It wasn't pointed down or anything, was it? Plus, you showed me the August trifecta."

"Please," her breath puffed in my face, "like they'd be so obvious as to point at what they're actually looking at. But they didn't bother to change the focus. They have it zoomed out too much. You can see the trifecta with the naked eye. Look." She outlined the three stars with her fingertip.

I blinked and looked up at the black sky. She was right, I could see the three stars almost as vividly as I'd seen them in the telescope.

"Real astronomers would want to see Saturn's rings, not stuff you can go outside and see for yourself."

"So if they aren't watching the sky, what are they watching?" I could almost feel eyes on me. Whose eyes I had no idea, surely not Will's. Maybe he wasn't so wonderful after all. "Figures." I straightened my knees to get up.

Shanda grabbed a handful of sequins, holding me in place. "They're watching something here on campus, or someone. It could be anything. But if I were a creepy stalker with a telescope, I'd watch everything. And everyone."

3

I tugged open the dusty blinds with a *whoosh* that echoed off the hardwood floors of room 210, my boarding school dorm for the next nine months. The windowpane stood tall and alone against the far brick wall, like a sentinel on guard. Nothing could go wrong on its watch. Famous last words, right?

A perfect view of the river loomed beyond the glass, juxtaposed against a serene lawn. The green contrasted with the deep gray water, merging into a peaceful palette. If I closed my eyes, I could almost hear the gurgle of rushing water.

The faint refrain of *Lucy in the Sky with Diamonds* jingled from the depths of my purse. I dug out my cell phone. "Hello?"

"Lucy," Mom's pitchy tone bordered on shrill, and just like that *Poof!* the peace was shattered. "I didn't hear from you last night. Is everything okay?"

"Not really." I bit into my tongue. She definitely didn't want to hear all my doubts about Nexis. I tucked myself into the cubby of brick around my window, drawing my knees up to my chin. "Sorry, Mom, but orientation was out of control yesterday. By the way, it's nice to talk to you, too."

"You should've called sooner. That rushed call from the airport doesn't cut it." Her voice shot up to the stratosphere. "How's your dorm? Are you making friends with your roommate?"

"Yeah, she's from New York and promised to show me around. I can't wait." A school-sponsored bus ride from the airport didn't count as my first

18

trip to the city. Not that Riverdale and the school didn't have their charms, as in far away from Indiana.

"You'll love New York in September, it's beautiful." Mom's worried tone evaporated. What a relief. "Once you get into Nexis, you'll be all set."

She sounded more like a game show host than a mother chatting with her daughter, always pushing her own agenda on me.

I gritted my teeth. "What if I don't want to join Nexis?"

"Now's not the time to be unreasonable." Her voice switched straight into Mom Mode. "We're talking about your future here. Don't you want to get into Yale?"

All the fight left me at the mention of Yale. Both she and Dad graduated from Yale, and James was supposed to go, too. We were all heartbroken when he disappeared to Europe and cut off contact with us. All we got was a postcard every few months. How could I disappoint them now? Especially when I had a chance to find out why he ran away.

"I'm sorry, Mom. It's strange being at the same school James was. It's like his shadow is everywhere."

"I know, honey." The sugar returned to her melodic voice and my jaw relaxed. "From what I hear, Nexis has a great leader this year. Did you look up the Stanton boy like I told you to?"

"Not on purpose." I huffed into the phone. "So don't get any ideas about fixing me up. I don't need any more drama, please."

Sometimes she could be so clueless. Good thing she didn't know her Stanton boy was a hottie.

I swiveled on the windowsill. As the sun lowered, a golden tint highlighted the tiny wave crests, muddying the rest of the Hudson.

"You're right." She sighed through the phone. We both had a hard time apologizing. "Want to talk to Dad?"

I braced my arm against the brick. Ready for impact in T minus ten seconds. "Sure, put him on."

"Hi, honey." Dad's soft tone threw me off. No more grilling me about college? He'd asked about it all summer, if he was home. Why stop now? "Glad you made it there in one piece. You put any more thought into a major?" Goody, the impatient tone I expected all along.

"I'm not even in college yet, give it time. I'll figure it all out soon, you'll see." Unacceptable by Dad standards. I only had two years to get into Yale.

What did I get myself into? I banged my head on the glass. Maybe the river could tell me what to do.

"You're right, sweetie, but now's the time to start preparing. That's why we sent you to Montrose." Did he mean that for real or as in, don't waste our money young lady? Bring on the guilt trip.

"And I thought you sent me away to avoid any more scandals." An edge of bitterness crept into my voice. My scar tingled at my temple, as if it could read my mind. As if it could remember the accident that brought me to this place, a thousand miles from home.

"On the contrary, we sent you to Montrose for your own protection. Not to mention a good education." His calm monotone spoke more than what he actually said. At least to me.

"Any word from James?" Even my sister, Paige, and her incessant beauty tips would be a welcome distraction right about now.

"James found his calling painting the Venice canals." A crisp edge sliced through his voice.

"Funny, I didn't know he could paint."

"Me, either." That familiar baritone laugh rumbled from the phone. How I wished I could reach out and hug him, tell him I wouldn't turn out like James. "Paige is out with her friends somewhere."

Mom yelled in the background. Snippets of garbled conversation filtered in snatches.

"Okay, Natalie, I'll tell her," Dad practically huffed into the phone. "Your sister's at the movies, okay? Now don't you listen to your mother. You stay away from boys, even that Stanton one."

"Relax, Dad, I think guys are scum, too." I hugged my knees and pressed my cheek against the cool glass. If he were here, he'd reach out and ruffle my hair.

"Good, that's what I wanted to hear. Don't forget that we love you, Lucy." His voice cracked when he said my name. Dads could be so silly sometimes.

"Love you guys, tell Mom. Bye now." I hung up the phone. Only a few days on my own and I missed them already. So much for independence.

The door swung open with a bang. I jumped from my window perch.

Shanda scurried in with a tower of boxes and dropped them on the floor. Her boxes and suitcases formed a mountain of stuff in front of her closet. It dwarfed my tiny pile of luggage. She peeled back the accordion doors and hung up armfuls of clothing.

"I'm just going to set up the room." Her designer clothes belonged in a celebrity closet, not a prep school dorm room.

I gasped, such gorgeous fabrics. "Is that cashmere?"

"You bet." Shanda draped the green sweater over my arm. "It's so soft."

I scrunched the silky wool between my fingers. "Heavenly. Maybe I should unpack my stuff, too."

With a flourish I went to work dressing up the bulletin board over my desk with bright fuchsia polka-dot paper and my family photos. What a cute, scrapbook kind of window into my life back home.

Something scraped against the wood floor behind me and I whirled around. "What in the world?"

She had the whole room laid out. Our beds pushed against the far brick wall, a white fuzzy rug in the center, flanked by black butterfly chairs. Posters hung all over the white cinder-block walls. Mostly bare-chested boys, but some pictures of Paris or New York.

"Silly putty." Shanda hoisted the package like a trophy.

My gaze flicked to the pinups. Heat curled up my neck. "That's not what I'm worried about."

Was she really one of those girls, the pop star obsessed, boy-crazy kind of girl? Because her rocker tee and faded jeans said she had more edge than that.

"You don't like it?" Her almond eyes batted at me, those bronze-glossed lips curving into a cute frown that probably worked on Daddy.

I shook my head. No pouting princess would change my mind. "Those have to go."

"My boys?" She rushed to the nearest one, tracing his smile with her finger.

Why didn't she get it? A muscle in my jaw twitched out of control. How could I forget about guys if they were everywhere? "Listen, I love the chairs, the rug is fine, but there's no way I'll put up with half-naked boys staring at me 24-7. Buhbye."

"What are you, a prude or something?" She twisted her lips and laughed in my face. The nerve.

"That's ridiculous." Every muscle in my body tensed. In the last six months only Becca and Jake ever made me this mad, and they turned the whole school against me.

I forced my eyes shut. *Calm down.* They were only posters, but they reminded me of Jake. And not in a good way. "They make me uncomfortable. Can you take down the guy posters? The rest are fine."

"That's fair, I guess." She yanked them down one by one, firing a glare at me each time. She arranged the pinups in her closet like a shrine. Gimme a break.

"Thank you." My heartbeat still thundered in my ears. So much for roommate bonding. Can we hold the drama, please?

With a flourish I sucked in a deep breath and walked out of our room, into the hall.

Now seemed like as good a time to meet my suitemates. Hopefully they would provide a much-needed distraction to my roommate spat. Their names, Mindy and Brooke, were taped to the doorframe on either side. I knocked and hoped for the best.

"Hello?" A brunette girl with blonde highlights opened the door, her smile wide.

I stuck out my hand. "Hi, I'm Lucy, one of your suitemates. Just thought I'd come over and introduce myself."

"Great to meet you. I'm Mindy." She shook my hand and ushered me inside. "Brooke's not here right now, she's at freshman orientation. Aren't you new, too?"

I nodded. "Yep, but I'm a junior."

"Oh, me too." She turned that warm smile on me and gestured to a purple fuzzy futon. "Sit down, won't you? We can get to know each other."

"Your room is starting to look good." Maybe a little sparkly and girlie for my taste with its pink, purple, and teal themed rugs and bedding. But somehow she made it look quite chic.

She plopped on the other end of the futon. "I just love to decorate, can't you tell?"

"It's like a designer magazine or something," I said.

"Thanks, you're so sweet." She leaned in, lowering her voice. "I'm not sure how much my roommate likes it. But we're working it out."

I huffed out a little laugh. "You don't say? Me and my roomie are having the same issues. I guess we just have different tastes."

She simply shrugged and crossed her legs. "That's what happens when you bring together different people from different parts of the country. But it also makes your life more colorful, don't you think?"

"I like that." I scratched my chin, settling into the futon cushion. "That's a great way to look at it." Maybe I could give Shanda a break and ease up a bit. Otherwise it'd be a long semester.

A warm breeze feathered my hair around me. I tucked the strands behind my ear, over the remnants of the accident. Sunlight slanted across the quad and tinted the grass lime green, the bricks orange. The bright colors ignited together, searing straight into my eyeballs. I lowered my head and focused on each step. One white canvas sneaker slapping the pavement, then the other. Mornings were the worst.

A jolt to my shoulder rocketed me off the sidewalk, right into the grass.

An angry guy whizzed past me. "Hey, watch it."

Where'd he come from?

"It's too early for rudeness." A frog sound ripped from my throat, but he was long gone.

I straightened my purple backpack and elbowed my way into the crowd. The flow caught me and pushed me forward. New Yorkers, everything moved so quickly. Until I reached the log jam at Trenton Hall.

I pushed my way through the swarm of people. High-pitched girly jitters blended together in a cacophony of chatter.

"Hey, Lucy." My suitemate, Mindy called from her group of posh girls dressed in perfectly ripped jeans.

I wiped my hands down my plain dark jeans and tugged on my aqua v-neck tee. Why hadn't I let Paige foist her Ivy League prep-school outfits on me? It felt too much like reenacting *Legally Blonde*, which so didn't work with my dark hair. My fashionista sister would fit in better at Montrose than I ever would.

"Morning, Mindy." I waved, but she turned back to her friends. Funny, she seemed much nicer last night when I introduced myself. Just as well. As if I really wanted to crawl back into the popular crowd.

I sidestepped the pockets of teenagers and trudged up a bazillion stairs to the landing of the three-story brick monstrosity. When I stepped into the marbled lobby, the babble reverberated straight at me like a locust infestation. Mom would tell me to stop and say hi to people, but the buzz seeped into my brain. The lingering side effects of my head injury, I guess. I punched through the mob straight into my first classroom.

Silence consoled my ears, I could breathe again.

In the middle of the stadium-style desks, I found the perfect spot and planted my stuff. Great view of the lecture area below, yet plenty of distance to hide behind. I fished out my notebook and gel pen.

"Hey." A bleach-blond guy in a muscle tee plopped himself down in the seat next to me. His arm dangled over the desktop, poised to brush my jeans. I recoiled as if he had fangs. "You're that girl from the thing Saturday, right? Can't hurt to make friends with a former Nexis president's sister. I'm Kevin from L.A., remember?"

"Right." My eyes narrowed at the spray-tanned hand he offered. I let it hang in the air. Wasn't he hitting on Shanda that night? Like I couldn't see right through him, just a carbon copy of my ex.

Finally, he retracted his orange hand.

Students filed in behind me, bringing their chatter with them. A tall man in tweed clomped down to the desk in the middle of the room. He scribbled "Mr. Harlixton" on the white board.

"Welcome to Western Civilization 101 where we'll be discussing the beginnings of civilization all semester. Just in time for you to figure out which campus civilizations you want to join. Choose wisely. Your future depends on it." His stern tone circled around the room.

"Pass these out." He strained the arms of his jacket, handing the front row a packet of papers. "You'll find the syllabus here and a list of campus groups. The Ivy League schools don't look kindly on fluff activities like party groups that masquerade as legitimate organizations."

Dad would love this guy. Great minds and all, he'd say.

Mr. Harlixton jabbed his finger into the packet. "Read the attendance policy in your syllabus to know many times you can 'not show up' and still pass. If you have questions, come talk to me after class or take advantage of my office hours, listed in the syllabus. Did I mention you need to read the syllabus?" He glared at the front row. My spot looked better and better.

Faint giggles erupted around the room and Mr. Harlixton's face softened slightly. "Now, on with the story of civilization."

He perched on the desk and crossed his legs. Could I clap now? What a brilliant performance, if you wanted to scare off slackers. No way was this teacher as scary as he pretended.

He launched into a story about ancient Mesopotamia. He covered every bit of history a book would, but he made it come alive. For some reason he kept citing Bible passages in his stories. Kind of an odd thing to reference in a history class. Maybe the Ivy League schools wanted their students to be well-versed in all aspects of life. Before I knew it the bell rang and storytime, aka class, ended. Zippers swished and papers shuffled as everyone left.

I jogged up the stairs and parted my way through the Red Sea before Kevin even moved. I flung open the side door, smack dab into some guy's broad shoulder. His backpack hit the marble with a clank.

"Sorry, about that." I glanced up, right into familiar blue eyes that matched my shirt today. Would he think I planned it?

My nerves kicked into hyper-drive, like a hamster spinning its wheel in my stomach.

I fidgeted with my bag strap, snagging my paper cut. It throbbed. "Don't draw any blood today."

Bryan swiped his bag off the floor and swung it over his shoulder in one fluid motion. Then he smiled at me. The real kind, not like Kevin's fake one. "Still in one piece, aren't you? What class are you coming from?"

Always answering me with questions. Could he be more annoying? Still, the hamster wheel churned my eyes into the ground. "I just had Western Civ."

"With Mr. Carter or Harlixton?" His words jumbled together. Was he nervous, too? Good.

"I have Harlixton. Why, is he bad?" I gazed up at him, chewing my lip the whole time.

"No, Harlixton's great. You'll love him." A light turned on in that ocean of blue. "If you had Carter I'd have to pray for you. Really pray."

"That bad, huh?" How sweet was that? Yeah right, stupid traitor thoughts. I'd have to murder them later.

25

"One day in Carter's class I raised my hand to tell him to shut up and stop repeating himself, but my friend stopped me. I ended up banging my head on the desk to keep myself awake." His eyes practically sparked when he laughed.

"Wow, that's bad. I mean, you seem like a pretty sane guy." For a control freak, maybe. Much better.

Kevin picked that moment to burst into the hall. "Get a load of this guy, giving us an assignment the first day of class."

"Reading a syllabus doesn't really count as an assignment." No way could I juggle two guys at once, especially ones I didn't want to juggle. I waved and headed for the door, but they both followed me like puppies.

"Very funny, you're one of those girls, aren't you?" Kevin brushed my arm.

My whole body tensed up. The hamster wheel stopped cold.

I flicked off Kevin's hand, ready to slap him if he made another move. "That's what my parents are paying for."

"Let's hope they get their money's worth." Kevin stepped toward me, but Bryan edged closer. "Me, I just want to get by and have fun."

"Isn't that the Nexis motto?" Bryan puffed out his chest like an action figure. He stared down Kevin, who glared right back. Cage match anyone?

"I've been waiting for an easy teacher." Kevin inched forward.

"Shoulda gone with Carter." I got him good. Before he could fight back, I pushed open the front door, shielding my eyes from the sun. From up here the quad looked peaceful. I booked it down the steps, ready to inhale the sweet smell of freedom.

"Burn!" Kevin gasped behind me, his long legs matching me stride for stride. So much for freedom. This guy couldn't take a hint. "Have you heard Bryan's story about how boring Carter is?"

I turned on my heel to channel all my annoyance into one laser glare. "You walked in on the middle of it, right?"

"What's up now? This girl's got game." Kevin stumbled into Bryan, who checked me out like I was under a microscope, same as Kevin. Guess players ran in packs.

"Now you have to make it up to me and my poor bruised ego." Kevin's lip lowered into what must be his most charming poor-me face.

Wouldn't work on this girl. I busted out laughing. "Yeah, right."

"I'll show you around the city. What's the harm in that?" He nodded at Bryan who couldn't stop staring at me.

I cocked my head and narrowed my eyes at him. His hang loose expression didn't waver. "Doesn't sound so innocent to me."

"Don't worry, I'll chaperon. How's Friday?" Bryan had HOPE scrawled across his face in giant letters. So adorable, especially after he showed his guy colors only seconds ago. How could I say no to that face?

I chewed my lip for the fiftieth time this morning. No way could I hang out with two guys by myself, Dad would definitely disapprove. What if they knew something about James? Kevin was some kind of Nexis leader, right? I shifted my bag to my left shoulder, and a crazy idea popped into my head.

"I don't know, why don't I talk to my friend and get back to you?" Shanda would die before she'd ever agree to a double date, especially in a city she knew like the layout of Tiffany's.

"I'm gonna hold you to it, chica." Kevin resorted to the he-man nod. Gag me.

"Fine then. See you around, I guess." I flipped my hair behind my shoulder. When I stole a backwards glance, they both stared after me. I waved goodbye to a grinning Kevin and a jaw-dangling Bryan. So much for playing it safe. Hopefully Shanda wouldn't kill me.

4

Wispy shapes moved and danced like clouds around me. A white horse pranced on the fluffy clouds with a tall rider, his face vaguely handsome, vaguely familiar. The white-clad rider dismounted and floated into the wind.

"Oh, c'mon. Just one more minute." I jerked out of dreamland and clamped the pillow over my eyes. Even my subconscious betrayed me. At least Prince Charming had no specific face, and no specific eye color.

"Wake up, sleepy." Shanda snatched the pillow from my face and snapped open the blinds.

Stripes of light burned across my lids and I rubbed the sleep from my eyes. "Why are you punishing me?"

"You don't want to be late for class, do you?" She clanked her dishes into our little in-room sink. "How about some breakfast?"

I padded over to the windowsill and flicked the blinds shut. "You mean like eggs and toast?"

"No, I mean like cereal." She huffed and handed me a bowl. "I'm not your mama."

"Too bad." I shuffled behind her to the mini fridge by the door she'd set up as a clever little kitchen station. Grabbing a bowl, I poured in cereal and milk. "Still tastes good."

She moved to the mirror, dabbing on her makeup. "I'm a gourmet chef, you know."

28

Suddenly the door popped open right in my face. I slapped it back with my palm. Nothing like a door handle in the gut to wake you up.

A blonde girl burst into the room. Geez, knock much? "Hey girls, sorry to interrupt. I'm Monica Belmont, your dorm assistant this year. I haven't met you yet, so I wanted to stop in and say hi."

She flipped her golden hair over the shoulder of her perfectly pressed coral tank top, her tawny cat eyes glinting as she stared me down.

"I'm Lucy, this is my roommate, Shanda Jones." Mom would applaud my manners, especially in the face of a door.

Shanda barely glanced up and made a mad dash to her closet. Mom wouldn't call that entertaining properly. What would Shanda's mom would say, or did she even have a mom? She never mentioned her.

"I thought it was pronounced Shawnda, like Wanda." Monica's southern drawl stretched each syllable like pink taffy.

"No, it's Shan-duh." She enunciated both parts. "People get it wrong all the time."

"Then I don't feel so bad." Monica's candy laugh grated my ears, too early for that much sugar. "I'll be popping in now and then to check on you. My suite is down the hall in 201."

"Good to know." Shanda turned back to rummaging around her closet.

Monica didn't seem to notice her clipped tone. "There's an informal Q&A session tonight at the library with the Nexis president, if you're interested in joining. All the officers host one. Since I'm club secretary, mine's Thursday if you can't make it tonight. So if you have any questions, just pick a night and we'll be there."

"Great." Shanda inched toward the door for a water bottle, as if to herd her out.

"I'll scoot on outta here and let you two get to class." Monica flashed her perfect white teeth and waved goodbye.

As soon as the door closed, Shanda almost spat out her water. "Who says the word scoot? And who scoots, anyway—can you scoot?"

She dug through a box until she found a pair of black boots. She pulled them on and freestyled around me. "I'm the Queen of Scooting."

She strutted her stuff like Michael Jackson. I busted out laughing. "Is that scooting? Looks like a moonwalk to me. All you need is a sequined glove."

"That's a Shanda scoot." Her cackle echoed off the walls. She studied her bare wrist, announcing in a *Gone with the Wind* accent, "It's time for us to scoot to class. But I haven't a thing to wear."

My foggy brain suddenly flashed back to drama club and the Georgia accent they made me practice for hours. "Don't be silly, Scah-let, dahling. I saw all those gah-geous clothes you was unpacking. How about this one?"

"Too bright, why do I own orange pants? Your turn." Her accent faded out as she pranced to my closet, flapping a sequined shrug in my face like a pompom. "How about this?"

I batted it down. "Not on your life." Back in my flashy days with Jake, he loved the bling like he wanted to show me off. No more trophy girlfriend for me.

She pulled out a suede belt, offering it with a new kind of smile that lit up her whole face. "Try this. I bet it'll go great with your dark hair and those big brown eyes." She shoved me in front of the mirror.

"Not bad." I wrapped it around my waist. "Too much with the glitter on my shirt?"

"No way, the shimmer brings out the gold flecks in your eyes. It's fabulous." Guess our roommate spat was over.

A musty smell wafted to my nose as soon as I pushed open the library doors. I inhaled the familiar smell of books. A good smell, one of possibilities. Libraries had always been a safe haven for me, a calm place to sift through the muddle of my thoughts.

Tall wooden stacks beckoned to me, like they knew exactly what I needed. I reached out and rubbed the dimpled spine of a book near the aisle. Shanda's elbow rammed into my back and prodded me forward.

She followed me past the stacks to an open table in the middle of the study area. "Where are all the guys? I thought there'd be at least someone cute to distract me or I never would've agreed to this." Her annoyed pitch echoed off the coffered ceilings of the immense room. No wonder everyone spoke soft.

"Could you be any louder?" I hissed at her. Half of the creaky wooden tables were littered with clumps of study groups and loners on laptops. Back at Alton High nobody would be caught dead in the library so early in the semester.

"This was your idea. It's not like I care about the half-baked Nexis Society." She clanged her bag on the table, but her tone hushed to a murmur.

"Don't you?" I cocked my head at her, but she dropped it.

I settled into a seat at the middle table with a perfect view to hide behind my book and hawk the main entrance. Boy, did I ever have questions for these guys. Like why was my brother the only Nexis president to skip out on a chance at an Ivy League education, even though he was accepted to all the top schools? Maybe they couldn't answer my questions, but I wouldn't know until I asked.

A bleach blond guy flung open the glass doors. That had to be Kevin, but he wasn't alone.

I elbowed Shanda in the ribs. "Quick, time to play it cool. Here comes your Nexis man candy."

She twisted her neck in his direction and smacked my arm. "Quiet, girl, now who's being loud?"

Another glance at him and she turned right back, eyes more alive than ever.

"Not exactly what I meant by playing it cool."

Kevin cleared the aisle for his friend, like a bodyguard. Lost behind surfer shoulders and that spiky hair, I strained for a glimpse of his mystery friend. Would it be Bryan offering a tour of the city, or the Stanton boy with the right amount charm? Maybe this wasn't such a good idea.

The Stanton boy breezed past the stacks to our table, silver-grays flashing. "You girls have some questions?"

Shanda pointed to me and wrangled Kevin into the chair next to her. "So how have you been?"

Her words faded as I focused on the sculpted face of the guy next to me. Will looked good in his dark jeans and navy t-shirt. His sandy hair held a hint of gold under the light, but all natural unlike Kevin's bleach job. Inked strokes of an arm-wrap tattoo peeked out under his right sleeve, drawing my eyes to his biceps. If I were bold like Shanda, I'd just ask about it. But I wasn't even supposed to be on the market.

He straddled the chair next to me. "Hope you and your friend are intrigued by what Nexis has to offer."

I sucked in a breath, unable to tear my eyes away. All of my James questions hammered into my brain, but I held my tongue. As Mom would say, there was a time and a place for everything. "I'm definitely intrigued."

"You want to learn some real history?" His fingers brushed mine as he grabbed my Western Civ book, opening to a picture of Noah's ark. "For instance, you think you know this story, right?"

"The flood?" The question prickled my skin, or maybe it was his proximity. I squinted at the book. "Everyone knows about Noah's ark. They even made a movie about it."

He shook his head, then came close. My heart practically stopped. His cinnamony breath spiced the air between us. "Sure, but not everyone knows the real story."

His eyes narrowed into lines of steel, like his opinion of me hinged on my response.

Sweat droplets bubbled on my palms and I wiped them on my jeans. "What do you mean? Like there's some secret to the flood that I've never heard of?"

"Maybe you know more than you think." He ran his finger down his jawline, then slouched back, nodding at me.

Did I pass the test? Those steely eyes analyzed me, as if they could read my mind. Goosebumps popped up on my arms.

"Shouldn't I be asking the questions?"

"I'm just trying to figure you out." His lips curled up in the most adorable grin. It shivered straight through me. "I think you're a natural for Nexis, and the Ivy Leagues."

A voice boomed from the stacks behind me. "You Nexis extremists don't need any more new recruits."

I spun around as Bryan stomped over to our table. What was he doing, hiding back there? His aqua eyes seared the air like light sabers as they leveled right into me, but his gaze didn't give me chills like the Stanton boy. Was that a good thing, or a bad thing?

"Cooper." Will's lips twisted into a scowl and he stood up, inches from Bryan. Did Bryan bring out the fight in every guy he met? "Like the Guardians need any more brainwashed cult freaks trying to shove their beliefs down everyone's throat."

"What did you say?" My heart jangled in my chest like a tambourine. Whoever these Guardians were, they didn't deserve to be called freaks. Especially if Bryan was one of them. Just like I didn't deserve to be called a prude. "Whatever happened to tolerating other people's beliefs?"

Shanda snorted out a laugh that sent me over the edge.

"That's it." I slammed my book shut. Not this again, I had my fill on unnecessary mockery in Indianapolis from my old friends, but even at a prep school? Shouldn't they be beyond petty bullying? I scraped my chair back. It screeched like I'd stepped on a cat's tail.

All eyes turned my way. "Excuse me. Why on earth do you think it's okay to call anyone a brainwashed freak? Grow up." Was Will just another jerk like Jake turned out to be? Maybe I assumed too much, or maybe this school really wasn't as perfect as I'd imagined.

His glare turned from Bryan to me. In an instant his face softened. "That's not what I meant, Lucy."

"Forget it." I tried to focus all my anger into the globe pendant on the ceiling. The ball of energy still roiled in my stomach and I couldn't calm it down. I shoved my books into my bag.

"I've got to go. I'll see you around." I raced to the door.

"See you at the next meeting." Will's voice cracked as he called after me.

Shanda mumbled something about giving me some space. Such a good call.

With my fist I punched open the French doors, stepping into the cool night air. How could I get so mad over one little comment and forget all my questions about James? The sidewalk burned from the day's heat as I inhaled a deep breath. The purpling sky soothed my inner rage, making the world feel halfway normal again.

"Wait up." Bryan's footsteps pounded after me. "That was pretty cool. No one stands up to Will like that, he thinks he's the big man on campus."

I kept walking, my heart still beating a syncopated rhythm. "I'm tired of putting up with jerks like that. Especially at a supposedly enlightened prep school. It gets on my nerves."

He jogged ahead, stopping right in front of me so I had to look at him. Normally I'd find that cute, if I wasn't so annoyed.

"Guess what? There's not as many 'enlightened' people as you might think." He made air quotes with both hands. "On top of that, some people who say they're enlightened are the exact opposite."

"What do you mean?" Like a magnet, my gaze moved to his face. The dusky hues of the sky turned his eyes robin's egg blue, calming the angry remnants of my silly outburst.

What could Will possibly think of me? Probably that I'm imbalanced or something. Good thing Bryan didn't seem to mind.

"It's hard to explain. Some of us are all about truth and the rest are just playing games. Hey, if you're in Harlixton's Western Civ class, I can help. There's a huge paper coming up, right?" He held out his hand. His eyes countered mine, practically daring me to take it.

What an odd way to change the subject. I shook my head. "I'm not going back in there. I don't care if he meant something else, it's a poor choice of words."

He cocked his head at me and laughed. "You're a firecracker aren't you? Don't worry, that's not what I meant. You think you can trust me?" His hand still hovered in the air.

"Good question." I inched mine closer until I barely tapped his palm. He gripped my fingers, hauling me down the sidewalk.

"Where are we going?" Great, what'd I get myself into now?

His white-toothed grin glowed under the lamppost. "The best place to study true ancient history."

5

The chapel shimmered against the navy sky. All the air whistled from my lungs. "Breathtaking."

Okay, maybe the uplighting on the scalloped arches had something to do with it. Still, the beautiful stonework made the church look like it belonged in Europe instead of a boarding school along the Hudson. I climbed up the cobblestone steps behind Bryan. The wooden Gothic door creaked as he opened it.

We stepped through the marble arches of the foyer and into the sanctuary. Even after the beauty of the outside, the sanctuary lived up to the hype. Dim shadows hid the stained glass windows on the outer walls, but a spotlight illuminated the back sphere of rose and blue glass with a golden cross in the middle.

"Wow, this place is gorgeous. You guys study here?" I tore my gaze from the magnificence only to find him twenty feet ahead of me.

"No, not in the sanctuary. We use the chapel library. It has some of the oldest history books around." He motioned down a tiled hall. "This way."

My ballet flats clicked against the hand-painted tiles, reverberating so loud I switched to tiptoes. Deep laughter rumbled ahead of me.

He peeked at me over his shoulder. "What are you doing?"

I clenched my fingers into a fist at my side. As if I didn't remember the last time this boy laughed at me. "Well, excuse me, I don't want to disturb anything. Or anyone."

"Relax, it's not like there's monks here or something." A beam of light spilled into the hallway from an open door, enough to spotlight his shaking head. "Here we are. Ladies first."

As I slipped past he bowed ever-so-slightly, like his small effort at chivalry could make up for his rudeness. I flipped my hair over my shoulder and flounced into the dimly lit library, where five unfamiliar faces stared back at me.

An auburn-haired beauty waved from the far wall of ceiling-high stacks. At her side, a younger girl with dishwater blonde hair offered a meek smile. It was my freshman suitemate, Brooke. Sitting at one of the few tables in the cluttered room, an orange-haired boy smiled at me with freckled cheeks.

The girl at his side swung her springy orange curls around and I blinked. "Wow, you're like a carbon-copy of your brother."

"Good thing they're twins." The voice came from a dark-haired guy by the lead-paned window. He didn't even glance up from the piles of books strewn in front of him.

"Yeah, caught that." I turned my back on him to take in the view. Cedar shelves lined each wall and most of the floorspace, with niches carved out for the window and a few tables in the middle. The coolest part was cloaked by darkness in the back corner of the room.

"Is that an actual turret?" Even though the tower was tiny, the bookshelves wrapped from the bottom to the very top. "Amazing. It's like a castle library."

Bryan cleared his throat and nudged me into the center of the room. "Everyone, this is Lucy McAllen. She needs help in her Western Civ class."

I cocked my head at him. "Do I really?"

"You've come to the right place then." The guy by the window finally glanced up from his book pile. "By the way, I'm Tony Delgotto."

Bryan smacked his forehead. "Right, that's my sister Brooke over there in the stacks, then Felicia Morales, and the twins here are Laura and Lenny Brewster."

"Hi, everyone." I forced my lips into some form of greeting and dumped my bag on Laura and Lenny's table. "It must be so much fun being twins."

"I love it, but he hates it." Laura's high voice held a surprising warm tone that soothed my ears.

"Only because she won't do cool pranks like switch places." Lenny had a lower voice than I expected, especially compared to Laura.

"Like I want anyone to mistake me for a boy." She shrugged off his comment and scooted out the chair beside her. "Come sit by me. What are you looking for?"

"I'm not really sure." I slid into the wooden chair. "Bryan said I might need some extra help to ace Harlixton's class."

"Is that what you said?" Tony tilted his chair back and kicked up his feet. "Nice."

"Don't listen to him, he's always giving Bryan a hard time." Laura snapped her book shut. "What'd you cover in your last class?"

"We spent the whole first part of this week on Creation and the first ancient civilization. It was kind of strange, actually ..." Not as strange as his random question. I unzipped my bag and fished out a notebook. "But if that's what Ivy League schools want their applicants to know, who am I to argue? I think we'll be covering the flood next week. You know, get all of the Bible stuff out of the way."

Everyone stopped cold and zeroed in on me, eyes wide.

"So soon." Bryan eased himself into the chair beside me. "That's faster than usual."

"Maybe she can't wait." Lenny whispered to Bryan, but his eyes never left me. Creepy. "Maybe she needs to know before it's too late."

"He's certainly not backing off." Tony's gaze flew over my head, straight to Bryan like I wasn't even there. Hello, could he be any ruder?

Bryan closed his eyes, fingers rubbing a hole in the collar of his gray t-shirt. "I don't know, I think there's still time."

An ache crept up the back of my head. Were they really talking about me? More like they were talking above or even around me—and it really burned me up. "This is getting ridiculous. What's going on, guys?"

I tried to stare them down, but no one would meet my eyes. Except Brooke, who peered at me from behind her wide-rimmed glasses. Her small smile released the tension in my shoulders I hadn't even realized I'd tightened.

"I think Bryan's right." Felicia crossed the room, perching on the chair opposite me. "There's still time."

I couldn't take much more of this. If they were talking about me like I was invisible, I might as well leave the room.

"I think I should go now." I stuffed my notebook in my bag and slung it over my shoulder.

"No, Lucy, don't go." Bryan's hand reached for mine, his fingers soft on my skin. A scratchy current in his voice betrayed a hint of desperation. It hit me in the pit of my stomach.

I released my grip on my bag.

"Thank you." Those aqua eyes turned on me full force, begging me to stay.

If I were just any gullible girl, I would've melted into a puddle on the floor. But could I really believe any of this guy's mixed signals? And what about his friends?

I folded my arms across my chest. Then I met his gaze, full on. "What's going on here?"

He flinched, but didn't look away. "I'm sorry, I'm being rude. There are things that go on at this school that most people don't know about. We don't want to scare you or anything."

"Too late." I crinkled my eyes until the image of him narrowed. "What kinds of things?"

"Secret societies." Lenny's low voice carried those words louder than his whisper.

"Lenny, hush." Laura elbowed his ribs. "You can't spring something like that on a person. That's not how it works."

He elbowed her back. "Well then, how does it work? She has a right to know."

I nodded at him. Finally, someone who was being honest, even if it all sounded like some kind of practical joke.

No one cracked a smile, let alone a laugh. Every face held grave expressions, which could only mean one thing. "You can't be serious. You're telling me Montrose has secret societies, like the Skulls or something crazy? Wait, are you talking about Nexis?"

Bryan gritted his teeth and glared at his friend. "You just have to be careful about who you make friends with, what groups you join. That kind of thing."

"You can't tell me what to do." Goosebumps peaked on my arms. James would never lead any sort of secret society. No way would my parents approve of that, let alone practically force me to join.

He narrowed his eyes at me. "Hey, I'm not telling you what to do. Obviously, you can fend for yourself. You should've seen the way she told Will off earlier."

"No way." Brooke gasped and all eyes turned to her. She looked at her canvas shoes, red splotches dotting her cheeks. "What? He can be so scary. It's cool that she stood up to him."

"It was pretty cool." Bryan squared his shoulders and angled toward me. "Come talk to me if something weird happens. Especially if it involves a campus group. Promise?"

"You mean like whatever this is? Sure, you got it." I shrugged, but I couldn't help rolling my eyes at these people. Just because some guy with gorgeous eyes asked me to go against my parents, it didn't mean I had to listen. "I'll figure this out for myself, you know, whatever it is."

"It's a deal then." He pulled a pen out of his pocket and grabbed my hand.

"What're you doing?" I wiggled and tried to pull my hand away, but he wouldn't let go. He marked my palm with his digits.

Then those dangerous eyes returned to me. "Promise you'll call me first if you run into any trouble."

He brought my palm closer and blew on the wet ink. Tingles shot up my arm.

"Yeah, right." I turned away from him.

"I hope you do." He let go of my hand.

Somehow, it felt cold without his warmth.

I raced out of the library, down the hall, and pushed open the heavy front door. I tilted my face to the moon and the stars, but my hand still tingled where Bryan etched his number into my palm.

So soon. Even the next day, Bryan's words echoed in my mind as I elbowed my way past the Trenton Hall crowd. I found my usual seat in Western Civ on the third row next to Mindy. The whole class sat clumped up front and center with their notebooks out, pens ready to write. Did everyone but me think the whole world hinged on what Harlixton was going to teach today?

Long, horizontal windows on the back wall framed the clouds outside. Rays of light and shadow dappled the lecture stage. Damp air hung above the classroom almost like the smell of spring—freshness about to burst into something new.

Mr. Harlixton uncapped a black marker and scribbled, "The Flood" on the white board. "Alright everyone. Open your books to chapter three on the flood. Those of you with Bibles, turn to Genesis, chapter six."

I blinked but pulled out the heavy textbook from my bag. Mindy opened her pink leather Bible, so did the girl next to me. All over the room, people cracked open the good book. Every student had one today. Apparently I was the only one who didn't have a Bible for this class. Weird, I couldn't remember Mr. Harlixton saying it was a requirement. And it definitely wasn't in the syllabus. It seemed like an odd addition to a history class.

He smoothed down the fuzzy hair fringing the edges of his bald spot. "Today we'll discuss the precursors to the flood and theorize what made God angry enough to drown the entire Earth in water."

He paused. A hush filled the room.

I glanced at Mindy if only to gauge her reaction, but her eyes were glued to the man behind the podium.

"There are basically two camps who interpret Genesis six differently. As you see, it talks about the Nephilim, a creature who was said to be half man and half angel. Most scholars conclude that 'sons of God' means the godly line of Adam's son, Seth. But some scholars argue it means angels, or fallen angels, actually demons. They are one and the same, don't forget that part."

I'd never noticed the part about angels marrying women. How did I miss that? The flood story I'd heard in Sunday school was about Noah's ark and all the animals.

I tapped Mindy's shoulder. "Can I borrow that?"

She nodded and slid the Bible into my lap.

I scanned the passage again, and there it was in Genesis chapter six, verse four, all about these Nephilim creatures. Still, it didn't make any sense.

Murmurs buzzed behind me, but I tuned them out to hear Mr. Harlixton. "One camp contends that God sent the flood because of the

Nephilim. This camp is further divided into many different sects, but for our purposes, I've lumped them all together. We'll go into more detail in a minute."

The girl on my left whispered to her friend. "Or just go join Nexis."

"Shut up." Her friend hissed at her.

What did that mean? Maybe these girls were some of the cult-people Will had been talking about.

"The other camp takes the passage literally and believes that God sent the flood to destroy all men. Because it was mankind who was so sinful. It had nothing to do with the Nephilim. This camp makes up most of Christendom. But as I alluded to before, there are certain sects in Christianity that hold to some form of the first camp's view. Some more adamantly than others."

He chugged a glass of water, leaning against his desk. "So let's go back to the first view. Some theorize that the Nephilim were the top dogs in Noah's world. About the only thing this chapter says about Nephilim is that 'they were the heroes of old, men of renown.' As you can imagine, there are some sects who worship the Nephilim, and others who say they were the beings who corrupted mankind. Any thoughts?"

A wave of mumbles swept around the room. The girl next to me shot her hand up. "Do the Nephilim still exist?"

Mr. Harlixton's eyebrows waggled. "Great question, Cora. The only other mention of these creatures is not direct, but a mere allusion to them in the book of Revelation. So it is possible they do exist now. Or they could exist again."

Her hand shot back up. "If they do exist, then it would involve angels marrying humans, right?"

"Yes, indeed." Mr. Harlixton pushed up his glasses. "That would be a scary idea to consider."

"Why is that so scary?" Cora asked.

"Because angels are said to be ten times more powerful than we are. And any angel who would come to earth, marry humans, and have half-human children would have to be a fallen angel, that is, a demon. Which is why people theorize that God wiped them out with the flood. Even the Nephilim, these half-angels, were more powerful and more prone to evil, allegedly."

The murmurs grew louder now, as spurts of arguments broke out behind me. But some strange fascination kept my eyes on the balding man in the front of the room like my life depended on what he had to say.

A guy in the front row raised his hand. "What about Noah? God said he was all right."

"Not merely all right. God said Noah was blameless, the only righteous man." Mr. Harlixton grabbed his marker and scrawled *Blameless* on the board.

I squinted, zeroing in on the word blameless.

I concentrated so hard on that one little word that it melted into a black and white puddle, swirling circles on the whiteboard. The puddle fizzled into a great beam of light that focused on a man. A middle-aged bearded man in funny clothing. "Blameless," boomed through my mind. "I will establish my covenant with you."

The booming voice came from a beam of pure white light that surrounded the bearded man. He nodded and bowed his head, then turned to me with his eyes closed. He opened them in a flash. From his eyes swirls of floating light and shadow streamed straight at me.

One man, called out above the rest.

To save the world.

To regenerate it.

And somehow I felt unworthy, like I didn't deserve such an honor. And it wasn't even about me. These were ancient words, from a thousand centuries ago, right?

Somehow they rang true in my heart. In my mind. In every part of my being. I could feel it in my bones.

Who am I?

I couldn't take it any more and clamped my eyes shut. The images danced in the darkness, then dimmed.

I lifted my eyelids, slowly.

The swirls of light morphed once again into the classroom. My back slammed against the chair and I couldn't focus on reality. I blinked several times to make sure the vision truly disappeared.

How long had I spaced out? Not long enough to fall asleep and dream something weird. Maybe this was some kind of literal daydream. Or I had one creepy, overactive imagination. Maybe it was my head injury, side effects that the doctor forgot to tell me about. Or else I was going nuts.

That felt more like some kind of vision than the aftermath of a car wreck. It's not like my head hurt at all. My mind waded through every plausible scenario that could make what I just saw okay. Nothing made sense.

"Heavy stuff, huh?" Mindy whispered to me. "You okay?"

"I'm not sure, I guess I don't really understand any of this." Definitely an understatement.

Mr. Harlixton cleared his throat. "Do you have something to add, Miss McAllen?"

I shook my head. The odd vision still lurked in the corners of my mind, threatening to overtake me again.

"Are you sure? Now don't be shy, ask anything you want."

"Well," I gnawed on my lip. "I have to admit, I've never heard any of this before, especially the fallen angels marrying humans part. It's a lot to take in."

A collective gasp rippled across the room, as if I'd just prophesied that the world would end tomorrow. Even Mindy jerked back like I'd jolted her with a taser.

"You're telling me you've never heard of the Nephilim?" She whispered the last word so soft I had to read her lips. "Not even from your family? Or your brother?"

"My family?" I searched her face. Totally serious, but she had to be kidding, right? "What would my family, or James, have to do with any of this?"

"You're joking, right?" She hissed at me with a glare that said don't-mess-with-me.

I met her glare full-on, until the corners of her eyes softened. Did she know James when he was here? Maybe they dated or something and things ended badly. She definitely fit his usual girlfriend type, perky brunette and all, but a little young for him.

"I think that's enough on this line of discussion for now." Mr. Harlixton's voice raised to a firm tone. The mumbling silenced. "Now let's talk about the second camp."

I slunk down in my chair. That's what I got for speaking up. The next part of his lecture droned on about the Sunday School version of the flood, so I tuned out.

When the bell rang, Mr. Harlixton stopped me at the door. "I'm sorry I put you on the spot today. I had no idea you knew so little on the subject."

I swallowed the lump in my throat. Dad would not be happy about this. "Am I too far behind to catch up?"

He motioned me to a far corner of the room, away from the loiterers glommed up by the door. "It's not that. I'm afraid I've put you in a very dangerous spot."

"Dangerous? What do you mean?" My old goosebump buddies prickled my skin.

"I don't have time to explain now," he whispered. "Come by my office after class Monday. Be careful this weekend, and choose your friends wisely."

I nodded. What an odd, almost Bryan-like, kind of warning.

Somehow my feet found their way out of the room and down the hall toward the front door. But my mind still lingered in that classroom. Mr. Harlixton couldn't really mean dangerous, but the way he said it made things seem more dangerous by the second.

What could Mindy possibly know about my family that I didn't know? I raced up the steps to catch up with her, but she sprinted down the hall with those long legs like some crazed bad guy was chasing her. Did she think I was the bad guy?

6

"Mindy, wait up." The rubber soles of my flats squeaked across the marble. Her question about my family blared like a fog horn in my mind.

Suddenly she stopped at the door of Trenton Hall, holding it open. What's so special about my family? I almost asked, but my mouth was glued shut. The question hung in the air with the rest of today's uncertainties.

I caught up with her and we descended the stairs together. A gust of wind whipped my hair across my face. I brushed the dark tendrils away, raising my face to the sky. Sure enough, gray clouds chewed their way through the horizon.

Splat. A drop of rain pelted my face. "Better run for it."

"I can't get wet or it's bye-bye sleek hair, hello frizzy mess." Mindy smoothed down her stick-straight golden brown locks, hoisting her bag over her head.

We sprinted down the cobblestone path as raindrops pelted the sidewalk around us. I pedaled my legs as fast as they could go, but she reached the cafeteria first.

"Wow, girl." I huffed in the thick air. It took way longer than usual for me to catch my breath. "You should be a track star."

We reached the overhang as rain showered the quad behind her. "Anything to save my hair."

"Don't worry, it's still perfect."

She curled up those pouty lips as we scurried inside the cafeteria to a mess of food smells. My stomach gurgled, probably because I'd neglected it since breakfast. The sharp sting of pepperoni hit me first. It simmered in the pizza oven on the back wall. Then the meaty smell of boiling hot dogs mixed with the greasy goodness of fried chicken. Montrose spared no expense to ensure all the regions of the country were represented, even in the cafeteria. But pepperoni couldn't cover up the damp odor of wet teens streaming inside from the rain.

"That could've been us." She handed me a tray and headed for the salad bar.

I followed her, adding a small salad to my plate. Mom would be proud of that, at least. She'd probably hate the self-serve giant sandwich with too much cheese, or something ridiculous. Sometimes Mom could be an uber-health nut, if it suited her.

Mindy topped her salad with piles of veggies. I loaded up my sandwich with the final touch, honey mustard, and scanned the tables for Shanda. No luck. The crowd pushed me to the checkout line and I got separated from Mindy.

After I swiped my card, I spied a couple of red-heads lounging at a big table by the front windows.

Felicia motioned me over, a small gesture that pulled me out of my inner ramblings and back to the real world like a lifeline.

I set my tray down across from her, next to Laura. "Hi, girls."

"Lucy, I'm so glad you found us." Laura put down her sandwich and flashed her warm hostess-with-the-mostest smile.

Felicia munched on her hot dog, her green eyes bright and friendly. "Me, too. I can't wait to hear about your class today."

"Really? It's just a class." I swung my bag off my shoulders. "Okay, maybe a little weirder than normal."

"Wait." Laura held up her tiny hand. "Don't say any more till the rest of the crew gets here."

"Why?" I scrunched my eyebrows at her, stuffing my turkey sandwich into my mouth to keep from saying something rude. The deli turkey was salty and delicious, especially paired with the juicy tomato and crisp lettuce. I could still make a mean sandwich, even if I had no idea why everyone cared so much about my Western Civ class.

Laura shrugged her red-orange curls off her shoulders. "So you don't have to repeat yourself. They'll want to hear about it, since it's everyone's favorite class. I know I'd hate having to tell the same story over and over again."

"Good call." I nodded at her, unscrunching my eyebrows. Still, the imminent threat of retelling Harlixton's odd class had me on edge. I twirled my silver ring around my finger, hoping that rubbing the family heirloom would suddenly make everything clearer. Did I really see some strange guy kneeling before God? Better keep that part to myself, or the school nurse would pack me up and ship me off to psycho-land.

Mindy wandered among the tables and I waved her over. She settled herself in next to Felicia.

"This is my suitemate, Mindy Donovan." I introduced her to Felicia and Laura.

The gingers exchanged odd looks. What was that about? I opened my mouth to ask, right as the guys yelled at each other across the cafeteria, heading to our table. I bit back my question and glanced up into those famous eyes. Bryan closed his trap, while Tony cocked his head at Lenny.

That made two things I'd have to ask about later.

Tony pulled out the chair next to Mindy, and Lenny plunked down beside him. That left one chair for Bryan, the one next to me. His lips twisted, not exactly a frown, but not really a smile either, until his shoulder grazed mine. I scooted closer to Laura and we all munched in silence.

"Hey, girl." Shanda waved at me across the dining hall.

Bryan snagged a chair from another table, sliding it between us. My jaw clenched as if he'd dissed me. Where'd that come from? I stuffed my sandwich in my mouth to distract myself from any more hormone-induced silliness.

"Thanks, Bryan." Shanda plopped into her seat next to me. "What'd I miss?"

"Lucy was going to tell us all about Harlixton's class." Laura nudged me and I put my turkey and cheese down. Everyone stopped what they were doing at looked at me. My face flamed.

I took a cool sip of iced tea. "There's not much to tell really. It was a little odd, that's all."

Mindy coughed. "Odd is an understatement."

"Really, how interesting could this class be? Western Civilization sounds like such a drag." Shanda slurped her smoothie.

"Thank you," I nodded at her, "except this time it was anything but boring. He asked to see me after classes."

She cackled loud enough the whole lunch room could hear. "Uh, oh, you must be in trouble."

The warmth from my cheeks burned down my neck. "It wasn't that big of a deal. I said that I had no idea what he was talking about. I think I'm just behind and he wants to help me catch up."

Bryan cracked a huge grin that lit up his whole face. "You're serious, you've never heard about the other angles of Genesis six?"

"Not really, it was all kind of strange." I shook my head at him, but his smile only widened. What an odd thing to smile about.

"Awesome." Tony pumped his fist. The small gesture lightened the tension at the table. They all stared at me like they'd just won the lottery, all except Mindy and Shanda.

"Really?" Such a strange reaction, especially from the guys.

"I don't get it." Shanda turned to me.

"You and me both," I whispered to her.

"What's not to get? There's two sides on this campus and you have to choose one. If your family didn't already choose it for you." Mindy pounded her cup down so hard the table shook. All the grins evaporated.

"What? It's true." She crossed her arms over her body and glared at me.

"What are you looking at me for?" That strange damp odor hung in the air, like a shadow over my head. It threatened to suffocate me with accusations and implications.

Something must've happened, something major.

Whispers swirled around me. *"It's your fault. It's all your fault."* Yet no one at the table opened their mouth. They just stared at Mindy.

How could it be my fault, or worse, what if the whispers were right? Did this have something to do with James?

I propped my elbows on the table. "You mentioned something about family in class, my family specifically. Does this have anything to do with my brother?"

Mindy flinched like I'd slapped her. Those goggle-sized eyes told the whole story. "You mean he never told you what happened here?"

A bitter laugh escaped my throat. Shadows from the storm outside dappled the tray in front of me. "Please, after graduation James jetted off to Europe. No phone calls, no emails, no communication of any kind. He practically abandoned the family, abandoned me."

"Lucy," her face crumpled. "I'm so sorry. I had no idea. I always thought ..."

"You thought what?" I snapped at her with more venom than I intended. Too much talk about James always brought out the worst in me. I'd be happier if Paige had been the one to take off without a word. But not James, my big bro, my confidant, my grounding influence. His absence carved a hole in my life that could never be replaced. My insides ached.

Her eyes glistened with tears. "Maybe we should talk about this later." With that she bolted out the door, straight into the rain. It must be a big deal for her to ruin her hair like that.

Something was wrong, seriously wrong. No one around here even knew James very well, except Will. Could I really talk to him about it, especially if he was mad at me right now? But where else could I turn?

The clouds parted and splatters of sunshine washed onto Shanda's forehead.

"What was that about?" She hissed in my ear, sending a chill up my neck.

"I have no idea." I clawed through my long hair, wrapping it into a bun. Anything to clear the what-if thoughts from my head. When I let go, soft waves feathered down my back. I stared out the window as the raindrops petered out. The rest of the crew mumbled things behind me, but I tuned them out.

Suddenly I felt like Switzerland, stuck between two sides. Even though I'd just met Mindy, she was quickly becoming one of my favorite people. Had I misjudged her so badly? I'd misjudged Jake, and look how that turned out.

James could've told me what happened anytime in the two years since he'd left me in the lurch. Especially if it involved Montrose. He knew I might come here someday. I missed that lopsided smile of his, the way it somehow made everything better. I'd always figured he wanted to rebel against Mom and Dad and their ridiculous Ivy League, high-society expectations. Maybe there was more to it.

Shanda's ebony fingers filtered the light into confetti before my eyes. "You okay?"

I nodded at her, but I didn't dare meet her eyes, or anyone else's in the group. Then a familiar smell wafted across the table, soapy with a hint of spice.

Will plopped himself in Mindy's spot and turned his gray eyes on me. I forced down a smile, but it played with the corners of my mouth.

Kevin scraped up a chair next to him. "Hi, guys, mind if we join you?"

Tony scooted away from him. "Whatever."

My sandwich lay half-eaten on my plate. The sight of it made my stomach flip-flop, like it couldn't take any more stress. "I've got to get to English. I'll see you guys later."

"Bye, Lucy." Bryan's concerned expression did nothing to calm my nerves. Maybe not nothing. He edged closer and whispered, "Don't forget our deal."

I nodded. His smile almost looked genuine, but was it for Will's benefit or mine?

"I'll come with." Shanda palmed her smoothie, slinging her bag over her shoulder.

Outside I inhaled a giant gulp of damp air. The rainclouds thinned out now, but water still clung to the trees, the grass, the cobblestone.

"Wait up." Will's voice called out. More footsteps sloshed behind me.

"You girls walk fast." Kevin puffed as he sidled up to Shanda. "How you been?"

Shanda's usual cackle teetered into a giggle.

Will caught up with me as I lagged behind the flirting spectacle in front of me.

"Kev's always good for a laugh." He stayed by my side as we headed to Salinger Hall where all the lit and art classes were held.

"I can see that." If Shanda's ebony cheeks could turn bright red like mine, they'd light our way to class like Rudolph's shiny nose.

Will tilted his jaw my way, with that cleft scrunched into his chin. Oh, to have such perfect genes. "You okay? You seemed upset back there. If it's about the other night, I'm really sorry. I hope you know I wasn't talking bad about you, just religious nuts like that Bryan kid. He gets to me."

"No, it's not about that. I feel kinda dumb for overreacting. Believe me, I've got bigger problems." Yet his comments about Bryan drew a hot breath from my lips. Figures they'd both be territorial, a typical guy thing. "My suitemate brought up my brother. It's kind of a sore subject."

"You're not dumb, but I'm glad we're cool." His gray eyes wrinkled like a smiling cat, as if he really meant it. "I wonder how your brother is doing."

Could such a gorgeous guy have a deeper layer of meaning? Before Jake, I always took things at face value. Now I had no clue.

"How well did you know James?" I jumped a puddle and planted my feet on the sidewalk.

He turned to face me. "I was only a freshman when he was a senior. He was president of Nexis then, always the life of the party."

A picture of James sliding down the dorm's grand banister in his PJs popped into my head. His shaggy hair mussed up, that goofy grin all over his face.

I cracked a smile. "That's definitely James. He's probably the life of the party wherever he is now."

The grit of rough fingers brushed the hair off my cheek. A chill crept down my spine at his touch. I stopped and fixed my eyes on Will's. They held me in place. "Someone so beautiful shouldn't be so sad."

Tears rushed to my eyelids. One spilled over, trailing down my cheek.

With his index finger he wiped it away. "I'm sorry, I know you said it's a sore subject."

"You can say that again." I wiped my eyes and studied the wet toes of my canvas Toms. I hadn't even noticed before.

He nudged me with his shoulder, out of my thoughts. "Hey, I'm sorry I can't make the double date thing on Saturday. I've got a Nexis council meeting. It's kind of a big deal."

"What double date thing?" Did my heart just stop?

"Shanda didn't tell you? She and Kevin were trying to do some sort of double date thing this weekend. I thought it was your idea."

"Right, I forgot about that. I was trying to distract Kevin." I bit my lip, peeking up at him behind my lashes. Wasn't the double date supposed to be with Bryan, not Will? But I couldn't ask him that. Already, this was getting too confusing.

"Yeah, don't take it personally. He hits on everyone." He turned those gray eyes on me full force, running his hand through his sandy mop. "But if you're free next weekend, I'd love to take you out. Just us."

"Really?" For the first time today a surge of warmth flooded through my body. He didn't mention the word date, so maybe he actually wanted to hang out. Because hanging out would be okay. But dating definitely was out of the question. "I think that'd be fun."

"Great, let's get you to class." He pressed his hand against the small of my back, leading me to Salinger. Strange, how the warmth of his hand comforted me and sent chills up my back, all at the same time.

7

Humid air pressed down on me, clogging my lungs as I pushed open the glass door to Nelson Hall. The gray heaviness outside had somehow seeped into my dorm, my thoughts. Did Will just ask me on a date, or was it some sort of friendly Nexis way to get me to join up? Maybe it was somewhere in the middle. Questions swirled around in my brain, colliding headlong into what Bryan offered the other night. Sure, I could be friends with guys, but probably not any guy like Will or Bryan. They were both way too charming to be any girl's friend.

"You got a sec, Lucy?" From behind the giant mahogany desk the forty-something dorm mom waved at me, her frizzy fake-red curls bouncing. "I haven't talked to you much, I hope you're settling in all right."

"No complaints so far, Miss Sherry." I edged toward the stairs. Couldn't she see the dark cloud hovering over my head?

Her hands cinched her plump hips. "Now don't play coy. I'm sure a pretty girl like you has lots of friends, and lots of guys chasing her."

Flames fanned up my neck, but I mussed my hair to cover it. Time to pull out one of those homecoming queen smiles Mom taught me. "Well, that's very nice of you to say."

She motioned me toward the front desk. "Since your dad's on the board, we all figured you'd start as soon as your brother graduated. But after what happened to the Donovan girl, you can hardly blame them. So sad really."

"You mean Mindy? What happened to her?" I looked around the room as if she was hiding behind the couch, plotting this whole thing. But the lobby was strangely empty.

The desk dug into Miss Sherry's belly as she leaned forward, lowering her voice a notch or two. "No, this was before Mindy's time. I meant her sister of course."

"Say what?" All I could do was stare blankly like an idiot.

She laughed. "Your face is too funny, like someone kept it a secret from you on purpose."

"Right." Somehow, my head bobbed, but I couldn't feel it. My whole body felt numb. "Why wouldn't they tell me?"

"I'm sure your parents just wanted to protect you." She shrugged like it meant nothing, yet somehow I knew it meant everything. "I'm sorry I brought it up, me and my big mouth. I never meant to upset you."

She ran her fingers through her short fluff, her dark eyes surveying my face.

"So what happened—"

A flash of blonde hair appeared at my side, and I turned to see Monica's white smile. "Hey, Lucy, don't let me interrupt something. I'm just here for the weekly check-in."

"Don't worry, sugar. Everything will be fine." Miss Sherry's bracelets jingled as she patted me on the shoulder.

I could only nod at her. She clomped out from behind her desk and herded Monica into her office.

Okay, maybe I was totally paranoid, but something weird was definitely going on there. All I could think about was Mindy, how something bad happened to her sister. But what did it have to do with my brother? Maybe I didn't want to know.

I shuffled up the stairs and down the hall until I reached Mindy's door. Muffled noises seeped under the cracks, crying noises. I raised my hand to knock, but chickened out and tiptoed to my room instead. She probably needed to be alone, and so did I.

As soon as I closed my door, I headed for the window and curled up in my little nook. Rain pattered against the glass, a random lull that soothed the questions away.

"There you are, I've got something to tell you." Shanda burst into the room, plopping her stuff on her bed and opening her laptop. "Don't worry, you'll thank me later."

"Famous last words." I hugged my legs, resting my chin on my knees.

"Aren't you just precious?" Shanda closed her laptop and perched on my bed, curling up her legs just like me. "You know, Bryan's not exactly cute, and he's only a junior. What about Will? He's so much hotter, and a senior, too. They're both completely into me."

"Is that your best Lucy impression? You need to keep practicing." I pressed my fingertips against the cool glass, tracing the droplets. "And you're wrong about Bryan. I think he's cute."

"Cute, but not hot, right? At least not as hot as Will. He's super fine. You've got to admit."

I just shrugged at her. "So what if Will is hotter? I still think Bryan's cute, too, but it's not all about looks for me. I'm attracted to who a guy really is, and no amount of hotness can make a jerk attractive to me."

"Don't I know it?" She snapped her fingers in my ear. "Girl, you've got it. Two guys after you in a matter of weeks, and you already got them texting you? It's not even homecoming yet."

Suddenly the air stilled, even the raindrops practically froze in mid-air. "There's a message on my phone? I didn't give either one of them my number."

The window ledge couldn't hold me as I tumbled onto the bed, plowing into my nightstand. Tremors seized my hands, but somehow I gripped my cell. Sure enough, a text appeared from Jake. *Miss you babe, let's meet up before you leave. Hope it's not too late. Call me.*

"I'm gonna kill her. How could she do this?" I slammed the phone on my bed, but it bounced once, landing as soft as a happy leprechaun. How pathetic, just like that messed up girl who ratted me out.

"Sorry, I didn't mean to spy." She swiveled her four-inch heel into the wood floor. "Your phone was just sitting there, buzzing away. I didn't mean to look. I put it right back."

I punched the delete button until my index finger turned white. Paige couldn't be that stupid, could she? "Not you, my sister. She obviously gave Jake my new number. That's the last thing I wanted. I just wanted to be free of that jerk."

55

I cratered my face into the pillow.

"That was your ex? What a creep." She eased down beside me on the bed. "Okay, I've waited long enough. Time to spill it. What happened between the two of you?"

"If you must know…" I let my words trail off. I couldn't look at her, so I rolled over and examined the ceiling. Plastic stars stuck to the drywall in some sort of constellation probably leftover from the last girl.

Shanda huffed next to me. Better just rip the band-aid off and be done with it.

"Fine, not like it's something original anyway. Same old sad story. I'd been with Jake since freshman year. When his dad bailed on the family, he got crazy jealous all of a sudden. Like any guy who said hi to me wanted to steal me away, even my guy friends. So I confided in my best friend, Becca, that I wanted to break up with him. Since he was a year older, she told me to wait till after prom."

I glued my eyes to the stars plastic stars above, not daring even to take a peek at her. She didn't say a word. "Okay, lame excuse, I should've broken it off then. A week after that, I caught him going to second base with Becca. I ended it. Then I drove my mom's Mercedes into a tree."

"You what?" Her screech filled the room. Probably echoed down hall, too, then around the world. Yikes, some reaction.

I tilted my head just in time to catch that same expression I always saw when the truth came out. A mixture of pity and sadness in her eyes, her jaw dangling open like a horror-movie poster child.

"Sorry, but dang, girl, that sounds really bad." She made a valiant effort to close her gaping mouth. "Can I see?"

"You mean the freak show. Why not?" The numbness crept in as I parted my hair and bent down. "I was out for six hours. Had eleven stitches."

Her fingers grazed the bumpy scar. "Ouch, that looks bad. How long ago was this?"

"Six months." My eyes welled up. I wiped the mist away and fingered the jagged path in my hairline.

Then a strange thing happened. The numbness released me as if it wasn't so bad somehow, now that someone at Montrose knew the whole truth.

I flipped my hair back into place. "That's not even the worst of it. Becca spread awful rumors about me all over school that I was crazy and psychotic. All my friends avoided me like the plague. It was a nightmare."

She inhaled a sharp whistle. "Does that mean you chose to come to boarding school?"

Her question caught me off guard. "I never really looked at it like that. My Dad always wanted me to come here and go to Yale like he did. After two years trying it my way, I didn't fight too hard to stay home."

"Wow, I thought I had it bad, being shipped here because Daddy's too busy working." Her hand smacked her lips, as if she hadn't meant to say that. She picked up my phone and shook her head. "Man, so he's a cheater, with your best friend? That's rough. I can't believe he texted you now like you're still with him. Sounds like he's the psycho."

I threw my hands up in the air. "Thank you! Tell me about it."

She leveled her gaze at me. "How long are you gonna let some loser keep you from dating?"

The full weight of her question hit me. My neck throbbed and I rubbed the kink away. "Jake can't keep me from anything, I'm just not ready."

"Seriously?" She arched back, eyes wide as I'd ever seen. Why was that the most shocking part of my story? "Personally, I believe in the rebound guy. It's worked for me on several occasions. Who wants to be tied down by a guy in high school anyway? This is the time to be free and have fun."

"That's my plan, just without a guy." I retreated back to my spot in the windowsill.

The clouds still colored the world as gray and moody as I felt. I pressed my forehead against the cool glass. Outside, the raindrops wept along with my insides.

"Okay, I'll stop grilling you." She smoothed out the wrinkles on my bedspread, like nothing ever happened. If only I could smooth out the mess of my life so easily.

I couldn't stand the gloom any more. I darted across the rug, pulling her into a big hug. "Thanks for listening, even though you made me tell."

"How else are we gonna be best buds? Dishing about guys brings girls together." She wriggled away and curled up with her laptop again. "Speaking of guys, I hope you won't get mad at this. I kinda booked a double date tomorrow with Kevin and Bryan."

"You what?" I inhaled sharply, but couldn't keep the smile off my face.

"You knew already." She peered at me over her laptop screen. "Was it Bryan? I knew he had it bad for you."

"You really think so?"

"It's so obvious."

"Well, it wasn't him." I twirled a stray lock of hair around my fingertip. "It was Will, and he kinda asked me out for next weekend."

"No way." Her laptop slid off her legs, and she lunged to catch it. "I was trying to get him to come with us instead of Bryan. Apparently Kevin's not Bryan's biggest fan. But Will bailed at the last second. Glad he made his own date with you."

"I don't know if Will really asked me out, like on a date." I nibbled on my bottom lip. "It could be more of a hangout kind of thing."

"Hang out? Will? Yeah, right," she said. "He gets points for boldness in my book. Does that mean you want to call off the double date?"

I stared at her, not saying a word.

"That settles it, then." She snapped her laptop shut with a flourish. "You're taking my advice whether you want to or not. You'll go out with us and Bryan tomorrow, and Will next week."

"Hang out, really, and tomorrow's more of a group date."

"Whatever you want to call it, you're playing the field. Which field I don't know, but it's still my best advice. You've got to see what's out there."

"Even if it has awkward written all over it?" I kicked a pillow from my bed at her.

"Don't I know it? I couldn't let you loose in my city with two hicks like Bryan and Kevin. What if something happened? I couldn't live with myself. What would I tell your parents?" She flashed a smile at me and padded toward the bathroom.

As she turned on the shower, I flopped across my bed. So Montrose wasn't quite the fresh start I wanted. It was just like any other high school, except now I had a new friend.

Maybe Shanda had a point. Was I really running away from Jake? Obviously that plan backfired because my past found me again, at least in text form. If Montrose could protect me from the big bad world, now was their chance to prove it. Why did even the mention of my ex get to me so much?

Time to forget about Jake and focus on something positive, like what disasters prep-school boys and Shanda could find in New York City on a Saturday night. Finally, something worth looking forward to.

8

"Wow, it reeks in here. Smells like a homeless guy's cardboard box. Glad I wore perfume." As the car rumbled down the track, Shanda elbowed closer to me in the jam-packed tin can. She pinched her nose with one hand, gripping the subway rail with the other. "Who knew you could cram so many people into one car? I can't believe we had to take a train for this. I haven't been on the subway in years."

"Poor spoiled rich girl." Kevin slung his arm around her shoulder. "I hope you can survive one night of roughing it on the subway."

"I doubt it." She smiled up at him like she'd forgotten all about the twenty-plus people surrounding her.

"Gross." The car lurched to a stop and I bounced into Bryan's rock solid chest. Probably a six-pack under there. My mouth dried up.

Maybe he'd think I was talking about him. Why didn't Shanda pull me aside and shake some sense into me? This guy was too gorgeous, not to mention way out of my league.

People rushed out as the doors opened, the perfect opportunity to put some much needed space between me and Bryan.

The silver peep-toes I thought were oh-so-cute only an hour ago now dug into my feet as I scooched away from Mr. Tall Dark and Handsome. But they perfectly accessorized my flowy purple dress, which matched the three-stone amethyst ring on my left hand. Plus, those extra few inches of height might pay off later.

We piled off the train at the next stop and Shanda yanked me up the cement subway steps. My heels pinched with each step. At the top, I walked out into the most breathtaking scene ever.

Neon lights lit up the darkness. Storefront signs, billboards, marquees, all colored the night sky as bright as a runway. I twirled to take it all in, my skirt ruffling around me. "Times Square, how fabulous is this? Look, it's a life-sized Hello Kitty doll."

"Beautiful, isn't it?" Bryan's eyes flashed at me. Was he talking about me or Times Square? Certainly not Hello Kitty.

Heat rose to my cheeks. I stopped spinning and smoothed down my dress. "Yeah, that Hello Kitty is a real bombshell."

"Wait till you see the restaurant I picked out." Kevin sauntered to the curb, his spiky hair blocking the fuzzy feline face.

I pulled my phone out of my clutch and tilted to the left to see around him. "Great, now she's gone."

"Shush, you're ruining this beautiful moment for Lucy." Shanda looped her arm through mine. "This is one of my favorite spots in the city. I'll always love Times Square. It's always bright, always loud, always changing."

"Always commercial."

"Bite your tongue." She kicked Kevin's shin.

"Hey, I was just kidding." He hobbled into the crosswalk. "C'mon."

"Fine." She huffed and we followed Kevin across the street, then down the dirty sidewalk.

The whole time I drank in every color, every flash. Until I face planted into Shanda's braids.

"The Hard Rock Café?" She halted in front of the glittering two-story guitar, her nose wrinkled like we stood in front of a truck stop or something. She punched his arm, shoving him against Bryan.

"Give it a chance, I've got connections." Kevin pulled out his cell, speaking in rapid-fire Spanish.

The crowd parted and a hostess appeared with menus. He dragged Shanda through the maze of tourists milling around the entrance. Bryan and I pushed people aside to catch up.

The hostess led us up a curvy staircase to a booth by the window. "Your server will be out in a sec. Later, Kev."

"See you, Carmen." He waved as she scurried off.

Shanda glared at Carmen's back. "How did you do that?" Her question held a brittle edge.

"My best friend from Cali's girl. We all grew up together, yet somehow she ended up in New York, too." Kevin shrugged and slid into a giant U-shaped booth right in front of the immense bank of windows. He patted the seat beside him. "What's the big deal? I come here a lot."

"Whatever it takes to get this view." She scooted next to him, bouncing on the red leather bench and turning her face to the window. "Times Square is amazing from up here."

She pressed her nose to the glass. I slid in next to her, gazing out the window. The lights twinkled back at me through the tinted pane.

"Stop that, who knows what's on that window." Kevin tugged her arm until she sat down. "At least wait till after we eat to get all germy."

"You guys ready to order?" A waiter hovered over our table.

"It's not rocket science, everything's good here, right, Jeremy?" He nodded at the waiter and started us off, then we all gave our orders.

As the waiter stalked off, Kevin put his arm around Shanda and said something in a low tone. She giggled like a middle-schooler.

"Gag me." I veered away, right into Bryan's stare, like a tractor beam reeling me in.

He bent down, his voice low. "I had no idea they'd hit it off so well."

"Funny how opposites attract." A shiver crawled down my neck and I backed up. "Where are you from?"

I did not just do that. Now who's dishing out pick-up lines?

His eyes wrinkled in the corners, like he knew every silly schoolgirl thought running around in my head. "Harrisburg, Pennsylvania, it's a couple hours outside Philly. I go back when I can for breaks and holidays. I still miss it."

"Close to your family?" Great job, number two on the first date list of obvious questions. That could be construed as a general, friend-type question right? I wish. Proof positive that I had no idea how to just be friends with this guy. I sipped my water, smoothing the napkin over my dress.

"Pretty much." That intense blue-eyed stare fixed itself on me. "My mom is a high-profile psychologist, she's been on TV shows like Good Morning America. Dad sort of manages her career because she travels around the country giving lectures and stuff, that's why we go to Montrose. It's because of her I'm thinking about psychology as a career. She really loves her job, but it's difficult to not bring it home."

"You mean she analyzes you a lot?" I pictured him lying on the couch, his mom perched in a recliner with a pen and paper. Poor guy.

"All of us really." He shook his head, draping his arm around the back of the booth. At least my side of it. "Poor Brooke, she still hasn't figured out the tricks, but Abby taught me years ago."

I curled my lips at the mental image—him in the middle of a sister fight, whistle in his mouth, ref's jersey. "Bet that was fun growing up with two sisters."

"We had some interesting moments." His eyes sparked like there was so much more to tell. "But Abby pretty much ruled the roost with an iron fist."

"Sounds like you're as close to Abby as I was to my brother." I let my eyes fall to the tabletop. I wish I still had a great relationship with my brother like Bryan did with his sisters. I scratched a chip in the wood with my fingernail, anything to avoid those eyes.

His fingers brushed mine, sending a shockwave through me. I gazed up at him, then caught a glimpse of someone standing over our table.

Jake.

My heart thudded in my chest, loud as a thunderstorm. It was all I could hear. A dark shadow hovered next to him, bringing a damp smell with it.

"No way." I blinked, but he still stood there, the shadow too. Something curdled in my throat. I could practically taste the fear, and it was coming from the wisps of dark smoke emanating from the scary-movie-like creature next to my ex. This couldn't be happening.

"That's not Jeremy." Shanda eyed the stranger. When she glanced over at me her expression died. "Do you know that guy?"

"Lucy, you okay?" Bryan grabbed my hand and squeezed it. "Who is this guy?"

Did he use a stun gun on me or something? I couldn't move, couldn't form a coherent sentence. Maybe it was the weird shadow. It had feathery tendrils that curled around the jerk's throat.

I rubbed my eyes again, but it didn't go away like my other vision. Was this a nightmare? The lump in my throat dropped like a bomb, exploding fireflies in my stomach.

"Sorry to interrupt like this." He pulled up a chair and parked himself at our table. Typical Jake. And the shadow stayed put. "I had to see Lucy. She and I go way back."

He shook Kevin's hand, then Bryan's. "I'm Jake, her boyfriend."

Disgust gurgled in my stomach, mixed with Jake-rage. Who did he think he was? Showing up here like this? Suddenly the shadow's tendril drifted from Jake's side of the table toward me. Before I knew it, an icy grip encircled my throat. I clawed at my throat to get more air. My fingers froze like they'd wrestled a Popsicle, the cold shivering down to my feet.

Words were impossible, breathing difficult.

He reached over to shake Shanda's hand. She didn't budge, just blinked at me. "You mean ex-boyfriend, right, Lucy?"

I tried to nod, but I couldn't move. Like I'd suddenly turned to stone. The panic welled up with a fire, burning in the corners of my eyes.

Then the waiter came over with our food, nodding at the new guy. "Did I miss someone?"

"I'll have the Hard Rock bacon burger and a chocolate shake." Jake shot me his I'm-so-charming face. Yeah right. "You don't mind if I join you, do you?"

"Not at all." Kevin popped a fry in his mouth.

Shanda and Bryan just stared at me.

With a surge of strength I shook my head hard, too hard. The shadow tightened its grip around me.

"You feeling okay? You don't look so good." Bryan brushed my hair back. His touch sparked the shadow and made it slither back to Jake's side.

Panting like I'd run a mile, I gulped lungfuls of air. No way could I meet Bryan's stare, full of questions. I had to think. What could I possibly say that would make any sense of my antics?

"Jake, what brings you to New York?" Kevin asked.

"That's a funny story." His eyes roamed over me like a piece of meat.

The anger swirled inside me, mixing with the fear and sheer panic until I couldn't take it any more. Acid burned in my throat. I clutched my stomach, gonna hurl.

"I could lie and say I was in the area. But it's not true." He reached for my hand. His touch burned my fingers and I jerked back.

"How's Becca?" I spat out the words like they were a disease. As far as I was concerned that's what he was, too. Biting into my lip, I glared my worst evil-eye at him.

"It's over now," he snapped. "That's why I'm here."

Shanda's face scrunched up and she rubbed my forearm. "How can you come here and say these things to Lucy. In front of her friends that you don't even know?" She threw down her napkin.

Bryan slid his arm around my shoulders. Even Kevin tensed up.

A glimmer of hope surged through me. I clenched my teeth, time to get it together. No more creepy shadow to hold me back. "Why don't you just leave? I don't know why you came, but I don't want you here. Please go."

Jake's face softened. "Luce, I miss you, that's all."

"Maybe you should take this outside." Bryan's jaw tightened into a straight line, his eyebrows bunching up. He couldn't be serious, like I'd ever let this crazy guy get me alone.

"I won't go anywhere with him. It's over, it's been over for months. I'm not discussing it." Flashes of hot anger seethed under my skin ready to electrocute that crazy shadow if it came any closer. I kept my voice steady, loud and firm. "Leave."

"How can you say that, it wasn't all bad, remember?" Jake jerked back in his chair like he'd been slapped. The smoky darkness lingered at his side. "I'm sorry, Luce, can't we just get over it and move on?"

"Stop it," Bryan cut in. "You're upsetting Lucy, can't you see that? You heard the lady, it's time for you to leave."

He squeezed my shoulder, but kept his angry eyes on the cheater. What a hero.

Jake slammed his fists on the table, hard. Everyone shot back against the booth.

"I'm not leaving till I get an answer."

"You got your answer." I stood, the words like a choke collar around my neck as the shadow lunged at me again. I jumped back and the wraith's claws missed me by mere inches. I couldn't let this guy win. I curled my fingers into my palms, clenching every muscle in my body. Something surged within me, burning my lungs. I felt powerful and alive, and I didn't care any more. Jake needed to get this through his thick skull. "Leave or I'll have my buddy here get the bouncers."

My eyes were stinging again. Great, here come the waterworks.

"Get out of here." Bryan towered over me, fists balled. "Or else."

"I don't think so." Jake growled, shoving his chair to the ground. The dark wraith billowed taller. "You don't understand what's going on here."

I wrapped my hand in the crook of Bryan's bicep, praying someone would come to my rescue.

"I understand perfectly." His arm encircled my waist.

Kevin rose from his chair. "Man, don't make me call security."

"That isn't necessary." Jake eyed Bryan and Kevin. The shadow whispered something in his ear, and he glared at Bryan's arm around me.

"Look," Bryan's face twisted, his jaw set, "this is your last warning. Get out of here. Now."

Suddenly the shadow morphed into a hulking man, fists raised. He made a jab toward Bryan's face, when out of nowhere a pillar of pure light shot down from the ceiling, halting the sinister arm mid-punch.

I gasped, and whipped my head toward Bryan. Blinking like a fool, I couldn't believe my eyes. But it looked so real.

At Bryan's side stood a cloud of the brightest white you've ever seen, outlined in the shape of one burly dude. He shone like the sun and flashed like lightning, his sculpted biceps refracting rays of light in every color. Breathtaking in beauty, if the light wasn't so piercingly white.

A sense of awe descended upon me. All the noises in the crowded restaurant faded into the background, hushed by the dazzling sight in front of me.

The shadow-ghoul aimed another swipe, but the white-lightning man blocked the dark punch with one shining blow. Then he landed an uppercut right under the wraith's ghastly jaw. Shards of every color whizzed by me like diamonds exploding in every direction.

The shadow man exploded in a puff of flame and smoke, blowing hot wind on my face. Then *Poof!* he evaporated into thin air.

It felt as if time stopped. All I could see was this immensely beautiful creature in front of me who saved me from a fate I didn't ever want to imagine. And one word filled my mind.

Angel.

He winked one golden eye and blasted skyward, leaving a wake of light that seared my retinas. For a few seconds it was burned into my brain—unmistakable. The translucent outline of feathery wings. But then he disappeared through the restaurant ceiling. I could only stand there in utter amazement, my eyes fixed on that one spot, as if by sheer willpower I could make the glorious creature descend from the heavens and explain himself.

Like why me, for example? How come I was the only one who could see what just happened? And how would I ever be able to explain any of this to a mere mortal?

"Maybe I'll see you around." Jake's voice was haughty, more like his usual self. Completely oblivious to the duel between light and shadow that just totally rocked my universe.

I lowered my gaze back down to the earthly fight in front of me. It all seemed so pointless now.

Bryan grabbed a handful of Jake's shirt and raised his fist. A low snarl escaped his throat. "If I ever see you hanging around Lucy, even on campus, you'll wish you never set foot in this city."

"Okay, man." A hint of fear clouded Jake's eyes. Way to go Bryan. "Relax, I'm going."

"Just let him go, man." Kevin cocked his head at Bryan.

He released Jake's shirt and my evil ex stalked off, squinting daggers over his shoulder the whole time. Bryan stared Jake down until he punched open the front door.

Then the waiter came back. "Everything all right, Kevin?"

Suddenly my entire body started shaking. The restaurant whirled around me, whizzing in circles like a funnel cloud of light and shadow. Did I really just see angels fighting wraiths? How crazy was that?

Bryan unclenched his fist, his fingers grazing my cheek. "Are you okay?"

"I don't know." Everything spun by too fast, except Bryan's face. Worry lines etched between his eyebrows, then it all faded out. Like I'd fallen into an abyss, and I'd keep falling forever. My knees buckled under me, but strong arms gripped me on either side. Bryan's arms.

9

Vague shapes greeted me when I opened my eyes, wisps of gray mist outlined by shadows. A dark hand pressed something cold against my forehead. Too cold. I jerked up and the world righted itself again.

Shanda rubbed my forehead.

"What happened?" I searched the dining room. No strange images of shadowy figures and lightning men fighting, just worried faces from Shanda, Kevin, and Bryan. Disappointment seeped down the back of my throat. Back to reality.

"I think you passed out." Shanda peeled back the icy napkin from my forehead. "Any better?"

"Getting there." I tried to force out a smile, but it hurt my head. A fleeting thought passed through my mind, like maybe what I just saw was all in my head. But yet I knew, deep down, it was real. It felt so real.

Bryan flagged down Jeremy, another worry line creasing over the bridge of his nose. "Get her a milkshake, quick."

Jeremy pulled the pen out from behind his ear. "What flavor?"

"It doesn't matter, chocolate I guess. It's an emergency." He rubbed my hands between his, faster and faster.

Jeremy zigzagged among the maze of tables, like I'd started a fire or something. It was almost laughable, if I had an ounce of energy to laugh.

"What are you doing?" The friction from Bryan's hands warmed me, surging through my body, pushing back the fog.

A muscle in his jaw twitched. "I don't know, just trying get your circulation going I guess."

Jeremy reappeared and plopped the shake in front of me.

Bryan ripped open the straw, dunking it in the cold liquid. "Sip this, slowly."

The icy chocolate goo sluiced down my throat. It tasted good. Then a fleeting sadness hit me. I couldn't stop picturing the fight—the real one, with the angel and the shadow. And I just wanted the golden-eyed angel to come back. My head throbbed again. "Did that really just happen?"

"What a jerk!" Shanda shouted as if she couldn't contain it any longer. "I can't believe he drove all the way here from Indiana. What a creep."

"I'm sorry I asked him to join us." Kevin slumped over the remnants of his burger.

"It's not your fault. He would've sat down anyway. He thinks he owns the whole world." Was my head the punching bag in that fight? It sure felt that way. I closed my eyes and rested my cheek on Bryan's shoulder.

Without saying a word, he reached over and stroked my hair.

"Mmm, that feels nice," I murmured. "I'm just glad you made him leave."

"No kidding, man. You saved the day." Kevin pumped his fist in the air like he was Rocky.

Shanda batted his arm down. "Guess it paid off, having friends here."

"You got that right." Bryan lifted his hand from my head and picked up a French fry.

"Tell me about it." I would give Kevin a fist bump, if I had any strength left to move.

Bryan dangled a fry in my face. "Maybe you should eat something."

"If you insist." I munched on the cold fry, as if simple carbs could magically imbue me with enough courage to say what I knew I had to say. "I'm sorry to put you in the middle of that. You deserve an explanation."

"Don't worry about it." His hand returned to my hair. "That part's up to you. It's not like you owe me anything."

"Really?" When I lifted my eyes to meet his, the look on his face wasn't the normal sad mixture of pity and horror. A glimmer of understanding lurked in his eyes, like maybe he could relate.

69

"At least your ex doesn't go to Montrose. Of course, mine never stalked me like yours has, at least not that I know of."

"Please," Kevin exhaled sharply, "like Colleen would ever stalk you. She's way too good for you ever since she left the Guardians and joined Nexis."

"Is that what you and chapel your friends call yourselves? How fitting." Then it dawned on me. "Wait, you dated Colleen?"

"That's right," Bryan interrupted, giving Kevin the cold shoulder, "but that was a long time ago."

"So was Jake, or so I thought." The words eeked out in a low whisper, as if someone punched all the air out of me. The truth of what I'd seen swirled around with the straw in my shake. No way would these guys believe my angel fighting shadow story. Even I didn't know for sure if it was real. So I focused on the present reality. "I was so shocked at first to see him, then mad. Seething mad. When I'm that upset, I can barely speak, you know? I don't know what I would've done if you weren't here."

With that I shoved a few fries into my mouth. Maybe I could hold off on the breakup spiel as long as possible. Once was enough for one week.

"I should've said something sooner." His voice grew loud enough that Kevin and Shanda put down their sandwiches. "I saw him hanging around outside the student union earlier today."

"On campus?" I almost choked on a fry. "I can't believe him!" Nausea slapped me in the face like a giant wave, my hands shook, my heart fluttered again.

"How'd he even find us here? It's not like this is anywhere near campus." Shanda eyes widened. "He must've been following us. That crazy stalker."

"Stop it, I don't even want to think about it." Images of the shadowy hand around my throat sent a chill through me. Bryan's fingers brushed mine with a spark, like the angel when he appeared. In spite of the Jake trauma and the angel/shadow drama, I still felt electricity whenever Bryan touched me.

"Isn't there something we can do about it?" Shanda turned her head toward Kevin who only shrugged.

"We should alert campus security," Bryan switched to a matter-of-fact tone, "and your dorm mom. Other than that, there's not much we can do, sorry to say."

"What about a restraining order or something?" Shanda shredded her napkin into confetti.

"Not without any threat of violence." Kevin clicked his tongue at her. "I heard it in my Criminal Law class. Besides, that wouldn't stop an attack, just put him in jail if he tried anything. It makes me sick."

"It's not that bad, he's not violent or anything." Still, I shuddered at the mere idea of it. "I'd feel better if we alerted campus security, like Bryan said."

I wobbled my bottom lip at Shanda, praying she could read my mind.

She pushed back her chair and hooked her arm in mine. "Don't worry, I've got your back. I'll go with you when we get back to campus."

"I think we should all go with Lucy to talk to campus security." Bryan's hand found the small of my back and led me out of the restaurant, just like Will the other day. But I couldn't think about that, not now.

"Good idea." Shanda nodded, catching up with Kevin.

Bryan's pace slowed and I slowed with him. "How about you come to our next chapel meeting? There are some things I want to show you."

The idea rolled around like a loose pinball in my brain. Nothing made sense any more. After what he did for me tonight, how could I turn him down?

"I'd like that." I smiled up at him and let him lead me down the busy sidewalk. After tonight, I might let him lead me anywhere.

Remnants of the weekend still slithered in and out of the corners of my mind. Jake showing up out of nowhere, the dark wraith versus the angel of light, smoke clashing with lightning. The images swirled in my head for the entire hour of Western Civ, until all I wanted to do was run out the door and into Bryan's arms. But I couldn't be that girl, the stupid schoolgirl always chasing some guy. Instead I trudged up the steps, into the mass exodus from Harlixton's classroom. The paneled hall felt cold, no Bryan in sight. I'd give anything for his arm around me, even if I wasn't supposed to want it. Kinda unnerving, really.

71

"Wait up, Lucy." A voice called from behind until the man himself stood beside me. "How are you doing today? You look great."

Those aqua eyes burned two little holes in me. I could've melted into the floor. "Thanks to you."

"Did you hear anything from campus security? I got this." He lifted the bag off my shoulder, brushing back my hair.

I turned away from the burning blue and smoothed my hair back in place, grazing the scar with my fingertips. "Besides the standard, 'we're looking into it?' Nothing yet."

"Then he's still out there." He practically punched open the outer door. Then his hand steadied and he held it open for me. "I knew it, I should've reported him when I had the chance. I'm such an idiot." His voice turned gritty.

At the bottom of the steps I slowed my stride and cocked my head at him. "The last thing I would call you is an idiot."

"I don't know about that." His hands pressed down on my shoulders, holding me still. Yet the horizon swayed. "Listen, that's not all I'm worried about. I know you probably won't believe this coming from me, but Nexis is not what you think they are. Trust me. Can you tell me what happened at that meeting in the observatory?"

"How'd you know about that?" This time I couldn't look away, no matter how bad I wanted to. "I wish I knew who to trust. I don't even know if I can trust myself any more." The truth hummed around in my skull.

All the color drained from his face, contrasting like night and day against his dark hair. "Please, God, tell me Will didn't hurt you."

"Will? What are you talking about?" Fear clouded his eyes. I shook my head at him. "No way, the meeting was weird, but he never laid a finger on me. Except to save me from falling off the ledge."

A grin split his face. Shades of cream and beige flushed his cheeks. "Thank God. Are you sure that's all?"

"Pretty much." That night was pretty strange. How could I have forgotten? "He showed me some weird book."

"He what?" Air whooshed from his lungs in a minty blast. "How could they let you anywhere near the Nexis book? You're not even a member yet. I thought it was under lock and key."

Really, was that all he cared about, the stupid Nexis group? Not the fact I almost fell from a five-story tower? I kicked the toe of my blue Toms against a crack in the sidewalk. "What's the big deal? It was kind of weird. You don't have to get mad about it."

His mouth hung open. I could've practically picked his jaw up off the cobblestone. "Mad, you think I'm mad? I'm in shock. It could've been much worse, he's a very dangerous guy. The book part is extra strange, even for him, like he's got something planned for you. It definitely puts a wrench into things."

"Are you for real?" Could he be right about Will? I squinted at him, studying his strange expression. Taut jaw, eyes steady and calm, no shifting off to one side, definitely not lying. Maybe just a hint of the furtive I'm-keeping-things-from-you look. "Is he that bad?"

"I'm afraid so." He wrapped his hand around mine. "Let's get out of here. There's some things I need to tell you. That I should've already told you."

"What about lunch?" Crickets chirped in the empty quad. Across the lawn, the lunch frenzy spilled over from the cafeteria. It'd be a madhouse in there right now.

Car keys jingled in his hands. "I know a great diner in town. My treat."

He tugged me down the sidewalk to the parking lot, stopping in front of a beat-up Corolla.

"Won't we get in trouble for leaving school?" I never thought of Bryan as the bad boy who skipped class. Next thing you know he'd hand me a leather jacket and lead me to his real ride, a motorcycle. Adjusting my black leather jacket, I glanced back to the campus—so small from this distance.

"Don't worry about it, we'll be back before our next classes. Hop in." The car door groaned as he opened it for me. "This is Old Faithful. She got my sister through high school, now she's all mine."

I slid into the passenger seat, smacking my forehead on his Betty Boop air freshener. Her rotten strawberry smell clawed at my nose. "Back it up, Betty."

Bryan climbed in the driver's side and started the car. "What'd you say?"

"Nothing." I eyed Betty's dark lashes. "Just having a conversation with Betty there."

His rumbly laugh filled the tiny car. "Brooke insisted on that. You know, you're the only girl I've had in here besides my sister."

"Good." His hand brushed mine as he fumbled with the gearshift.

Five minutes later he eased into the parking lot of the Riverdale Coffeehouse. Inside we were shown to a vinyl booth by the yellow-gingham-curtained window. The waitress penciled our order on her notepad and left us alone in the practically full dining room.

I bounced on the burgundy bench. Not quite the picture of freedom and rebellion I'd imagined. "Okay, what's the scoop on Will?"

"You first." He scooted forward, his elbows grazing the Formica. "Tell me what else happened in the tower."

"Not much. Well, except one thing." I stopped bouncing. "Shanda is really into astronomy. After the meeting she told me Nexis wasn't using the telescope to check out the stars. They're watching the campus."

The waitress came back with our iced teas and Bryan pressed his lips together until she stomped off. "That sounds like the opposite of a star party. More like a stalker party, and Will's got you in his sights. Honestly, that's what scares me the most."

Peach-flavored tea hit my tongue as I sipped, refreshing in spite of Bryan's stalker party accusation. Jealous much? "Yeah, right, like they need me for anything. What's so scary about him anyway?"

He gulped down his Coke, scratching his chin. "That's the thing, I'm pretty sure he only wants you in his group because of your family."

"Because James was the last president, or because Dad's on the school board? My parents were the only reason I subjected myself to that meeting. I wanted to run for the hills. Literally." For the first time I'd vocalized the truth, and now I couldn't stop the dam. "I never want to end up like them, or James for that matter."

"You won't end up like your brother unless you want to." Bryan's hand crawled across the table, his fingers sliding around the amethyst ring my parents gave me as a sweet sixteen present. "But there's more to it than that. It's about your family's legacy."

Just then the waitress appeared with my sandwich and Bryan's burger. He shut his mouth again until she left. Who was she gonna tell anyway?

I hoisted my sandwich high enough to cover my mouth. "What do you mean by family legacy?" I whispered behind the chicken parm, just in case it was actually as big a deal as Bryan imagined.

He hacked up a storm, almost choking on a fry. "You're a funny girl, you know that? But we can't discuss it here. We'll have to wait until Wednesday, in the chapel."

"Seriously?" A mouthful of marinara stuck to the back of my throat. I slurped down my tea as fast as it would flow. "What does your little group know about my family?"

"Sounds like more than you do, apparently. Believe me, the Guardians are no little group." He glanced around the dining room. "Be sure to keep this to yourself, though."

I nodded, lowering my voice like I was sure Nancy Drew would. "I won't spill a thing about the Guardians, whoever you are. But you, mister, never answered my question. Why's Will so scary?"

"It's not just him, it's his group. Nexis is more than a school club, they're international and they've got scary plans. The justification behind them is even worse." He folded his arms across his chest. "Will is their fiercest recruiter in several decades. He's heartless, especially when he doesn't get what he wants. The fact that he's after you, so soon, really bothers me."

I sucked down my tea until the cup emptied. Obviously, Will wanted me to join his super secret club, but why? And why did Bryan care so much? Jealousy could do weird things to people, even halfway normal guys. Besides, there was no way I could stop anything Will or Nexis had in mind. One little girl from Indianapolis? Sure, I wanted to make my own mark, but this was getting out of control. Whatever Will or Bryan wanted from me, they couldn't both be good.

10

With my pencil, I traced a feathery outline of the white image branded into my mind. Those delicate wings, so alive, so full of light in every shade. How could my simple drawing recreate their splendor? I smudged the edges with my index finger, but it only diluted the white, as if the wingtips were singed by the shadow. That's not the way it happened, not in my mind. I ripped off the page and crumpled it in my hands.

It felt wrong to be so heartless, yet wrong to draw something untrue to what I'd seen. Could what I imagined somehow be real? It'd felt so real two days ago. But if it wasn't real, then I needed to have my head examined. I chucked the paper wad into the trash.

The last bell rang and I shoved my sketchpad and pencils into my bag. Maybe I was going crazy, seeing strange things like angel fights, shadowy wraiths, and an old man praying. With my fingertips, I grazed over the familiar bump under my mass of dark hair. Could it be my head injury from seven months ago, or something else? Something bigger than I could fathom in my own little world?

The mad end-of-the-day rush carried me down the cobblestone path from Salinger and across the quad. I fought against the flow all the way up the steps into Trenton. If only I could push back the image I'd seen in Harlixton's class, the bearded man, kneeling, with black and white and gray swirling around him.

I trudged around the halls like a reluctant mouse who didn't really want to find her way out of the maze. On the left I found a door with a golden plaque that read Mr. Harlixton. Rocking back on my heels, I fiddled with my sweet-sixteen ring, wondering if I really wanted to go in. The temptation was too great, so I peeked my head into the closet-sized room.

The balding man arched back from the stack of papers in front of him. "Miss McAllen, please take a seat." He gestured to the only chair in the cramped room not piled with books or folders. "Do you have any idea why I wanted to see you today?"

I scooted the chair in front of his wide desk. "Because I'm behind in Western Civ. My dad really wants me to get into Yale, and I have to keep up my grades. So I'll take any help you can give me."

His pot-belly dented into the desk. "Is that all your father said to you? He hasn't told you anything about Genesis six or any groups on campus?"

I inched back in my chair. "Not really, except for Nexis I guess. My parents both really want me to join."

"Interesting." His office chair squeaked as he shifted his weight back. "Why do you think that is?"

I shrugged. Maybe he should have a couch in here or at least an easy chair if he planned to offer therapy sessions. "I don't know, I always assumed it was because of my brother."

"Yes, that's probably it." He unhooked his glasses from his ears. Then he whipped out a white handkerchief, rubbing the smudgy lenses. "I'm still surprised your parents never told you more about Noah or the flood."

"Why would they?" I cocked my head at him. This was getting a little weird.

He folded the handkerchief into a neat triangle, then placed the glasses back on his face. Papers swished across the desk as he angled forward, eyes trained on mine as if the whole world were about to end. "Because you have a significant choice to make, right here, on this campus."

I froze under his beady-eyed gaze, still as a deer in his headlights. "What do you mean?"

"There are two groups on this campus." His words poured out slowly, like he didn't want to spook me into running for the woods. "They believe diametrically opposite things about the passage we discussed in class on Friday. They are both backed by strong supporters of the school. So unfortunately, Montrose has been forced not to take sides. These groups recruit members for their cause. You, little lady, are the highest priority for recruitment by both groups."

"Me, seriously?" Oxygen seeped from my lungs like a deflating balloon. I gulped in stale office air. "Why would Nexis and the Guardians want me?"

"Good girl, at least you know who's after you now." His deep voice hit a grave note.

"After me?" I sputtered. "But why me? I'm nobody."

He shook his head. "Unfortunately for you, that's not true. Trust me, I wish I could tell you more now, but you probably won't believe me. I don't think you're ready yet."

Could he be any more cryptic? His blank expression held a hint of kindness, like he told the truth as best he could. But the questions assaulted my brain. "You can't tell me all of this and leave me hanging. Please, give me something I can use."

"Fair enough." His elbows clanged on the desk, his voice low. "First I'd send you to the chapel study group to get you caught up on your history."

"I was there last week." I squinted across the desk at him. Why did I think he already knew that?

"They meet once a week, but you can certainly go on your own and do your own research." The way he emphasized *your own* made it sound like a command, not a suggestion. "Focus on Genesis and Noah. You'll figure out your place in all of this soon enough."

That last part hit me in the gut. If I had to figure out my place in the Nexis/Guardian tug-of-war, the sooner the better. Before someone else figured it out for me. "Is that all?"

"No." Mr. Harlixton scraped his chair back and stood up. "You need to be very careful. Don't believe everything these people tell you, especially about your brother."

"My brother, really?" The words clanged in my ears as I rose to my feet. I racked my brain for all the things James ever said about Montrose, but I couldn't remember anything specific. "What do you know about him?"

"Just be careful." He nodded toward the exit as a honey-blonde girl waited in the doorway. His voice crescendoed and his lips curled, almost like a smile, but not quite. "Okay, Lucy? I'll see you next week, same time."

"But—" His eyes hardened, so I clamped my mouth shut. "Next week then."

"Good luck." He called after me as I squeezed by the girl on my way out, her green eyes slicing into me. Colleen, from the Nexis meeting. No wonder Mr. Harlixton ended the conversation.

How much did she hear? With a slight nod in her direction I booked it down the hall, gunning for the nearest exit. Those catty eyes glued on my every move, like she saw right through me. A chill crept up my neck.

Nexis or Guardian? I had no idea which side to choose. Harlixton pretty much vetoed all the hopes I had of not taking sides, being my own personal Switzerland. How in the world could my strange visions be of help to anyone? More importantly, how would I ever know if I chose the right side? After all, I was just one girl.

A rosy hue lit up the wooden altar of the chapel sanctuary. I tiptoed to the nearest hand-carved pew and kicked back to watch the stained-glass sunset. Evening rays slanted through the multi-colored panes, splashing the room with faded light. A mosaic waltzed across the floor tiles, the entire formation an intricate dance more spectacular than each piece on its own.

"Beautiful, isn't it?" I stiffened and turned toward the voice. Bryan rested his hand on the back of my pew. "You ready?"

"I could watch this all day. Can't you guys meet out here instead?" The world made more sense here in the chapel—next to Bryan. Less overwhelming. So peaceful I never wanted to leave.

"Hey, good idea, for another night. We've gathered up some books in the library that you'll want to see." He tugged on my hand and I followed him down the cold tiles.

"Why do I have this funny feeling? Like there's some big secret about my family and it's not good?" My questions clashed together like cymbals, one on top of the other, echoing down the hall. I cringed. "What a mess," I whispered to my shoes. I always blurted out my ramblings, even the intensely personal ones. This time, it felt okay, like he'd understand.

"You decide your own destiny, good or bad." He swung open the library door. It creaked on its hinges.

I scrunched up my forehead in the way Mom hates. She insists I look like a worried bulldog, but seriously, what a strange thing for him to say.

I opened my mouth to object, then clamped it shut. Maybe I could at least wait and hear him out, then make my decision. I tripped over the door jamb and crashed smack dab into his back. "My bad."

"C'mon, it won't be that awful." With his palm he steadied my elbow, leading me to the table by the lead-paned window. Piles of books littered the tabletop. Dad would love this, all the antiques and old books.

The redheaded trio of Lenny, Laura, and Felicia made Brooke's dirty blonde hair stand out even more. She stared back at me as I eased into my chair.

"Where's Tony?" I glanced around the shelves, but the dark-haired Italian didn't slink out from behind the shadowed stacks.

"Soccer practice." Laura answered from her seat next to me. With tiny hands covered in hospital gloves, she flipped through the gilt pages of a decrepit book. "He may show up later, but tonight is really all about you."

"Goody, another weird old book," my mouth blurted out on its own again. Perfect. I faced the window and inhaled a deep breath. Something big was about to happen, I could feel it hovering in the room whether I was ready or not. Outside the sky darkened into shades of blue and gray. The uneven glass painted the clouds with a watercolor glow. "Okay, whatever it is, please be gentle."

Bryan angled his chair toward me, his knee inches from mine. "How much has your family told you of their beliefs about the flood?"

I chewed on my lip, raspberry lip balm smacking my tongue. Was this a trick question? It felt like a pop quiz. "Not much, just the usual Noah's ark Bible story. Why?"

"Nexis believes your family is descended straight from the line of Noah's firstborn son, Shem." Lenny's deep voice did nothing to calm my nerves. Neither did those strange words.

"Say what? How is that even possible?" I combed my fingers down the length of my hair, twirling a long strand around my pinkie. "What, because I've got dark hair and dark eyes? We're not even Jewish, I don't think."

Laura rubbed my shoulder with her tiny fingers, like there might be more to come. "It has nothing to do with what race you are. It's more of a specific covenant with God, the one in Genesis six to be precise." She inched the yellowed book toward me.

A black and white drawing of a man in a robe stared back at me. He was kneeling before a great beam of light. I blinked, then blinked harder. The picture was unmistakable.

It was the same as the vision I had in Harlixton's class. The caption read *Noah's Covenant*.

"Covenant." The word whispered in my ears over and over again, like it came from somewhere in the room. I glanced from the stacks to the turret, even out the window. No one lurked in the corners or in the shadows. I closed my eyes and the whispers stopped.

When I opened them everyone stared at me. I probably had some wild, rabid look on my face right about now. Great, now they just thought I was nuts. At this point, I'd say the same about them.

"Okay, so there's some kind of covenant. What does that have to do with me?"

"Firstborn descendants of Shem are marked. They're supposed to have special gifts." Felicia thrust another book at me. "No gift is the same, some know things, like the difference between good and bad. Some have premonitions."

"Wait a minute." I stared straight into her green eyes, almost like Colleen's, only less catty. "I'm not even the firstborn."

"But your dad is, so that makes you a descendant of the firstborn." Her voice lowered to a whisper as one polished nail landed on a drawing in the book. "One appointed firstborn has the most powerful gift of all."

My lungs froze in my chest, as if waiting to breathe until she finished her sentence. Dare I look at that picture? I forced my gaze down to the drawing in front of me, similar to the one Laura showed me first. This time the man had wispy shapes of light and shadow swirling from his eyes.

I lowered my lids and the vision came back to me. In full color. It was the exact same image—in my mind and on paper. And it was too much.

I opened my eyes. "Technically, if you believe the Bible, then every person on earth is a descendant of Noah. So how could I be the direct firstborn descendant of Noah's firstborn son? The odds are like one in three billion." No way, it couldn't be me. I couldn't stare at it any more. With a flourish I pushed it away.

Bryan jammed his hands over mine, rough but gentle, sliding the book back toward me. "This is a rendering of an ancient prophesy. That once every century, when they turn eighteen, one appointed firstborn descendant of Noah will have the power to see the unseen."

In front of me the drawing came alive. The beam of light shone from the book straight into my eyes. When I turned to Bryan the same white light backlit his face, only in a dimmer form. A halo almost, highlighting his profile. It burned my eyes, but I couldn't look away.

Could he be creating that light, or was I losing it again? He pointed his finger at a paragraph about the descendants of Noah. The words jumbled together. "The unseen, what does that mean?"

The halo moved with him as he dipped his head to meet my eyes. "It's from the Bible—Ephesians chapter six, among other places. It refers to the unseen battle between heaven and hell."

That had to be it. A sudden shiver raised the hair on the back of my neck. Maybe it was all real, the vision I saw at Hard Rock. Was it some kind of supernatural battle? "Whoa, you're kidding, right? That's the gift, the power to see angels and demons? Creepy."

"Yes, very creepy, if used the wrong way." Laura's index finger drew a line under a passage in the book, but the words still didn't make much sense.

Wisps of cold wove their way under my skin. The world around me stood still. And suddenly it made perfect sense.

I turned to Bryan. "So you're saying Will thinks I have some kind of power and he wants to use it for Nexis?"

"You, and future generations." He nodded around the table, the light behind him fading. "See what I mean? Very perceptive."

"That's so stupid, I'm the middle child," I screeched like a terrified bat. "If that's what they actually believe then they should be after James. Wait, is that why he's in Europe?"

"I don't know." Laura peeled off one glove and reached over to pat my hand. Warmth seeped from her soft touch, warmth I needed desperately. "I know this is a lot to take in, let alone believe. We're only here to help."

I exhaled the breath I'd sucked in for too long. In some strange way what they were saying was starting to make sense. James wouldn't abandon me like he did unless he had no choice. But the idea wasn't as comforting as I thought it'd be.

Clip-clomps of heavy feet pounded from the hallway, one by one, until a dark figure filled the doorway.

"And we're also here to protect you." Tony's deep voice echoed like a gong in the quiet room. That boy could win a James Dean lookalike contest. All he needed was a leather jacket over that blue and gold Montrose Soccer uniform.

"Is that why you guys call yourselves the Guardians? What is there to protect us firstborn descendants, or whatever you call us, from?"

"From Will and his family's stupidity, but most of all from Nexis." He straddled the back of a chair next to Bryan. The Montrose logo on his jersey peeked between the slats. "They have big plans. If they think you're the Seer or you have an equally powerful gift, they'll need you to complete their mission."

"The Seer. Is that what you call this one supposedly special relative of mine?" It sounded like a Lord of the Rings character. Yet it clicked, right into place. Did that mean my hallucinations were part of this unseen reality? Could I actually be the Seer? No way, not in a million years. It didn't add up. Except it did explain my visions—and proved I wasn't crazy.

Maybe I could trust these people. The smallest flutter of courage rose from my gut. I opened my mouth.

"It's insane." Tony's words cut me off. "It's too early in the century for a Seer to come along."

Scratch that, at least someone would think I'm crazy, and he'd probably be right. Maybe they were the crazies, not me. Yet I couldn't deny the things I'd seen. Not any more.

"Nexis and the Guardians have been fighting over the Seer for centuries. The Seer could come along early, if Nexis has really big plans this time around." Bryan's eyes softened. "After all, only God controls his own covenant. Still, it's unlikely."

"Just think of it like this," Laura bumped her shoulder against mine, a smile lighting up her face, "either way, you will have some kind of gift in two years, one that will help you out in a lot of ways. Whatever it is."

"I know it's a lot to take in. We just wanted to prepare you, especially since Nexis is after you, too." Bryan's hand brushed over mine. "You don't have to understand it all right now, or even believe. Promise me you'll reserve any judgment for a week or two. I'm here if you have any questions.

It's kind of my job to help newbies figure things out. Feel free to do your own research, too, whatever you need."

Those words punched me in the gut. "If it's your job and everything."

If I thought I was confused before this conversation, I was dead wrong. I'd reached the epitome of confusion. Even so, their words held a ring of truth. This biblical legend could explain my strange visions. Until I knew for sure, I couldn't reveal them to anyone. After all, I wasn't eighteen, or even the firstborn. It had be some kind of fluke—or some kind of lesser gift.

"I've got a lot to think about." I must've stood up, because Bryan followed me to the door.

"Take all the time you need."

I wandered down the hall, opening the front door with a creak. Crisp night air hit me in the face, like everything else at this school.

My goals at Montrose were simple, start over and make my own mark, apart from my family. Now I couldn't get away from them, even here, like my destiny was already planned out. The claws of fate had their hooks in me—a fate I'd never asked for, never planned for. All I wanted to do was run away.

11

A pillar of afternoon sun striped across the foot of my bed. I slipped my bookmark into the conjugation page of my French book and tiptoed to the window. Washes of feathery white smeared across the blue sky. I could almost hear the birds chirping. I found the lever at the bottom and cranked the creaky handle with my fingertips until the window jutted open.

Something banged behind me so loud I jumped. My elbow hit the crank.

"Ow." The sore spot smarted as I rubbed it.

"Sorry, I knocked." Mindy hovered among the butterfly chairs, eyelashes quivering. "Can we talk? I think you deserve an explanation about last week."

A breeze wafted across my face, smelling sweet and crisp with a late-September chill. I pulled on my sweater. "Let's sit."

Mindy plunked down in the chair opposite me and clasped her hands in her lap. "I didn't mean to accuse you of anything. Especially at lunch like that, in front of all your friends. I'm really sorry."

"It was kind of weird." I couldn't see her eyes through the sandy fringe she'd let fall across her face. "I didn't even know you had a sister, let alone that she knew my brother. Are you guys close?"

Silence shrouded the air, even the birds stopped chirping to hear what Mindy said next. "Maria and I were close, until she died two years ago."

Tears rolled down that Miss America face, smudging her mascara, streaking her makeup.

"I'm so sorry, I had no idea." I palmed the tissue box, nudging it against her knee. Any words of comfort I could fathom got stuck on the tip of my tongue. She wouldn't glance up, yet I had to ask. "How did she die?"

She sniffed and dabbed her face. "It was here at Montrose. They found her in the river."

"Ohmigosh!" The screech escaped before I had a chance to check it. Horrible images floated in my mind. "That's so awful."

She wailed into the Kleenex, blowing her nose with a loud honk. "I always thought James knew more than he let on. I don't know what I was thinking, I'm totally irrational sometimes." She balled up her tissue, her pageant face completely gone now, her red nose splotchy, eyes puffy.

Tears welled up just looking at her, but a seething pulse drummed into my ears. I wanted to scream. How could she accuse James of being involved? Could either one of us be rational here?

"I don't understand why James would know anything."

She yanked out more tissues, wiping off the streaks of black eye makeup. "They were dating at the time, some people said they were about to break up, just rumors of course. I wish I knew the truth, though."

Her head bobbed back and forth as another sob racked her shoulders. "According to Colleen and Monica, he was the last one to see her alive."

Her words buzzed like a live wire, as if she'd just slapped me in the face. They electrocuted my brain with a life of their own, lacing the air with resentment, bitterness, betrayal.

And then the room started to spin.

Her splotchy face once backlit by afternoon sunlight was now fading into deep shadows, twisting and twirling around me.

My dorm room merged into a mish-mosh of colors swirling together in one fuzzy blur. Like it was supposed to be that way all along.

I gave in to the spinning. Who was I to say no, to stop what needed to stay in motion?

I let the whirlwind take me wherever it wanted to go, into a chasm. I was falling into an abyss, unknown, unseen, cloaked by mist. A hand reached out.

Somehow it was James I saw in the fog.

He clawed at the mist, searching for me, trying to show me the way. But I fell too far, too fast, too deep. He was gone, and nothing but gray surrounded me.

Just like that I was back in my dorm, staring at my suitemate, her face clouded with confusion. How long was I out this time?

Mindy mouthed goodbye and slipped out of the room.

I didn't want to move, but I had to. I had to find a way out, or something bad would happen, as if the fate of the whole world depended on me. I picked up my keys and headed out the door.

One thing I knew for certain, Colleen and Monica were just plain wrong. I had to get to the bottom of this.

"One hour, the countdown is one hour." Shanda screeched at me as soon as I opened the door. "You should be getting ready."

I rubbed my eyes and set my books down on my bed. Had I really been in the library all afternoon? I'd read about angels and Nephilim, those infamous half angels that everyone had theories about, as if they even existed. I came back more confused than ever. Surprise, the Bible doesn't say much about angels, at least not a whole lot of specifics. You really had to dig for it, but I guess I dug around a little too long.

Lucky for me, this dorm party was only one floor down. I hopped in for a quick shower and when I stepped out of the bathroom, the sickly-sweet smells of hairspray and perfume hovered in the air. How was my roomie almost all primped up and ready to go?

I dragged the brush through my hair as I blowdried, then flat-ironed a cute flip on the ends. Not a huge departure from my usual straight style, but a definite improvement. More casual, and it brought out the copper highlights in my walnut hair.

I dabbed on my last coat of lip gloss. Mid lip I flinched at a creaking sound to my left as the door slammed shut. Did Shanda leave without me? I tiptoed to the door and peeked down the hall. She was long gone.

"Someone's overeager to hang out with boys." Probably a certain surfer boy.

"Not me." Mindy popped out of her room, yanking Brooke down the hall. She gave a meek little wave. "See you down there."

"See ya." I couldn't look at Mindy, so I glanced at Brooke instead. Bryan's sister couldn't be more unlike him, a mousy dishwater-blond girl with thick bangs, but seriously cute glasses. If anyone could get that girl to open up, it'd be Mindy. My heart still ached for her loss, in spite of her obviously misplaced anger issues.

Tonight I couldn't focus on what she'd said to me. I needed to shove it deep in the furthest corners of my mind.

I padded back to the mirror for a quick double check. My blue jersey skirt flared with a hint of flirty, like the purple shadow on my eyelids. Not half bad.

"Time to blow off a little steam." I raced down the hall, almost crashing into the lobby door. "Great, exactly what I need, the imprint of a door on my face." I flung it open and scurried down the stairs.

When I reached the lobby, a silver balloon bonked my forehead. Miss Sherry had rearranged the room into clumps of couches and chairs with board games on every coffee table. There wasn't an empty seat in the crowded lobby. Guess we were kind of starved for entertainment in Riverdale.

"Lucy," Shanda called out from her spot on the couch between Bryan and Kevin. "There you are, get over here."

"Hi, Lucy." Bryan stood, motioning to a spot between him and the arm of the couch. "You had a chance to look into things?"

"Sort of." I wriggled in next to Bryan, good thing I spent extra time primping. Might've given it another five minutes if I'd known I'd be crammed so close to one of my McDreamies. "I'm not really sure what I'm looking for though."

"I could help you sometime, if you want." His gaze burned into me. I shrugged and kept my mouth shut.

"The Midwesterners here taught us a great game." Shanda pointed at the twins as they organized homemade cards on the coffee table. Mindy and Brooke sat on the opposite couch with them.

"Everywhere's the Midwest to you." I laughed. "It's like there's the East coast then the West coast, and everything in between is the Midwest."

"Good one." A low voice filtered down from above my head as something pounded into the back of the couch, one on either side of me. I whirled around, coming face to face with a pair of familiar gray eyes. "Nice to see you, Lucy."

"Hi, Will." My face was inches from his half-smiling, half dare-you-to-move expression. It never wavered, that grin and those eyes almost laughing at me. Was this a game to him? Probably. I couldn't stand it any more and turned around. "You win."

"Okay, they're from Kansas." Shanda huffed on Bryan's other side. "Will, why don't you join us?"

He pulled up a chair close to my side of the couch. "So what are we playing?"

I felt Bryan bristle next to me. When I stole a glance at him, a muscle in his jawline twitched. How cute was that? On a whim, I reached over and patted his shoulder. The twitch stopped.

"Mafia." Shanda handed me two cards, and I passed one to Will. "We're starting a new game."

Not at all like McAllen family game night. It was a piece of cardstock with a drawing of a red-headed kid labeled townsperson.

"We made the cards ourselves." Laura's little-girl face beamed with pride and she fanned them out on the table with her tiny hands. "Cute, huh?"

My head bobbed. "I don't get it."

Bryan came close, like that wouldn't distract me. "A few cards say Mafia, everyone else is a townsperson."

"There's also a sheriff and a doctor," Lenny chimed in. I still had to swallow a laugh at his deep voice, especially right after Laura's high pitch.

"The point is to figure out who the Mafia are and vote them out. Make sense?" I lost the rest of Bryan's explanation in those blue wonders. If eyes really were a window into someone's soul, I would never need to worry about this guy. All of a sudden he paused.

Right, my turn to say something, anything. "I'll pick it up once we start."

"Everyone close your eyes and wait for my instructions," Laura announced.

"Really?" I closed my eyes only because everyone else did. How stupid, until I caught a faint whiff of Bryan's woodsy aftershave, so yummy my toes curled. I opened my eyes a crack to see Bryan's hand inches from mine. Much too soon for PDA.

Wait, did Shanda move?

"Everyone, open your eyes." Laura's head swung around the circle. "I'm afraid the Mafia has axed someone. Will, you're out."

"Darn." With an exaggerated motion he snapped his fingers and threw his card on the coffee table. Yeah right, didn't fool me.

"Who could have killed Will?" Laura eyed each of the nine people in the group. Maybe Lenny was one of the Mafia. He wore a nervous grin, like he was trying to act all innocent.

"It was Lucy." Shanda lunged across Bryan and jabbed her finger in my face.

"No way." Bryan brushed her back to her spot. "She didn't move an inch."

"Me?" I scooted forward, arching my neck to face Shanda. "On my first game, I pulled a Mafia card. Yeah right."

"Likely story." There was a gleam in Shanda's eye.

"What does everyone else think?" Laura asked the group. No one knew what to believe. "No proof, no decision, everyone go to sleep."

"Thanks, Bryan." Somehow I was inches from his face. Better back up, his lips were dangerously close.

"You're welcome." Those lips curved at me as he closed his eyes.

Somehow I could feel Will's stare burning a silver hole in the side of my head. I forced my eyes shut.

This time Shanda didn't move, probably still guilty.

"The doctor has saved Lucy," Laura burst out as I opened my eyes.

The group erupted with shouts. Mindy and Bryan accused Shanda, but Kevin insisted I was part of the real Mafia trying to frame her. Precious, really.

Out of the corner of my eye, I caught Will staring. His face lit up and he nodded at Shanda. It was all the confirmation I needed. "My money's on Shanda as the ringleader."

"You're a feisty one, huh?" Kevin tsked his tongue at me.

Bryan busted out laughing. "You got that right."

Bet he just wanted to make my cheeks burn. It worked, too.

Lenny and Shanda ganged up on Brooke, who never said a word. She only rolled her eyes. The discussion ended with uncertainty.

In the next round Laura announced that I died. "Guess that's what I get for talking."

"The dead don't speak." Laura whispered behind her tiny hand. I zipped my mouth shut.

"Keep your eyes open, I bet you were right. You'll get 'em next game." Bryan's hand brushed mine, sending a shock wave up my arm. His touch was different than Will's. It was electric, good enough to be scary.

Will inched his chair closer. "The dead should stick together." Can we say creepy?

"I guess." His gunmetal eyes practically bored into my skull. Suddenly, I loved the arm of the couch for being my buffer between me and Will.

I scooted closer to Bryan, but Will just propped his elbow against the couch arm. That fire in his eyes suddenly reminded me of Jake, and it was too soon. The blood curdled in my veins, I was trapped. Silver on my left, and blue on my right.

Drastic times called for drastic measures. I couldn't think of another way out, so I slipped my arm under Bryan's.

His head spun toward me, his wide eyes narrowing as they locked with mine. At least he smiled. "What's going on?"

I nodded toward Will and scooted next to him. "Just go with it."

"Only if I get to call you honey, or sweetie, or babe." Bryan's breath warmed my face.

"No problem, babe." I said out loud and silently mouthed thank you.

Will stood up, kicking his chair back with an ear-piercing screech on the hardwood floor. Conversations lulled as all heads in the room turned to see what he would do next. His commanding tone bellowed across the silence. "Are you engaged or something?"

"What?" I gasped so loud it bounced all around the room, probably around the world.

And then everyone's eyes were on me.

I buried my head in Bryan's shoulder, his jaw rested on my head. It I wasn't mortified to the core, it might've been nice.

12

"That ring's on your engagement finger, right?" Will's question hovered over the party like some kind of accusation, and the room buzzed with whispers. He betrayed no embarrassment at all. None.

I couldn't believe it. In fact all I could do was blink at him, then down at my ring. A plain silver band with intricate carvings surrounded by three sparkling purple stones. Nothing like an engagement ring.

"It was my sweet sixteen present." When I turned to Bryan for backup, instead of the outrage I expected to see, his face scrunched into a frown.

"Hey, wait a sec, can I see that? What's written on the inside?" Bryan yanked the ring off my finger, holding it up to the light as he examined the inscription. "Gratiam Coram Domino."

"What's it to you?" I snatched the ring back. My heart slowly sank into a puddle on the couch cushions, like the rest of me. "It's some verse from the Latin Vulgate. It's a family heirloom."

"Sorry, I was just curious." He slumped next to me like a deflated balloon, then whispered in my ear. "It's Genesis 6:8 isn't it?"

"I don't know." I crossed my arms and glared at him. "How would in the world do you know what it is?"

"I'm sorry, this isn't your fault." He looked around at the group and scooted away from me. "I'm just confused, that's all. We should talk about this. Later."

"About the ring? How did you even know there'd be an inscription?" I hissed back at him. "And you're the one who's confused?"

A sadness filled his sea-blue eyes as they roamed over my face. "I can't explain now. Later, I promise."

Later was all I ever had with this guy. If only I could rewind the last few minutes, to see that smile on his face again.

"You promise?" I held up my pinkie finger.

When he hooked his pinkie around mine, the corners of his mouth curled. "Promise."

I couldn't stand the heaviness in his sigh, like something weighed down on him. All because of a ring? I squinted down at it, the center stone glinting back at me.

"Now that we've established Lucy is not engaged, can we get back to the game?" Shanda's annoyed timbre silenced the hushed murmurs.

"Go for it." Will plopped back down, a satisfied smile on his face.

Everyone closed their eyes for the next round, except Will. He kept smiling at me, a smug grin like he'd just won a battle. The anger seeped from my pores until it pooled in my balled up fists.

"I think I need a Coke." Without a glance back, I shot up, weaving across what was left of the party toward the kitchen. A nice moment ruined, and I didn't even do it myself. I smacked the kitchen door so hard it almost came back and hit me in the nose.

"Watch it." Will's arm slid around me to prop open the door. "Don't hurt yourself."

"Smooth." I spun on my heel shooting flaming arrows at him with my eyes as I backed into the kitchen. "So, you want to tell me what that was all about?"

"Calm down, you don't have to get so mad. Though it's pretty cute." He sauntered up to the stainless refrigerator and opened the door, as if the last few seconds hadn't happened. "Coke, right?"

"Fine, whatever," I mumbled, but it wasn't fine. Hot anger still sizzled up and down every nerve ending. "I don't get what happened out there. Besides me looking like an idiot in front of a whole bunch of people. Thanks for that. I guess you bring it out in me."

"C'mon, it wasn't that many people. I'm just trying to watch your back, Lucy." He tossed me a can of Dr. Pepper. "Sorry, no Coke."

"That's my favorite, anyway." I popped the top and sipped the fizz. The coolness slid down my throat, evaporating some of the rage.

"I had a feeling." Will plunked down on a barstool at the center island, patting the seat next to him. "Come sit by me, I don't bite. You know, I used to find James in the kitchen late at night, totally asleep."

"Really, that's what you want to talk about?" I rubbed my fingers against the cold aluminum. No random comment about my brother could make up for what he did, even if that lopsided expression on his face looked like he actually meant it.

"Don't you know how much I want to tell you everything?" He combed his short sandy hair with rough strokes. "If you'll just come to the Nexis initiation, I'm sure I could bend the rules a little."

"After that fiasco out there you think I can believe anything you say?" The words burned like fire in my mouth. I doused my tongue with sweet soda bubbles.

"Listen, I know I owe you an explanation." He twisted his stool and lifted his chin toward me, his best feature. As if I'd be helpless against his charm. "I didn't mean to make a scene."

Acrid laughter rose in my throat. "Ha!"

His hand shot straight up, like he was about to swear on his Dr. Pepper can. "Honest, I didn't mean for it to go down like that. You weren't picking up my subtle hints. That guy was reeling you in."

"What, so you were jealous?" The smoldering ball of fury simmered down, a little bit. Of course he really didn't mean to embarrass me, he just couldn't help himself. Hmm, smug or cute?

"We were supposed to go out this weekend, and then you're hanging all over Bryan. I don't like that guy. He's bad news." He slammed his can into the counter.

I jumped back and bumped into an empty stool, which seesawed back and forth. "You never called to set something up."

"Yeah I did, don't you check your messages?"

I tugged my phone out of my pocket. It showed four missed calls today, after my talk with Mindy. "Oops, I didn't notice."

"No kidding, I guess you forgot about me." His voice softened on those last words.

"That's not true. And it doesn't give you the right to embarrass me like that."

Sandy tufts of hair fell around his eyes. "I know, I didn't mean to make such a big deal out of it. I just lost it. I'm sorry."

The muscles I'd tensed slowly relaxed, the anger evaporating, too. Those annoying little butterflies swarmed in my stomach, enough that I couldn't deny it. I was still attracted to him, even if he was utterly obnoxious. "If you hadn't been so rude about it, I'd almost think you were kind of sweet. Wanting to look out for me and all."

He looked up. "Really? Most girls would call it possessive."

"They have no idea what it's really like, then." If you wanted possessive, you didn't have to search any further than my ex.

Will tapped the countertop with his fingers. The soft sound brought me back to him. "I'm sorry, I heard a bit about your last boyfriend. One drawback of our moms being friends. Anyway, you deserve better than that, and definitely much better than that Bryan guy out there. He broke my friend's heart and kicked her out of the Guardians. Plus he's ultra-religious. Trust me, he's the wrong guy for you."

"You mean Colleen?" When he nodded, I stuck my hand on the swaying stool, trying to regain my balance. After what Mindy said, it was hard to get on Colleen's side. But Will was obviously right about Jake, could he be right about Bryan, too? "So what does that make you?"

"Just a guy who wants to be with you." He inched forward, eyes searching mine. They stayed locked on me for one long moment.

"I, uh ..." My lips parted, but no sound came out. I didn't know what to say to that. Against my will, my heart flip-flopped around in my chest. I couldn't move. He had some kind of hold over me, like a snake charmer luring me under his spell.

A shadow crossed his face, his expression turning hungry. He bent his head toward me, lips inches from mine.

Suddenly an image of Jake and Becca flashed into my mind. Why couldn't he stay in Indiana? But this time it was different, Will was there, too. Whoa, that couldn't be right.

I jerked away, yanking myself free from whatever strange force just pulled me into this guy's tractor beam. The can tipped and spilled Dr. Pepper all over the counter, wafting a dampness through the air.

"What was that?" I put some much-needed distance between us, tearing off paper towels from the roll by the sink.

"I'm sorry, I couldn't resist." He hung his head, but his face lit up in that annoying half smile.

"You're not sorry, not even close." I tossed a paper towel at him.

"Too soon?" He stared me down like an eager pup waiting for a scrap.

"I wish it wasn't." The paper towels sopped up the sticky liquid at my fingertips. "I wish I was normal, like every other girl who doesn't have a care in the world."

"You're not normal, you're Lucy. We can take this as slow as you need. Okay?" His smile widened as he reached over to help clean up the mess.

"What? No." Objections piled up in my head, and I shook them free. "We're not taking anything slow. I can't date you, or anyone. Not yet." What would Bryan say if he saw us? How had this happened? And why did Will think he could embarrass me in front of everyone and then try to kiss me? Thank God I hadn't let him. I traced my lips with my fingers, those traitors.

"But Lucy, I have feelings for you." He grabbed my hand, his thumb caressing the back of my sticky palm. "And they're not going away."

The softness in his gray eyes cracked any resolve I had left, but couldn't break it. "I'm sorry, I just can't go there. Not right now."

"If that's what you want." He climbed down from his stool, his smile gone now. "I bet they're wondering about us. Why don't we head back to the party?"

"Good idea." I followed him to the door.

He turned and offered me a real smile, so his chin cleft showed. "Don't make me wait too long."

"If you're waiting for me, it'll be on other side of never-gonna-happen." How could I make promises I couldn't keep? Mom would probably kill me right now, but it was still too complicated.

I didn't want to go back to the party. Part of me wanted to go back to my room and analyze what just happened. Part of me wanted to kick myself. Then it hit me—I couldn't go back in there and face Bryan.

"Do me a favor."

"What, sweetie?"

"Don't call me that." I could've smacked that smirk right off his face, but I played it cool. "I'm beat. Tell everyone I turned in for the night."

"You got it. I'll see you tomorrow at the initiation. Don't worry, I'll figure out a way to tell you what I can about James." He reached over and ruffled my hair, much like Dad always did. It sent a shiver down my neck. He waved goodbye as he pushed open the kitchen door.

I crushed the empty soda can with one hand, then chucked it at the door after him. Why did he try to kiss me, then blackmail me with promises about my brother? Why did I let him get that close?

I trudged up the back stairs to my room.

Better question, why couldn't I stay away from this guy? It felt like I was sucked into the moment, almost like he had me under a spell. The complete opposite of Bryan.

Last week I might've chosen Will. Before the ring debacle tonight, I'd started falling for Bryan.

Maybe these flip-flopping feelings meant I shouldn't be on the market right now. My stomach clenched. Deep down, I knew I'd have to choose one, eventually. Right now, I just wasn't ready to let go of either one of those guys, let alone choose between them.

The smell of burning wax singed the air as I stepped into the dark dome of the observatory. Shanda's gasp drew my eyes upward. The giant telescope hung from the cavernous ceiling like a chandelier, the dome completely closed in for tonight's initiation. Did I really want to know what happened to James this badly? If Will was really going to tell me the truth, I knew I couldn't turn down this opportunity. Even if I had to join the Nexis ranks.

"So wrong." She whispered as Mindy prodded us into the center of the room. The only light came from the flickering white pillar candles evenly spaced in a wide circle. Their tongues of fire floated in mid-air above the dark circle, the iron stands practically disappearing into the charcoal floor.

Faces emerged from the shadows, one by one. Cloaked in black robes shrouding their heads, they surrounded us. Something prickled the back of my throat with a taste like acid, a definite sense of dread. But I had to do this, for James.

"You have been carefully selected to join an elite international group." A commanding female voice spoke from my left. All heads turned toward her. "Only twelve members from each class are offered this opportunity every year. Juniors, welcome to the Nexis Semigod Nations."

"The what?" Shanda snarled in my ear. "Are they serious?"

"I hope not." I hissed at her and Mindy hushed us. My brilliant plan to give Nexis a chance didn't seem so brilliant any more.

"If you survive the night, you will become a Nexis member forever." The male voice boomed from my right, and my focus shifted to him. "We have chosen you, but you must also choose us. By completing a series of trials you will learn about the group, what we believe, and what your role will be. Choose wisely."

Those words rang like a gong in my ears. Hadn't I heard them before? Harlixton said that same phrase to me in his office.

"First you will learn the twelve tenets of the Nexis Nations." Another girl's voice, higher-pitched this time, chirped from dead ahead. Sounded like Monica's candy voice. It rubbed me raw just thinking about what she supposedly said about my brother. "At each ceremonial flame you will collect an item that represents one tenet of Nexis truth. Once you collect all twelve you'll have everything you need for your survival kit. Then you will move on to the next task."

"The first tenet of Nexis is the most important." Will's clear voice rang out from behind me. The whole group spun around and gathered in front of him.

He hoisted a giant antique magnifying glass in front of the flame. "Seeing is believing. Find the one who sees, and the rest will believe."

His gray eyes narrowed at me as if I were under the magnifying glass. A chill shot up my spine. He passed me an odd-shaped canvas bundle tied with twine. "Hand these out around the circle."

I reached for the bundle and grazed his palm. Suddenly a black shadow slithered across his hand, then up the sleeve of his black robe. I shook my head, but the snake-like shadow lingered, shining in a dark coil on top of his cloak. This couldn't be happening, not again. I closed my eyes and inhaled a deep breath. It was so dark I couldn't be sure I saw anything clearly.

I opened my eyes, and the shadow morphed into a cobra that writhed up his neck.

"What the—" I jumped backward. The package tumbled from my hand, crashing onto the hardwood floor. The canvas came loose and magnifying glasses spilled everywhere.

Yet that wasn't even the strangest part. Will's gray eyes sparked at me like he knew everything I'd just seen.

He slid his hand across my upper arm, those gray eyes softening in a wash of concern. "Are you okay?"

I blinked at him, the vision gone now. I swung my gaze around the room. Candles illuminated only faces in the crowd, eleven uncloaked ones stared at me. Had I imagined the whole thing?

"I'm sorry, I'm so clumsy. Please continue." I crouched to my knees to pick up the magnifying glasses.

"Here, let me help." He knelt beside me, scooping up the plastic toys. "Good thing I got the cheap ones, huh?"

"Yeah, that makes me feel better." I sneaked a peek at him, catching an eyeful of that adorable cleft under his grin.

He turned to me with a kinder look than I deserved and grabbed my elbow to help me up. This time his touch felt normal, no strange images. I must've been seeing things. I'd always been afraid of the dark, especially when I was little. Mom said it was only my overactive imagination, and I desperately hoped she was right.

"You'll need these for your survival kit. They'll be crucial in the next task." He passed out the magnifiers.

Each inductee moved on to the next station until I was all alone beside him.

"Don't be so nervous. It's adorable, but completely unnecessary. You got this, sweetie." His whisper sent another shiver crawling down my neck. I snapped my head his way. It wasn't what burned my nerves.

"I'm not your sweetie." I hissed at him.

"Not yet." He edged close to me, close enough I caught a familiar whiff of spice. "But you will be, as soon as you're ready."

I clenched my teeth down hard, but I couldn't let it go. Not this time. "I hate arrogant guys."

"I'm not arrogant, I just know what I want. Do you?" His white teeth glowed in the candle flickers.

I pursed my lips together and narrowed my eyes at him.

"Don't look at me like that or I'll have to kiss you for real this time."

"Enough." I backed up, but his hand clamped down on my shoulder, holding me in place.

"Just finish the next task and bring back the book. Then I can tell you everything you ever wanted to know about James."

"Is it really worth it?" A tremor laced my question, so close to him in the dark. How I hated the weakness it betrayed.

"Absolutely." He squeezed my shoulder, pressing his lips against my hair. "Now go on, you don't want them to leave without you."

He nudged me toward the next station, his laughter rumbling in the darkness.

13

The chapel clock struck midnight as eleven juniors pounded down the sidewalk of the dark quad beside me. Why was I doing this? The sky grew blacker as we left the path and skirted along the edge of the woods. My parents couldn't possibly have done this too, but James was always up for anything. Did they have this kind of Nexis initiation? The questions halted as we froze in front of the library doors, our final destination.

Mindy reached out to yank the doors open. A brave first step, but the steel-encased glass barely moved an inch. "Now what?"

"Step aside." The recruits parted for her as Shanda pushed her way forward. "I've got this."

She unhooked a bobby pin from of her hair and straightened out the metal. With deft fingers she inserted it into the lock and twisted as if she'd picked locks all her life. A minute later, the doors popped open like magic.

"How'd you do that?" I squinted to read her expression in the darkness. An unmistakable hint of pride washed over her face.

"Used to do it all the time before we moved up in the world." She folded the bobby pin and stuck it back in her hair. "It's a good skill to have."

"Yeah, if you want to go to juvie," Mindy whispered in my ear.

I sucked in a breath, just like everyone else.

Shanda yanked the girl in by her shirt and her jaw jutted out. "You don't know what I've had to do to get by. So don't lecture me on the ghetto, and I won't lecture you on what it's like to be a Barbie. Got it?"

"Got it, sorry." Mindy's arms flew up in surrender until Shanda released her collar.

The rest of the group marched into the library, Mindy rushing to catch up. But my feet refused to budge. If I stepped across that threshold, there was no turning back. I'd be breaking the law, even if it was only a prank.

"C'mon, girl." Shanda tugged on my arm. "I'm not doing this without you."

If I could somehow get through this, Will would tell me everything I wanted to know about James. Or at least more than I already knew, right? I gritted my teeth and let her drag me into the dark library. One of my favorite places for solace. Now a misguided gang of teens disturbed its peace.

A loud beep hammered my ears, echoing up every aisle.

"Great, you set off the alarm." Shanda pointed at my feet. Sure enough, a red laser dotted the ankle of my black pants.

In a mad dash, the group herded back toward the front door. Someone called out in the crowd, "Wait."

Two dozen feet halted.

An Asian guy pushed past me and typed some buttons on the keypad. Suddenly the beeping stopped, and we all just stared at him.

"What?" He shrugged. "I work here."

"Might've mentioned that sooner." Shanda punched his arm, her face scrunched up like an anxious schoolgirl for the first time tonight. "Now we have to do this before security gets here."

"Sorry." He bolted the door. "Maybe that'll hold 'em off for awhile."

"Good job, Tim," someone yelled out.

"They'll have a key." Shanda rolled her eyes, but he just shook his head. "We've probably got ten minutes. Let's get this over with."

My roommate of all people knew the exact ins and outs of breaking and entering. Why didn't that surprise me?

"Everyone fan out to different stacks." Mindy waved her arms like a flight attendant as she scurried backward down the center aisle. "We've got to find this book, or we're not getting in. It's got to be pretty old."

"Didn't know she wanted to get into Nexis that bad. Go Barbie." Shanda hushed her usual cackle to a mere breath.

"It's probably in the rare book collection, over there." Tim motioned to the back corner.

"Show us." I snatched Shanda's arm, following him until we reached the glass doors of the back section, covered in shadows, of course.

Did my parents break into the rare book room? Did they smash the glass into pieces, or try something else? Even worse, did they know I'd have to do this, too? There's no way they'd encourage some random crime, not even a harmless prank like this, not *my* dad. Did they really want me to get into Nexis this bad?

He pressed some buttons on the keypad lock and the doors opened. No glass shattering tonight, probably why Nexis recruited this guy. Sadly enough, there really was no turning back, not now. I had to see this through if I had any prayer of not getting caught. I inched my way into the dark room.

Pungent odors of old leather and aged parchment clung to the air. Every shelf was made of the same cedar wood as the chapel library. How were we going to get out of this one in ten minutes? More like eight now.

Shanda motioned for me to case the back aisle. She and the other guy took the first two stacks.

I tiptoed to the last row by myself, holding up my cell phone for light. It cast a bluish glow over the books. I ran my fingers across every spine, then something pricked my middle finger.

"Ouch." My finger throbbed its own little heartbeat as drops of blood hit the carpet. I pressed my thumb against the wound.

"Where'd that come from?" With my left hand I wrangled the book off its shelf. Caramel leather bound together the rough-edged parchment, an embossed seal in the center. I touched the metal lines raised in a symbol I could've sworn I'd seen before, an angry-eyebrowed jack-o-lantern with a mouthful of fangs. The metal burned my fingertips.

Suddenly the room went completely black. And disappeared.

Long grasses appeared on the horizon, rustling in the wind.

Flaming torches popped up all around me.

I stood in the middle of a circle, six cloaked figures in black surrounding me. Some men, some women, all with angry eyes that glared fireballs at me.

James emerged next to me.

I reached for his arm, but my hand went right through him like I wasn't really there. Or he wasn't. This was getting weird now. Flames cast tendrils of shadow on each face, clawing at James like an apparition.

Cynical laughter rippled around the circle. "You're crazy."

"You've been corrupted." A screech cut across the sphere.

"For your crimes, you are banished." The hiss was right next to me.

"Banished." The word echoed five times, each figure nodding in agreement.

James crumpled to the ground at his pronouncement. A choked scream escaped my throat, but only silence came out. Two guys grabbed him by the shoulders and hauled his wriggling body out of the ring of fire.

"James!" My voice was mute. I reached out for him, but they'd already dragged him out of sight.

Only four remained in the circle, plus invisible me. I strained to hear the whispers.

"Overseas."

"Silence."

"Sister."

Then the field faded into utter blackness.

A distant thud crashed around in the dark.

Something smashed down on my foot, crushing my big toe. Suddenly I couldn't feel it, like I'd gone numb, my whole body really.

Darkness twisted into shades of gray.

The dim shadows of the library returned.

I bent over to pick up the book. The pages fluttered in front of me, as if they wanted me to read them.

A young woman stared back at me from the yellowed parchment, with a far-off expression and a strange sort of halo behind her head. Her eyes were dark and shadowed, hollowed almost. She held a tray with bulging circles on it. Were they eyes? An odd feeling slithered inside my body, like I should know exactly what the picture meant. Only I had no clue.

I slammed the book shut.

"Did you find it?" Shanda peeked into the space I'd left in the bookshelf. "Is that it?"

I nodded and opened my mouth, but nothing came out. Just like that vision of James, or was it a hallucination? My fingers flew to my temple, rubbing the scar under my hairline, but I couldn't blame this on the accident any more.

Finally my voice croaked something out. "Let's get out of here, before I really lose it."

"There's no time to go out the way we came. We'll have to sneak out the back, c'mon." She yanked me toward the end of the aisle. I blindly followed, my body still numb. The images of James, the field, the circle, snapped like camera flashes in my head. His tortured face, the flaming torches, their haunting eyes.

Beside me Shanda raised her voice. "Guys, we got it. Follow us out the back."

We tumbled down the back steps and into the dewy grass. Under my arm the book radiated heat, as if those torches singed it somehow.

I thrust the horrible book at Shanda. "Here, take it. I don't care what he or that stupid group has to say about James. I'm out."

She tucked the book into her giant purse. "Who said what about your brother? Is something wrong?"

"It's nothing." I sucked in a breath of cool night air, but my cheeks still burned. "I'm just tired, it's been a long night."

"Are you sure you want out?" She squeezed my shoulder. "Look, don't decide anything tonight. I think they'll cut you some slack. You found the book, so they've gotta let you in."

I stared at my hands. "I don't know what I want."

"Why don't you sleep on it? I catch you back at the dorm, okay?" She waved and followed the rest of the troops to the edge of the woods.

I watched her disappear into the night.

Campus looked too much like that horrible field where James was dragged into the shadows. And I couldn't do anything to stop it.

Too many images collided in my head, of James, of Nexis, of my own sanity. If there was any shred of it left.

Sunday morning brightness floated over my face from the corner of my dorm window. I rubbed the grit from my eyes and rolled over, but sleep eluded me. It had eluded me all night, ever since my vision of James only

105

hours ago. More like a walking nightmare. His face, contorted with fear, filled my waking thoughts. I prayed to God it wasn't real, that it was all in my imagination.

I pieced it together with the other strange things I'd seen and heard over the last month at Montrose—the odd chapel conversation, the blameless man in the spotlight, the weird visions from Hard Rock, then last night. I had no idea what was real any more. Maybe I should see the school counselor.

In one fluid motion I peeled back the covers that clung to my body and swung my legs over the side of the bed. I pulled on jeans, then grabbed my soft navy hoodie in case the late-September morning held a chill. I slipped my feet into my canvas shoes and padded to the sink. The cool water soothed my warm cheeks, but failed to wake me from my daze.

Shanda slept soundlessly as I tiptoed out of the room and down the stairs to the lobby. The house looked so still and peaceful at this hour. At my touch, the front door creaked open and I stepped into the cool air. Gray clouds covered the sky.

Grateful for my hoodie, I zipped it up and went wherever my feet decided to go. Toward the student union. Would the counselor's office be open this early? Probably not on Sunday.

I pivoted off the path into the dew-drenched grass until I found the steps that led to the river bank. As I descended the uneven flagstones I slowed my pace.

At a landing carved into the hillside, a white-washed pergola hung over a mosaic stone patio. A cement bench rested on the hillside's wall, but my arms reached for one wide column of the pergola.

The wind whipped my hair in front of my face. I hugged the column and faced the wind. My tangled hair flew behind me. How I wished the strange nightmare of last night would fly away, too.

The river below me gurgled with life and freedom. James would have loved it. In an instant, hot tears sprang to my eyes.

"James." I whispered his name into the wind, but it made no difference. The tears streamed down my face until I tasted their salt. "Wherever you are, I hope you're safe."

Something rustled behind me. I snapped my head around.

Bryan shoved his hands into the pockets of his jeans. "Sorry, didn't see you there."

"It's okay." I wiped my eyes on the sleeve of my hoodie, glad I hadn't bothered with any makeup on my way out.

He moved in front of me, his broad shoulders blocking some of the wind. "Are you okay?"

Those images of James wouldn't go away, the flaming circle, the cloaked figures. They haunted me still.

"I don't know." I refused to meet his gaze. Instead, I ran my hand through my hair. Halfway down, it snagged on the tangles. "I don't know what's real any more."

"You look like you need to sit." He eased onto the cement bench, and I moved next to him. "Do you remember our deal?"

I nodded, tears clinging to my lashes. I couldn't keep my voice from shaking. "I'm so confused."

"When I'm confused, I just go with my gut. What's your gut tell you?" He wrestled his arms from his bomber jacket and bundled it around me.

I wrapped it tighter, snuggling into the fleece. At least someone knew what I needed, even though I hadn't noticed the cold until now. Maybe if he knew what happened last night or the night before he'd take it back. I swallowed and inhaled deep.

"My head tells me to do what my family wants and go to the final initiation so I can get into Yale." The images rushed back and I closed my eyes to shut them out. But that only made them clearer. I lifted my face to the gray sky. "But my gut tells me there's something I'm missing, something I'm not aware of yet. Maybe something my brother figured out before he disappeared, before they made him disappear. But that just sounds crazy when I think about it too much."

Those aqua eyes glowed against the steely sky. His Adam's apple bobbed with an audible gulp. "I think you're right about James. He was on to something, that much I know."

"You knew my brother?" I reached for his hand and he flinched like I'd shocked him. His fingers were hot under mine.

I studied his face, strong cheekbones outlined by dark stubble, eyes darting back and forth. Not in a sinister way, more like he struggled to recall something.

"Only through my sister." His eyes stopped dead center and his jaw dropped. He stared at my hand over his. "How could I have forgotten? It's as clear as day right now. I was still in junior high, but I remember Abby's story. About the Guardians taking someone in right before graduation, after Nexis ousted him. Apparently he was afraid of something. He stayed out of sight and wouldn't go anywhere but class or the chapel. He was never alone, always with two of the Guardian's biggest guys, like bodyguards. Right before graduation he moved into the chapel and slept there. She said it was the weirdest thing. It had to be James."

Did that mean I wasn't crazy? Maybe my visions were trying to tell me something, maybe they were real.

When I shivered, Bryan looped his arm around me, scooting me closer. "Can't believe I remembered that all of sudden."

If this was true, then Will lied to me when he told me about James. Why would he leave out something like this? He was a freshman then, but he still had to know more than he let on.

That creeped me out even more. I nestled into Bryan's side. "But why would James leave without a word to any of us?"

"I don't know," he whispered into my hair, "but you said it yourself that your family wants you in that club. Maybe that's why."

I shook my head. James knew me better than that. "But that didn't include me. I couldn't care less what club he belonged to."

He drew back to look at me. "I'm sorry. I'm not helping, am I?"

My lips curved at the beautiful concern in his eyes. "I don't know about that. Things didn't make sense until you told me to listen to my heart. At least I don't think I'm crazy any more. That's a big improvement."

"Good to know I have some effect on you, even if it's only keeping you sane." A laugh rumbled from his chest. "I believe I said, go with your gut, not this mushy heart stuff."

I didn't have the energy to laugh. Still, the burden of uncertainty over James lifted like a weight off of my heart. If this story was true, then my visions were true, too. I let my shoulders relax and my head sink onto Bryan's firm shoulder. As he stroked my hair, I closed my eyes. I barely noticed the bright light I saw instead of darkness. It wrapped around me, filling me with peace as I drifted off.

When I came to, strips of sunlight beamed between the wooden slats in the pergola's ceiling. I sat up and rubbed at the knot in my neck. "How long was I out?"

Bryan stretched his long arms to the sky. His fingertips skimmed the vines that hung from the wooden slats. "Less than an hour. You needed the rest."

I yawned, arching my back. "Probably because I didn't sleep at all last night." The images of James in his terror were gone now, and a strong sense of peace surged through me.

"Maybe I should walk you back to the dorm so you can get some rest." He helped me up, putting his hand on the small of my back to steady me as we climbed the stairs. "Why couldn't you sleep?"

Even if he proved to be a good pillow, I couldn't mention the strange vision, let alone what almost happened with Will the night before. "I think I was just worried about James."

"I'm sure he's fine." Bryan slowed his pace as we neared the girls' dorm house. "If you want, maybe I can do ask my sister about it. Try to find out what happened to your brother."

"That would be great. You'd really do that for me?" It finally felt like someone understood my dilemma, at least a little bit. And to have another person take something off my plate of worries—priceless. Could such a gorgeous guy really have a good heart? That might be too hard to resist.

"Anything for you." He veered to a path that led to the back door of the dorm.

"Do you mean that?" I gazed up at him until he nodded, but a question lingered in my mind. "Okay, here goes. I was wondering why you freaked out about my ring the other night."

"Oh, that." He scratched his chin and wouldn't meet my eyes. "It's just an indicator of how important you are. The fact that Will knows it, that's what made me mad."

"I see." I nibbled the inner edge of my lip, willing him to clarify what that meant.

"Don't you worry about it, that's my job." His strong palms rubbed into my shoulders.

At the door, he reached for my hand and pulled me closer. I ran my fingers across his five o'clock shadow, examining that soft expression in his eyes. It melted my insides. With a mind of their own, my toes arched until I stood inches from his face. I tugged on his t-shirt until his lips met mine. When I pulled back, his arm slid around my waist, bringing me in for another quick kiss. Then he dropped his arm and jerked back.

"I'm sorry." His voice cracked. "Didn't mean to be presumptuous."

"Don't be sorry, it was nice." I grazed my fingertips across my lips.

"If you're sure." His blue eyes burned into mine, searching for something. "Get some rest, Lucy, and be careful."

"I'll see you in class tomorrow." He stumbled backward and cold air filled the space between us.

"Right, can't wait." I murmured, unable to look away. Instead I reached back, found the doorknob, and waved goodbye as he walked away. "See you tomorrow."

Lack of sleep could do crazy things to a girl. With Bryan I forgot to check myself. It came natural, easy and uncomplicated, like freedom for a change. And it felt good.

14

Crisp wind blasted my face as I followed Mindy out of the dorm and down the cobblestone. The chill crept down my neck and I wrapped my soft sweater around me. Another sign October had come to New York, along with the trees dotting the once-green landscape in bright red, orange, and golden hues.

Mindy's perfectly-highlighted head slipped past me when we reached the quad, disappearing into the crowd. Almost like she wanted to ditch me. After our strange conversation about her sister, we still weren't exactly on good terms.

The rest of the girls from my dorm herded me up the old stone stairs for the junior assembly in the chapel.

Candles in red hurricane globes glittered in the foyer. The arching stone cavern swallowed up all the light. Gothic chandeliers hung on wrought-iron chains from the vaulted ceiling. They cast dim circles of yellow around the room.

Hundreds of Montrose students and faculty filled the great sanctuary. The faces all merged together, yet I couldn't make out anyone I knew. Mindy, Shanda, even Will, were conspicuously absent. Not a single Nexis member in the room.

From the front of the room Lenny motioned me over. The stained glass cast tinged shadows across his and Laura's faces.

"Man, what was up with Will the other night, total wacko, right?" He fiddled with the pegs on his guitar, a light maple color with wicked flames patterned into the wood stain. Laura jabbed her mic in his side, but he dodged it. "You coming to the library this weekend, Lucy? I could really use some help with English."

"Sure, why not? I love English."

"I know you do," Lenny peered into my eyes. "I'm just glad we're in the same class. Cuz I suck at it."

I breathed out a laugh. "I'm sure it's not that bad. What are you—" A swift blow to my shin stopped me mid-sentence. I glared down at the tiny foot, Laura's foot. Was she grinning? "Ow, what was that for?"

With the same brown eyes as her brother she stared me down. "Don't you have other plans this weekend?" She nodded three rows back. Of course, Bryan wanted to meet at the bonfire to talk. His words, not mine.

My heart clenched. How could I be so cruel in the face of such vagueness? "Right, I guess I could squeeze you in Saturday or Sunday afternoon."

He slid his fingers up and down the frets. "Can't, I promised the guys I'd help with the set up. Maybe next week?"

"That works." I forced my eyes to study his face, if only not to turn around in search of you know who. "Set up for what?"

He coughed and stared at me like I'd asked when the moon launch was. "Where have you been? The hall decorating contest is next week. You know, the Montrose Halloween shindig. Each floor decorates their hall. Whoever wins gets a pizza party. We're reigning champs three years running." He let out a whoop and pumped his fist in the air.

"You've probably been too busy to notice. Our floor is doing something really fabulous this year. You're going to love it." Laura magically whipped a clipboard out of her bag. "I'll sign you up to help with me at the end of the month. That'll be the final night, so it'll be all about the finishing touches."

"Why not?" I nodded at her and she penciled me in. "Is this really a month-long thing?"

"For our theme, it has to be. We're going all out." She shoved the clipboard back in her bag with a glare in Lenny's direction. "Time to dethrone those boys who only clean their rooms once a year."

"Better to clean it for open dorms than not at all." Lenny flicked his guitar strap at Laura.

James and I used to be like that. What would he think of my life here? Of the Guardians, of Bryan? Why couldn't I stop thinking about him for five seconds?

I couldn't stand it any more. I peeked over my shoulder to see Bryan in the third row next to Brooke. She ushered me to sit next to them.

"Go on." Laura's little hand shoved me forward. The lights dimmed and all the chatter died down as I wove myself into a seat between the Coopers.

A chorus of groans creaked from the ancient wooden pews as everyone took their seats. Late morning sun spilled in from the East windows, snatches of blue and gold filtering through the glass. The colored light danced around the congregation.

"Welcome to our special junior assembly." My English teacher, Mrs. Erickson, tucked her short blond hair behind her ears and pushed up her black frames. "We have many distinguished guests and alumni from around the world. Be sure to introduce yourself to someone new today. You could be shaking hands with a senator or an ambassador, or some future ones."

The junior band tiptoed to the platform as her speech ended. Laura stood behind a microphone off to the side. Lenny picked up the guitar, its glossy flames reflecting back at me.

A shaggy-haired guy took center stage and asked us all to stand. He nodded to Lenny who shredded the guitar into a fast song I'd never heard before, but it could definitely be on the radio. Who knew? Lenny was way cooler than I ever imagined.

The band followed up with three other songs. I basked in the glow of stained glass and rocked out with each song, my kind of school-sponsored event. What a great way to make this old chapel come alive. When the band finished their last number, I clapped and cheered with the rest of my class. Then Mr. Harlixton took the podium.

He spoke on a strange topic, Daniel's prophetic visions, but his narrative came to life with his storyteller's voice, just like in his classes. Yet his story sank deep into my bones, more so than ever before. When he illuminated some great truth from the Bible, his words made me want to go back and read the passage again. Maybe I was more like Daniel than I realized.

As his talk came to a close, his face hardened and he stared right at me. "I hope you each catch the vision for your life. You have a purpose here, and if you keep looking, that purpose will reveal itself to you."

Crystal clear, those words rang through my head. *Vision. Purpose. Reveal.*

I peeked at him through my lashes, and his gaze was still set on me with a question mark all over his face. Like he wanted to make sure I got the message. I blinked and sat back in the pew with a creak that echoed in the quiet.

His eyes narrowed as he nodded. "Thank you. You're dismissed, everyone."

Around me, students gathered their things and filed out of the sanctuary. As the crowd swarmed out, Mr. Harlixton's words bounced around in my brain like ping-pong balls. *Vision. Purpose. Reveal.* The words latched ahold of my thoughts and wouldn't let go. They played a repeating rhythm in my head, over and over again. What did they mean, to me?

Bryan nudged me forward. "You ready? I'm starving."

"Yeah, sorry." I trailed behind Brooke and Bryan out of the sanctuary.

On the steps, the brisk air nipped at my cheeks. As soon as my feet hit the sidewalk, a cold hand grabbed mine. Familiar gray eyes stared back at me.

"Lucy, I need to talk to you." Will tugged me down the sidewalk.

Bryan turned in a split second and barreled right into him, jostling him into the grass. "I don't think so, buddy, you better back off."

After that odd assembly, there was no room in my brain for this kind of boy drama. "Better just get this over with. I'll hear him out and meet you in the cafeteria. Save me a seat, okay? I'll be fine, promise."

"Fine, I'll see you later." He shoved his hands in his pockets and shifted his weight. His blue eyes seemed to get paler as he glanced from me to Will, finally resting on me. "If you're sure."

Slowly I nodded at him, but he just shook his head and stomped off. "Great." I mouthed to the gray sky.

"Finally, I thought he'd never leave us alone." Will sprawled out on a stone bench under a cluster of red maples. His gray eyes matched the sky, enough so you'd think the whole thing was some kind of elaborate photo shoot. He patted the space beside him. "Have a seat, I won't bite."

"You said that before. I'm not so sure." I stood tall, dropping my bag on the spot where he wanted me to sit. "What do you want?"

"Listen," he slung his arm across the back of the bench, "I didn't want to be the one to have to tell you this. But your mom asked me to watch out for you, so here goes. First you disappear in the middle of an important initiation. Now it looks like you're falling for the wrong guy."

"First off, that was no ordinary initiation, more like some kind of test. Well, I failed." Miserably, I should add. His eyes widened and his chin tilted, like he wanted me to challenge him. Game on. "Two days ago you almost kissed *me*, remember? You're just mad because the guy I'm falling for isn't you, right?"

"Ouch, that hurt. You don't know how much I care about you." His game face fell and suddenly his hand curled around mine. I wriggled my fingers against his, but he clamped down tighter. "Maybe you're right, but not just for that reason."

"Okay then, what is it? Spit it out already." I pursed my lips together. Could I really trust his perspective?

"Feisty today, aren't we? I like it." His eyes dropped to my mouth, with traces of a grin creeping up his face. Then he cocked his head at me. "First off, Bryan's little group is completely messed up. They only want you for your abilities, you know? They don't care about you at all."

"What?" I backed up, sliding my hand from his grip. How could he possibly know about my so-called abilities? I hadn't told a soul. Two could play this game. "Abilities? Just because my daddy's on the school board and my brother used to be your president doesn't mean I have any abilities. I'm nothing special."

In an instant his smile faded. "Is that what they're telling you? Don't believe it for a second. You may not know it yet, but in a few years you will. By then they'll have you under their thumb. Do you really want to be a pawn in their little game?"

"Better to be a pawn in yours, I'm guessing. Exactly what game might that be, anyway?"

Those platinum eyes were stuck on me like Velcro, and I couldn't look away. The breeze died down, the air stilled around us.

"You wouldn't believe the truth if I told it to you." He stood too, closing the gap between us. His cinnamon breath warmed my face until my cheeks blazed.

Yet I couldn't pull away, those hypnotic eyes held me in place with some strange sort of fascination. A shiver slithered down my neck.

"I'll be the judge of that." My voice wobbled, a chink in the armor that finally gave me the freedom to break his gaze. Wind rustled through the maple tree. A red leaf drifted on the breeze, landing in my lap.

"Thanks for watching out for me." I said it more to the maple leaf than him. I didn't want to think about the initiation, or Colleen and Monica's accusations. He didn't add anything more, if there really was anything more. "You better say what you wanted to say, or I'm taking off."

He reached out one finger and grazed my chin, guiding my face toward his. "I doubt he's told you what really happened, but Bryan broke my friend's heart last year. He dumped Colleen for not conforming to the strict Guardian rules. Then he kicked her out. That's why she joined our group. I just don't want the same thing to happen to you. You don't deserve that kind of heartache."

Could he really be so low? What if someone pranced around campus telling everyone about me and Jake, from Jake's perspective? I'd kill them.

The anger practically steamed from my pores until I wanted to scream. "Why should I believe anything you say?"

"I knew you wouldn't believe me." His jaw clenched. He punched his thigh, then his head snapped back to me, a fire in his eyes. "Why would I lie?"

That really burned me up. "As if I know the inner workings of your twisted mind. I don't know why you'd lie, but you lied about James. Why wouldn't you lie about this?"

"What I told you was entirely true." His arms crossed over his chest like he wasn't going to budge.

"Liar." If only I could punch him right now. I balled my fists up, clenching them to my sides. "I know he was kicked out of Nexis. What did you do to him?"

"I didn't do anything to James." He reached across the gulf I'd carefully crafted between us and grabbed ahold of my fist.

The harsh vision came back to me, the field, the figures. I yanked my hand back. "Nexis threw him out. How could you keep that from me?"

"I'm not supposed to tell anyone. How did you even find out? You're not a member. Look, I'm sorry, Lucy." His fingers ran up my arm, brushing back my hair. I flinched as his nails grazed my skin. "If you become a member, I can tell you everything. I promise."

"You haven't denied any of it. Can you promise it won't turn out like it did with James? That I won't be banished from the country for God knows what reason? Blamed for someone's death?" Tears stabbed my eyes.

"What are you talking about?" His eyebrows scrunched into that V shape I used to think was cute.

"I'm talking about Colleen and Monica accusing my brother of being the last one to see Maria Donovan alive." My voice was booming now, shattering the silence of the quad.

"What, why would they say that?" He pinched the bridge of his nose, air whooshing from his lungs. "It has to be a misunderstanding. They didn't actually say he did anything, did they?"

"They implied." If only I could bore holes into him with my eyes. "If you think I would ever join a group who kicked out my brother, whose members implicated him in someone's death ..."

"I still don't know how you found out about James. I wanted to tell you myself."

"Please, wouldn't you like to know?" Why was I still sitting here, listening to all this garbage? Like he had some kind of spell over me, a cobra staring me down with its sick fascination. No more. I snatched my bag off the bench, threw it over my shoulder, and stormed down the cobblestone.

"Lucy, wait," he called after me. "Don't be like this. You don't understand, I have so much more to tell you."

"Too little, too late." I ran across the quad as fast as I could, as far away from him as I could get.

I'd made my choice, and Will knew it now. What would he do? If he was mad enough to confront me like that, what about my parents—would he tell them? But above all those questions, one blared through my brain like a fire alarm.

Why would my own parents want me to join Nexis after what happened to James?

Maybe they didn't know, they certainly hadn't seen my vision. On the other hand, maybe Bryan made up the whole thing about his sister and James. I pushed that question back into the shadows. I couldn't think about that now, even entertain the idea. Will practically admitted that Nexis threw James out and my vision confirmed it. Period.

15

With a quick knock I burst into Harlixton's office, ready to pound a gavel on his desk and demand some answers. Silence and the stench of despair filled my nostrils, seeping into every pore. A deadly aroma of French press and moldy books, the hollow cry of a neglected office. It reeked of so much more than stale coffee. If only my frustrations could drown themselves in the murky darkness.

On the wall, the clock ticked as I cleared off a chair to wait for my teacher. Maybe it knew more than I did, that time was running out. I couldn't just go with the flow and listen to whatever Will or Bryan said. Not this time.

Mr. Harlixton bustled past me with a stack of books up to his chest and dumped them on the floor. "Miss McAllen, right on time I see. You'll have to forgive my oddities. You know some people say that a messy office is the sign of a productive person. At least I do."

"Never heard that one." I crossed my arms, leaning on the edge of his desk. "I know your little speech in junior assembly was meant for me."

"Possibly." He scratched his chin and stared right back at me.

"What I don't know is why would you single me out like that?"

"Let's just say I wanted you to come and find me. There are too many people watching me. If you didn't seek me out on your own, they'd get suspicious."

"What does that mean?" I threw up my hands like an exasperated little girl. But I couldn't help it, this was getting too weird. "Why does everything have to be so cryptic around here? I just want some answers, and I want them now. I don't know what to believe any more."

"I see. Then you must've heard a bit from both sides by now." He pushed up his glasses as an expression of utter calm swept over his face. So calm it hit me like a splash of cold water on my cheeks.

I snapped back in my chair. "Yeah, you could say that. It's been interesting on both sides, especially with Bryan's crew."

His loud laugh roared around the small room. "Is that what you call them? Boy, would he get a kick out of that."

"You can't tell him I said that." The plea came out high and breathy. For the first time since I arrived at Montrose, I desperately wanted to sink into the dark depths of my past where things were so much easier.

"Calm down, I have no interest in matters of the adolescent heart. I'm more concerned that you figure out what is true and what is false." He waddled over to the pile of books he'd left by the door. "I pulled these from the school library. Feel free to peruse them and take whatever you need. I recommend the top three."

"Are you for real?" In a few steps I stood next to him, plowing into the ten-book tower. With titles like *Angels, Angels, Angels*, and *The Nephilim Conspiracy*, I wasn't sure what to choose. Flipping through the dusty hardback books, I settled on the top three, plus a few with lots of pictures.

"Thanks for this. I researched in the library on my own a few weeks ago, but didn't find much. It's so overwhelming." The real question, the reason I'd ran straight to his office, paused on the tip of my tongue. I bit it back, for now.

He crammed the remaining books onto his shelf. "Just doing my job. You know, half the kids come here fully brainwashed by their parents. The rest are like you, stuck with parents who want them to choose a side, but won't educate them. That's why you're here."

"What do you mean?" The books weighed on my arms, but his words burrowed into my brain.

"You want the truth?" He zeroed in on me with those beady little eyes behind his thick lenses.

My arms went slack, the books dive-bombing into a pile at my feet. Slowly I nodded. "I need the truth."

"Brace yourself." He rolled up his shirt sleeves and plunked down in his seat, motioning me to do the same. "The academy was founded by the Montrose family, Nexis leaders whose sole purpose was to recruit future Ivy Leaguers into the ranks of Nexis. Within a few years, the Guardians discovered their plot and threatened war if they kept recruiting innocents, as they called you teenagers. A truce was negotiated, allowing Guardians free access to recruit as well. So innocents had a choice."

Pressure built up between my eyes as I wrinkled my brow at him. "I don't get it, why don't they just duke it out?"

He only shook his head. "At that time, neither side was strong enough for all-out war. Now, I'm sorry to say, both sides are too strong. There'd be too many casualties. Instead, it's all about clandestine missions and turning the right people."

He openly stared at me this time.

An ache spread across my forehead as his implication lapped into my mind. "By 'the right people' you mean me, don't you? But seriously, why me?"

He lowered his voice a notch. "With your gift, you can tip the balance of power to whichever side you choose. Your parents sent you here to join Nexis, not the Guardians. Why they didn't indoctrinate you more, I have no idea, but it hasn't always been that way."

"What?" The idea kicked my mind into overdrive. To think, my parents could've pushed Nexis on me since birth, but they hadn't. "Wait, you mean some of my relatives were Guardians?"

"Until recently." He turned his face away from me, toward a picture on the wall. "For centuries actually, on your father's side. A few generations ago, that all changed. Which is why it is so critical for you to learn all you can. You have to make the right decision. It will impact future generations."

Perching on the wooden chair I squinted at his painting, a landscape of a lone tree in the forest on fire. Shapes flickered at me in the waves of fire. A lone branch emerged from the flames, then the rest of the tree. Something niggled at my mind, but I couldn't make sense of it.

"Why would my parents keep all this from me?"

"That's what I can't figure out. Maybe because you're the middle child, and not yet eighteen," he chewed on his pen cap, eyes glazing in a faraway stare, "but I don't think so. It must have something to do with your brother."

At the mention of James, I couldn't hold back any longer. The words tumbled out of my mouth. "Do you know what happened to him? Can you even tell me?"

He swiveled back in my direction, shaking his head. "I really wish I did. I'm pretty sure he was kicked out of Nexis, I have no idea why. If he never told you or your family, then it's probably extremely bad. I'd go on, but I don't want to alarm you."

"I think I'm already alarmed enough as it is." I combed my fingers through my hair, pulling out the knots as I bent down to pick up the scattered books. "Maybe these will help."

"I'm afraid you won't find much about the Nexis sect in these books. They're a very secretive bunch. You'd have to be a member to know it all. Although once you're in, it's hard to get out safely."

James' face flashed in my mind, shadowed in torchlight. The breath caught in my throat. "You mean James might've been in danger for leaving?"

His shoulders slumped as if I'd punched him in the gut. He barely nodded. "That's my guess, but I hope I'm wrong."

Suddenly, the blood pounded in my veins and my brain sputtered to life again. I knew what I had to do. "I have to learn everything I can about them."

"Now we're getting somewhere. I hoped you'd say that." He rubbed his hands together, a smile creeping up his face. Then he opened his desk drawer and slid out an ancient skeleton key, with a modern-looking key hanging next to it.

"For me?" I snatched the wrought-iron keychain from his hands. "Cool, what're they for?"

"The big one is for the chapel door, the small one for the library. I suggest you do some extra research in there. Those old texts will give you a much richer history than these contemporary books."

He wiped his hands on his plaid dress shirt. "Be very careful with those old books. They have some bias in them, but you'll find more information on Nexis, even if it's from the opposite side. Things aren't always as good, or as bad, as they seem. Keep that in mind."

With that he scooted me toward the door. In the doorway he stopped, whispering in my ear, "Keep those keys to yourself. Don't share."

"Got it." I shoved the keys in my pocket and took off down the hall. Nothing could stop me from finding the truth now.

Burning candles flickered in the chapel foyer, a faint smell of wax in the air. Stained glass spattered rainbows of dusky light on empty pews. My wedges clicked against the marble tile en route to the library.

The door creaked open at my touch.

"Oh, it's you." Mindy lifted her head from the book she hunkered over at the corner table. Her eyes said it all. "What are you doing here? Wait, don't tell me, you procrastinated on that Western Civ paper, too. Shocking, since I heard you were next in line for the Nexis throne, or something."

I glared her way, squinting daggers. Just because I was James' sister? She couldn't be that clueless.

"That's a sick joke." The words burned like acid in my throat, then it dawned on me. "Where'd you hear that?"

"Please, it's all over school." She shoved her book aside, and matched my gaze with withering fury. "Your dad's on the school board, your mom was homecoming queen, your brother was president. It's only a matter of time."

My jaw dropped straight onto the carpet. Air puffed from the gaping hole, but I couldn't wrap my mind around her words.

"Deny it all you want, we all know it's true." An odd sort of smile played at her lips, kind of like Will's under the maple tree. Too creepy. "I bet even your precious roommate is jealous."

"Don't believe everything you hear." So, that's what this was about. Did I really have to deal with her as if she were an arrogant guy, my own suitemate? I wanted to wipe that smirk off her face. "That's not the whole truth. Someday you'll have to learn to think for yourself. If you can ever grow up and stop believing idle gossip."

"Whatever." She flipped her hair at me, as if I cared one iota. "Go do your stupid research."

"Fine, I will." I turned my back on her and beelined across the room to the card catalog.

Without another word, I yanked open the top drawer of the skinny five-tiered file cabinet. It banged open, almost dumping its yellowed index cards all over the floor. I thumbed through the angel section, scouring the tiny type for books on Nephilim, or Christian sects.

"Jackpot." I fist-pumped the air, reading the card again. These books were in stack number seven, the dark corner of the library. With a gulp, I swallowed the lump of fear creeping up my throat. Time to be brave, if not for me then for James.

I zigzagged to the other side of the room, then tiptoed down the last aisle. At the end of the row something banged into my shin and I almost face-planted right into a tall ladder. It completely blended in with the cedar shelves. Pushing aside the ladder, I scanned the numbers, then the titles, but the books I wanted were nowhere in sight. They had to be in the turret.

The dimly-lit tower extended up twelve feet or so, with old books stacked around its three sides.

"Impressive." The only light seeped in from two porthole windows ten feet up, highlighting the section I needed. That meant one thing, time to climb the ladder. It creaked on its rusty hinges as I rolled it into place.

If only I could swing around like Belle from *Beauty and the Beast*, it might be less creepy. But I was on a mission—a mission to figure out why James disappeared and why Nexis kicked him out. I couldn't fail this time.

On shaky legs I climbed upward, rung by rung. With even shakier fingers I pried the thick leather spines of two books from their hiding places. As I descended, the ladder wobbled beneath me. Belle would've never had to put up with this.

Finally my feet touched ground again. I lingered in the musty old corner. The cool darkness cradled me, ten times safer than Mindy and her misplaced anger.

I spread my books out on the nearest table, turning my back on her even though she was on the other side of the room. The first dusty tome listed a bland paragraph about the Nexis sect, but no juicy details. I shoved that book aside and moved on to the next.

"Please let me find something, anything." This decrepit book had a whole chapter on the Nexis Semigod Nations, the same name they used at the initiation. According to the author, the sect was actually a collection of clans across many countries, called Nexis Nations. They held to "extra-biblical" views of the reasons God flooded the Earth in Noah's time.

Nexilim, as they preferred to call themselves, believed that God used the flood to wipe out all the Nephilim because they had grown too powerful, almost godlike. These half-angel beings were so powerful they ruled humanity. A drawing in the book depicted a figure with broad shoulders standing a full head and shoulders higher than any man.

The Nexis goal was to create Nephilim in the modern world by convincing fallen angels to marry and have children with Nexis women.

"How would you do that?" I whispered to myself, hoping Mindy wouldn't notice from across the room. She didn't move a muscle.

The book put forth an even scarier idea—that these Nephilim children would be brought up under Nexis control. So one day all Nexis Nations would be populated with these Semigods. In turn, they'd rule every country on Earth with Nephilim as their heads of state.

This was too much. I couldn't wrap my mind around it. Question after question pelted my brain, pummeling me in the forehead like a tether ball hitting me again and again.

"Ick, is that what they want from me?" I stared at the page until my eyes lost focus. None of it made any sense. Why in the world would some ancient group with an elaborate scheme hold secret meetings on a prep school campus?

In a split-second the room dimmed. I blinked. The inky letters on the yellowed page shifted, like something out of a movie. Slowly, some grew larger and glowed with a yellow light. I snapped my eyes shut. When I opened them again, the letters were still the same.

What could this mean? Was it something I had to decipher?

I pulled out my notebook and wrote the letters vertically. Sure enough, they spelled out Nexis Semigod Nations. Weird.

I glanced back at the book and now the letters were glowing brighter, a strange gilt-halo effect that erased everything else on the parchment. The highlighted letters seesawed around the page and then *Poof!* they rearranged.

I penned the letters vertically again, next to the Nexis column. A phrase that sent a chill to the depths of my bones.

GENESIS SIX DOMINATION. Side by side with Nexis Semigod Nations, the phrase contained the exact same letters. An anagram.

I slammed the book shut. So that was the true purpose behind Nexis. Their one goal for centuries, to dominate the world according to Genesis six with these Nephilim beings. Could they really find a way to recreate the terrifying Nephilim creatures God destroyed in the flood?

Hold the phone—did they want to use my gifts to do it? Better yet, did they know about the visions I was seeing? That must be why Will wanted to be with me so bad.

Too much. I gasped and suddenly forgot how to breathe. This couldn't be real. This had to be a nightmare or just another vision. But if my vision about James was true, did that mean this was true, too?

Mindy quirked her head over her shoulder to glare at me. "You look awful. What's the matter, find out your perfect world isn't so perfect?"

"Just stop. I can't deal with you right now." I held up my hand in front of my face. Anything to shield me from the ugly truth. "You know, if you didn't believe the lies about me, we could actually be friends."

"Yeah right." She swiveled away from me again.

And the room started spinning with her. My head lolled down to my hands. The darkness of the tabletop soothed the spinning, if only for a few seconds.

Loud footsteps clomped on the thin carpet, heading straight toward me.

"Lucy, didn't know you'd be here." Even Bryan's calm voice couldn't soothe the rocking in my brain. Who could be calm at a time like this?

An inch at a time, I raised my head. "What, I can't come here on my own?"

"No, just surprised to see you here." He wrangled a spot in the chair next to me, carefully avoiding eye contact. As if that mattered now.

"Join the club." I pursed my lips, eyeing the back of Mindy's head. "I give up, I don't know what to think any more. This is too much. It's just too much."

"What's too much? What've you got there?" He picked up the book, brows scrunched, blue eyes clouding over. "Is that why you came here, to see for yourself? You don't trust me?"

"After Will's little speech, can you really blame me?" I clamped my hand over my mouth. The book dropped to the table with a thud. "I'm sorry, I didn't mean that. Right now I don't know what to believe."

"Why don't we go sit in the sanctuary? You love it in there." The blue calmed again as he rubbed slow circles on my back. "Maybe I can help you figure this out, if you'll let me."

"No need to move, I'll leave. I'm done anyway." Mindy hoisted her bag over her shoulder, closing the gap between us until she stood next to my chair. "Listen, I'm sorry about earlier. I guess things really aren't so perfect for you either."

"You can say that again. Thanks." A weak smile was all I could offer her.

"You take care of her. Bye, Lucy." She waved her perfect little wave and disappeared out the doorway.

Bryan leaned over my shoulder to examine the earth-shattering book, his palm still circling my back. "So this isn't about me, it's about them."

I nodded. "Is this true? Is that what Nexis wants, for me to marry a fallen angel and make half-angel children? Because I know what fallen angels really are, they're demons. Hello, check the Bible."

He only nodded his head. "Hey, I'm not disputing that."

"So it's true then?" For a long minute I let myself gaze into those mesmerizing eyes, hoping this was all a dream. Maybe I should tell him what I saw. Would he believe me, or just try to use me like Will?

He gave me a head-bob, the final nail in the coffin of the ugly truth I just figured out. "I'm afraid it's one of the possible scenarios, according to our intel."

"Your intel? Does that mean you're spying on Nexis?" I stared at him, hardly believing what I was hearing.

"Not me personally. But the Guardians, yes." He just shrugged. "Each side spies on the other. It's the only way to get ahead."

"Really?" I blinked like a fool. How could he be so calm about such crazy, out-of-this-world, completely unbelievable stuff? Did I really want to be caught in the middle of this clandestine game of chess? No matter what side I chose, surely it was a game nobody could win—let alone one teenage girl from the middle of nowhere.

He kept nodding, but it didn't make his words easier to swallow. "Some of our sources say the Stanton's want you, or your descendants, to have a Nephilim child. But there's no way Nexis would stand for it. In theory, if the Seer had a Nephilim child, that family could rule Nexis. Which violates one of their main tenets of belief about equal power among Nexis nations, or some garbage like that."

"I just don't get it." His words held no meaning, giant waves of nothingness crashing around in my brain. "It doesn't make any sense."

"Essentially, they want to rule the world." A hush fell over the room, like a calm before the storm. "They actually think their crazy plan will bring peace to the nations of the earth. At least that's what they tell themselves."

"Yeah, right." The force of it all smacked me head on. "We're not just going to roll over and let some wacko group take over the world. I know I wouldn't. There's plenty of militant groups who'd fight. Governments, too."

"That's why they recruit Ivy League families, to get into all kinds of power positions like the government." His hand on my back stopped, mid circle. "Of course, Nexis believes there won't be a fight. Nephilim are supposed to be that strong. The Bible says they stood head and shoulders over any man."

I nodded slowly as the pieces of the puzzle finally clicked into place. "So that's why they're here at Montrose. Didn't they read the part about David and Goliath? Or that part about the Flood wiping out the Nephilim? As if God would really allow any of it."

He resumed the circles, slower this time. "But the Nephilim did exist, Goliath, too, and they created so many problems that God had to wipe them out. That's why the Guardians were formed. We believe our purpose is to oppose Nexis, and eventually demolish all their entrenched schemes."

"I see." I gripped the edge of the table, my only anchor. "Hold on a second. Did you just say you thought I was the Seer?"

His mouth curled up and he nibbled on his bottom lip. "Caught that, didn't you? I think that's what Nexis believes, anyway."

"And what do you believe?"

"I don't know. I didn't think it was possible, but right now I just don't know." His eyes met mine, and I couldn't pull away.

"And that's why you need me. Just like Nexis does."

"Again, I'm afraid you're right." The calm on his face softened into sadness. He wrapped his arm around my shoulders. "Sometimes I wish you weren't so perceptive, you know."

"Wait a minute." I nestled into his collarbone, unwilling to watch his eyes cloud over again. "You said Will might have something else planned for me?"

"I don't know for sure. We only have circumstantial evidence from our sources." His muscles tightened against my cheek. "We're still trying to figure out what the Stanton family is up to. It's all just conjecture right now."

"Out with it, Cooper." I couldn't stand it any more. He knew more than he was letting on. How could I ever trust him, or the Guardians, if they didn't tell me the whole truth. "Just tell me, whether I like it or not."

He gulped in a giant breath, so big his Adam's apple bobbed against my temple. "Okay, here goes. Another theory is that Will's family is pushing him to date you, even marry you so whenever you have a family, they'll be in control of the next Seer."

"Double ick. That's messed up." The idea of it churned my stomach into a spinning whirlpool of sludge. "As if I'd ever marry him, let alone be controlled by him, or his family, or anyone else." In my mind, that included the Guardians, too.

"I'm sorry, Lucy." He murmured against my forehead. "I shouldn't have said anything. It's too soon to know for sure."

"No, I'm glad you told me." I couldn't move, my limbs were stiff as a plank. "It's better that I know now, before it's too late."

With his free hand Bryan scooted the book closer, and flipped it open right to where I left off. "What'd you find out?"

I blinked, and the letters lit up again, waltzing around the page. Any second they'd spell out that awful phrase, the anagram of doom. I slammed the book shut like it was a disease.

"Enough to know one thing for sure. I'm never joining Nexis. Ever."

16

Night air hissed in from the cracked window, softly, like a whisper. I could almost hear Will's voice on the breeze, calling my name. His face floated unbidden into my mind, sitting on that bench under the maple tree. Why couldn't I get him, or his family's scary plans, out of my head?

I slammed my face into the pillow, hard enough to send his gray eyes out of my mind. The wind blew across my bed and I shot up to close the window. If only I could block him out, too. Outside, the sun disappeared though the trees as the sky purpled with deep hues, then faded into navy blackness.

Uncertainty curled up like a vise grip in my gut. This new revelation didn't sit well with me. No matter how much I wanted to believe my parents had it right, there were only two possibilities. Either they didn't know what Nexis was really about, or they wanted to use me just like everyone else. A shudder crept up my spine. That couldn't be true, could it? My parents loved me, that much I knew.

So what about James, where did all of this leave him? Maybe he figured it out too late and wanted out. In the end, I guess my options were the same as his. Get pushed around by everybody, Nexis, the Guardians, my parents. Or choose for myself.

A star winked at me through the glass, reminding me of my obligation— the bonfire tonight. I lingered in the window, not ready to get all dolled up just yet.

My gut told me which way to go, but who gave me that whole listen-to-your-gut speech? No, there had to be something I was missing. Something that tugged at the corners of my mind, but I couldn't grab onto it.

I slipped down from my perch and padded to the mirror. With a wide-toothed comb, I parted my hair down the middle and twisted each side into pigtails. Then I bowtied them with blue and gold ribbons that shimmered in the fluorescent light. "Perfect."

"You look hideous." Shanda practically shrieked in my ears. "Why don't you just paint your face with Montrose colors and do cartwheels?"

"Wouldn't want to steal your thunder." I dangled the leftover ribbons in her face. She gagged. "Seriously, you should come."

"No way, I won't be caught dead at a smelly fire." She ran the mascara wand over her thick lashes. "Besides, I have a date with Kevin."

"You're always with surfer boy lately. What's the matter, he's not into football?" I balled up the rest of the ribbons and chucked them at her.

She batted down the blue and gold satin. "Yeah, he's sane like me. We'll have way more fun than you, at some lame pep rally."

Bobby pins poked into my skull as I secured the ribbons in place. "C'mon, it's the first one of the year. You can't miss it. I'm meeting the suitemates, Laura, and Lenny in the lobby, just in case you change your mind."

"Not on your life. I'll be the only one having a good time tonight." She put the final sprinkle on her eye makeup.

"Suit yourself." I zipped up my navy Montrose hoodie and sashayed out the door. If only my gloomy thoughts would stay home for the night.

The girls and Lenny waited in the lobby, not one of them in school colors. Not even the girls. Apparently, no one else did peppy. Maybe I'd hung out with jocks too long. Jake's friends would've mocked me all night if I didn't wear the right shade of Alton High red.

"How cute are you?" Brooke checked her hair in the mirror. "Maybe I should change."

"She's right, those are adorable." Mindy smoothed down my pigtails. The first gesture of affection I'd had from her in awhile. Maybe things could finally go back to normal.

"You know, I did bring some extra ribbons in case mine fell out." I slid the sapphire and gold satin out of my jeans pocket. "Have at them."

"Really?" Laura squealed and fingered the blue one.

"Don't take too long." Lenny plopped on the couch, crossing his legs like he knew she would be awhile.

The girls grabbed for the ribbons and went to town. Mindy worked a long gold ribbon into a stylish headband, while Laura looped a big blue bow around her ponytail. I split Brooke's hair into loose pigtails, then double-knotted them with blue and gold ribbons.

She grinned back at me in the mirror. "Now I look as cute as you."

"Cuter." I poked her button nose. Her cheeks pinked up.

"Better, don't you think?" Laura waggled her ponytail at Lenny.

He lumbered to the door, holding it open for us. "Just don't put any on me."

"Don't be silly, you'd just look tacky in ribbons. Too bad we don't have any face paint." Brooke linked arms with Lenny as they marched across campus.

He rolled his eyes at her. "Yeah, too bad."

Mindy hooked one arm around Brooke's and the other through Laura's, who roped me with her tiny arms onto the end of the chain. I'd created three monsters. More like a band of peppy Rockettes ready to high kick it all the way to the bonfire.

"I've got all the ladies tonight, so you'll have to share me. Speaking of sharing," he shook his shaggy red hair from his eyes and craned his neck down the Rockette line. "Lucy, you know Will still talks about you like he's got a chance."

"What?" I dropped Laura's arm and halted in the middle of the path. "You've got to be kidding me. We had a huge fight and I haven't spoken to him since."

"Must be clueless." She patted my back and prodded me forward. "Or just plain arrogant."

I crunched my sneakers into the dead grass as we followed the path toward the practice football field.

"I guess absence makes the heart grow fonder." Mindy batted her eyelashes at me. "Good thing Bryan's not that way, or he'd be sick of you already. You've been with him every day."

"Have not." I huffed like ten-year-old me after I got busted for stealing Paige's Barbie doll. Didn't fool my little sister then, not fooling anyone now.

"Yeah, right, you eat lunch and dinner together. Then you're at the chapel library after that." Mindy flipped her hair over one shoulder, catty eyes flashing at me. She kept awful close tabs on me. A little jealous maybe, or did she still think I knew something about Maria?

"Please, we're just friends." The words tumbled out of my mouth, but even I didn't believe them.

Lenny stared me down. "Will thinks you're just friends with Bryan, too. He doesn't care that you ignored him."

"Of course not. God told him to marry Lucy." Laura's comment sent the group into hysterics.

"Say what now?" I grabbed her shoulders, forcing her to look at me. Could she really joke about such a thing? "You wanna run that by me again?"

Her eyes inflated to the size of the moon behind her. "Lenny didn't tell you? Kevin let something slip to that effect. I'm sorry, Lucy, I didn't mean to make fun of you. I just assumed my brother already told you." She elbowed her twin in the ribs.

The night wind whipped my pigtails around, sending a chill down my neck.

"Why would I tell her? It's completely nuts." Lenny slapped her elbow away. "She has enough on her plate right now. No need to pile on some crazy guy's idiotic nonsense."

"So true." I nodded at Lenny and we exchanged knowing glances. Maybe what Bryan said about Will last night wasn't so far off after all. Still, the idea of it kind of unhinged me. Marriage, at sixteen? Ick.

"Yeah, it's beyond wacko." Mindy gave me a small smile and came closer.

"Thanks." I quirked one side of my mouth at her. Maybe we could put our silly little fight behind us now.

Our group merged with the crowd in front of us. A roar rippled through the huddled mass as the first branch caught fire.

I shook my pigtails, but it didn't clear my head. Now I knew enough to stay away from Will, even with his irresistible bad-boy charm. Maybe he overestimated that charm, or I'd simply underestimated him, period.

A shadowy figure bobbed its way through the mess of teenagers. Before I knew it, Will's gray eyes found me in the crowd. He pushed people aside until he stood next to me.

"Hi, Luce, I've been trying to find you everywhere. You're adorable. Love the pigtails." He flicked one in my face.

The shiver on my cheek felt more like a slither. "Don't call me Luce." That's what Jake always called me. I backed up into Lenny's shoulder. "That's creepy."

"No, it's romantic." Mindy giggled and the girls laughed.

Lenny muscled his arms across his chest and scowled at him. Bryan would be proud.

The dense crowd thickened by the minute. Even with a blazing fire twenty feet ahead and the warmth of my hoodie, goosebumps popped up all over my arms. "Look, Will, I hate to break it to you, but I'm not into you."

"I don't believe you." His chin cleft quirked at me. Then his beady eyes honed in on me as if they alone could convince me of anything.

I scanned the crowd for a quick exit. I'd never escape without him following me like he did in the kitchen. Who knows how he'd act without the group? I shuddered.

I planted my hands firmly on my hips and steeled my gaze. "Don't you get it? There's nothing between us."

"You and I both know that's not true. Just wait and see." His creepy grin widened.

Butterflies on caffeine swirled in my stomach. "I've had enough stalkers for one year. Just leave me alone."

"I'm no stalker, I just know what I want." In his dark jeans and black leather jacket, he practically blended into the night. Only his gunmetal eyes glinted as he edged closer, his breath hot on my face. "You're the firstborn, which means I'll never leave you alone."

Laura, Lenny, Brooke, and Mindy's stares bounced from Will back to me like a tennis match. Eyes wide as tennis balls, too, stunned silent. Some help.

I clenched my fists at my sides, fingernails digging into my hands. The butterflies were hopped up on Redbull now.

"I'm not the firstborn, you've met my brother." I screamed with all the air in my lungs. Yet it made sense somehow, explained why my mother always pushed me so hard. Like no other child.

"Yes, you are." He leveled his gray eyes at me. The bonfire raged behind him, but his eyes, his voice, transcended the chaos. Calm as still waters. "You know, for someone who's supposed to be good at seeing things, you're pretty blind to what's really going on."

In the corners of my peripheral vision, I saw the group staring at him, but I couldn't tear my eyes away. Everything around him blurred.

"What are you saying?" Wood smoke hovered in the air, weaving its way in and out of the crowd, clinging to my ribbons. It clogged my nose, my thoughts.

"Lucy, don't you know how much I care about you?" He turned toward the fire, then back to me. "What do I have to do to get through to you?"

The distant orange light edged the silhouette of his face. Those steely eyes pierced into the shadows, dead set on me, waiting for an answer.

My stomach clenched into a thousand knots I could never untie. I had to ask, I had to know, now or never. "Why didn't you tell me about James?"

"Please, like you didn't already know. Deep down, you knew." His soft tone jarred the knots. They buzzed in my middle like a hot wire, ready for the onslaught. The firelight soared higher, the teenage roar rippling through my objections.

"Excuse me, I certainly did not." How could I ever imagine it? A secret so deep it cut through the entire McAllen family, my very being. Every idea, every belief, every hope held captive by my mother's indiscretion. "Like I would guess something that awful about my own mother. How could she?"

"What is it that really bugs you the most? That she did it in the first place, or that she hid it from you?" Firelight danced in his eyes, as if he were a stand-up comedian, mocking my pain.

I gasped. Why didn't he just sucker punch me in the gut? Air puffed from my lungs like he had.

"Try sixteen years of lying, of keeping secrets. Then I had to find out on my own from some guy who—" Suddenly my hand shot up, ready to smack the smugness off his face.

His fingers clamped around my wrist, held my arm still, even as I lunged forward with all the strength I had left. "Some guy who what? Tried to be gentle about the truth and not dump it on you all at once. What do you have to say to me? Just tell me."

The words burned and choked my throat, all of them. So many things I could say to him. "I can't believe you. What you did to James. How could you?"

His eyes narrowed at me, his lips twitched like he wanted to laugh. My hand squirmed in his grip of iron. "That wasn't me, I was just a freshman. The council did that."

Like he couldn't have stopped Nexis if he wanted to. Excuses, all of it.

Finally, I wriggled free of his grasp. "But how could you not tell me sooner? I thought you cared about me."

"Of course I do, that's why I didn't tell you. It's a family thing. James isn't here, and your mom wasn't about to go into the sordid details. I'm sorry I had to do it this way."

"As if that's any excuse."

His lips curled and he stepped closer. I could smell the cinnamon over the wood smoke. "Soon you'll be unblinded. Then we'll be together, forever. You'll see. I knew it was you the moment I saw you."

So he thought I would be the Seer, but he didn't know about my visions yet. Score one for Lucy. The smoky-spiced air caught in my throat. I backed up, an odd feeling settling in my stomach. I didn't want to be the Seer. He couldn't be right. And nobody told me what I was or wasn't going to do.

"We'll never be together, not now. So you better get over it, or leave me alone." I drew my right arm back, angled for a jab.

Firm fingers gripped my arm, locking it in place.

"She said leave her alone." The gruff voice came from behind.

My insides melted at his breath on my neck, a soothing warmth that banished the goosebumps. I turned around to meet those darling blues.

"Bryan?" My arms went limp. Was he taller now? His eyes seared into Will like a western showdown.

"Yeah, Will." Lenny stood taller, too. "Stop bugging Lucy. Go hang out with your Nexis friends. Look, they're over there."

"Fine." He shoved his hands in his pockets, eyes stuck on me. "This isn't over."

He stormed off into the crowd.

"Sheesh," Mindy breathed. "No more hanging out with that guy."

"He certainly can't take a hint." Laura's little laugh put the group at ease.

"I wonder if I can find a new suitemate," Lenny said. The girls laughed, but it was off-kilter.

"Better ask your dorm parents. I don't want you hanging around him any more." Laura's shoulders quivered. Their discussion of Lenny's dilemma faded into the background.

My heart still thudded in my chest. On tiptoes I arched as close as I could get to Bryan's ear. "Thanks."

The musk of his piney aftershave mixed with the smoke of the fire. It hit me in the pit of my stomach. I sank down on my heels.

"No big deal." He brushed aside a strand of my hair, his fingers soft on my face.

"It's a big deal to me." My words tumbled out fast and breathy. "Nothing phased him. He said he'd never let me go, it was creepy." Even thinking about it made me shiver.

He rubbed my arm, more chills trickled down my spine. "Here, take my jacket."

"I don't know what I would've done if you hadn't shown up." The familiar fleece lining rubbed against my cheek. I closed my eyes, inhaled the scent.

"From the looks of it, you could've knocked him off guard." His hand covered mine, balling it into a fist. "Where'd you learn to do that?"

"My dad made me take self-defense classes a few years ago. I've never used it before, so I probably couldn't actually hurt anyone." Will's face came to mind as I pulled my arm back.

"You've got pretty good form." He wrapped both hands around my arm, one at my bicep and one at my elbow, then rotated my arm around. "If you've only got one punch, you better make it count. An uppercut would do the trick better than a jab, since you're a girl and all."

"What're you saying, I'm weak?" My arm felt feeble in his strong hands, not that I'd ever tell him that.

"Just compared to a guy. Body leverage is key." He thrust my arm forward until my fist tapped his face. "See, lights out. Your jab would've distracted him enough so you could run away. Maybe left him with a black eye."

"That'll be the day." I rubbed my fist. "If you hadn't shown up I might've spent the night in the slammer."

"Glad I got here just in time." The firelight flickered in his blue eyes. Suddenly he dropped my arm and his eyes fell with it. "I finally got ahold of Abby. She's been avoiding me, said she didn't want to tell me what happened with James."

"Why not? I'm his sister." Or half-sister. Could it be true? The fire wobbled behind him, the crowd undulating around me, as if the earth was about to give way. "Does it have something to do with what Will said? He said I'm the firstborn, and I almost believed him."

His eyebrows scrunched up, his fingers massaging his forehead. "Abby said she wouldn't say anything unless we figured it out ourselves. She said it was too personal, not her secret to tell."

He snatched my hand, dragging me away from the crowd.

"Where are we going?" I couldn't see his eyes. Shadows covered his face as we trudged up the grassy hill. Then we hit the cobblestone, a lamppost spotlighting his cinched-up forehead. His gaze cut right through me, like he could see something beyond me, on the other side of me.

He squinted for practically all eternity. Then his eyes widened in an instant. "Maybe that's why he got kicked out. Why it's you and not him."

Black dots flashed before my eyes, the world swayed back and forth. My knees wobbled.

"No, it can't be true." I clutched his forearm as he wrapped it around my waist. Finally his blue eyes found me. The horizon stilled for a minute.

"What if it is true, what if James is really your half-brother?"

"No." Sparks of light and shadow swirled before my eyes, stinging every part of my body. Fire pulsated inside me until it morphed into a core of fury in my chest. I balled my fists up, but my uppercut drooped halfway there as my knees buckled beneath me.

Bryan caught me, steadied me, but I flinched against his strong arms, fury still burning inside.

Behind clenched teeth I managed to say, "He can't be right."

"I hate it, too." Those aqua eyes roamed my face. "But it's the only explanation that makes any sense. The Seer is always the firstborn, so maybe it's you and not James, and that's why Nexis kicked him out."

"No way, I just can't believe it." I shook my head so hard my hair whipped me in the face. "I can't be the Seer, it's all completely ridiculous. I'm done talking about it."

I clomped down the hard sidewalk, booking it toward my dorm. At least some part of me knew where to run.

"What if you are the Seer?" His soft voice grew louder the closer he got.

I whirled around on my heels and stared him down. "Honestly, I don't care who the Seer is. I just want my brother back." Something inside me snapped and I let loose, pounding my fists into his chest. They bounced right back off his solid muscle. So I flattened my palms, smacking him until my hands hurt. Like a little girl.

"I'm sorry, honey." His arms wrapped around me, tighter this time, pinning my arms to my sides. He stroked my hair, nudging me into his shoulder like my beating hadn't even hurt him.

"I don't know what to think any more. Every time I think things can't get worse, they do." I buried my face in his warm sweatshirt and let him lead me back to the dorm. What if he was right? There had to be a reason James left. Could this be it? "I'm sorry, I'm too old for tantrums. I don't know what I was thinking."

At the front door Bryan enveloped me in his rock-solid arms. "I shouldn't have pushed you like that. Whatever happens, we'll figure this out together. We still have two years before we know if you're the Seer. And I'm not going anywhere, okay?"

"Good." I wrapped my arms around him, too.

He bent down, his face inches from mine. He pressed his soft lips to my forehead. "Goodnight."

Somehow I walked into the dorm, away from him. My cell phone practically burned a hole in my pocket. I knew just who to call, no matter how late it was. They needed to hear this, even if I had to wake them up.

17

"Hello?" Dad's groggy voice croaked back at me through the phone. One peek at the clock told me I should've waited till tomorrow. My room was like a dungeon, dark and cold. But an angry inferno still burned me up inside. I couldn't let it go.

"Sorry to wake you, Dad," I said, my voice loud and snappy. Wait a sec, did he even know the truth? Maybe he didn't. I bit my tongue.

Shanda mumbled something at me and rolled over. I slipped on my flip-flops and padded out of the room, leaving her alone in the dungeon. Flapping down the stairwell to the empty dorm lobby, I inhaled a deep breath—willing calm to spread through me as I exhaled.

"Hey there, Monkey." He cleared his throat. His pet name for me hung in the air, like a sliver of hope I could almost reach out and grab. "Is everything okay, it's midnight there, right?"

"I don't know." Such a Dad question. The anger softened into a sadness that wobbled my voice—sadness for him, sadness for me. I couldn't be the one to tell him, not if he didn't already know. "I want to know what happened to James. Did he get kicked out of Nexis? Why would you guys still want me to join? I just don't understand."

"What do you mean, what happened to James? Calm down, sweetie, you're not making any sense." His baritone faded into the background. Random noise filtered through. Was that Mom's voice? Great, I'd woken them both.

A blonde head burst through the front door and I flinched. Monica flounced past me, trotting up the stairs.

"Lucy, you shouldn't have called so late." Mom's stern voice blared from the earpiece. "Why don't you worry about normal teenage things like boys and clothes instead of James? You should have a nice boyfriend by now, like that Stanton boy. What's wrong with him?"

"Mom, I want to know what happened to James, not talk about my boyfriend." I clapped my hand over my mouth. Too late.

I flicked my gaze to the second floor landing just in time to see Monica flee into the stairwell. Great, it'd probably be all over school by Monday.

"Your boyfriend?" Her screech buzzed into the phone so loud I whipped it away from my ear. "Who is he?"

"No one, Mom." She would hate the way I rolled my eyes now, but seriously, c'mon. "I don't have a boyfriend, just a guy friend or two. That's not even the point. I want to know about James."

"Lucy," she sighed into the phone. "We haven't heard anything new in ages. That can't be what this is about."

"It's not." I sucked in a breath, the words on the tip of my tongue. Not here, in the dorm lobby. I tiptoed into the kitchen, plopped on a counter stool, and sucked in a deep breath. If I could get through this, I could get through anything.

"Is James really my brother, or my half-brother?" The words tumbled out before I had a chance to check them. "Please, just tell me the truth. I deserve to know."

She breathed into the phone, but didn't say a word. A low gasp came through the speaker.

"How did you find out?" Her choked words were soft and breathy. "I'm sorry, honey. You weren't supposed to know until you turned eighteen."

"Mom!" I screamed into the phone, not caring if I woke up the whole house. "How could you keep this from me for so long, then send me here?"

"You were supposed to join Nexis and become a great leader." She hissed through the phone. "They would've helped you figure things out. You'd be set up for life."

"You mean like James? I don't want to be brainwashed, thank you." I tightened my fists to hold back the tide of anger surging throughout my body.

"Have you joined the Guardians or something?" Her words sounded like an accusation, like it would completely ruin her life. "You don't think they're brainwashing you, too? Don't be so naive."

"I haven't decided yet." A hint of gravel tinged my voice, as if I could snap any second. "Just give me one good reason to join Nexis. One that doesn't involve exploiting me."

"Because you can change the world." Her tone turned sugary real quick. "Nexis is all about bringing our society to new heights. Lifting the whole planet out of its petty wars and rampant capitalism. There could be a new reality—peace and prosperity for every person. Who doesn't want that?"

"At what price, Mom?" Her words cut into me like a razor blade. She believed every word. The truth shined straight through her words, like a faraway star twinkling in the darkest night. "You can't possibly be so deluded that you don't realize the cost. The resistance, the bloodshed involved—"

"Don't you speak that way to me." Her terse words were even, smooth and cold with an icy edge. "You are my daughter, and you'll do as I say."

"Excuse me? I am your daughter, but I won't do as you say." I dug my nails into my palm until my knuckles turned white. "You can't even tell me the truth. I don't even know who my brother is, or who his father was. Do you?"

The volume of that statement reverberated back to me. Who was I, really?

"Young lady, that's none of your business. I've heard enough of this nonsense." The sinister note in her voice sent a shiver down my neck. "If you won't do what I want then I will come there and make you."

"What?" I slapped my hand on the kitchen granite. "How exactly can you make me join Nexis?

"There are ways, Lucy girl. You won't like them very much. Don't make me fly out there." So cold. She didn't sound like my mom at all.

All the energy drained from my body and so did the fight. I slid down from the stool, my eyes welling up.

"Whatever, it won't change my mind." I huffed into the phone.

"Then I think this conversation is over." Her venom got cut off by dead air.

Did she seriously just hang up on me? Wow, I thought I had issues. She couldn't be more clueless. All along I'd assumed Dad really wanted me to join Nexis, but it was Mom the whole time. Was it her idea to send me to Montrose?

Lucy in the Sky with Diamonds ... buzzed in my ear. Not this again. Mom better not be calling to apologize for hanging up on me. I hopped down from my stool, stomping down the checkerboard tile to the fridge. With a bang I thrust open the door and yanked out a Dr. Pepper can.

"Okay, what's the deal?"

"Lucy?" Bryan's voice came through the phone, not Mom's. "Everything all right?"

"Sorry, I just had a fight with my Mom." I blew all the pent up rage from my lungs, taking a swig from my soda can. "She's still gung ho about me joining Nexis. She even said she'd fly out here and make me join. Yeah right. Then she totally hung up on me."

"Ouch, that sounds rough." Silence on the other end.

I angled the phone away my face, but the call hadn't ended. If he was waiting for me to cough up the truth about James, that'd be on the other side of never-gonna-happen. No way I was ready to admit the truth to anyone, not even him. Not yet.

"Maybe I can cheer you up." It came out like a question, like he wasn't sure.

"Doubt it, unless it's really good." I paced across the kitchen, a vain attempt to work out my frustration. Maybe if he was here, that'd cheer me up. Then again, maybe not.

"Felicia's first exhibit opens tomorrow at a gallery in the city. You think you're up for that?" His voice cracked at the end of his spiel. How cute, he sounded just as anxious as I felt.

"Why not? I could use a distraction right about now. I'll be there."

Air whistled into the phone. "Great, we'll leave Friday after dinner. I'll meet you in your lobby, around seven?"

"Sounds perfect, see you then." He could probably hear the smile on the other end, but who cared. Another chance to see Bryan. Wouldn't exactly call this one a date, right? More like a desperate attempt to cheer up the girl who just found out her brother wasn't her brother. At least he gave me something to look forward to, something that calmed me down to just a simmer.

White dust puffed up like smoke in the dark sky, shrouding the street in gray mist. It felt like I'd landed on an alien planet, where the truth I'd always taken for granted turned into lies. I didn't really belong in this city, or home, or anywhere. Suddenly the path I'd planned for my future, for Yale, seemed hidden in shadows. The gray mist fogged up everything in sight, my way more uncertain than ever.

"C'mon, Lucy." Bryan guided me out of the bakery haze, like my own personal seeing-eye dog, away from the 23rd Street subway station. The crowd of faces blurred into an amalgam as I passed, until they didn't even look like faces any more. I needed someone else to see things for me right now, because somehow I missed it.

How could I be so blind to my family, my own mother? Her despicable lies, pushing me toward Nexis the whole time—even after she'd sacrificed her own son on its altar. A shudder racked my shoulders and I bumped someone's elbow.

On the sidewalks of Chelsea the blur finally lifted, faces blaring into full focus. A guy yelled at me to buy a pretty watch, another thrust his bootlegged movies at me, some guitarist crooned in front of an open case. But nothing touched me. Somehow I felt more alone than ever, cut off from my family, my lifeline. It was frayed and broken in so many pieces I'd never be able to put it back together again. Not the way it was before.

Around the corner a line of people clogged up the sidewalk. Bryan squeezed my hand. "We made it."

That small gesture, the tiny glimmer of hope on his face fizzled up my arm. I squeezed back.

"I can't see anything." I arched on tiptoes, still barely taller than his eye level.

"Here we go, the Montgomery Gallery of Fine Art." He put two hands on my waist and lifted me up onto a bench like I weighed five pounds. A swarm of butterflies buzzed in my stomach.

The wind picked up and I rushed to smooth down my black tulle skirt. Good thing I wore leggings and boots tonight.

A pewter cursive sign was backlit like a work of art. I dug my camera out of my purse and snapped a photo. That's when I spotted two tufts of red in the sea of black-clad New Yorkers. "I guess Laura and Lenny beat us here."

"Let's go stand by them." He slid his arm around my torso and helped me down. His broad shoulders squared a path through the line until we caught up with the red-heads.

"This is so cool." Laura squealed as we approached. "I'm part of some actual New York nightlife."

"Too bad you're too short to see any of it." Lenny's deep laugh rumbled from his chest. "Not that there's much to see."

She fluffed her loose curls. "I'm not too short to see our friends coming this way."

Tony sauntered up to us in his signature black leather jacket. "You guys are easy to pick out of a crowd."

"And you blend right in." I curled my lips at him, as if there was some life left in me yet.

He just smiled back and tugged on his leather lapels. A blonde head peeked over his shoulder.

"Here's your ribbons back." Brooke held out the blue and gold satin, reeking of wood smoke.

Memories of that horrible bonfire gushed back. Will spewing out the wretched truth that clogged my lungs, made it hard to breathe. It was too much right now.

I pushed his words back and pushed her hands away, swallowing down the bile burning my throat. "You keep them. You might need them again."

"Thanks." Her face lit up like I'd done her a huge favor. Quite the opposite, really. She tucked the ribbons in her purse, out of sight, out of mind. The bonfire images faded into the crisp night air. I inhaled a fresh breath.

Then the doors opened and the crowd herded us into a white-walled room with black floors.

Bryan rested his hand on the small of my back, sweet but not possessive. Butterflies zigzagged up my spine as he led me around the gallery.

We shuffled around the front area of landscapes on one side and photography on the other. Bryan, Tony, and Lenny lingered over the landscapes. Brooke and Laura oohed and ahhed over the trick photography.

Then we hit the impressionist alcove. Each painting was a masterpiece of sheer beauty full of light and color that chinked open the dark corners of my blurry gray world. To me, they spoke volumes. Maybe there was still something in this world I could cling to—life, beauty, love. It was all still there, whether I could see it or not.

"C'mon. Since we're the only ones here not related, you'll just have to pretend I'm your big bro." Tony practically yanked me into the next room, where a fire-engine red wall showcased modern art. Chaos on canvas.

"You're like five months older than me." Still, my heart clenched at his words, wanting so badly to cling to the straw of hope he offered. I shoved his leather shoulder. "Ick, get me out of here, I don't get any of this stuff. That one over there has some cool paint splatters, but c'mon. I could totally do that in art class."

"With paint filled balloons. Wouldn't that be fun? Especially if we could throw darts at Will's face." Laura's giggle echoed around the tiled room.

"Nice one." The urge to laugh bubbled up inside, but it wouldn't break free. Like I hadn't fully vanquished the numbness yet. "Didn't know you had it in you."

Bryan cleared his throat. "Sorry to break up the Will-haters club, but it's time for Felicia's show upstairs."

I followed him up the open staircase, more like a slip-and-slide for my boots. Just my luck, I'd trip and fall on my face.

"You're such a klutz." Lenny offered his hand and helped his sister up.

"You try being a girl in heels." Laura gripped her flowy peasant skirt. "It's harder than you think."

"I'll take your word on that." Bryan grabbed my elbow, but his rough fingers only sent my inner butterflies into a frenzy, making my legs wobble.

At the top we stood at the back of a crowd huddled around a white curtained entrance. A woman in a silver dress tapped the microphone and the murmurs silenced.

"Ladies and gentlemen, I'm honored to have you here for our young artist showcase. Our featured artists are all in high school and were chosen based on their originality and diversity in their subject matter. Montgomery Gallery is proud to showcase these pieces of ingenuity and imagination. Each has a story to tell, so take the time to appreciate each one." She pulled the curtain's tassel and it dropped to the floor.

"Found the food." Lenny rushed to a table covered with trays of hors d'oeuvres. He managed to balance a tower of food on one tiny plate. "What?"

"Score." Tony rushed to fill his plate, too.

Laura rolled her eyes at them and followed me and Bryan around the room.

"There's Felicia." Bryan pointed to a flash of auburn surrounded by reporters with notepads. They snapped picture after picture, like strobe lights in a nightclub.

I halted in front of a collection of black and white night snapshots. Blurry neon and twinkling stars, like she might've caught a glimpse of some of the weird things I'd seen since coming to Montrose. Yet there was a simple beauty in all the chaos, the way the light streaks blended into something glorious.

"Felicia's work is fabulous." Then I moved to her mixed media section, compositions of photo backgrounds with a poem or quote, dried flowers, and fabric overlays. A description of the materials hung on small plaques next to each work. In a word, gorgeous.

But the real beauties were two enormous oil paintings. One painted entirely in pastel colors with a pair of shadowy, semi-translucent figures in the center entitled, "A Walk with the Father." The second was flanked in bold hues of red and orange surrounding a blue and black center, simply called, "Ramifications."

"Must be some kind of pain or suffering." Brooke cocked her head at the bold painting.

I stared at the pair of paintings, gnawing on my bottom lip. "You think? Maybe that *Ramifications* one could be, I guess."

"Hey, Felicia," Tony shouted across the gallery.

Bryan jerked back as a streak of green flashed toward us. His eyes rested on the auburn beauty in front of us.

"Hi, guys. Glad you're here." Her emerald dress matched her kitten eyes that stared right back at him. Her smile sagged as she smoothed down her hair. "Hectic night."

Bryan wrapped one arm around her in a side-hug. "Your work looks great."

Her eyes lit up at his touch, at his compliment. Somewhere deep inside, an old ember burned.

"I really couldn't have asked for more. My pieces are professionally lit and displayed. The gallery even promoted this event well. I've talked to a ton of reporters. Not the Times or anything, just small markets. Still, it's been a blast."

"Way to go, Felicia." Lenny cheered, pumping his fist over the crowd. "These are awesome."

"Calm down." With her tiny hands Laura wrestled his arm down. "No need to cause a ruckus."

"You're no fun. Everyone likes a good ruckus now and then." Lenny winked at me as if my traitor thoughts were written all over my face. He slung his arm over Felicia's shoulder. "How about a teeny hubabaloo?"

Laura rolled her eyes then burst out laughing. "Do you mean," she said between giggles, "you mean, hullabaloo?"

Lenny held his head high. "No, I mean hubabaloo. It's my new word, like hubba-hubba, with the added bonus of a ruckus."

"So you think my art is attractive?" Felicia narrowed her eyes at him.

"You bet. I'd say they're quite something." Lenny wriggled his way out from under her glare. I gulped back a laugh. "Especially those paintings."

"Thank you, everyone." Her face bloomed as red as her hair. "It's an exciting night for me."

"We wouldn't have missed it." Bryan rested his arm on her shoulder. She pressed her cheek against his hand, closing her eyes.

The ember inside me sizzled.

He patted her head, then slid his hand back. "What're friends for?"

She flinched, turning a catty glare on me. "I better get going, my dad wants to do a celebration dinner. Thanks for coming guys, I'll see you at school."

Felicia waved goodbye and headed for the stairs, toward a man in black-framed glasses with salt-and-pepper temples. A strange silver necklace gleamed from his neck—a pyramid pendant with an oval in the middle.

My next breath beat against the bars of my ribcage. An image flashed in my mind, of him dressed in all black.

Felicia kissed his cheek. How did she know him? He wrapped his arm around her shoulder, smiling down at her almost like a father would.

I backed up, right into the wall. My fingertips bumped against a tiny symbol on the corner of Felicia's painting, *Ramifications*. A swirling eye inside a triangle, dashes radiating from the outer corners.

The same symbol he wore.

Red and orange brush strokes blurred into oblivion, until the colors burned like flames on my fingertips. A shriek almost ripped from my throat but some strange Latin words, the name for that symbol, screamed back at me. *Signum Videns*. Lack of oxygen blurred the gallery into splotches. Slowly I sucked in a full breath.

The revelation finally eeked from my lips. "It's the mark of the Seer."

18

"What about the Seer?" Like a knock on the door of my sanity, a gruff voice pulled me out of the fire, back into the real world. This time it was Tony's pale face and dark brown eyes I stared into. He shook my shoulders, but his words barely registered. "Talk to me, Lucy."

"I thought I saw ..." My finger traced the outline of the symbol on the painting, then swiveled to the stairs, his escape. "With Felicia."

He examined the painting. "Felicia? Of course she's not the Seer."

I honked out an ungraceful snort. "No not her, the guy with her. He had on a necklace, with a strange symbol."

"You mean this one?" When I nodded, his forehead scrunched up like he didn't believe me. Then his eyes widened and he scratched his chin. "You know, now that you mention it, he did seem kind of familiar. Show me."

"What, are you from Missouri or something?" For the first time he looked at me like I was crazy. "It's the Show Me state. Nevermind, c'mon."

Without a glance back at Bryan, or anyone else, I clutched Tony's arm and dragged him down the stairs to the front door. We raced down the sidewalk, mauling through the crowd, until we hit the subway station.

"There." I spotted a flash of green dress, aiming his head in their direction.

She brushed back her auburn hair and he pecked her cheek. A streetlight caught the silver, reflecting it back to us. It was only a profile shot, the necklace barely visible. Then they disappeared into the shadows.

Tony stopped two feet from the entrance, mouth dangling. "Okay, that was a weird symbol, but I think I've seen it before. What was he doing with Felicia? He's old enough to be her father."

I thumped his shoulder. "Brilliant, Watson. My thoughts exactly."

He shook his head back and forth, like a sad bobble-head staring down the gaping hole of the subway steps. "What's so important about it? Why can't I remember where I've seen it before?"

His questions huffed white clouds into the air. They thinned out, dissipating into the inky black sky. My insides squeezed into tiny knots, as the street noise filtered in and out, blurring into a dull roar. I didn't have any answers. I just threw up my hands.

"I don't know."

Footsteps pounded the pavement behind us, high pitches and low tones flitted above the din.

Brooke reached us first, gasping for breath. "What was that? You guys just took off."

"Like the place was on fire or something," Lenny chimed in, the only half-smiling face in the bunch.

Bryan reached for my hand, but it felt limp in his grip. "Are you okay, what happened?"

"I, uh ..." I whipped my head toward Tony. His pale face stared back at me, contorted in an odd expression. "We had to see something for ourselves."

He zipped up his leather jacket, his tough guy persona roaring back in a flash. He inched his way in front of me, protective, almost like James. "Lucy saw something strange, said it had something to do with the Seer, so I had to see it for myself."

"Hush." I drew my finger to my lips. "Not here."

"But that doesn't explain anything." Brooke's lips furrowed into a frown. "Like why you went running out of the gallery."

I couldn't look at her, she wouldn't understand, none of them would. "I don't know if I can explain, it sounds impossible."

"But Tony saw it too, right? You have to tell us." She crossed her arms in front of her tiny frame as if she'd never budge in a million years.

I exhaled a breath at Tony and he nodded. We both stared at the subway entrance, hoping she'd pop up and explain herself.

"I saw Felicia with ..." The words, the truth, stuck to my tongue, unwilling to move.

This time Tony threw up his hands. "She saw Felicia leave with a strange guy, probably her dad. He had on a really weird necklace. Some kind of ancient symbol totally different from any Guardian or Nexis symbol."

Slowly, each of their faces fell like dominoes, one by one.

Bryan dropped my hand. It thudded to my side. "What are you say, she's a traitor? That can't be true, no way. She's been my best friend since middle school. It just can't be true."

"No one's saying that." Tony put a hand on his shoulder, staring him straight in the eye. "It's just shady. She saw the symbol, I saw it, too. It's true."

"Fine, you both saw some symbol." Bryan shrugged Tony's hand off, edging away from me with a face full of too many emotions to name. "Maybe it doesn't mean what you think it does, maybe it's a mistake. We'll have to investigate."

With a nod, he punctuated the end of his sentence like it was some kind of final word. And it burned away the knots inside me. As if he knew everything, as if he didn't trust me, after all we'd been through.

"Great, investigate all you want. I'd start at the gallery. The symbol is right there on her painting. Figure it out for yourself." The burning inside washed away as a flood of unshed tears beat against my eyes like river rocks ready to overflow. I couldn't stand him any more, that sick expression all over his face. I huffed and whirled down the steps in front of me.

Tony clutched my bicep, halting me on the second step. "Lucy's right, not here. We have to get out of here, find someplace secluded. We'll hold a special meeting, without Felicia, okay?"

"Fine, but where, and when?" Bryan's eyes exploded like fireballs aimed at Tony, even me.

"The chapel, at midnight. I'm going to find out what that symbol means. We'll have to sneak out after curfew, but I'm going with or without you." I didn't wait for a reply. I snapped my head around and marched down the stairs.

Darkness covered my dorm room, but I couldn't sleep. Shanda's breathing rose and fell in a hushed rhythm. I stared at the ceiling, transfixed by the glowing stars above my head, drawing my own constellations. The questions whirred among the plastic stars like a celestial carnival ride, counting down until midnight. Like why all of a sudden Bryan didn't believe me, and why he stood up for Felicia. As if I'd made up something horrible about her. It just didn't add up.

Gingerly I rolled over, the green numbers of my alarm clock glaring 11:45. I tapped my fingers on the comforter. I couldn't wait any more. Slipping out from under the covers, I padded across the white fuzzy rug to my closet and shimmied into the first pair of flats I found. Then I lifted my Montrose hoodie from its hook and slid Harlixton's keys from their hiding place into the front pocket. Slowly, I closed the door until it clicked.

This late at night the hallway was dark, with creepy shadows. I shivered and zipped up my hoodie.

In front of me, Brooke's dark blonde head poked out her door. Her lips curled up. "Nice PJs, purple stripes go great with silver flats."

"I don't have anyone to impress." I twirled away from her, if only to choke back a bitter laugh. "That's me, on the cutting edge of fashion."

Laura tiptoed up to us in dark jeans and a black hoodie, almost identical to Brooke's outfit. "Looks like some of us aren't used to covert operations."

"Well I'm glad you came, too." I snorted out a giggle, quickly smothering my hand over my mouth. Laura tsked her tongue at me, like she was actually serious. "Oh, c'mon. What are they going to do to us, throw us in detention?"

She tucked her red hair under her black hood and tugged on the tassels. "I'm not talking about detention."

"All right, I get it." I shrugged my navy hood over my head. "Okay, I'm serious now."

Brooke nodded with wide eyes, pulling her hoodie up, too. "Now you look like the Unabomber in funny pants."

153

"Better than Little Black Riding Hood over here." I elbowed Laura as her eyes sparked at me, but her lips curved slightly. "Okay, Miss Director of Clandestine Affairs, lead the way."

"That's more like it." Silently, she motioned us down the back stairs and into the kitchen. She made a beeline for the sink, opening one of the windows. "Hurry up, before someone comes down for a midnight snack."

I hopped up onto the counter, swung my legs out the window, and shimmied down the siding until my flats found the dewy grass. Brooke thumped her knee against the windowsill, so I unhooked her leg and eased her down.

Laura's tiny feet made no sound on the grass as she jumped down, pointing at Brooke. "You're the tallest, shut the window slowly so you don't wake Miss Sherry."

Brooke silently obeyed, then glided with us across the empty lawn. Dew soaked into my flats, squishing between my toes. Maybe Laura was right about my crazy outfit. As the night chill whipped around us, we huddled together. A warmth seeped into my heart as we skirted buildings, slinking through the shadows until we reached the back side of the chapel. After my outburst, the fact that they still went along with my nutty idea meant only one thing. Somehow I'd made friends at this school. Real friends.

"I've always wanted to try this. There's a secret entrance back here. It looks like it's been bricked over, but it's not." Laura tapped on the red bricks until her knuckles found a hollow one. When she twisted it to the left, the brick whooshed aside to reveal an ancient, almost decrepit, door.

"How're we supposed to get in?" Brooke peeked around my shoulder, as if the old door would jump out and bite her.

"With these." I stuffed my hand into my hoodie pocket, hoisting the keys into the air.

Moonlight washed over the shiny metal key, slanting strange lines on the wrought-iron skeleton key. Laura nodded at me as if she approved, while Brooke's jaw dropped.

Footsteps crunched behind me, heavy by the sound of them. About time the boys showed up. Bryan led the black-clad trio, his eyes on the keys dangling from my hand.

"Where'd you get those?" Rough fingers clawed my forehead.

I wrenched my arm away from him. "Guess someone doesn't know everything."

Nostrils flared as his breath steamed up the chilly air. "Just open the door already."

"Fine." I whipped my head around so hard my hood drooped back. My hands shook as I cleared dirt away from the rusted lock. With a sharp motion I thrust the giant skeleton key in and pushed on the weathered wood.

Flashlight in hand he edged past me, his wet sneakers squeaking across the tiled hallway. He twisted the library doorknob. "It's locked."

"Oh ye of little faith." I jingled the keys in his ear, squeezing in next to him. "Got it covered."

A puff of hot air warmed my neck as I unlocked the door for everyone. The other four trickled inside, but Bryan just stood there beside me. When I turned to him, his eyes trailed their way down to my pants, then my feet, taking awhile to get there.

I glared at him, wrinkling my eyebrows as if I could ever figure this guy out. Let him mock my crazy outfit all he wanted. With a flourish I flipped my hair out from under my hood and flounced into the room.

"Stop being such a baby." Brooke's jaw jutted out at her brother. "We came here to figure this out fairly. Let's get it over with so I can go back to sleep."

"Fine, I'll listen and try to keep an open mind."

"Thank you, that's all I'm asking." She rolled her eyes at him, turning to me. "Who wants to go first?"

I chewed my lip and glanced at Tony, his dark hair highlighted by the moonlight from the window. "I don't really know where to start, I guess at the gallery. I saw this strange symbol around Felicia's dad's neck, then on her painting. Suddenly the name for it popped into my head, the mark of the Seer—"

"Why didn't you tell me?" He drew in a sharp breath, the hollowness in his voice hitting me in the stomach.

"Are you even listening?" I could practically feel his stare, but I just looked straight ahead. "Tony was right there and the guy had just left. You weren't close enough."

155

He puffed out his chest. Silence hung heavy in the room. Nobody asked me to elaborate and I wouldn't volunteer any more details, no way.

"It still doesn't prove anything."

On my heel I pivoted toward him, a hard line chiseled into his jawbone.

It burned my eyes into slits. "Do you want to go back to that gallery and see for yourself?"

"Maybe I will." He stared me down, as if he could get me to surrender.

"Be my guest." I pursed my lips at him. "But you won't catch me stepping one measly toe in that building ever again."

"Enough, we're getting off track." Tony sliced his hand into the space between us. "My turn. All I remember was how Lucy almost fainted, like she'd seen a ghost or something. I went over to help her up. She pointed to a weird symbol on one of the paintings, Felicia's paintings, and mumbled something about the Seer and Felicia. I told her to show me."

"That's when you raced out of the gallery." Brooke adjusted her glasses like giant microscopes as she studied my face, then Tony's.

"That's right." He leveled his gaze at her. "We followed them down the street. At the subway entrance I saw his profile. He definitely had the symbol around his neck, the same one on the painting." He crossed his arms in front of his chest, angled at Bryan like some kind of guy challenge.

"So you're saying Felicia's dad is part of the Watchers, Felicia, too? That she's some kind of double agent?" He squared off in Tony's direction.

"That's it, that's where that symbol is from." He dropped his arms and smacked his forehead. "I don't know how deep they're in, I'm just telling you what I saw. What we saw. Do you really think we can trust her?"

"Of course I do, she's a member of the Guardians. A full member." Bryan turned back my direction for a nanosecond. Long enough it burned me.

"And yet, she put some kind of Watcher symbol on her painting, whatever that means. Strange, don't you think?" I stepped in, matching his pointed stare.

He backed up. "It's still not enough proof to convict her."

"What are you talking about?" I pounced forward, caught in some kind of cage match. "I'm not asking you to convict her, or whatever you "full members" do. I'm just asking you to believe me. I've never even heard of the Watchers, or anything else you've been keeping from me. Why would I lie?"

"Lucy, I'm not saying you're lying." His hand eased out, caressing my elbow. "I just think you might've seen things wrong, misunderstood something. There's got to be some other explanation."

"All I wanted was a little trust, but I guess I'm asking too much." I jerked my arm back. Pressure pounded up my eye sockets, threatening to spill over. I bit into my lip, hard. As a tear slid down my cheek, I ran across the room, into the darkness of the turret.

"Don't be like that. C'mon, Lucy." His words faded into the shadows, but his footsteps clomped closer. In seconds he stood over me in utter darkness, no flashlight in hand. Moonlight from the portholes slid along the outlines of his features, outlining his forehead, eyelashes, the tip of his nose. Gritty fingers brushed my cheek. "I'm sorry, I really am. I want to believe in both of you."

With his breath on my forehead, his hand on my cheek, I could barely breathe let alone think. "I get that, but I know what I saw. There has to be some kind of explanation."

His mouth curved up as he came closer. "We'll find it, together."

I nodded up at him and he pulled me in, wrapping his arms around me so tight. I hugged him back, not ready to face the others just yet.

He pulled back an inch. "Hold up, you said the symbol was the mark of the Seer, right?"

Again I nodded, craning my neck up at him. "You think we could find it in one of these books?"

His lips spread, white teeth gleaming down at me. "It's scary how you read my mind sometimes."

A thousand tingles fluttered up and down my arms. If he was right and I said another word, somehow I knew he'd kiss me. And I couldn't take that right now. Even one kiss could completely unhinge the tenuous peace we'd just brokered.

As if he'd turned the tables on me, he put some distance between us. "Bring the flashlight over here."

A circle of light bounced around the turret, onto Tony's face. "I've got the girls searching the card catalog for books on symbols."

"Guess everyone can read my mind." Suddenly the space between us grew cold. "Lucy found some great books in here last week, maybe we'll get lucky."

All my questions about this new group he mentioned, the Watchers, would have to wait. But I wouldn't forget, they were burned into my brain.

The boys each took a section, pulling out books, scanning the indexes. I ended up in the back section without a light, so I dug out my cell phone and scanned titles. They were hard to make out in the bluish glow, but something else caught my eye. The shelf's boards were lined with carvings, intricate shapes in the wood.

And there it was.

The strange swirling eye inside a triangle, dashes radiating from the outer corners. My fingers bumped across the indentations and I dug out a clump of dust. As soon as I pressed into the triangle, a metal clanking sound clicked into motion like giant gears turning.

The shelf shot back a few feet, then shifted behind the section beside it. A gaping hole opened up in the wall.

"What was that?" Bryan aimed the flashlight at me. Its light spilled down a wrought-iron set of stairs curling into the abyss. "What'd you do?"

"You said to find the symbol." I pointed to the shelf carvings. "I pressed it and poof, there you go."

"Cool." Lenny peeked his head into the opening. "A secret passage."

"Way to go." Tony held up his hand and I high-fived it.

"Let's check it out." I gnawed on my bottom lip, shifting toward Bryan.

His mouth curled up again, and this time I wanted to smooth my fingers against his lips. But now wasn't the time.

"Hey girls, we found a secret passage. Anyone ready for an adventure?"

About time he listened to me for once.

19

A gaping black hole stared back at me. Secrets lay buried down there, I just knew it. The way you know it's about to rain, or where to look for the moon. I grabbed the flashlight from Bryan and tiptoed down the creaking steps, swiping at cobwebs the whole time. Ten or twelve feet later my shoes hit some kind of crumbling stone floor, about as far down as a basement.

The circle of the flashlight illuminated a picture of truth right in front of me. As the others clambered down the spiral staircase, I stood perfectly still, palm flattened against my chest. Carvings etched into the ancient stone depicted intricate scenes. On a square tile the flashlight beam highlighted a group of men chiseled into the stone, one head and shoulders taller than the rest.

"It's a Nephil," Lenny breathed in my ear. "They're the whole reason we exist."

I wanted to ask him to explain why the Guardians had to exist, but I didn't. I already knew the answer. One group wanted to bring these strange creatures back, the other wanted to stop them. Plain and simple, yet centuries had passed without changing the problem.

"I heard the Watchers built secret tunnels and passages, but I never imagined in a million years it could be here, at Montrose. It was all just legend." Bryan eased the flashlight from my grip. He shone it around the circular stone vestibule, lighting up an archway that opened into a long corridor—leading straight into darkness.

"You did not hear about this." Brooke shoved his shoulder and the beam faltered. "How is it you always know everything?"

He aimed the spotlight at her. "I don't know everything. Harlixton gave me a book that mentioned a legend of secret tunnels, that's all."

"So you didn't "hear" it." Her fingers bent and lifted in air quotes. "You actually read about it."

"Now who knows everything?" He turned back toward me and exhaled a sharp breath.

Dust blew off the wall, revealing another carving next to mine, at the entrance of the tunnel. With shaking fingers, I brushed the remaining dirt away. "You've got to see this. Do you think the whole tunnel is lined with them?"

A picture formed as the dust cleared. Noah's ark. I tried not to think about the strange words from my even stranger vision in the chapel library just last week. But sure enough, they came blaring back through my mind. *Genesis six domination.* The Nexis motto.

"There's only one way to find out." He flashed the light down the tunnel.

I couldn't see anything but blackness.

"I got this." Tony whipped out his pocket knife. In a few minutes he rigged the flashlight to dangle from pieces of fishing line, the knife anchored into the ceiling.

"Impressive." I bumped his fist, careful not to add the extras I shared only with James. Wherever he was, I had a feeling he'd be happy knowing someone else had my back.

The group fanned out down the arched tunnel, cell phones in hand, fingers digging out dirt. I started with the pictograph closest to the light. As I sifted away the dirt with my fingers, a startling scene stared back at me. A bearded man, arm outstretched, knife held high over a child on a pile of branches.

My heart skipped a beat or two, then pounded wildly against my chest. "So it's all true. Even Abraham was a Seer." There was no question in my mind any more. This was real, which must mean I really was the Seer. Why it was all happening now? I needed more answers.

"Cool, let me see." The rigged up light illuminated Lenny's orange hair, casting strange colors on the stone picture. As if the branch altar were alive with fire.

"Come see mine, I've got Jacob's ladder." Laura's voice echoed off the stones.

Five heads jostled each other to get a peek of the two foot square carving. On tiptoes I craned my neck around until I could see the whole picture. A robed man, wrestling with lines in the shape of a wing, on a ladder.

Somehow, an electric current zapped the musty, dank air. How did I, or my family, fit into such lauded history? It all seemed unreal.

I couldn't take my eyes off the scene. Jacob's vision of heaven was famous, so he was obviously the Seer. The puzzle almost snapped into place, but something was missing. "Wasn't he the younger son?"

"In those days, the father could choose who to give his blessing to. That's what happened with Jacob, because Esau turned down his birthright." Bryan's eyes locked on me, like a heat-seeking missile.

"As if seeing is a blessing." The words trickled from my mouth, barely a whisper.

"What'd you say?" In the dark, his hands landed on my shoulders, turning me toward him.

I didn't know how to answer him, my mouth just hung open. If I really was the Seer, which was still a long-shot, could I turn down the "gift?" But then it would just go to Paige and she'd have to deal with all of this. And I couldn't do that to her, not even hypothetically.

"Guys, you gotta come see this. Bring the flashlight." Tony's voice rang out from deep in the dark tunnel. Saved by the baritone.

Lenny doubled back around us to unhook the flashlight, traipsing through the blackness ahead.

I lingered, unwilling to go into the unknown, not yet. With my fingernails, I dug out dirt from all corners of the stone tile. In the lower right-hand corner, I uncovered a symbol. The same one I'd seen on Felicia's paintings.

"C'mon, they're leaving us behind." Bryan tugged on my hand, but I wouldn't budge. "Hey, is this the symbol? I've seen it before, somewhere."

161

Black shadows engulfed his body as if he'd disappeared into the darkness. When I flashed my phone at him, he was running his fingers along his chin scruff.

"What is it?"

His eyes ping-ponged from the symbol, back to me. "It's the Seer's symbol, alright, a Watchers' symbol."

"So wait, there's a Seer's symbol and something called a Watcher and you knew about it all along?"

He raked his fingers into his two inches of hair. "There was an old legend in one of the books Harlixton gave me. The Watchers built 'sanctuaries' near important Nexis or Guardian places so they could keep an eye out, police things if necessary."

"Great, another weird group." The light from my phone dimmed, submerging his face in shadow. "Who are the Watchers? What do they do, besides watch?"

His choppy laugh fragmented off the stones. "They're the ones who think Nexis will bring about the end of the world. They hate how the Guardians handle things, so they formed their own group."

All light from my phone faded and blackness surrounded us with its silence. His calloused palm encircled mine.

"Don't be mad." His words floated around in the darkness, like an apparition. "I seriously just remembered this. One of the Watchers' goals is to mark the Seer, so both Nexis *and* the Guardians know who it is."

"What does that mean?" I tried to drop his hand, but he clamped down tighter. "For a Guardian guru, you sure forget a lot."

"I don't know, it was all just legend. Until now. I never thought it would play out in real life." Suddenly a square light cut into the darkness, his phone aimed at my face.

A patch of light in the shadows was all I saw. I held up my phone to see his face, too. "If Felicia's dad is a Watcher, allegedly, then they probably know everything the Guardians are up to. At least here at Montrose."

"They don't know the whole truth. Montrose is just a small piece of the pie. There's Guardian outposts all over the world." The way he said that, his eyes wide, stole my breath away.

"The whole world?"

I heard his head rustle before I saw him nod. "You're right, I need to research the old legends. See if I can find any parallels to what's happening right here and now."

A sudden chill crept up my spine. I gripped his hand. "This is way more than I ever bargained for."

He squeezed back. "You're telling me. That's life, honey." With a soft tug, he led me deeper into the tunnel.

As I followed him into the shadows, the truth pierced me like an arrow between the eyes—he'd really given up a lot for the Guardians. A normal life, a normal school, maybe a girlfriend or two. I wasn't sure I was willing to give up that much. Not yet, anyway.

Dark heads huddled around the flashlight. Just another weird carving, in a really bizarre underground tunnel. Goosebumps prickled up and down my arms, as if they knew more than me. Then I saw it.

A young girl with a halo around her head. Hollow eyes, a vacant expression, arms outstretched with a tray in front of her. The loudest gasp ever ripped from my mouth, stole my breath away. Five heads turned my way.

I gulped in lungfuls of musty air. "Are you kidding me? This is the girl from the Nexis book. Was she a Seer, or something? This is getting too weird."

With their faces engulfed in shadows, each pair of eyes captured the light, illuminating the truth even in the dark silence. To them, this wasn't brand new information, they already knew. More than that, I glimpsed the faintest hint of surprise when Brooke glanced at her brother.

"That's St. Lucia. You really haven't told her anything, have you?" Her full lips jutted out, almost in anger. Those normally soft eyes narrowed into slits as she stared him down. Maybe I should've been taking notes from this girl all along. "Well, you're just going to have to tell her everything now."

"I know." In slow motion he wagged his head up, then down, as if he didn't want to admit the truth. "I guess I just wanted to protect her from all of this."

"Hey, I'm right here." I elbowed his ribs. "Just tell me the truth."

"Okay, I can do that." He hung his head, barely looking at me. "I'm sorry, I assumed we had more time, that Nexis would leave you alone until senior year at least. Boy, was I wrong."

"Dead wrong." Tony's whisper sputtered like gravel into the thick air. "Now not only Nexis is involved, but the Watchers, too."

"Wait," I blinked at their shadowed faces, "you're saying her name is St. Lucia?"

He nodded. "Was."

"And you couldn't tell me any of this before?" Fire flared through me, from my fists down to my feet until I couldn't take it any more. I hurtled myself down the tunnel, away from those lit-up stares. Jagged rock bumped against my fingertips, unyielding as the tracks of sewn-together flesh hiding deep beneath my hairline. The stone scratched into my skin. All of a sudden I stopped, as my nails traced unknown ruts in the rock. Were there carvings on both sides of the tunnel?

A vague whisper hissed in my ear, forming a faint word. *Look*.

A chill crawled up my skin, steeling my stubborn resolve. I planted my shoes against the dusty stone floor and forced my gaze in the opposite direction of the others following. Whatever lurked behind me in the darkness couldn't stay hidden for long.

Pounding footsteps echoed off the arched stone. Tony shined his light on my face, then his chin dropped to his Adam's apple. "Whoa, this has to be a Watchers' tunnel for sure. Check this out."

More clomps resounded behind him, until everyone crowded around me. Slowly I turned on my heel. A strange pile of carved rock-like shapes reached high into the sky, with figures trying to climb the makeshift tower.

"Is that what I think it is?" Heads bobbed up and down in the spotlight. I narrowed my eyes at the stone tile, but I couldn't make sense of it. "I don't get it. What does the Tower of Babel have to do with anything?"

Bryan cleared his throat. "It's where Nexis started. When they couldn't reach heaven on their own, they worked up a new plan to make their own heaven on earth."

"More like dominating earth, actually." Lenny's deep voice rumbled on my right.

Genesis six domination, the words were back again, this time they almost left my tongue. Tingles crawled up and down my neck. "That's just crazy. They've really been at this for tens of thousands of years?"

"Afraid so." His giant paw landed on my shoulder.

I gulped, bit my lip, willing myself to ask the question I didn't want to ask. "And that's why they want the Seer so bad, to finally get what they want?"

He stared down at me. "That's it exactly."

Strange fascination gurgled in my throat, a bubble of curiosity I couldn't shove down. Maybe this was the time. My time to be brave, and find out the truth. I swallowed down the lump of fear before it could shoot up again. "Have they ever had the Seer on their side before?"

"No, never. Not that they haven't tried. They've managed to get themselves in other positions of power and killed several Seers for not joining them. Even people they thought were Seers, like Joan of Arc."

"Joan of Arc, really?" This time a softer grit of sandpaper grasped my hand. Bryan.

"Her and many more, though she wasn't actually the Seer of her generation." The goosebumps popped up my arms again. He squeezed tighter. "I think it's time you found out the truth, before it finds you first."

I nodded at his shadowy face, but the dark and light shapes blurred until he was unrecognizable.

"C'mon." He tugged my hand, like he'd done so many times before.

This time a strange cold seeped into my skin. Even his soft voice, his warm touch, couldn't melt my heart. If I was the Seer or even if they thought I was, would I meet the same fate as Joan of Arc did—a trial by fire? Or would it just happen to someone I love instead? The cold enveloped me, sapping away all my steeled-up resolve.

Numbly my feet trudged forward, deeper into the tunnel. The musty air lost its edge, smelled fresher even, calling me to be still. And I knew what I had to do.

I let go of Bryan's hand, stopping dead in my tracks in the middle of the tunnel. I clasped my hands together in silent surrender, as if God or my angel could really hear me. *Where are you? Without you, I'm completely lost.*

"Lucy, we're almost there." Bryan's hand brought warmth this time.

I whispered my thanks to the ceiling. Almost like God was telling me he'd heard, and given me friends to help me along the way.

We found ourselves in another circular vestibule with a spiral staircase, much like where we'd entered at the library. I was the last to climb the stairs. I stumbled across the uneven doorstop, landing on my knees in the dewy grass. Tony and Lenny pushed a stone panel back into place until it looked like there was no door at all.

Stars greeted me in the cool night sky. "Where are we?"

He wrapped his hands under my shoulders, pulling me up in one swift motion. "Behind you."

I whirled around, my face inches from the observatory tower. "Cool, unless Nexis knows about this."

"Get back. We don't want them to spot us." Laura yanked me against the brick wall with the rest of the group, her voice low. "I don't think so, that door hasn't been opened in a long time. Shanda was right. I bet they've been searching for this all year."

"Creepy, sis," Lenny whispered. "Do you think that tunnel goes anywhere else?"

"Like where?" She rolled her eyes at him.

"Like a secret passage to a Nexis underground lair? Woooo." He reached out and waved his hands in her face like a cartoon ghost.

"Or a Watchers' den where they monitor us like puppets in a play." Yep, that was me—always blurting out exactly what I was thinking. But if we found a secret entrance in the chapel, there had to be others.

Crickets chirped happily in the crisp night air, oblivious to our earth-shattering problems.

Bryan looked at me, head cocked. "Why would you think something like that?"

I dropped Laura's hand. "Strange symbols, underground tunnels, forgotten legends. At this point, it seems like anything is possible."

Lenny nodded. "I'm with Lucy, I don't like this at all. There's gotta be more to it."

"Maybe." Bryan scratched his chin, glancing away from me. "I'll look into it."

"You do that." I shrugged off his dubious maybe and glanced around at the rest of the group. "They've got an eye in the sky and we're stuck here. Now what do we do?"

A flash of something gleamed in Tony's eye. "What if I can distract them somehow? And find out if Felicia's working for them at the same time?"

"I'm listening." Beside me, Bryan's voice turned gruff. He reached for my hand, as if for the first time I might be able to give him some measure of strength. I squeezed back. His puffed out chest deflated.

Tony whipped out his cell. "I could call her up and say we've found some kind of secret chamber, across the river. Maybe they'd leave the tower."

Bryan shrugged, with my hand still in his. "I guess it's worth a shot. Let's put it to a vote. Just nod if you approve."

Laura nodded on my left, then me, followed by Lenny and Tony. Brooke peered over at Bryan and bit her lip. Slowly, she nodded, too.

With an emphatic nod, Bryan gave his final approval. But his lips twitched, as if it wasn't his first choice. Again, I squeezed his hand. His eyes softened as he stared down at me.

"Here goes." Tony dialed the number, gulping in a deep breath. Suddenly his lungs heaved and his voice turned breathy as he panted into the phone. "Felicia, you won't believe it. We've found something, a secret chamber under the Watchers' field. But it's too dark tonight. We're going to meet up at dawn tomorrow to explore it. You in?"

At my side, Laura stifled a giggle. Bryan just shook his head and slumped down against the brick tower.

"Great, bring all the flashlights and candles you've got, okay?" He clicked off the call and stuck the phone in his pocket. "Now, we wait."

"Brilliant." Laura golf clapped at him. "You should really take up acting or something."

He raised his eyebrows, taking a slight bow. "I just might."

"Shush." Brooke slammed her finger to her lips. "They might hear us."

"Sorry." Laura mouthed, still smiling at Tony.

I slunk down the side of the tower on the grass next to Bryan. The wind whipped at my face, and I wrapped my arms around my knees. His hand found its usual place on my back, rubbing circles, only this time it wasn't for my comfort.

"What if this actually works?" His hushed words floated up, into the cold breeze. "We'll have to treat her like a traitor. This can't be happening after all these years."

"We'll figure that out when the time comes." My words weren't really about Felicia, like my mouth knew more than my brain.

167

Vibrations trembled behind the stone tower wall, then stomping, probably heavy footsteps down a certain wrought-iron staircase. A door creaked open and slammed shut. Kevin's bleached head barreled into the darkness, his legs churning in the fastest sprint I'd ever seen. Soon he was out of sight, headed straight for the field across the river.

"Well, I guess we know the truth now." Tony's whisper was solemn, as if he never really believed it could be true. "I'm sorry, man. I hoped we were wrong."

"Me too," I whispered so low I wonder if he even heard me.

He grabbed my hand and pulled us both up, his face full of weary lines. "Let's get back to the dorms. We'll deal with this tomorrow."

In an instant he let go of my hand took off running.

I tried to keep up, but halfway across the quad my legs turned to mush and cold air seared into my lungs. I slowed the pace, but he kept on running into the night. The white outline of the hawk's wings on his jacket practically flapped in the darkness, almost as if he were really flying. Tony and Lenny disappeared after him until all the boys were out of sight.

I whispered to the starry sky, "Help him figure this out."

Laura and Brooke finally caught up to me.

Brooke nudged my shoulder. "He'll be fine, he just needs some time to cool off."

"You're right, I know." My hot breath steamed into the cold air.

Laura's lips curled up. "Let's sneak back in the way we came."

I nodded and followed them into the shadows, wishing I could turn back time to the way things were before I saw that symbol—the mark of the Seer.

20

A thunder rush of wind and metal blew in my face as another train raced into the station. The blast whipped my hair around me.

Suddenly I felt eyes all around me, staring.

The world went black and gray.

One thing remained—the eyes.

Tenuous trust, shattered in an instant, as if someone knew the secret we found last night, and they weren't going to let us get away with it.

The darkness closed in, a gray mist suffocating like fog around us.

Only I could see, everyone else was blind.

A message burned in my heart, telling me I had to lead the way. I had to show them the truth. Strong hands thrashed at me from either side, but I danced around them. Away from their clutches, toward the light that burned so bright I fell to my knees. I bent my head and nodded, accepting my role even if I didn't know the details, didn't know the cost.

Colors filtered through the mist, and the subway station reappeared.

The world was right again.

The vision vanished as quickly as it came on.

They kept getting weirder, not to mention more pointed. This one felt like a turning point, like I couldn't go back any more.

"Clumsy girl," Tony gripped my arm, hoisting me to my feet. "Someone's got to look out for you."

I blinked until the fog cleared. Better play it cool, like nothing just happened.

We climbed from the subway to East 103rd Street in Harlem, a trio of two-by-two ark buddies on a pilgrimage ordered by our fearless leader. When I sneaked a peek at Bryan, his lips were twisted, his eyes skittering over everyone and everything on the crowded sidewalk. Just a hint of fear, small but unmistakable. He hadn't answered my calls all day. I was determined to give him his space, as if I had a choice.

The overcast sky dimmed to a darker shade of gray, Brooke following right on her brother's heels as he led the way past eclectic New York shops and beautiful old brownstones to Lexington Avenue.

Tony lagged behind with me as we shuffled down the crowded street. We turned the corner into a construction zone, which lasted until we reached 104th.

"Smell that, it's heavenly." Laura inhaled, lingering in front of a fragrance shop on the corner.

I caught a whiff of exotic sandalwood. "If only the rest of New York smelled this good."

"True dat. No time for window shopping, little sis." Lenny shoved her down 104th as Tony pulled me along the sidewalk. "Pick up the pace."

"Hey, I go at my own speed," she cried and punched Lenny's bicep.

"Yeah, why don't you stop and smell the sandalwood?" I twirled my dark hair into a rope and whipped it at Tony. "We could pass for brother and sister I guess."

"Funny." He pursed his full lips that any girl would pay to have. Under the glare of the streetlights, his dark hair really contrasted against his features.

"Wow, your skin is paler than mine. Anyone ever tell you, you look like a vampire?" I hissed at him.

He jerked his face toward me as he bared his teeth. "If I was, you wouldn't be around long enough to tell anyone."

A large Latina passed us, covering the eyes of her two kids and huddling them to her side.

I cracked up so loud both brother and sister pairs turned around. "Watch out, Tony Cullen is scaring the locals."

Laura and Brooke busted out laughing, but Bryan and Lenny furrowed their foreheads like I'd asked them to multiply square roots.

Tony just hung his head. "You don't want to know."

It felt good to smile, even laugh again. Things had been way too heavy lately. Maybe this so-called field trip was just the thing to lift me out of my funk. Even Mr. Tall Dark and Brooding might have a little fun. Yeah, right.

We crossed Third Avenue into the residential area of 104th Street. Circles of light haloed the gum-dotted pavement every few feet as the street noises died down. Tall brick buildings covered with evenly-spaced windows sprouted on our right, then on both sides of the street. I scooted closer to Tony. "Are these the projects?"

He shrugged, eyes darting around. "Not the scary ones you see on TV. These are mostly remodeled co-ops. Don't worry, there's a police station a couple of blocks over. It's perfectly safe."

I wanted to run up to Bryan and wrap myself in his arms, but I had to be brave. *Silly girl.* I bit my lip, trying not to let the shivers crawl up my spine. From our spot in the back of the group I herded the sheep forward until we crossed Second Avenue. We passed a few oddball shops and brownstones that screamed old New York. Then we came to our final destination.

"Beautiful." I whistled out all the pent-up air in my lungs.

A massive circle of stained glass glowed in the gathering dusk from several stories up. We stopped in front of the enormous stone church. Above the door it read *St. Lucy's Church and School.* "Awesome, I have a church and a school. Does that mean I'll have to become a saint to get my full inheritance?"

Bryan ignored me and checked his watch. "Good, we're on time. I told Father Patrick about half past eight. I said we're doing a paper on St. Lucia and we had to interview a priest. I know, I hate lying to a man of the cloth. But we have to know more about her, and they're not all sympathetic to the Guardians. Some are, some aren't. We'll have to see."

I glanced over at Tony and he shot me a quirky look. We followed the siblings up the steps to the church. In the doorway I stopped.

A strange sensation of utter sorrow mixed with determination submerged in the pit of my stomach, but I pressed on.

171

A hush fell over us, bright soprano voices feathering the air of the grand stone foyer. A long high note pierced through the cracks of the sanctuary door, then faded to silence. I tiptoed across the tiles after Brooke and Bryan.

"Choir practice, ugh." Tony whispered to me.

"It's gorgeous." I held one finger to my lips, pausing mid-step.

Another muted refrain rang out, the low alto rising in a soporific crescendo. I arched up to my toes as the music swelled, peeking into the triangular window of the nearest door.

"C'mon." He grabbed my hand, yanking me down a dim hallway. "If anyone's destiny depends on this, it's you."

"For your information, if anyone isn't quite ready for her destiny, it's me." I waved my farewell to the beautiful music, my beacon of hope that melted away the dark subway vision.

Thick eyebrows waggled above his pale, bluish lids. "Ready or not, here it comes."

"I don't need a babysitter, you know?" I wriggled my hand free to walk at my own pace.

"Somebody thinks you do." He cocked his head down the hall, toward the broad shoulders that disappeared into a doorway.

"Why can't he do it himself?" I stamped my foot like a toddler who didn't get her way. Exactly how I felt, too. "He's just mad about Felicia, but it's not like I'm the one that forced her to switch sides."

Yellow light spilled from the open doorway into the dim hall.

"Of course not, but it's totally rocked him. He says we have to go on the offensive now, whatever that means." He pulled me toward the light into the small library, whether I wanted to go or not. "Just keep an open mind, will you?"

I nodded at him, the smell of burning wax searing my nose. In a room as big as a bedroom, shelves of books lined the walls from plush carpet to coffered ceiling. The windows were draped with burgundy velvet. Candles flickered in gilt candelabras on the windowsill between the fabric panels. Old hardbacks stacked with ancient leatherbound volumes lined each shelf, all miraculously dust-free.

Bryan and Lenny stood in front of a large mahogany table in the center of the room, their sisters seated in Victorian chairs in front of them. Bryan scooted out the remaining chair, nodding at me to sit.

Then a black-clad man with a white collar bustled in. "It's nice to see chivalry hasn't died out in the teenage population." He adjusted his dark frames against his grayed temples. Those small, beady eyes reminded me of someone.

Bryan shook hands with the priest who took the remaining seat. "Thanks for meeting with us, Father Patrick. You'll be a big help to our project."

Father Patrick cracked his knuckles, then flexed his fingers. "You've been assigned one of the more interesting saints, I must say. What did you want to know?"

"We want to know the legend of St. Lucia." Laura's tiny voice sounded larger in this small space. She gulped, then turned to me. Silence hung heavy in the room.

Brooke glanced at me just like Laura had. Then she pulled out a pad of paper, her pen poised over it. "Tell us about how she became a saint."

One of the guys rested his hand on my chair. His fingertips grazed my shoulder, tracing the tiniest circle on my back. How could I concentrate while Bryan was doing that?

"There are many legends that surround her." Father Patrick's gaze swept over us in a wide arc. "The legend goes that she was martyred for her faith after she refused to marry a prominent man. He purportedly turned her over to the Diocletian's governor in Syracuse, who killed Christians in the Middle Ages. When she refused to recant her faith they tried to drag her off but couldn't move her, as if she were made of stone. Then they tried to burn her, but God saved her then, too. So they gouged her eyes out, eventually running her through with a sword. Because of her eyes, she's the patron saint of the blind."

My jaw dropped, but I closed it with a snap, biting into my cheek to stop the scream that rose in my throat. Still, my blood curdled. "Why would they gouge her eyes out?"

Bryan's hand clamped around my shoulder. Was it to comfort me or hold me in my chair so I couldn't run away? Brooke scribbled furiously on her notepad, filling page after page.

The priest eyes probed mine, sort of like the subway eyes. Then his gaze softened as he adjusted his collar. "I'm obligated to tell you that the Catholic Church doesn't endorse all of this as fact, since there's not enough evidence to support it. That form of torture wasn't common in that time, but was done on occasion. There is evidence on both sides, but the older sources do support the theory."

The rotund man moved to a shelf on the opposite side of the room, his black suit crinkling as he moved. "Wait, I think we have something that will help."

He pulled out a large brown volume and gently laid it on the table in front of us. With shaky hands he flipped through the ancient leatherbound parchment until he came to a picture. One I'd seen before, a woman with hollow eyes.

"It's also rumored that God gave her glorified eyes to replace the ones she lost. If that was in heaven or on Earth is much debated." Then he flipped to another picture, a drawing of the sandy-haired saint with jeweled eyes.

I gasped. I'd seen that image two times before, but never like this.

Behind black frames, his eyes found me. "Beautiful isn't she? Personally, I find it hard to believe the part about her eyes isn't true. All of the artwork from Medieval times portrays her without eyes, or with her eyes on a tray. Some even with her glorified eyes, like this rendering here. She's also the patron saint of the blind, like I said before."

He slid the book back and shut it with a bang. "Even though the evidence is scant, that is mostly due to the time period. They didn't call it the Dark Ages for no reason. Sometimes, you have to have a little faith."

I shot a sidelong glance at Laura and Brooke, but they wouldn't meet my gaze. Did they know about this? Why wouldn't they have told me already? Those questions twisted into an inner funnel cloud of what-ifs.

He threw his hands up and let out a long sigh. "But alas, I am among the few who still believe the old legends. If we could only discover why Diocletian would gouge her eyes out, everything might finally fit into place."

"Is there anything else you can tell us, about the eye myth in particular?" Brooke's pen paused for a split second. She actually met my gaze this time. "If that's okay with you."

"Let's hear all about it." I couldn't censor the blatant sarcasm. This saint's story, coupled with that picture I'd seen in the Nexis book, hit too close to home. I certainly wouldn't want to trade places with her. Why would I want to hear the rest of her sad tale?

Father Patrick glanced at the roman numeral clock above the doorway. "I wish I could stay and chat. Choir practice just ended. I've got to set up for tonight's mass."

"Wait." Brooke dropped her notepad, chewing on the end of her pen. "Are there any books you can point us to? I think this angle would be a great way to go for our paper. We'd need some good sources for our reference list."

"Only if you promise to be extremely careful." He circled the room, then came back with a stack of books. "I don't want to hear you in confessional crying about how you ruined two thousand years worth of history."

Brooke helped him lay out the books one by one on the polished table. "I promise we'll take good care of them."

"I'm leaving you in charge. I'll be back in an hour." He wagged his finger and walked out the door. Then he peeked his head back in. "You know my favorite part about St. Lucia? She is a picture to the church of how God's love is blind. Even when we can't see it, he loves us for who we are, not what we do."

"Interesting take," I muttered under my breath. "Not exactly a perfect analogy if you're the one getting your eyes gouged out."

"That was intense." Brooke held her breath until he left the room. "Why don't we each take one book and see what we can dig up."

She pushed an aged greenish leather volume my way. The book had a strange symbol on it, a winged cross in the middle of a four-pronged circle. Kind of like the stained glass window up front. "What's this emblem?"

Bryan peeked over my shoulder. "That's the Guardian crest."

The whole group except Brooke huddled around me to get a glimpse of the crest.

"Is this a Guardian church or something?" All eyes turned on me like a pack of hungry dogs.

Brooke gently shut her book. "Why would you think that?"

"Because of the stained glass window out front." As soon as the words flew out of my mouth she bolted out the door.

"Wait here, we're going to go check it out." Laura scuttled down the hall after Brooke.

Lenny eased down in the chair next to me. I'd almost forgotten he was there, he hadn't said a word most of the night. "You know, there's not a lot of Guardian churches left these days. We've lost some to Nexis, and some to the politics of the post-modern era. Soon we'll be living in a post-Christian age, at least that's what my dad says."

"How do you know this is a Guardian sanctuary?" Tony paced the length of the library, back and forth. "What if this is a trap? I don't like it."

A bubble of anger gurgled in my stomach. I pushed back my chair. "Now wait a minute, I didn't ask to come here. I heard we were going to learn something about Nexis, not some weird saint. I just noticed that the crossbars in the stained glass window and the Guardian symbol are similar. I didn't say I knew for sure."

He combed pale fingers through his dark hair, but his gaze slanted above me. "Just because a church was built with a Guardian symbol doesn't mean that they're still affiliated. For all we know they could've defected to Nexis fifty years ago. Besides, I wasn't talking to you, sis." He smiled at me, but his pacing resumed.

"You meant our fearless leader." I swiveled around the back of my chair. Bryan's hands still clutched the spindles and suddenly we were eye to eye. One staring contest I wasn't going to lose, not even to those gorgeous blue eyes. "You've had a plan all along, haven't you?"

He inched his face forward, those eyes zeroing in on my mouth.

I squinted at him, pursed my lips.

He backed up, slowly. "I want to stay ahead of Nexis, get a leg up for once. I wanted to see if this church was still a Guardian sanctuary, and I knew they had some great resources in this library. It could be a start to finding your brother. But I also wanted you to know more about St. Lucia. I did promise I'd tell you about her."

"Yeah, I got that much." I bit my lip, anything to stop my thoughts from escaping unchecked, but they overflowed. "So you think Will and Nexis want to gouge my eyes out? How would that help them?" My stomach roiled at the idea of it.

"If you were the Seer, then you couldn't help us." Lenny's calm tone put a chink in my anger, just a teeny one. "But you couldn't help Nexis, so it would be a last resort. Guardian legend says that St. Lucia wouldn't marry because her betrothed was a prominent Nexis member. He only wanted her because she was the Seer. When she refused to marry him, he turned her over to Diocletian's men with strict instructions to remove her eyes. They tried three times before they succeeded."

Tony stopped pacing. He plopped down on the tabletop and crossed his legs Indian-style, pulling a book onto his lap. "They'll do anything to have the Seer on their side. They've been trying for centuries."

"Well, I'm not the Seer, so we can all just go home now. Nexis can forget about me." Tears pooled in my eyes. Even I didn't believe me any more.

Bryan's hand covered mine. "What if you're the predecessor to the Seer? You're next in line, but we won't know till you're eighteen."

"What happens then, my visions get worse? Will I see things all the time?" I clamped my hand over my mouth, too late. The words had already escaped my lips.

Bryan's jaw dropped, so did Tony's and Lenny's. They all stared at me like I was crazy. Maybe I was.

Then Bryan's mouth slowly curved up, almost a smile. "I knew it, you saw something at the Hard Rock, and at the Nexis initiation. Am I right?"

I looked up at him and a tear trickled down my cheek. Heat seared my neck, singing my cheeks, but I couldn't look away.

His eyes sparkled, like they were lit up from the inside.

"How did you—"

Suddenly the door burst open. A strange man loomed in the doorway, almost identical to Father Patrick, minus a few pounds and a few gray hairs. His glare locked on me. "It's you. The moment I laid eyes on you, I knew. You're the next Seer, and you'll bear the same mark."

21

A small wrought-iron instrument gleamed in the man's right hand. He raised it over his head and edged across the room, straight for the candelabra. He plunged the metal rod into the flames until it glowed, a strange symbol reddening across the iron—a triangle with a swirling eye in the middle.

Then he lunged toward me.

He grabbed my wrist in a death grip and forced it close to the red-hot branding iron. Inches from my flesh, the glowing symbol still scorched my skin.

"Yeow!" The pain was stinging, and I'd do anything I could to make it stop. Thrashing like a wild woman, I kicked at his shin, dug my nails into his arm, and finally wrestled free from his bruising grip. Strong hands pushed me out of my chair, onto the carpet. I came face to face with Tony as he half-shoved, half-rolled me under the table. Chair legs dug into the growing rug burn on my shoulder. Then the chair flew back. A loud crash echoed on the other side of the room as something thudded to the floor.

Tony peered between the table legs. "Poor Lenny."

I bumped my head on the table frame as I scanned the lower half of the room. Someone lay crumpled in the corner, poor Lenny indeed. His chest rose and fell, still breathing. In the dark I made out the shapes of two sets of legs, one pair clothed in black, the other jean-clad.

In an instant a flash of denim flew up, disappearing as something slammed onto the table above us. A horrible squealing sound raked across the wood. I could only see the silhouette of black trousers now. Bryan was all alone up there.

I tugged on Tony's shirt. "Go help him. I can take care of myself."

He nodded and thrust an oblong object at me. "Just in case." Then he slid out from our hiding spot.

I could barely make it out in the shadows—his trusty pocket knife. What good would that do? I flipped out the knife blade like he said, just in case.

Another chair clanged across the room, then something whacked the tabletop above me. Ragged gasps sliced my eardrums.

I couldn't just sit here and let these guys take a beating for me, not when I could do something to help. In the suitcase-sized space I contorted into a back bend, hugging the bottom of the tabletop. I inched forward until I was peering over the edge.

Bryan lay sprawled out on the table, his lungs panting for air. Across the room Tony ripped books off the shelves, flinging them at Felicia's dad one by one. He chased Tony around the room.

I reached for Bryan's collar and dragged him off the table. My shoulder burned with his weight, but I couldn't stop now. When his feet hit the floor I tugged him into my hideaway.

"What should we do now, run or fight?" I brandished my pocket knife in the air.

Bryan almost smiled at my antics, wincing. "If only that were larger. We have to get you out of here." He dug out his phone and dialed 911.

"I assume you have a plan." I barely had to whisper with his face so close to mine.

Cuts scabbed up over his eyebrow, his nose bloody, a dark bruise swelled under his eye. My fingers brushed across his temple, combing into his hair. I felt the beginnings of a bump under his scalp. He winced again.

"I do now." His eyes widened at my touch. Slowly, he slid something out from under his arm. The Guardian book I'd been reading. "Just stay behind me."

I crawled out into the open, crouching behind him. He ripped out a page from the book. The loud paper-slash perked the crazed man's ears. He dropped Tony's shirt and turned toward us, his face ashen.

Bryan crumpled up the page and threw it at the candelabra. In seconds the paper burst into flames, licking the velvet curtains. He caught Tony's eye, nodding at Lenny. Then he wrapped his jacket around his right hand and darted across the room.

Hoisting up a candle, he chucked it at the priest.

Tony zipped to the other side of the room as the man's black pants caught fire. He screeched like the hounds of hell were after him. The ghoulish sound ripped through the air, even as tongues of fire scorched the room.

Bryan dove through the smoke, shoving me forward and we ran out of the room. Tony lugged Lenny into the hall and dumped him at my feet. Then they both doubled back to barricade the door.

I bent down to examine Lenny, who lay stiff as death. I glanced up for help, any kind of help. *Jesus, please get us out of here alive.* Only framed pictures of the parish priests stared back at me, one drawing my attention. The photo labeled Father Patrick was of an older man, but he was bald, no gray head of hair. So who was the "Father Patrick" we'd just met?

Out of the corner of my eye, Lenny's chest moved a millimeter and my heart stopped. Was he all right? I had to find out. I slapped his face, and a moan escaped his lips. I almost jumped for joy.

"Thank God." I breathed, then an idea seized me. I flipped down the blade, calling out to Bryan and Tony. "Catch."

Tony caught the pocket knife with one hand. "What am I going to do with this?"

I threw up my hands. "I don't know. Shove it in the door jamb or something."

He mumbled things at Bryan, but I didn't have time for that.

I slunk to me knees next to Lenny. "You okay, buddy? You need to get up, we have to get out of here."

"What happened?" He rubbed the goose egg on his forehead. "Are you okay?"

How could he think of me first at a time like this? I smiled and helped him up. "I'm fine, let's get you out of here."

Faint sirens sounded as I limped with Lenny across the tiles.

"Okay, we're coming." Bryan yelled down the hall. "Get ready to run."

I pinched Lenny's cheek. "You ready?"

"Sure." His eyes glazed over like he couldn't focus.

The guys' footsteps thundered behind me. I pedaled my feet with Lenny under my arm, but his weight was like an anvil on my already worn-out shoulders. Tony and Bryan rushed to my side, snatching Lenny's arms.

"Start running," Bryan screamed at me, his eyes wild. "The cops can't find you here."

I opened my mouth to ask questions. I'd never seen his eyes like that—full of fear, even pleading. Desperate.

With a quick nod I raced down the hall, out the front door. I almost tripped over Laura and Brooke on the steps sipping Cokes.

"We have to get out of here." I shot them the wild-Bryan eyes. One look at my face and they dropped their Cokes on the sidewalk.

We took off down the street, sprinting in the opposite direction of the sirens, past dark doorways and storefronts until we hit the end of 104th Street. My lungs burned as if I was still back there, in the fire, but I had to keep going.

Then we rounded the corner and ducked into the First Avenue Deli.

"What happened back there?" Brooke panted and pressed her face to the window. "Are the guys okay?"

"I don't know, he just attacked us." I gulped and heaved at her side. "Felicia's dad just showed up, but even worse, I don't think that priest really was a priest. His picture wasn't even on the wall."

"What?" Brooke gasped. "What do you mean?"

"I mean, something really strange is going on here. Maybe he tipped off Felicia's dad, or maybe he's one of the Watchers, too." I grabbed Brooke's hand, then Laura's. "At this point we can only hope God is really on our side."

Laura pulled us into a booth and stared out the window. "It may be their only hope."

"They have to be okay, they just have to be." I closed my eyes, water pooling, stinging as I pressed them tighter to keep the tears at bay. I squeezed Laura's hand, then Brooke's, saying my own silent prayers. *What's happening out there? Please help those poor guys. Don't let them get hurt or in trouble because of me. I can't handle that right now. Keep them safe. Please.*

Neon lights burned into my eyeballs. The flashing billboards of Times Square glowed brighter as the night grew later. I could almost feel the New Yorkers' stares as they wove around us, like they knew we'd almost burned down a church. Like they could see the horror cloaking us.

Laura stopped on the corner and turned to me. "Is this really a good idea? We're so exposed here."

"That's the point." Brooke reached around me, patting her shoulder. "If what Lucy says is true, they could be in real trouble. We can't risk getting caught."

"But we didn't do anything wrong." Laura bit her lip, eyes glittering with tears. I knew just how she felt. "How do you even know they'll figure it out?"

Brooke's face split into a grin, kind of like her brother's did sometimes. "Please, he's like Bryan's favorite part of Times Square. He talked nonstop about this guy all summer break. I think he'll be here."

"We've got to find him first." An ache clenched the pit of my stomach, as if I'd never see the Guardian guys again. Their terrified faces faded in and out. Lenny collapsed, Tony handing me the knife, Bryan's bloody nose and bruised eye.

Goosebumps popped up on my arms. I cinched my leather jacket tighter around me. "They have to be okay."

"There he is." Brooke pointed down the block. "C'mon, girls."

She grabbed my hand, then Laura's, and we raced around the thick crowd like bumper cars strung together. Two blocks later the dulcet melody finally hit me. A tourist group clapped in time to the music, bagpipe music.

"What is that?" Laura whispered as we huddled in. "It sounds like 'When the Saints Go Marching In,' but it's hard to tell."

"I'm no saint." A bitter laugh escaped my throat. "Is he the only bagpiper on Times Square?"

Brooke's eyes went wide. "Uh-oh, I didn't think of that. Bryan just said whenever he needed to think, he'd come here."

"Kind of strange, huh?" Those big eyes told me I'd said the wrong thing. "I'm sure they'll find us. Don't worry."

The music lilted around the people in front of us, calm and slightly off-key. Then the song turned somber, a haunting tune that thinned out the bright-shirted tourists until only the three of us remained.

Laura bit her lip. "What if they went to the hospital, or they got hauled in for questioning or something? It could be hours."

"Then they would've texted or called us by now." Brooke tugged her phone out of her pocket. She held it in front of Laura. "See, no messages."

"Not if they're in jail. They'd only get one call." Laura's eyes went past us, then her whole face lit up. "Wait, there they are."

The three guys straggled towards us, Lenny limping along on Tony's shoulder. Behind them Bryan's face emerged from the shadows. Something inside me snapped at the sight of him.

I let my feet run free, picking up speed until I practically barreled into his chest. I flung my arms through his unzipped bomber jacket and buried my face in his t-shirt. "I'm so happy you're okay."

His hand trickled down my hair, pressing me into his warm shirt. My tears finally spilled over, soaking the black cotton.

"You don't have to worry about me, I'm not going anywhere." His breath tingled my ear.

With one rough finger he traced my jaw until it reached my chin, tilting my face toward him. A weak smile shimmered in my watery eyes.

"I was so worried." The words came out in a choked whisper. I reached up to wipe my eyes, but his hand stopped me.

He brushed away my tears with his fingertips. "Don't cry, honey. I'm just glad you're not hurt. I'd do anything to protect you." His fingers laced through mine.

The butterflies swirled inside at that word, honey. Then they crash-landed in a fiery pit. "That's what I'm afraid of."

"I'm so glad you figured out my text." Brooke's squeal broke us apart. She wrapped her arms around his waist. "Don't scare me like that again. I was worried sick."

"Sorry, sis. We're fine." Bryan huddled the group together, lowering his voice. "We told the cops we saw the fire from the window and rushed in to help. I think they believed us."

"How'd you explain your injuries?" Laura wrapped her arm around Lenny's back, propping him up.

Tony coughed. "Smoke inhalation. We said the guy was wigging out by the time we got to him, which is mostly true. They took our statements and patched us up." The corners of his mouth arched up.

"They didn't ask about Bryan's black eye?" My hands flew to his face but stopped mid-air. I didn't want to hurt him. Tears threatened again. "I don't know what's going on, but I'm pretty sure it's not worth this. Maybe I should just go back to Indiana."

The group burst out in protest, Bryan's stern tone silencing the others. He snatched my hovering hand. "I don't think so. You can't go back to the home turf of your crazy ex, he's a stalker. How would that be any better?"

"At least no one else would get hurt because of me. I couldn't live with myself if something happened. To any of you." I looked around at this amazing, ragtag group.

"Lucy, you can't go. We need you." Bryan squeezed my hand, so soft. Tingles zapped to my toes. "Everything's fine now."

"Then it's settled." Brooke grabbed his other hand, dragging me with him. "Let's go see the famous bagpiper you're always raving about. You'll feel better."

"Good call." Lenny stepped forward with a slight hitch in his step. "I could use something fun right about now."

Tony shook his head as we approached the musician. "What's so fun about a Scottish dirge?"

"I know more than that, laddie." The bagpiper's accent sounded half-Scottish, half-Irish. "Good to see you boys made it out okay. We've got a cleanup crew on the way to the church, so just pretend like you're regular teenagers making fun of the street performer."

I scrunched up my eyebrows and stared at him, but he just swung his pipes around.

"It's okay, he's one of us." Bryan's whisper warmed my neck. I relaxed my shoulders and leaned against him.

The bagpiper's green and white kilt with blue stripes was frayed at the edges, fading in spots. Good thing the giant bagpipes covered most of his outfit.

"It's my family kilt," he responded to my silent question. "The blue stripes mean that we're Highlanders."

"Yeah, right." Tony mumbled under his breath. "He's probably just a fan of the TV show."

"Shush." Brooke shot him the evil-eye and turned to the bagpiper. "Will you play us a song?"

"Of course, lassie, if you'll do me a favor first." Still with the Scottish accent? Not fooling anyone, buddy, except maybe Brooke.

"Okay, anything." Her sandy head bobbed like an anxious puppy.

"Me throat's parched from playing all night. You mind going into the Marriott here and getting me a glass of water?"

"Of course not. Anything for the bagpipe maestro." She trotted off toward the hotel.

"Now." Mr. Bagpipes licked his lips at each of us. "What shall I play for you? I do show-tunes, standards, or a traditional bagpipe lullaby, if you prefer."

"No thanks." Laura's scowl wrinkled up her face.

"How about 'Fly Me to the Moon?'" Bryan's arm slid around my waist, pulling me closer.

"Good choice, lad," the bagpiper beamed. "One of me favorites." His accent landed on Irish this time, unless my Alton High drama teacher had it all wrong.

"Let me work some kinks out." He touched the pipes tenderly and twisted the tuning pins.

"Wait for me." Brooke jogged up to us. "Here's your water, sir."

"Thanks, lassie." He sipped it and poured the rest into a tasseled leather pouch at his hip. He handed the cup back to Brooke. "Do you mind?"

"Not at all. So what will you play tonight?"

"Your strapping young friend requested '*Fly Me to the Moon.*'" He blew into the pipes, horrible screeches tearing through the chilly night air.

"Strapping friend?" Laura giggled under her breath. I elbowed her in the side, if only to suppress my own laughter.

The bagpipes sang out their somber melody, filling the space between us with its slow, slightly off-kilter melody.

Laura jerked on my arm. "Get a load of that, he's trying to do a jig." Sure enough, the burly man bent one knee then kicked out his foot, switching legs to do it all over again.

I couldn't hold back, and suddenly busted out laughing. Laura cracked up too, whether at me or the bagpiper I couldn't tell. Her high-pitched giggle rang out like a siren, louder than the Times Square noises around us.

"Hey, what is this? I don't play for no cynics." The bagpiper's face grew redder by the minute. Then he waddled close to Bryan and whispered, "The cleanup crew just reported in, the Watchers are here. Not sure why they're being so persistent. They've never wanted to risk exposing themselves before now."

Bryan's eyes landed on me, his fingers encircling my singed wrist. I winced.

"Oh, I see," the piper's eyes widened. "You'll have to hide out in the Marriott until the coast is clear. Get back to Montrose before they catch you. It's the only safe place left."

Bryan nodded at him and grabbed my arm.

"Get out of here, or I'll clobber you with my pipes." He hoisted up his bag.

"Funny, no accent now," I whispered to Bryan as we walked away. The boys and Brooke straggled behind.

"Heard that." He picked up the pace and ran after us. In an instant it turned into a foot race. Six teenagers verses one kilted man, with bagpipes flailing on his back. Probably looked like a comic book scene to anyone else on the street, hopefully even the Watchers.

"Quick, in here." Tony pulled Brooke into the revolving door of the Marriott.

Bryan and I smushed into the next section, Laura and Lenny right behind us.

"Man, that guy sure knows how to waddle." Lenny did a jig around the room like a hunchback puppet trying to dance.

Laura let out her siren giggle and I couldn't help it, I totally cracked up. Our laughter hit the marble-encased foyer and bounced right back at us. A few guests stopped and stared.

"Shush." Laura sucked in air to stifle her giggles.

"You started it." I gasped. "Man, that was loud. Everything echoes off of marble."

"Hey, guys, I've got an idea." Lenny's face perked up for the first time tonight.

"Great, not another one of his ideas." I followed the twins over to the bank of elevators. When I turned to Lenny, the smile on his face said it all.

"I've got a plan to pass the time. Who's in?"

22

Soft music trilled through the otherwise silent lobby. Laura's neck craned up and down the glass-encased elevators as she eyed Lenny. "Elevator tag, really?"

He flashed his goofy grin at her. "What, we have to lay low and pretend like we're normal teenagers, right? Might as well have some fun. We'll do brother-sister teams, Tony and Lucy can team up."

"You're so immature." But she smiled back at him, not fooling anybody. "You're on, but let's make it interesting."

He scratched his unmarred chin. "Losers have to buy the winners' subway ride back to school."

"Not interesting enough." Tony's sneakers squeaked across the marble. "How about the subway ride, plus loser buys the water bottle to throw at the bagpipe guy?"

Bryan and I busted out laughing, but Brooke's jaw dropped. "What if you threw it too hard? We could really hurt the poor guy."

"Me, who says I'll be losing?" Tony glared at Brooke, who scoffed and rolled her eyes. "Don't worry, it'll be the all clear signal. If he tosses it back to us, we head back to Montrose."

"Fine, deal." Brooke pumped Tony's hand. "We'll take the right side, you take the middle, Laura and Lenny, you're on the left. All three teams must ride to the top floor, then run down the hall to the next set of elevators. Whoever makes it down first, wins. Racers ready?"

"So official." Tony saluted her, sauntering to my side.

Brooke, Tony, and Lenny poised their hands over the buttons.

"Go." They pressed their buttons simultaneously ... and we all waited.

Laura checked her watch. "So this is what elevator tag is like."

Then the bell dinged and the doors opened for Tony and me. We waved at the real siblings as Tony sang out, "Hey, hey, goodbye."

Passengers shot us puzzled stares as they exited. If I wasn't so amped up, I might've been more self-conscious. But a nervous energy zipped through me, like something good was about to happen for a change. We scurried on and Tony hit the door-close button.

He grinned. "I can't believe I'm acting like a middle schooler."

"Me, either." I cracked up, then my smile faded. "Did you already know that bagpipe guy was some kind of Guardian lookout?"

"Sure. He's more like an informant, really, between sectors. A middle man. We tell him stuff, he tells us stuff." He pressed his nose to the elevator glass, looking out at the courtyard as if that were a normal everyday comment. "They're only a couple of floors behind us."

The car jerked to a stop on the fifth floor.

"What do you mean, sectors?"

"There's Guardian groups all over this area, it's a big city. We have to stay in contact." He shot me an enough-with-the-questions expression.

"Fine, I'll take what I can get." My breath caught in my throat. "They're about to catch up."

Who was I to question the Guardian system? After the church, that awful man with his branding iron, that terrible fire—I'd survived. It felt good to be alive, unmarred. Mostly. Thanks to my Guardians and their informants like the bagpipe man, we might actually stay that way.

Suddenly Brooke and Bryan's elevator shot ahead, while ours stopped.

"Man, they're passing us." He was just as into this game as I was, maybe more so. The Coopers waved, Bryan shooting finger pistols at us while Brooke stuck out her tongue.

"How mature."

"Going up?" A fortyish man asked when the door dinged open.

"Yes." I frowned, batting my eyelashes at him. Wow, my competitive side would do anything for this win.

"I see. I'll catch the next one."

"Thank you, sir." Tony jabbed the button and we were off again. Still anyone's game. I spotted Brooke and Bryan's car stopping below us.

"What's up now?" I cheered and high-fived him. As we passed the Cooper car I pressed my hands to my lips, blowing kisses at the glass.

"Don't be such a baby, sis." Tony rolled his eyes, but his half-moon smile said it all.

I grinned back at him. "Who cares as long as we win?" At the top floor the elevator dinged and the doors opened. Cold air blasted my face as we raced down the hallway.

"Which way?"

"This way, come on." I yanked his arm, veering from one hall to the next set of elevators. Across the open courtyard, a bell dinged. "No way."

The Coopers stepped out of their elevator.

"Faster. They're coming." Tony bellowed behind me.

My jog shifted into a sprint. When I reached the other elevators I banged on the button, hard. My flats didn't stop fast enough and I flailed about like a pinwheel, almost smacking my head against the wall.

"Great, they're catching up." I panted out ragged breaths.

"Come on, stupid elevator." He kicked the door.

The Coopers buzzed down the hall, Bryan towing Brooke behind him. He practically strutted up to us and pressed his button.

"So, you thought you could beat us?" Brooke squinted at Tony as she approached.

"Game's not over yet." Tony countered, crossing his arms over his chest.

"We'll see who has the last laugh." Brooke nodded at Bryan. They grinned at each other like fools. Odd, I never smiled at my brother like that unless we were about to pull something big.

Then the elevator dinged and the doors burst open. That's when Bryan snatched my hand and yanked me to his side.

"Hey, what are you doing?" I whirled around to see an evil grin on his lips.

"Lucy." Tony's hand stretched toward me, but Brooke side-tackled him and they crashed into the elevator. The doors shut behind them, Brooke's muffled giggle seeping between the crack.

I stuck my hands on my hips, puffing out my bottom lip. "That was a dirty trick."

"Sorry, Brooke's idea." That evil grin said otherwise.

"Sure it was." When the next elevator opened, he nudged me inside. I stared up at him, hand stuck in his grip, familiar tingles sizzling up my arm.

"I didn't say it was a bad idea. I did give up a chance at winning." The smile softened, spreading to his eyes now.

"And you stole my chance." My heart fluttered in the cage of my chest. *Quick, say something.* I blurted out the first thing on my mind. "You're still holding my hand."

"So I am." He inhaled a deep breath, staring back at me. Something flickered in his eyes. All of a sudden, he bent down. "Lucy, I—"

As he inched closer my heart drummed faster, his minty breath filling the car. I closed my eyes, his mouth lightly brushing my lips. He moved his arms to my waist, wrapping them around me, pulling me closer. His lips pressed into mine, firmer this time.

Then he pulled away, one hand stroking my cheek, his blue eyes larger than ever as they searched my face. I gazed back at him, but he didn't move. He just stood there, frozen like an exquisite statue. That's it, after weeks of build up?

"I don't think so." I arched on my toes, pulling him back to my lips.

"Much better," I murmured against his mouth, relaxing into his arms. This is how kissing was supposed to be, no expectations, just chemistry.

Suddenly the elevator alarm sounded, shattering the best moment of the night. The car halted, mid-air. I jumped back, bumping into the metal rail between me and the glass. Bryan's hand rested on the red stop button.

"I knew it. I can't believe this." His eyes widened, then narrowed into a glare. "Why didn't you tell me?"

"Tell you what?" I stared past him through the glass window of the car. Hanging in the middle of nowhere, uncertainty thundered in my ears.

He cocked his head at me, blue eyes drilling deep. "Why didn't you tell me about the visions?"

This again. My heart almost stopped. What could I possibly say, that would make this any better? My eyes darted around the small space. It closed in on me, I couldn't escape. I blinked hard, but his eyes still bored into me. The air clogged in my throat like I could hyperventilate any second.

I spewed out the first coherent words. "I don't know, it's pretty crazy. How could you possibly understand about my visions? Why don't you think I'm crazy?"

"Honey, I know you're not crazy. I'm sorry I got so mad." He reached for me, wrapping me up in his arms again. One hand nestled my head into his shoulder. It felt good to rest there. "You must be the predecessor to the next Seer. Those things you see are pretty scary."

"No kidding." I lifted my head, watching that strong profile. "But how do you know what I've seen?"

Those blue eyes seared into me. I could've melted into the floor. "Just now, when I kissed you, I saw some pretty strange things." His fingers toyed with my hair, like it was no big deal.

All of the air blasted from my lungs. Relief flooded my body, as if a heavy load magically lifted off my shoulders. Finally, someone who could help me understand my scary visions.

I collapsed into him, letting his strong arms hold me up. "You really saw something when you kissed me, or when I kissed you?"

Laughter rumbled in his chest. He planted a kiss on the top of my head. "I wasn't expecting that last one, but I saw something both times."

"Really? What did you see?"

"First I saw that man with the golden eyes, in a hospital surrounded by white light. He made you feel better. Then I saw that shadow snake slithering up Will's shirt. Gave me the creeps." A shudder racked his body. "Now I wish you would've listened to me and stayed away from him."

"Wow, I almost forgot about the man in the hospital. He felt so real." My mind flew back to those horrible days after the wreck—the hospital, the recovery, all of it. Bryan saw the whole thing, or at least part of it. Somehow that felt more intimate than kissing, like he could see into my soul.

"You have quite a gift," he whispered into my hair. "I'm not sure how I could see what you've seen. I'm shocked, in a good way."

"This is so weird." I nuzzled into his shoulder and closed my eyes. Finally I could breathe easy, now that someone else knew exactly what I'd been going through. "Funny how you saw two random visions."

Bryan stepped back, tilting my chin up. When my eyes fluttered open, dazzling blue filled my sight.

"What do you mean, random? How many visions have you seen?" His eyes weren't angry, just searching.

"I don't know." I broke his gaze. Could I be honest with him? After all we'd been through, he might be the only person I could trust. "Maybe five or six actual visions. Sometimes I just see shadows or light around people."

"Oh, really?" He pushed the stop button again. The elevator rumbled back to life. "Anything around me?"

"Definitely a light." I smiled up at him. The vision of the fight came back to me. "Even a man of light when you stood up to Jake. Your guy totally punched out Jake's shadow. It was awesome."

"What? You saw an angel fighting a demon?" His hands moved to my shoulders. "Are you sure?"

I tried to shrug, but his hands weighed down on me. "Yeah, I think so. It's not like they tell me what side they're on. It's usually obvious. When I thought he was an angel, he nodded at me like I was right on. That was the first time I saw anything remotely human, except for that Noah vision."

"Noah vision?" Suddenly his face fell, arms drooping to his sides. He paced back and forth, then turned to face me. "This is so much bigger than I thought."

The elevator dinged and we split apart.

"Stupid bell." With my fingers, I combed away the tangles in my hair. What did he mean? What's so important about the Noah vision? I shouldn't have mentioned it, but I thought he could handle it.

Bryan's eyes lingered on me. He swiped his palm across his lips before the doors opened. Good call. My plum lip gloss all over his face would be a dead giveaway.

The doors opened on Brooke and Tony strutting around the elevator lobby. He crossed his biceps over his chest, glaring at us. "Where were you guys? You weren't that far behind."

"There you are. We won!" Brooke danced around and high-fived Tony. "You know what they say, all's fair in love and elevator tag." She narrowed her eyes at me. "Why are you acting weird?"

I bit my lip, peeking sideways at Bryan. Maybe we should just tell them the truth, that we were making out and Bryan saw my visions, so I'm really not that crazy. Nope, still sounded crazy.

Bryan threw up his hands, nodding at me. "We were just trying to catch you, but it didn't work."

I lifted my hands, too. "Yeah, too bad. We lose." Admitting defeat was about right after what happened up there.

"Okay, I get it." Tony's head bobbed back and forth between us with a gleam in his eyes like he knew the truth. What, did my bright red lips give it away? "You don't want to pay for the subway, but I say you still have to buy that water and throw it—"

"You mean toss it gently." Brooke stared him down. "It's not a baseball game, no one needs to get injured."

He turned toward her. "Fine, toss it to the bagpipe guy."

"Deal." Bryan pumped Tony's hand, nodding his all-knowing nod. "Now let's go find some bottled water."

"Meet you in the lobby." Brooke grabbed Laura's arm and walked off with Lenny. She turned, tossing her head long enough to wink at me. Great, now my cheeks burned bright. That girl was good, not to mention subtle.

Bryan led me down a dimly-lit hall to a bank of vending machines set back into an alcove. Only the machines gave off any light, almost mood lighting.

He glanced around before he opened his mouth. "Listen, I'm sorry about what happened back there."

I banged my head back against the Pepsi machine, anything not to look him in the eye right now. "I'm not sorry. If anyone has to know what I'm going through, I'm glad it's you. As long as you don't think I'm crazy."

Those eyes locked on me, covered in shadows. Machines buzzed, but he didn't say a word. Anger welled up inside me, balled up my fists.

"You know what? I don't care if you do, at least it's out there now." I couldn't read his express in the dark, and it drove me nuts.

"Of course you're not crazy." He reached across me to feed a dollar bill into the machine, trapping me against it. When he pressed the water button, his hand grazed my cheek. I searched for something in his eyes, hoping they'd tell me what he was thinking. They flickered and suddenly his hand moved behind my head, his lips melted into mine again.

I threw up my fist to push him away, but ended up wrapping my hands around his neck. His arms encircled me, pressing me up against the vending machine. He tasted sweet and minty, his lips soft, his breath hot on my cheeks.

Then he inhaled deeply and pulled away. I rested my hand on his chest. "What did you see?"

He exhaled a low whistle. "You were right about the Noah vision, that was definitely him. Because it was meant for you, that makes this so much more complicated."

"What?" I reached for his hand, but he stepped back. Cold air filled the gap between us. "I don't understand."

He wouldn't meet my eyes. "I wish I could explain it all now. As a Guardian, I'm just a protector. My job is to stop people from being duped by Nexis and protect them. But you, your destiny is so much bigger than mine. If you were only the predecessor to the Seer, we might've stood a chance. Now that I know who you are for sure, I can't risk being a distraction to you. The world would suffer for my selfishness."

"Me?" My hand flew to my chest. "Who am I? I'm nobody."

"No. Don't ever say that." He pressed his palms on either side of my face, forcing me to look at him. I wanted to look anywhere else, but he waited till my eyes settled on his. "You are the one. You're the Seer. Your destiny is to stop Nexis and save the world, and that's the only thing that matters right now. Even if it means we can't be together."

"I don't understand, I can't save anyone, not even myself. I wouldn't know where to start." Tears percolated in my eyelids. How could this be true? "It doesn't make any sense. Why can't we be together?"

"We just can't. If the Watchers know who you are, then Nexis will find out soon enough. When they do, and they figure out you're dating a Guardian leader, they could lash out. Even call for war." His expression shifted, his lips set in a line of stone.

"That can't be true. War?" Now that I wanted someone in my life, I couldn't have him? Plus I was destined to stop some crazy group, while going against my parents? Not to mention war, or at least rumors of war. It didn't make any sense. "If that is being the Seer, I don't want any part of it."

"But you are the Seer, and you have to remain neutral. For now." He rubbed my temples with his thumbs, as if that would help. "You see, if the Seer joins one side, any side, the other immediately declares war. That's why we haven't let you become a full member. Because we weren't sure."

"For now? What do you mean, for now?" I stared at him, willing him to make eye contact.

He stared down at me, holding his gaze steady. "Unfortunately, war is imminent. The Guardians in Europe are close to declaring war against Nexis. If they do, America will follow."

"Oh." The word tasted pathetic on my tongue. "There are Guardians in Europe? Is that where my brother is?"

"I think so, but I'm still trying to find out for sure." He combed his fingers into my hair, halting as they bumped across my scar. "What's this, honey?"

I bit my lip. The soft way he said honey, and the revelation about James sparked hope in my heart. Since he finally told me the truth, didn't I owe him the same? "It's from the car accident, after I caught Jake cheating. Eleven stitches, three days in the hospital."

"Ouch. That must've been the first vision I saw." He parted my hair, pressing his lips against the bumpy ridges. "If only I could make it go away."

"I wish." My scar tingled with his warmth and I huddled into his arms. "Me, too."

"Hold on a minute." He smoothed my hair back in place. "Maybe that's why your visions came early. Don't you think?"

"I don't know." With a limp effort, I shrugged my shoulders. "And I don't know if I care. Right now I just wish I'd never seen anything."

"Don't say that, honey. I'm right here. I'll be here to help you every step of the way. Don't worry." His words sounded hollow and empty after all we'd just shared. His cold hand brushed against the small of my back, leading me to the lobby like a little lamb back into cruel reality.

I sank my teeth into my bottom lip, fighting to keep the tears in check. The truth escaped anyway. "Good, because I need you."

His lips curved. "That's my job, after all. To protect the Seer."

Great, more hollow words hurled at my already bruised heart. I tried to push them away, like I pushed everything else away, but numbness wouldn't come. Instead my whole body ached, more than the superficial injuries from the fire. Why did it have to hurt so much? A sharp pain filled my chest, searing me straight through. Maybe he didn't understand how much I needed him. How could I make him understand? Even I didn't understand right now.

I followed him outside, watching as the bagpiper caught the water bottle and tossed it back to him. That was supposed to mean all clear, right? Nothing about this night felt all clear. My life felt muddier than ever, all because someone finally knew the truth.

23

The musty odor of books hung heavy in the library. A few deep breaths of that familiar book scent calmed me, like a splash of clean water for my lungs. Lenny's contagious smile helped, too. Hard to believe he'd been all bruised up only last weekend. We'd all agreed to lay low for awhile, until Mr. Fearless Leader could figure out what to do. That might or might not involve telling every Guardian I'm the Seer, he hadn't decided yet. As if it was his decision to make.

For the poor beat-up guys it meant wearing baseball caps everywhere, even class when they could get away with it. Faint brown spots still outlined bruised circles under the brim of Lenny's hat, but with his freckles and red hair no one noticed any more.

The hiss of whispered rumors pricked me like tiny little daggers. A week later, and the murmurs still followed us everywhere. I tried not to choke on the déjà vu, tried to forget about the Alton High rumors that sent me all the way to Montrose. What would they say if they knew I was the Seer, like Bryan did? Even I couldn't believe it was entirely true.

Lenny didn't seem to notice the whispers around us. He waved me over to his table, bathing me in his happy spirit. "You doing okay? You look a little stressed."

How I needed the glow of his unaffected smile, the warmth of his sincere tone. Such kindness made me want to dump all my problems on him. But I wasn't that brave, not after all I'd had to carry this week.

"I'm just trying to figure out what's what right now. It's all such a mess."

"You mean the open dorm contest?" A little kid grin spread across his face. "Your floor having problems already? We're gonna crush second floor Nelson."

I didn't have the heart to tell him what I really meant. Let him think I only had simple worries like school-sponsored contests. Innocence like his should be preserved at all costs.

"At this rate, you may be right." Instead, I flipped open my English textbook. "What are you having trouble with?"

Lenny spun his book in my direction. "I can't get a handle on this crazy symbolism. Especially in *Paradise Lost.*"

"Yeah, funny how everything at this school revolves around the Bible." I thought I'd mumbled so low no one could hear, but Lenny caught my eye.

"You want to know why?" He propped up his book, dipping his head behind it.

I swept my gaze around the room, only four other students. I almost laughed at his antics, until I saw the semi-serious expression on his face.

"Because the school board is split between Guardians and Nexis." His deep words were muffled behind the book, but still, they pinged at me crisp and clear.

"Really?" I had to know, so I dropped behind the book cover, my head next to his.

"These people aren't just teachers, principals, dorm parents. They're prominent leaders from both sides, sent here to recruit powerful people," he paused and lowered his eyes, meeting my gaze dead on, "through their kids. To develop them into the next generation."

"So this place isn't just a training ground for both sides?" I leaned in on my elbows as the realization hit me smack between the eyes. "It's like an army recruiter's territory, for kids who don't know what's going on, and their parents, too? Is that why half the school knows, and the other half doesn't?"

"That's one way to look at it. But you didn't hear it from me. Got it, soldier?" He clicked his tongue between his teeth, arching back.

"Got it." I slid my hand over my heart, but the weight of it settled me. The Guardian versus Nexis feud was bigger than I imagined. The truth sank deep down, a million zombie butterflies eating me up inside.

"Good." He bobbed his cap and that boyish grin returned. "Now back to *Paradise Lost*."

"Symbolism, right?" The type jumbled together, meaningless markings on a page. I scanned the first lines of the epic poem until the letters rearranged into words again. "I like to think of symbolism as a vehicle for truth beyond the words, a truth that resonates deep within. If the words of the poem make you think of something else entirely, it could be symbolism, especially if it's a deeper level. Does that make sense?"

"Not really." He shook his head. "Maybe I'll give it another try and see if I can find something new."

I read the text from my own book, searching for some hidden meaning that could make sense of all the Nexis/Guardian secrets floating around in my head. As if John Milton knew all the answers. The Puritanical language threw me off. I had to dig deeper.

Right away, the word pregnant from line twenty-two jumped out at me. On the page, an image appeared of a black shadow, its feathery tentacles wrapped around a woman's swollen belly. I shoved my book across the table, but the image lingered like mist in the atmosphere. A shiver zinged up my arm.

"There." Lenny's finger pounded into the pages. "Line twenty talks about wings, and the next line about a dove. Maybe he used those words to represent flight and the freedom it brings. That could relate to the freedom that heaven and Earth experienced before the fall. Does that sound right?"

I glanced up at him. A bright light burned out the shadows, washing away my dark vision.

Peace flooded my heart.

My eyes welled up. "That's really beautiful. Exactly what Milton meant." He had no idea of the gift he'd just given me—freedom from the darkness.

Halloween night I stepped straight from my dorm room onto the streets of Hollywood decked out in cardboard and paper-mache. Pink and gold celebrity stars lined the floor from the stairwell, past our room, all the way down to room 220.

To walk down our hall the judges had to enter through velvet ropes that outlined a bright red carpet path, flanked on both sides by giant gold-painted cardboard cutouts of the Oscar statue. Behind the giant Oscars hung more cutouts of cameras with blinking flashbulbs. Speech bubble captions by the cameras read, "Over here," "Who are you wearing?", "You look fabulous."

After the Oscar mob, the scene turned into Grauman's Chinese Theatre where Laura laid down movie star hand prints as tiles on the floor. Then the judges had to veer single file around the huge Hollywood Hill, a paper-mache monstrosity that engulfed half the floorspace.

Somehow she'd roped me into spray painting that giant hill until I'd sneezed green and brown paint. Shanda finagled the easier job of hanging up movie posters with flashing Christmas lights. Even the fluorescent lights overhead were covered in colored tissue paper, a different hue for each section.

"Nice." I nodded at Shanda.

"Way better than spray paint duty, right girl?" She elbowed my ribs.

I rubbed my nose, careful not to mess up Shanda's perfect make-up job.

Laura and Monica insisted all the girls on the floor wear red carpet attire and do our best Hollywood waves when the judges came by. Of course, Shanda dressed me up like a Barbie doll in her silver sequined one-shoulder cocktail dress. In our doorway, I waved like a pageant princess and smiled until my cheeks hurt while the judges passed.

At the end of the hall Laura hung cardboard that accordioned down gradually like amphitheater seats leading to the Hollywood bowl. On the stage, she tacked up a giant picture of all the Nelson second floor girls with pasted musical instruments and microphones in our hands. If those judges didn't award her the title over Lenny, they needed to have their heads examined.

As soon as the judges disappeared up the stairs to the next floor, Shanda grabbed my arm and shut our door. "Let's go see if the boys are any competition."

I ran my hands over my sequins. "Shouldn't we change first?"

"No way." Shanda twirled in her ivory satin halter dress. "Let's go show those losers how fabulous we are. Then they'll *know* we're gonna win."

"If you're sure." A frenzy of double-espresso butterflies fluttered up my arms. I cracked open the door and pulled my fuzzy gray scarf from the coat rack, draping it over my shoulders like a shawl. After all, maybe a certain someone needed to see me in Shanda's gorgeous dress just to remember I still went to Montrose. "Let's pick up Laura and Brooke on the way out. I'm sure they want to rub their imminent success in their brothers' faces right now."

"You just want to see Bryan." Her eyes gleamed at me, was I that obvious? "And why not? You look great, that'll show him. I'll get Brooke, you find Laura."

I huffed out a breath, practicing my best runway strut past the decorations in Shanda's super-high heels. Sometimes, I wished I hadn't told her about that night, the elevator. But of course she'd insisted she just "had to know" why we were acting like awkward middle-schoolers every time we saw each other between classes or in the dining hall. At least she never teased me in front of anyone else.

I found Laura with a trash bag in her hands and my Shanda-tude kicked in. "Girl, the night's only begun, let's enjoy this while we can. You can clean up tomorrow. Right now you've earned some well-deserved bragging rights."

"You sound just like your roomie. Maybe you're right." She giggled at me, grabbing her purse. "I'll get pictures of third floor Denby, and put them next to mine in the Brewster family scrapbook."

"There won't be any comparison." I pushed her toward Shanda and Brooke.

She paused at the end of the hall to tell Monica the judges had been by. The gorgeous blonde was decked out in a full-on red taffeta ball gown.

"Don't you clean up nice?" Shanda eyed Monica up and down. "Like one of those girls who hands out the statues at the Oscars. How perfect are you?"

"Thanks, I think." Monica smoothed down her dress with a frown. "Someone had to be the belle of the ball."

"Don't mind her, you look gorgeous." Laura tried to drag Shanda out the door, but the poor little girl didn't have enough strength.

"That's always you, isn't it?" Shanda flipped her hair over her shoulder and flounced out the door.

I clicked down the stairs after her with Laura and Brooke tumbling through the front door behind me. Once we hit the night air, she finally turned around.

"Before you say anything, I know, I shouldn't be so catty. I saw her flirting with Kevin yesterday. She just gets to me."

"Can't say I blame you there. For some reason she's always seemed just a little bit off to me." A gust of cold wind blasted us, so I wrapped the scarf tighter and picked up the pace.

"Right? Thank you," Shanda said, throwing up her right hand like she'd finally be vindicated.

Laura rubbed her shoulders and edged close to me, while Brooke huddled against my other side. My teeth chattered as I tugged down the hem of the tiny dress Shanda talked me into. It barely came down to my knees.

Shanda didn't seem to notice the cold. Blind rage probably kept her warm.

"Maybe it's not what you think. It could've been a misunderstanding," Laura said.

"I know, you're probably right. I should just let it go. He's my boyfriend, not hers." Shanda rubbed her arms. "Wow, it's cold out here."

"No kidding." I turned my head to Laura and Brooke, rolling my eyes.

Our heels clacked against the pavement, a hollow sound on the almost empty sidewalk. We scurried for the warmth of the boy's dorm.

The third floor of Denby screamed its superhero theme at us. Lenny had decked the place out with giant paper-mache versions of Superman, Batman, and all the comic book heroes. He also had painted life-size versions onto plywood and cut out holes in each face.

"C'mon, let me get a picture." Laura practically shoved my head into Wonder Woman. Shanda peeked through the Batman cut-out, scowling as Laura snapped the shot. "Now get me and Lenny."

She handed me the camera, then hollered down the superhero tunnel. "Lenny, get down here."

A bright orange head peeked out of a doorway.

"Nice costume, Lenny, are you wearing PJs?" Brooke cracked up as he shuffled toward us in his black cape and faded Batman t-shirt.

"It's not as nice as your lovely outfit, I must say." He eyed the purple flowy dress she'd borrowed from me.

Her ears and neck pinked up, not from the cold this time.

"Nice, Lenny. Smile now." I held the camera to my eye, stifling a giggle.

"Wow." Bryan's whistle carried up the tunnel as he approached. "You look amazing."

I snapped the photo and the world stopped for a second. Caffeine butterflies fizzed up my stomach as our eyes met.

"That's the idea." Shanda twirled in the ivory Marilyn dress that contrasted perfectly with her chocolate skin. "You should see Laura's Hollywood set designs, it totally blows this out of the water. She could go on Broadway with those babies."

Laura's blush highlighted the emerald green of her a-line dress. Made me wish I'd raided her closet instead, if I could fit into any of her doll-sized clothes. I toyed with my silver sequined hem again.

Tony sneaked up behind Bryan, eyes glued on Shanda. "So what, I got to use a chainsaw for these cutouts. How cool is that?"

"Don't do your victory lap yet." Lenny edged us out the door and into the stairwell. "Kevin's creation is ten times better than ours. You've gotta see the fourth floor. You'll freak out. Literally."

24

We trailed Lenny up the stairs, straight into a long black dungeon. The lights glowed red, the walls were covered in black plastic, skeletons dangled from the ceiling. Ghoulish sounds echoed off the cement-brick walls. The creepy, sweet smell of dry ice fogged up from the floor in a misty cloud.

Shanda batted at the little skeletons. The movement triggered a net of cobwebs that dive-bombed us from the ceiling.

I flung my arms over my head as the sticky gauze swooped over us.

"My hair." She shrieked and the boys laughed.

Goosebumps popped up my arms in a wicked tingle, sending all the butterflies screaming away.

Lenny pushed a button on the wall and the spider-web net retracted back in place with a mechanical sound. "Done this a few times." His slightly crooked smile was half-shadowed.

I nudged Bryan in front of me. "You block the creepy things, okay?"

"On it." His chest puffed out as he laced his warm fingers through my icy-cold ones. His next footstep triggered a crash of thunder and flashing strobe lights. "Cool."

"That wasn't so bad." I clutched his hand tighter.

In the misty darkness, Lenny charged ahead with Bryan and me flanking his six. A fog machine hissed on my right, smoke billowing up from the floor. Suddenly Lenny jerked out of the way.

Tendrils of slimy goop rained from the sky. A scream tore from my throat, so shrill it pierced my skull and reverberated down the hall. I flailed my hands in the fog shooting up from the floor, squishing my fingers into dime-sized balls.

"Gross." Strings of peeled grapes swayed from the ceiling like a disgusting beaded curtain.

Bryan parted the grapes enough so I could wriggle past. "That was a good one, huh?"

I shook my head. "Not really."

"And we have a winner." A door busted open, splashing light into the dark corridor. Will sauntered out of his room as Kevin victory-lapped around him, both applauding, of course. "Best scream of the night, by far. That'll go in the hall of fame."

His hypnotic eyes synced on me like a morsel to devour. I halted right there, fog swirling around my sequins, as if my heels were glued to the floor.

Kevin held up a tiny recorder and played back my horrifying scream. "Nice one, don't you think?"

"Give it here, you creep." Shanda lunged for his hand, but he chucked the digital recorder to Will.

"Don't worry, we're just gonna add it to our sound effects for the haunted house. You know, give the kids a treat." He tossed the recorder back to Kevin who dunked it in his pocket. "What're you doing with them anyway? You're not supposed to consort with Guardians."

"Excuse me?" Shanda stuck her hands on her hips. "Like I can't have friends?"

"Shanda, you didn't …" I said.

She just shrugged at me. "What can I say? When Dad found out he forbid me to join. I just couldn't resist pissing him off after he dumped me in this God-forsaken place."

"I think Nexis is the most God-forsaken place here," I mumbled under my breath.

She gave me the barest of nods so imperceptible to anyone else, it'd just seem like a twitch. "Kevin and I hung out with Bryan and Lucy at the beginning of the semester. Didn't hear anyone complaining then."

Will gritted his teeth. "He wasn't on probation. But you may be stuck there for awhile."

"Yeah right." She rolled her eyes at him, then reached for the recorder. "I can still have friends, especially if they aren't on anyone's side."

"I'm glad that's still true, for now." Will yanked his arm away from Shanda, but his eyes lingered on me like a cobra, holding me still.

"You have your fun with it while you can." Shanda stuck her hands on her hips. "But you better watch your back, 'cause I will find it and destroy it."

"Thanks, girl." I forced my hand in the air and she high-fived it with hard smack. The slap broke the trance enough that I stepped back from Will.

He grabbed my hand, twirling me around in some kind of dance move. "You're looking lovely tonight, Lucy."

"How can you say that after what you just did?" I glared into his eyes—big mistake. Those gray orbs circled over me, as if one stare could sizzle me straight through.

Bryan's shoulders stiffened. In an instant he blocked Will's sightline, standing toe to toe with the golden punk.

He thrust his jacket at me. "Here, take this."

Will threw up his hands in mock surrender. "Relax, Guardian de facto, she's safe for tonight. But I've got big plans for that little girl. She's mine."

"Yeah, right, in your dreams." I churned my fists into mallets as I wrapped the familiar bomber jacket around me. I glared over Bryan's shoulder, but the warm fleece didn't stop my shivers. Will's chin jutted out at Bryan, like an olive-toned dagger with sandy stubble—aimed straight at Bryan's smooth marble cheek.

"You better back off, Stanton. She's not ever gonna join you sick Nexis freaks." His white biceps bulged from his dark t-shirt as he put up his dukes.

"Wanna bet?" Will mirrored his stance.

"C'mon, let's just go." I tugged on Bryan's shirt. He didn't back down.

Kevin stepped between them, clamping a giant paw on each of their shoulders. "Chill out, guys. This isn't the time or the place for this."

"It will be soon." Bryan dropped his fists and slid one arm around my waist, herding me away from the golden cobra. Waves of sweet relief splashed over me with each step.

"I've got your number, Cooper. I'm coming for you." Will's threat boomed down the hall, echoing with a tinge of disdain.

"I'll be ready," Bryan growled so only I could hear. In the stairwell he turned to me, his face softening. "I'm sorry about that, I shouldn't let him get to me."

"Don't worry about it." I marched him down the stairs to the lobby, his shoulders slumped, head down. "Besides, I look better in your jacket anyway. I wear it so much it feels like mine now."

"You look cute in anything." He held the door open for me. I glimpsed a hint of a smile as he moved his arm across my shoulders.

We stayed that way, huddled against each other, all the way back to my dorm.

"You've come this far, why don't you come up and see our hall?" I dragged him up the stairs to the second floor, as if a bunch of high school Halloween decorations could really distract him from all our problems. "What do you think?"

"This is awesome, you'll definitely win." He forced his lips to curve, but they just twitched and drooped back down. "Way cooler than that messed-up haunted house. They'll never win. Their hall is covered in trash bags."

"Really? That's awesome." I pumped my fist in the air. "I knew we had it in the bag. Wait till you see the rest."

Heat seared up the back of my neck as I guided him down the red carpet, past the theater, and around Hollywood Hill. After our kiss, and now this almost-fight with Will, I didn't know how to act around him.

I stopped in front my door. "This is me, but you should check out the Hollywood Bowl at the end of the hall."

"I'll be right back." He took off down the corridor.

I tried to open my door, but something pushed back. I bent down, picking up a silver tray with a paper triangle on top. The note read, *Prize for the Best Scream Award.* How could that get around so fast? More importantly, who could've put the tray in my room? I thought we'd locked it.

When I lifted the paper, a pair of eyeballs rolled back at me.

In a split-second my dorm room disappeared.

The rest of the real word faded away, too.

As if I stepped through a portal to another world, suddenly I found myself in the archway of a Gothic cathedral. With a blonde girl dressed in white staring at me like she needed something. She held up her own silver tray—except the eyeballs were real this time. Lolling back and forth like they were still alive.

When she looked straight at me, I knew who she was.

Her eyes weren't eyes any more. They sparkled like diamonds.

She was St. Lucia, she had to be, just like the "priest" showed us at the church.

She stretched out her finger, not at me exactly, but over my shoulder. I swiveled around like a marionette.

Something was shrouded in the darkness.

Then the onslaught came.

Shadows laced with sparks and lightning rushed at me. Wraith-like claws lunged for us, shrieking and seething in a burst of fireballs that exploded like fireworks—aimed in my direction.

I screamed.

A flash of light snapped me back into the real world.

Girly jitters erupted down the hall.

I dropped the tray with a crash of metal on hardwood. A peeled grape squished under my heels.

What just happened?

I blinked, dazed and confused but back in my dorm room.

I bolted out of my room just in time to see snatches of brass and honey-blonde hair, along with a swatch of red dress zipping to the end of the hall. The door slammed as the evil blondes disappeared into Monica's room.

Bryan jogged up to me. "What happened?"

I retreated to my room, plopping with a thud into Shanda's butterfly chair. "I don't know, I had the strangest vision. I think Monica and Colleen got a picture of it."

"What? You're joking, right?"

I shook my limp head at him.

"That's perfect." He threw up his hands. "She's had it out for me ever since we broke up. It'll be all over Instagram, Twitter, everywhere, in five minutes." He scooped the tray off the floor, one grape skittering into the corner. He chucked the metal tray across the room, hard. It clanged against the cement brick. "Were there two of these?"

The expression on his face said it all. The fear in his eyes, mixed with anger. I couldn't get a sound out. I just nodded again.

"Worse than I thought." His phone buzzed in his pocket. When he pulled it out it had an awful picture on it. Me, with my eyes half rolled back in my head, a horrified expression on my face. "Much worse."

"Why would they do something like this?" I rubbed my fingers into my temples, closing my eyes. The vision of St. Lucia flooded back to me, her sunken eyes sparkling like colored diamonds of crystal, amber, and black. Those jeweled eyes seared through me as if they could see into my eternal soul. I blinked fast, forcing my eyes to stay open.

Bryan twiddled his thumbs over his phone's keypad. "Don't worry, I'll make sure this is taken down as soon as possible. But it may be too late."

Laughter wafted in from the doorway. So it began.

Shanda strolled through the open door, followed by Laura, Brooke, and Lenny. "Screaming Psycho? What is this, Lucy, some kind of joke?" She foisted her cell at me.

"Yeah, thanks for rubbing it in my face." I swiped it away like a cat. "Monica and Colleen's revenge, I guess."

Her laughter died a silent death.

"They sent it out to everyone we know, the whole school. It's gone viral. That's cyber-bullying." Laura's pale cheeks whitened a few shades. "I can believe Colleen capable of something like this. Are you sure it was Monica with her, and not Felicia trying to get back at us?"

I shook my head. "Not unless Felicia suddenly dyed her hair blonde and stole Monica's red dress."

She gasped. "How could she do something like this? I thought she was so nice."

Shanda slipped out of her heels, pitching them in her closet. "That's exactly what she wants you to think. I'm going down there to give those dumb blondes a piece of my mind."

She met my gaze and I pursed my lips at her, nodding my thanks. A sliver of hope swelled up in my heart with that determined look in her eyes.

Bryan nodded. "Take Lenny with you. Maybe he can work his hacker magic and erase it from her phone or computer, or both."

"So devious." Shanda narrowed her gaze at him. "I didn't know you had it in you."

His jaw stiffened back to marble as he matched her glare. "Only when necessary."

"I'm on it, let's do this." Lenny shot us two thumbs up. "You distract them with a cat fight and I'll sneak in, got it?"

"C'mon, Laura, you can play the peacekeeper and turn the sweetness right back on her." Shanda stomped down the hall, claws bared, the twins on her heels. Her shouts drifted down the hall, mixed with muffled voices.

What if Bryan's brilliant plan didn't work? I crumpled into a ball in the chair, head in my hands. "How did this night get so twisted? I don't even understand what's going on."

Brooke scooted a chair up next to me, shooting Bryan a sidelong glare. "Okay if I tell her?"

He barely glanced up from his phone. "Be my guest."

"This wasn't just some practical joke or even cyber-bullying." Her clammy hands clutched mine, forcing me to look at her. "This must mean they know what happened at St. Lucy's. Maybe even planned it with the Watchers as some kind of retaliation."

"No way." Slowly, my head bobbed sideways, like a robot. "Wait, retaliation for what?"

Bryan's fingers stilled. "For Felicia being banished from the Guardians."

"You banished her?" The horrible word reverbed in my ears, a dissonant chord. "Because of me?"

I glanced from Bryan back to Brooke, who dipped her head at him.

That marble jaw was firm. "It wasn't my decision, Harlixton and the other teachers made the final call. But your evidence, along with Tony's trap, put the last nails in the coffin. She didn't take it well."

"So she sent her father to brand me? How sick." I traced the faint outline of the surface burn on my wrist. "What do these people want from me, to finish what they started?"

"It's obviously a threat." Brooke's voice trembled. She squeezed my hand. "If you don't join them, they'll just keep doing horrible things like this to you."

"Like I'd have anything to do with the Watchers, or Nexis after this." A chill crept up my legs. "Do they really think torturing me is going to make me join them? That's seriously twisted."

"You said it." His words came out staccato, rough with electric fury.

His fury seeped into me, burning away all questions but one. "How can you be mad at me? You never told me any of this, and now you expect me to figure it all out? It doesn't work that way."

"Hold it." Suddenly he closed the gap between us, his hands wrapping around mine. "I'm not mad at you, I'm mad at Felicia, how she could betray us so easily. Being a Watcher is one thing, but working with Nexis is another. I can't believe they'd resort to such intimidation."

"Oh." My cheeks cooled and I met his gaze colored with soft washes of blue.

"I'm just worried." He squeezed my hands. "What if they're planning something else? We should figure out some way to go on the offensive again."

Brooke rubbed her palms together with a fiery gleam that stoked her pupils. "I've been waiting for this. We can't let that stupid church incident keep us from playing the game."

"It's not a game." I snapped my head toward her. Had Bryan's younger sister really just relished something dangerous? Sounded more like something Shanda would say, not Brooke. "What did you mean 'planning something else'? What're they going to do, gouge my eyes out?"

Bryan stamped his shoe into the rug with a bang. "No way, not if I can help it."

Questions hammered my tongue, about Nexis, about us, but my voice box was frozen. Silent.

Footsteps pattered down the hall as Lenny raced in, hoisting up a thumb drive like a victory flag. "Got it. There shouldn't be any more copies of it on the net either. I zapped them with my mad hacker skills."

"Way to go." Laura high-fived her brother. "Score one for the good guys."

"What did I miss?" He stole a bottle of water from the fridge and chugged it down. After five gulps he crumpled it up and tossed it in the trash can next to me.

"We're going to find a way to get the upper hand." Bryan stood up fast, leaving a wake of cold. "This time I want to get one step ahead of them. Once we figure out their plan, we can beat them at their own game."

"Just what we need, a little diabolical thinking." Lenny fist bumped him. "Does that mean we're going to watch the Watchers' Tunnel?"

"Drastic times call for drastic measures, but not that drastic." Bryan lowered his tone, hunkering down over my chair. The others crowded around me in a Guardian huddle. "It's too dangerous right now, especially with them hunting for that tunnel. They could use it against us, and then we'd be right back where we started. No I'm talking about beating them at their own game."

He crouched down next to me as a foreign expression washed over his face. Those eyes drilled into me with a focus I recognized, but not from him, from Will. The specimen-under-a-magnifying-glass stare. "Don't breathe a word of this to anyone, got it?"

All heads bobbed, all except mine. "I couldn't tell anyone if I wanted to." Because I didn't know what was going on, but I bit those words back.

"That's the spirit." Laura pumped her tiny fist into the air. Sometimes she had so much of her brother in her.

"Wait, not even Shanda?"

He shook his head, gaze set on me. "Not even Shanda."

I narrowed my eyes at that smug stare, as if he could control me so easily. How could he be so tender one minute, so cold the next? This push-pull tug of war was starting to wear me thin.

More footsteps clamored down the hall, and I dropped his icy gaze. The huddle broke apart as quickly as it congealed, leaving me on my own again.

Shanda flung herself through the doorway. Only she could stomp so loud in bare feet. "That felt really good. Did we get it?"

"We got it." Lenny waved the evidence above his head. "This calls for a celebration."

"How about a Shanda scoot?" I watched as she turned to her closet, a huge, triumphant smile on her face. If only I could tell her everything, but of course, Bryan was right. The less she knew, the better.

25

The overcast November day circled me, filling me with its cold, damp sorrow. Even the low clouds taunted me with random droplets as I crossed the quad, ready to open the floodgates on me. I double-timed it up the concrete steps to Trenton Hall.

As soon as I got inside every eye stared my way, mouths whispering, giggling, murmuring. "Crazy girl. What is she, possessed or something?"

"Here comes the weirdo."

"Was she having a psychotic break or what?"

"Someone needs to lock her up."

How could I be reliving this nightmare again? Different state, different school, same rumors. I stupidly wanted to make my mark. This wasn't what I had in mind.

I curled deeper into my suede jacket, focused on each stomp of my brown boots on the marble tile. Stares burned into my neck no matter how hard I wanted to stamp them out. Practically everyone saw Monica and Colleen's social media stunt calling me the Screaming Psycho, a label that circulated like gangbusters. Gossip always spread like wildfire, no matter how far away from home I got. The rumors followed me with only a slight variation this time. But they hurt the same. And I couldn't let them see that.

Bryan's dark head bobbed above the crowd. "There's my favorite brown-eyed girl. Can we talk for a sec?" He led me away from the crowd and up the first flight of stairs. We ducked into the second floor bio lab. "How are you holding up?"

"Okay, I guess." Understatement of the year. I rubbed my rubber sole into the linoleum until it squeaked. "The moron who invented the Internet really sucks."

"I know." With his finger he traced circles into my palm. My knees quivered. "Bullies are ruthless, especially when they're Nexis puppets."

"Let's not talk about them. What are we doing in here, anyway?" The air reeked of bleach and sulfur, a potent combination. I bumped my hip on the black tabletop full of Bunsen burners, rattling the beakers poised above each station. Not the ideal place for a heart-to-heart.

"Just wanted to find somewhere quiet where no one would bother us." Heat surged from his palm up my arm, straight to my cheeks. Suddenly he dropped my hand, fishing a spiral notebook and pen out of his backpack. "Time to do a little research on you."

"What do you mean?" His eyes bored into me with microscopic focus. Not this again. My cheeks cooled. "Should I be sitting down?"

"Probably." He clicked his pen, like he hadn't heard the blatant sarcasm in my question. The click echoed in the empty room. "It's time we dig deeper into those visions of yours."

"Is it safe here?" I clanked down on the metal stool, staring at him. Morning light streamed in from the window, the sun finally deciding to break through the clouds. His tall shadow washed over me, shielding my eyes from the light. "Shouldn't we go to the chapel, or the school shrink's office?"

"We don't have time for that. Besides, even the chapel could be compromised after the Felicia debacle." This wasn't Bryan any more. Not the same Bryan who calmed my tantrum at the bonfire and rescued me from the branding iron. This guy was completely different, staring at me with his ice-cold eyes. Almost a stranger. "Tell me more about the first vision you had on campus, the Noah vision."

"Fine, have it your way." I gulped. "It was right in the middle of class. A man kneeling before a bright light, a booming voice. The words *covenant* and *blameless* stuck out to me. Didn't you already see this one?"

"Yes, but I want to know your side of the story, what you felt." Somehow, his tone rang hollow, void of its usual warmth.

"So now we're on different sides? I really should be lying down for this, then. Shouldn't you charge a therapist's fee?" The words spewed out of my mouth in a breath of venom. I slipped off the stool and clawed his t-shirt, yanking those aqua down to my level. "Who are you, anyway?"

A blank expression washed over his face. He didn't waiver for a second. "I'm the same person I've always been."

"No you're not." I sizzled him with my best evil-eye, but nada, not even a flinch. "At least not the same Bryan you've always been. You're acting like a robot, weirdly calm about everything. What's up with that?"

He just stared at me, with that unwavering expression. I reached out and pinched his flesh between my nails.

"Ow." He recoiled, rising to his full height. For a second, his face shifted from the strange calm into a normal emotion, like shock. "What was that for?"

My lips curved. "Just checking to see if you're for real."

"This isn't a joke, I'm certainly for real." He crossed his biceps over his chest, squinting at me with those icy eyes. "And so is Nexis. They're hurling everything they've got at us."

"No kidding, like I haven't already felt their wrath." I folded my arms across my body, mimicking his condescending expression. "It's not the first time I've been attacked by bullies. These guys should really sit under Becca's tutelage. They could learn a thing or two."

He actually rolled his eyes at me, like a five-year-old. "It's more than a little cyber-bullying. They're testing the boundaries of the peace treaty with stupid pranks."

"So all this is about some stupid peace treaty, huh?" I curled my fists, as if my tiny little hands could ever hurt Mr. Perfect. "You think that makes it okay to test me like a lab rat? That's not gonna help either one of us."

"Maybe it won't, but I have to try something. Anything." He threw up his arms with a force that blasted my hair off my shoulders. "They won't be satisfied until they get their hands on the prize. If that prize wasn't you, I'd say go ahead, take it. But they want you. That's all they want. And I for one won't let them have you." He stooped down until his face was inches from mine.

His nostrils flared with each breath, as if he had so much more to say to me.

Let's see if he could fight it now. "Why not?"

I met his gaze, eyes locked on him, daring him to move.

He flinched, but didn't step back. Instead, he toyed with a tendril of my hair. "You don't know what they're capable of. Who knows what they'll do?"

His fingers trickled down my hair to cup my cheek.

Electric shivers shot up my spine. "I'm not asking what they'd do to me. Believe me, I hope I never have to find out. I'm asking why you care so much."

I held my breath, searching his face, willing him to make the first move. Silence fizzled in the space between us. His eyes softened, his lips parted, but he didn't budge. Still as a marble statue.

Was he scared *of* me or *for* me? Or both? Had I imagined everything I thought he felt for me? The stupid questions of a silly schoolgirl who couldn't let go of the one thing she couldn't have—the guy standing right in front of her.

The silence stretched on forever until I couldn't take it any more.

I sucked in the last remnants of oxygen left between us. "Ever since the elevator, the only way I can get your attention these days involves Will or some Nexis prank. Why is that?"

"Are you saying that you're doing these things on purpose, just to get my attention?" He didn't move an inch, but his expression crumpled.

"Are you kidding me, how desperate do you think I am?" I reared back, right into the stool. The metal contraption tipped, clanging to the linoleum.

"I'm sorry." His hand wrapped around mine, forcing me close to him again. "I didn't mean that."

His touch burned up all my stupid questions like kindling, leaving a void of tangled emotions. How he kissed me in the elevator, saved me from the fire, yet said we couldn't be together.

"For someone who isn't supposed to be with me for some stupid, made-up reason you sure find a lot of ways to be around me." I squeezed his hand, as hard as I could. So he could feel the pain I struggled with. "Like studying my weird visions in a science lab. Who does that?"

"Believe me, Lucy, the reason is real." He squeezed back with his strong, painless grip until I relaxed my hold. "Your visions aren't weird, they're important tools that can be used for great good. Or great evil. Don't you see why we need to know more about them, how they operate, so we can figure them out? Maybe then we could get a leg up on Nexis."

I ground teeth together. One emotion finally won out and it boiled deep down, tensing every muscle. "Did you ever think my visions weren't meant to be shared? Maybe they're meant just for me, and I shouldn't have to tell you anything."

"You didn't tell me about them." He dropped my hand and crossed his arms again. "You didn't trust me, remember? Instead I had to find out by kissing you."

Now I really wanted to pound on him.

Instead, I slapped my thighs and huffed out a hot breath. "You make it sound like a big mistake, like you never should've kissed me at all."

"That's not what I meant." He edged toward me. "You should've told me, that's all."

"Right now, you're not inspiring me to tell you all my secrets." As soon as I had the full weight of his iceberg eyes, I let him have it. "In fact, this little stunt makes me wonder if I should go to Nexis willingly. At least then they wouldn't keep torturing me like you are."

With that I turned on my heel and sprinted for the door, out of the lab.

His deep voice called after me, higher and louder each time, but I couldn't let myself look back. The tears sliced down my face, running into my nose, my mouth. I swiped at them with my leather-jacket sleeve, but more saltwater replaced them in seconds. I couldn't let him see me like this.

I punched open the lobby door, jogging down the steps, then across the quad. No way could I face any classes today. Score one for Montrose, zero for Lucy. And I certainly felt like a zero.

A string of endless gray November days followed our fight—unending torture. Wind howled against the glass as I perched on my favorite windowsill, my Western Civ book open. Black and white type jumbled together in a blur of nothingness, my mind seesawing back and forth between Bryan and the drama awaiting me at home.

I couldn't face him, especially if he just wanted to study me. So I avoided him, skipping chapel meetings, ignoring him at lunch, between classes. My own brand of punishment, as if some time apart would make him admit his real feelings for me. It worked real well, especially on me, until the one question I couldn't answer blared through my mind like a foghorn. *Why couldn't we be a real couple?*

To him, I was no ordinary girl. According to the Guardians I had a destiny, to save the world from Nexis. That was all that mattered.

"Whatever that means." I could picture the words on his lips, but I'd never understand why it mattered so much.

Rays of sunshine streaked between the clouds, pinging drops of warmth on my face. I read the same sentence five times. Finally, I chucked the book on my bed. It was pointless. Everything felt like it was piling up on me, a steady stream of boulders on my back until I couldn't take one more ounce of pressure.

Tomorrow I'd be on a plane back to Indiana, but how could I face my own mother? Deep down I knew I had to hear her out. I'd pushed it back for too long, sticking to superficial topics in our calls and emails. I had to deal with her sometime.

The door banged open and Shanda breezed into the dim room like a whirlwind, alive and alight with energy. "Lucy, get up and quit this moping around. You look like I feel."

"Uh-oh, what happened?"

"Nothing much, Daddy's taking me to the Bahamas. Same old, same old." She threw her jacket on the nearest butterfly chair and rummaged through her closest. "What a great time for a vacation, don't you think?" Her usual sarcastic tone was laced with a sour undercurrent

"For Thanksgiving?" I popped down from my perch. "What's gotten into you, Kevin busy tonight?"

Her dark figure flitted back and forth in front of me, dumping clothes and makeup into her suitcase. "Yeah, busy with Monica and I'm free, forever. So tonight we celebrate."

"What happened?" My heart sank for the tough girl who might not be so tough after all. "Are you okay?"

"Please, I'm fine." She wrestled a bikini from the bottom of her drawer. "It's you who's falling to pieces."

"Thanks for that." I crossed my arms at her. "Hey, wait a minute, don't try to change the subject."

She buzzed back to her closet, her shoulders slumping. "Okay, I caught him kissing Monica and dumped him. There, you happy now?"

"What a jerk." I squeezed her arm, her almond eyes softening. "I'm so sorry, Shanda, you deserve a lot better than that."

"You're right, I do." She hoisted the black and white bikini over her head like a trophy. "I deserve a beach party."

"Not exactly what I meant, but okay." I grabbed my pink suitcase out of my closet and started packing right alongside her.

"I know what you mean, but I don't want to think about it." Her lined expression broke into a grin. "I've just been dumped and the beach is the perfect place to celebrate life without boys, right?"

"Absolutely." I paused my packing to look at her. "But technically you dumped him."

"How right you are." Shanda danced over to me and grabbed my hands, twirling us both around the room.

"Hey, I wish I could go to the Bahamas instead of going home." I laughed as we spun around. If only I could celebrate a life without boys right along with her. But I wasn't ready to give up just yet.

The notes of *Lucy in the Sky with Diamonds* trilled from my bedside table, the display flashing Bryan's name.

Shanda shot me her patented evil-eye, but went right back to her suitcase.

On the last ring I answered the call. "What's up?"

"I can't take this any more." His words tumbled out, as breathy as if he'd just jogged a 5K or something. "I thought it'd be best if I just gave you your space, but this is killing me."

My lips curled up, didn't mean to make the guy desperate. Well, okay, a little desperate. I fumbled for the right words, but nothing came out.

"I guess I deserve it. Listen, I'm sorry about the science lab, I was way out of line. I wanted to get with you before Thanksgiving, but I'm leaving for Pennsylvania tonight. Can we meet up after break?" His voice cracked on the last words, an uncertain note that melted me down to my toes.

"How's a girl supposed to say no to that?" There was more sweetness in my voice than I intended. "I guess you could pick me up at the airport. If you want to." I twirled a strand of hair around my finger.

Shanda waltzed up to me, batting her eyelashes. Why couldn't I just play it cool? At least my roomie seemed more like herself again.

"Great. I'll be there, just text me with the details." His voice brightened like I told him he just won the lottery. "Call me over break if you need me, anytime."

"I will." I hung up wishing I could see him before he left. If only I hadn't frozen him out for so long.

26

Dad's salt and pepper Einstein hair stuck out above the mob crowding the airline gate. My breath caught in my throat, but Mom wasn't next to him. I exhaled the biggest sigh of relief in the history of the world, bobbing and weaving around the human clusters standing between me and my dad.

"Sweetie, you look so grown up." He wrapped his big-bear arms around me, ruffling my hair. Some things never changed. "Montrose must be good for you."

"Most of the time." I bit back any hints of sarcasm in my tone. The less he knew the better. "I missed you, Dad."

"Me, too, Monkey." His eyes glistened behind his turtle-shell frames, as if he wanted to say more. "C'mon, let's get those bags of yours."

"Just one this time." I followed him to baggage claim, his arm slung over my shoulders.

"Really? That's hard to believe." A laugh rumbled from his chest. The Dad of my childhood still stood beside me, even if everything else in my life changed constantly.

The baggage carousel spilled over with luggage, a mosaic of colors blurring into its own pattern. Dad plucked my pink suitcase from the baggage-go-round and like a twelve-year-old again I trailed him to the parking lot.

When I'd picked out that bright pink suitcase four years ago I'd filled it with jewelry, dolls, and dress-up clothes. Now it traveled all the way to New

York with me and back again, scuffed and frayed from the trip. If that bag could take a beating and keep going, couldn't I do the same? I knew I had to.

"Hop in, Monkey." Dad hoisted my suitcase in the back of the van, then opened my door. "I'm surprised you're letting me get away with it."

"That's the last one." I wagged my finger at him as he climbed behind the driver's seat. "I only hung upside down on the monkey bars after you took me to the circus."

"Ahem, every year from the time you were seven until you were twelve." He started the car and headed to the exit, punching some buttons on the radio.

"Alright, you had your fun. No more monkey talk." Still, a teeny smile escaped.

"We'll see." He laughed his gentle, rumbly laugh again, turning up the radio. "It's one of your favorite songs."

The sweet refrain of *Mrs. Robinson* played from the speakers. "I just love the Beatles."

"Didn't we settle this years ago?" Dad shook his head as he steered our new Mercedes SUV onto the highway. "It's not the Beatles, it's Simon and Garfunkel."

"No way." I pumped up the volume until the bass vibrated the speakers. "It sounds like the Beatles."

"I think you can take the word of someone who was actually alive when the song came out."

I tapped the title into my phone. "Then they covered it from the Beatles, because it's all over the Internet that it's the Beatles."

"And the Internet is so accurate."

The DJ came on after the song ended, announcing *Mrs. Robinson* by Simon and Garfunkel. "No way, that can't be right."

"You're so stubborn, just like your mother." His shoulders stiffened, like he didn't mean to mention her.

I turned down the volume until the car was silent. "Why didn't Mom come with you?"

"She had a lot of shopping to do with Paige. There's a big dinner tomorrow, you know." A muscle in his jaw twitched as he kept his eyes on the road.

I chewed on my lip. "You know what I mean. Why is she avoiding me?"

"She doesn't want to deal with what she did." The life drained from his voice. "She wants everything to be happy and normal."

Like mother, like daughter. "Does that mean you know?"

I stared across the car at him. Slowly, he nodded, as if the truth weighed him down as much as it did me. "I'm sorry I didn't tell you when I found out, after James left. I don't know if it was the right choice or not, but it's the choice we made, that I made. I chose to forgive her, to work on our marriage, keep the family together. It's been hard, but I try to forget about it as much as I can. You should really think about doing the same."

"Forgive her? Yeah, right." The word resonated in my mind, as if somehow it were possible. Maybe for my dad, who elevated himself to sainthood with all his forgiveness talk. But not me, I had a long way to go to reach Mother Teresa status.

He cleared his throat. "It took me awhile to get there, and a few compromises. But it was worth it. My family is the most important thing to me."

"I know, Dad." I wanted to pat his shoulder, but I had to know. "What kind of compromises exactly?"

"Well, marriage counseling for starters." He flicked on his blinker, exiting the highway. "But the biggest was about Nexis."

"Really?" I held my breath, waiting for him to continue.

"Before I found out about James, I considered myself neutral on the subject of Nexis. I believed her when she said it was the best way to get into Yale. After they kicked him out just because he wasn't in the Seer's lineage, I realized what Nexis really was. A secret society, one your mother's been a part of since she was a kid. And I told her I would leave if she tried to make you or Paige join Nexis."

"Really? I appreciate that." I exhaled softly, just to be sure I heard him right. "So grandma and grandpa started all of this?"

He shook his head as he stopped at the light. "Not just them. It's been generations of Talbots. They've been brainwashing their children for years. Which is why I wouldn't let them do it to you."

I glared across the console at him. "So all that talk about Nexis and Yale was you guys backing off?"

"That was mostly your mom's attempt to have her way." He shrugged, the corners of his mustache lifting. "Like I don't know my own daughter. It was all reverse psychology, sweetie. I let it go because I knew it would completely backfire."

"No way." I snorted out a laugh. "You were right about that." But something in my heart clenched. I didn't want to be a pawn in anyone's game, especially not between my own parents. "But how could you let me think all those things about Nexis and Yale?"

"Sweetie, I don't care what school you go to or what group you join." At the next stoplight he turned to me with those teddy bear eyes. "I just want you to find some direction, to find your calling."

"Thanks, Dad. That means a lot to me." Relief washed over me. "I want that, too."

"Growing up is hard, but part of being an adult is learning to let go, learning to forgive. It's freeing, even." He reached across the seat and ruffled my hair again.

I lifted my eyes to the clouds, a silent thought stuck to my lips.

Could I really forgive someone who lied to me for so long?

In an instant, the sky changed.

A bright whiteness lit up the car like a burst of controlled lightning, suddenly dimming as the man from the hospital appeared on my left.

His golden eyes warmed my face.

"Lucy, it's a hard choice, one of the hardest you'll have to face. You must choose the light for yourself, or the darkness will consume you."

I heard his words clearly, but his mouth never moved. As if the message was only meant for me. "I don't understand."

"You will, child. When the time is right, you will." His eyes expanded to ten times their size.

Then, in a blink, they transfigured into a thousand golden butterflies that fluttered away, dissipating back into the clouds.

And the sky was normal again, cars buzzing along the highway toward the horizon.

"I know it doesn't make any sense, but we're doing the best we can." Dad's voice filtered into my ears, breaking my trance.

"I know, Dad, I just wish things were different." My words eeked out softly, as if the angel would come back any second. In my soul, the world made more sense when he was here. But when he left, it scrambled my brain with layers of questions. Would any of my visions ever make sense?

"C'mon, Pinky." Dad rolled my suitcase up the brick path to our yellow-sided home, shadows of dread hovering as dusk settled in. To me, this little tidbit Dad offered about generations of Nexis members on Mom's side was all brand new information. She lived with her secrets for years, only admitting the truth after James found out. How could I really trust her? Did they tell Paige yet? Those pesky thoughts niggled at my dread.

Dad swung open our red front door, clunking my suitcase onto the carpet. Mom's dark head hovered over the sink, a potato in her hand. Her face lit up when she saw me and she dropped the potato with a thump.

"Lucy, my girl, there you are." She dried her hands and rushed up to me, damp fingers wrapping me in a hug. "How I've missed you. Sometimes I wish we'd never sent you to that school. It's so far away."

I hugged her back with stiff arms, almost robot-like. The warmth I'd hoped for didn't materialize, from her or from me. As if we both knew what was coming. "I've missed you guys, too."

"Natalie, let the girl get situated. She's had a long flight." Dad lugged Pinky soundlessly down the carpeted hall.

Still Mom clung to me, as if she couldn't let go. "I just hope you know how much I love you."

I sucked in a shaky breath. "I know, Mom, I love you, too."

When she released me, tears sparkled in her eyes. "If I could change the way I handled things, I would. But I want you to know that I love James just as much as you and Paige. Your dad does, too. He's a good man."

She waved her hand in front of her face, as if she were swatting at a fly. "Let's not worry about this now. You get freshened up for dinner."

"Sure, Mom." I mumbled as she planted a kiss against my hair. I trudged to my room, shutting the door with a bang. How could she just dismiss everything away with a swat of her hand? As if it was no big deal that James was my half-brother, lost in Europe.

The flowers on the wallpaper leered at me, the pink polka-dot duvet cover mocking me like they knew all along. I was such a child for believing otherwise. I flopped onto the bed, freshly washed with snuggly softener as if it were some kind of peace offering that could make up for years of lies. I wish.

A timid knock at the door nudged me from my self-inflicted agony. "Come in, Paige."

My little sister peeked her dark head in. "Hey, you. It isn't that bad being home, is it?" She plucked a tissue from the box, handing it to me.

I dabbed at my eyes. "No, it's just Mom. We're sort of feuding."

"Yeah, I got that." She plopped down next to me, flipping her hair over her shoulder. "What do you think?"

"They let you go ombre at thirteen?" The entire bottom half of her raven locks were streaked with caramel and gold highlights.

"Tweens even get a discount." Her amber-brown eyes lit up as she fingered the ends of her hair. "My own little rebellion."

I curled my lips at her. "I can appreciate that."

Her baby-doll smile faded fast. "Listen, you should try to make nice with Mom and Dad. I heard them arguing the other day about yanking you out of Montrose."

I jerked back, my heart in my chest all of a sudden. "Even after Jake stalked me on campus? No way, I couldn't stand being at school with him and Becca. I bet everyone still thinks I'm psychotic, as if they never knew me at all. I've got enough lies to deal with right now."

Her tiny hand covered mine. "I'm really sorry, I should've never given him your new number. If I had known ..."

"It's not your fault, you didn't make him come to New York." I squeezed her palm. "Just try to keep them off my back, will you?"

She squeezed back. "You got it, sis."

She tiptoed out of my room, leaving the door open. I padded to the bathroom, splashing water on my face and applying a quick touch up.

As soon as I reached the kitchen Mom handed me the salad bowl. I set it down and slid into my chair, sensing the cockles of my stubborn streak waking up inside me. Better to stay out of the way and not make things worse.

At dinner I quietly munched my salad, our traditional pre-Thanksgiving dinner to leave room for heavy feasting tomorrow. I answered every one of her questions with a simple yes or no, until Mom slammed her bowl on the table.

"Why are you being so sullen?"

"I'm just trying to be polite." I shoved another forkful of lettuce in my mouth.

"Right." She sniffed, her knuckles white on the bowl. "You're just trying to say as little as possible."

"Maybe so." I munched on my tomato slice, desperately trying to tame the spurts of anger buzzing through my nerves.

"That's not good enough." She pried her clutches from the bowl. "We need to talk about your hostility issues. I don't know if I want you to go back to Montrose."

"My hostility issues? I'm not the one slamming bowls onto tables. My hostility issues have nothing to do with Montrose." I didn't dare meet her gaze, staring at Paige instead. "They'd only be worse if I came home and you know it."

"Maybe so." Her words mocked me now. "But then we could at least work things out."

"Yeah right, Mom." Electricity lit up my insides until I practically turned incandescent. I couldn't take much more of this. "You think I would forgive you if you forced me to move home? Back to a school with my ex who spreads lies about me and stalks me five states away. How could that possibly help?"

"Honey, that was months ago. I'm sure Jake feels really bad and wants to make things right. Everyone else at that school has probably forgotten all about it by now." Her tone turned syrupy-sweet, as if she had any clue what she was talking about.

And that really burned me up. I dug my hands into my jean pockets. "You don't understand what it was like, Mom. He drove all the way to Montrose, then followed me into the city. If my friends weren't there, who knows what would've happened?"

"He only approached you when your friends were around. Maybe it's not as bad as you think it was." The coolness in her voice killed me, so nonchalant, so unaffected by what I'd just told her.

The anger-bomb exploded inside me, bits of fury hurtling everywhere until I practically screamed at her. "You didn't hear a word I said, did you? You just don't get it."

I wadded up my napkin, chucking it at my plate. With that I made a mad dash down the hall.

"Lucy, come back." Her voice faded the closer I got to my room.

"I'm not hungry." I slammed the door behind me. So much for trying to make nice. I punched my fists into the pillow, willing myself not to cry. She wasn't worth it.

Maybe I could try to show a little forgiveness. My dad managed it somehow, and if James were here he'd probably tell me to get over myself. She was still my mother, after all.

Just then my phone buzzed. "Thank God."

Shanda's number appeared, another person who'd tell me to get over myself. Funny how she just knew I needed to talk the exact moment I needed her. Though I highly doubted she'd be as hip to the forgiveness part.

27

Soothing smells of turkey drifted to my nostrils, curling tendrils of comfort around my foggy morning brain. Bright light burned from my bedroom window, dimming as I rubbed my eyes. Thanksgiving morning and the smells were still the same, warm and heavenly as always.

Maybe I'd been too harsh with Mom last night, even Shanda said as much. Maybe she really had missed me, was only watching out for me. I'd just have to make it clear that I had to stay in New York, and Jake was the reason—not her. That should do it right? At any rate, she'd have to notice a new measure of maturity, and maybe even thank Montrose for it.

I snuggled my fleece pullover on top of my Montrose t-shirt. If only it were Bryan's bomber jacket, I'd be in heaven.

After I wrestled the tangles out of my hair, I barefooted it to the kitchen. Mom hovered over the stove in Grandma's frayed apron, looking more domestic than ever. I wrapped my arms around her waist.

"Morning, Mom. Sorry about last night, I shouldn't have been so rude. You forgive me?"

"Of course, honey." She patted my hands and handed me the wooden spoon. "Why don't you stir the gravy for awhile? Mom could use a break."

"You got it." I took the spoon from her and dunked it in the bubbling liquid. Bits of unidentified meat floated up as I stirred. "This doesn't exactly resemble gravy."

She smoothed her palm down my hair. "Well not right now, I've only just started it. It'll be perfect in a few hours."

"If you say so." I craned my neck to face her. "About Montrose, it's not that I prefer being there over being home. It's just Jake, I can't be around him. You know what happened the last time."

Her fingers winged across the bumps of my scar. "I think we can all agree, we don't want anything like that to happen again."

"That's for sure. Then you understand?" A crick formed in my neck, but I had to see her face, read her expression.

"Completely." Her eyes smiled at me, a surge of warmth swarming into my body. "Let's not worry about this now. Let's have a nice Thanksgiving dinner."

"That sounds great." I smiled back at her, for real this time.

For the next few hours we worked on all the Thanksgiving staples, boiling potatoes, mixing pie dough, sieving gravy. My favorite was throwing together the green bean casserole, mostly because Mom hated the less-than-fancy dish and everyone else loved it.

Before I knew it, mid-afternoon rolled around. I wiped my hands on the frilly apron Mom let me wear. "Maybe I should go freshen up."

"Good idea." She poured the pot of potatoes into the colander. "Why don't you tell Paige to come set the table?"

"No problem." I untied the apron and hung it on the hook next to the hallway.

Suddenly the front door whooshed open, sunlight streaming its rays around a tall silhouette. For a second it almost looked like James, or could it be Bryan? My heart stuttered at each possibility.

Instead Jake's frame filled the doorway, that obnoxiously cocky smile spread across his face. My heart sank, as I steeled my fingers into fists at my side.

"Who invited you?" It could only be one person. I turned to my mother, the traitor. "How could you? After the accident, after I told you how I felt?"

"Honey." She rushed to my side, clasping my hand in hers. "It's not what you think. He just wants to apologize, to make things up to you. As your mother, I think you deserve that. I think we all deserve that."

Fire practically flared from my nostrils. "If you want to listen to his pathetic excuse for an apology, do it on your own time. As for me, I never want to see that jerk again." I sprinted down the hall to my room and slammed the door.

Anger crackled through me with nervous energy until I couldn't sit still for a second. I fished my cell phone out and sent the horrible truth to Shanda. *Mom invited Jake to Thanksgiving dinner. What a sick joke. I have to get out of here NOW.*

On a whim, I added Bryan to the message before I sent it. Seconds, minutes later, my phone lay silent. Of course, they had happy Thanksgiving plans to attend to. I curled and uncurled my fingers, electric fury zapping up and down my whole body. I couldn't take it any more.

I rushed to my closet, throwing anything that could fit into my suitcase. Then a firm knock rapped on the door.

"Can I come in?" Dad's voice rumbled through the wood.

"Fine." I kicked the suitcase into the recesses of my closet.

He opened the door, his stubbled face full of worry. "I'm sorry, Lucy, I had no idea she'd invited him. I'm sure she just wants to hear him out, but this probably isn't the right time or place for that. I'm not here to excuse her actions. So I've decided that we'll do whatever you want. If you want to send him away, I'll tell him to leave."

The fire inside died a little at that broken look on his face, like a wounded St. Bernard. "All I wanted was to have a nice dinner. I'm not sure what to do."

His mouth curved up an inch. "You say the word, and he's gone. No questions asked."

I swallowed the lump of dread rising in my throat. "Maybe it's time to be a big girl and face him. At least you'll be here. What's the worst that could happen?" Famous last words.

"That's my brave girl." He wrapped me up in a bear hug and kissed the top of my head. "Now put on something nice. You know how Mom feels about Thanksgiving."

"I know." I rolled my eyes behind his back. "I'll be out in a few minutes."

Dad ruffled my hair and gently closed the door behind him.

231

I rushed to my closet, pawing through my clothes. A hideous gold knit sweater from Mom's favorite old lady store stuck out like a sore thumb. I yanked it over my head, then slapped on a headband and some pearls.

If she wanted nice, I could play nice. I didn't even recognize myself in the mirror. Perfect, I cleaned up like a fresh-faced version of Mom's forty-something sweater-set friends.

With a flourish I flounced down the hall, smoothing down my stick-straight hair and adjusting my pearls. An evil idea crossed my mind that I should spritz on some of grandma's perfume, but I swatted the nuisance away like a true debutante. Instead, I breezed into the dining room, plastering a smile all over face.

"Dinner almost ready, Mommy, dearest?" The added Donna Reed sweetest did the trick.

Mom dropped the spoon in the gravy with a splash.

"You look lovely, as always, Lucy." Jake's tone was almost as fake as mine.

"Thank you, Jacob." I chirped at him, but I didn't even give him a second glance. Instead I pranced into the kitchen and pulled out the potato masher. "With or without lumps, Mother?"

"Whatever you want, sweetheart." Mom's smile faded as she watched me mash and mash the spuds with a pounding intensity. "That's enough, darling."

"All ready to serve then, I think." I ground my molars together as if I could crush her misguided plans with sheer will. "Shall we eat?"

"Of course. Good everyone's all here." Mom dumped the potatoes into a crystal bowl, scurrying to the dining room table as if she could escape the Donna Reed me.

Right on her heels, I slid into the chair between Paige and Grandma, leaving Grandpa segregated on the same side as Jake.

"How perfect is this?" Even the gender bias played into my hands. Yes, the 1950s were still alive and well-preserved in the McAllen household.

"Shall I say grace?" Dad coughed, hiding any semblance of a smile behind folded hands. "Dear Lord, we thank you for the wonderful gifts you have given us. Please help us to always be thankful for your blessings, and to remember you in all we do."

"Amen," I said, louder than the rest of my family. "Please pass the potatoes, Grandma."

She nodded her sage nod at me. "You're very chipper today, Lucy. That boarding school must be doing wonders for you."

"I'll say. It's the best place I've been in years." I nodded back, thumping a pile of mashed potatoes onto the gold-trimmed china.

Mom cringed at the end of the table, but just spooned more stuffing on her plate.

Jake cleared his throat, his beady little eyes swinging around the table. "I'm sure you are all wondering what I'm doing here."

"I for one couldn't care less what you have to say." Paige's angry words silenced the rest of the table. She just shrugged. "What? I made the mistake of trusting this guy once already, and he followed Lucy all over New York City. I won't believe anything he says, ever again."

"Thank you, sis." I squeezed her hand and she squeezed back.

"That's one of the things I wanted to apologize about." Jake put down his fork. "I should've never gone to New York. I had this intense desire to see you. When I saw you with your new boyfriend I got jealous and just snapped. I'm sorry I did that. I guess I understand now why you ran into a tree."

"What?" I slammed my fists against the table. The silver and china clinked with a satisfying shudder. "Running into that tree was an accident. I didn't stalk you across five states."

"So it's true then?" His spaniel brown eyes laid into me, as if that begging-pup act still worked. "You really do have a new boyfriend?"

I narrowed my eyes into a laser beam aimed straight at Mom, the heat sizzling from my hands to my face. "How could you tell him that? It's none of his business."

Her face crumpled. "I just wanted him to know you'd moved on, that you're over him."

"Of course I'm over him, whether or not I have a boyfriend." If this were a cartoon, steam would hiss from my ears. "Why are you talking to him in the first place, inviting him to dinner? It doesn't make any sense."

"Child, calm down. Here, have some of your favorite." Grandma patted my hand and stuck a spoon between my fingers.

"You're right." I couldn't stand that she and Grandpa were here, watching me totally lose it. I shoveled in spoonfuls of green bean casserole.

"Does that mean you don't have a boyfriend?" His eyes bored into my forehead until I couldn't glare at him any more. "Do you think you could ever forgive me, or even think about taking me back? Because I still love you, Luce. I'd do anything to get you back."

I just glanced at Mom and shook my head. "Do you get it now?"

She bobbed her head, as if that were enough of an apology.

"I think you better leave, son." Dad rose from his chair, thumping a hand on Jake's shoulder. My heart soared right into outer space as he herded Jake to the door. My hero.

"Goodbye, Lucy." Jake's body slumped in the doorway. "I hope you have a good Thanksgiving."

I didn't move, I just watched him leave. "Thanks, Dad, Grandma, Sis." I nodded at them.

For the next ten minutes we ate silently until I finished my plate. "Great food, Mom. May I be excused?"

"Yes." She whispered the word, as if she couldn't afford to waste any more air.

I trudged down the hall to my room and stared at my cell phone. Two messages, one from Shanda that read, *Bummer holiday drama. Wish you could come back early and stay with me but Dad's drumming up some Caribbean biznez.*

The other message was from Bryan. *That's messed up. If you need me, I'll drive to Indiana and pick you up in 9 hours. Just say the word.*

At least that was something to cartwheel about. I read the message again, slowly savoring each word. That text was a lifeline, buoying me up and out of the nightmare I was stuck in.

I texted him back. *That's sweet, but I'll stick it out. As long as you're still picking me up at the airport Sunday.*

Two seconds later my phone buzzed. *I'm there.*

My toes tingled. I clutched the phone to my heart and rolled over on my bed, staring at those two words until I drifted off to sleep.

Sunday, the blessed day was finally here. At least Bryan would be at LaGuardia to pick me up, hold my hand, maybe even kiss me or some other silly nonsense.

I dragged my suitcase off the walkway, heading for the pickup zone. At the front door, my face reflected back at me off the glass, almost like a ghost. I smoothed my hair down and suddenly Bryan's frame filled the window with a heart-melting sight. The translucent picture of us together looked too good to be true.

Against the deepening navy sky, his face lit up like the golden butterflies. They buzzed in the pit of my stomach as he opened the car door and took my hand. It slid into his perfectly, like a dream.

"You look great." His eyes roamed my face. How I missed this.

My knees went wobbly, those baby-blues clouding up my brain, until the one question I'd avoided for weeks barreled its way back. *Why can't we be together?*

"I'm sorry you had a bad Thanksgiving." His soft tone evaporated my feeble attempt to formulate words. "About the lab, I don't know what I was thinking. I just want to find a way to stop Nexis, so they can't hurt you any more. You mean so much to me."

Rough fingers brushed my cheeks.

At those words, my insides leaped. All I ever wanted was someone to protect me, especially as my family crumbled around me. Yet, something held me back, like a checkpoint in my spirit. And I knew it wasn't the right time, for me or for him. Just knowing I meant something to him—more than "like," more than friends—it was enough for now. It had to be.

"Thank you for that. I'm sorry I gave you the silent treatment for so long."

"Good, we've got that settled." The way his face lit up, how his lips curved and his eyes sparkled—with one look, he said it all. "Let's get going."

He dropped my hand and lugged my suitcase to his trunk, my cheeks tingling with cold.

I slid into the Corolla, winking at Betty Boop. "Don't worry, I'm not going anywhere this time."

"That's what she likes to hear." He hopped in, turned the key, and the engine sputtered to life. "Should I even ask about what happened?"

"It was horrible," I shrugged, secretly wishing he'd wrap his arms around me and tell me everything would be okay. In my dreams. "My dad was sweet as ever, I even made up with my sister. But my mom is just getting out of control."

"Do you think it's got something to do with Nexis?" The brakes squealed as he screeched to a stop at the light.

"I don't know, maybe. I just don't know why she had to bring Jake into it." I dared to peek over at him. That furrowed eyebrow thing, a faint trace of stubble, a whiff of his soap and I was a goner. But I couldn't fall apart now. I had to pull myself together, focus on the task at hand, otherwise he'd figure me out for sure. "I always assumed Dad was the one pushing Nexis on me. But that's not true, he told me he doesn't care about any of it. So it has to be all her."

"What does she want to do, force you to join Nexis?" Cars whizzed past his puttering Toyota, but he didn't even notice.

"She tried that already, it only made me want to rebel more. Now it seems like it's about punishing me for not joining." All my muscles tensed, even my throat clogged up. "She even threatened to yank me out of Montrose."

"Honey," he reached across the gearshift and grabbed my hand, "don't worry about that till it happens. We'll get you a scholarship, or appeal to your Dad. I won't let you go back to your old school. Not with that deranged ex of yours running around."

"Thanks." His rough fingers danced across my forehand, shooting firefly tingles up my arm. "I hope it doesn't come to that. It's just that Mom and I both have tempers, we're both stubborn, and we both hate apologizing."

"Tell me about it." He lifted his hand, leaving mine cold. I gasped. "Sorry, wrong thing to say. My mom would tell me I'm being passive-aggressive. How's that for honesty?"

"Better, I guess." I forced a smile at him, but his hand didn't return. "I guess I'll just try to get through the next month."

"Speaking of the next month, I have something to run by you." He veered toward the Riverdale exit. "Since you gave me the silent treatment the last few weeks, Nexis has left us alone. Maybe we should make a pact, you know, to cool it for awhile."

His cold tone blasted shivers down my arms, banishing the fireflies. I rubbed my arms, but the numbness crept in. "You mean like some kind of distance pact? As in stay away from each other in public or something?"

"I mean no contact, at least until I figure out what their next move is." His jawline hardened as he pulled into the parking lot.

"Really? If that's what you want, then why are you picking me up at the airport?"

"So I could tell you in person."

How he could switch from gentle giant to cold robot in an instant, I'd never understand. Inside, all my muscles seized up, but I willed myself not to shut down. This time, I had to be the bigger person, the honest one. If only to show him I was ready for more.

"I don't want to stay away from you. And I don't know if I can." I bit into my cheek, willing my voice not to wobble, the tears to stay at bay. "I don't think it's a good idea. What if something goes wrong?"

"Believe me, it's the last thing I want to do. But it may be the only way to protect you right now." He shifted the car into park, and hopped out in one instantaneous motion. "Laura and Brooke are full Guardians, they know how to protect you."

"That's just perfect." I fumbled with the door handle, unpacking my stiff legs from the car seat as if they were molded there. I didn't want to move, didn't want to accept this strange alternate reality I'd walked back into. But his jaw was set, and he was back in marble-mode as he launched himself out of the car. "I really hate this. And there's no way I can change your mind?"

"Not this time. I can't help but think Will's vendetta is more about me than about you." His breath puffed out a blast of steam. "I hate it, too, but this is the best thing I can think of to keep you safe."

He rolled my suitcase to the sidewalk and we slowly fumbled our way down the cobblestones in the dark. Suddenly he wrapped his arms around me, pulling me close. The suitcase clattered to the pavement behind us.

"You better figure this out, because I won't last long." I squeezed his waist, holding on for dear life. "I'll miss you."

"Me, too." He tilted my chin up, until his eyes found mine. Fireflies swarmed again as he pressed his lips against my forehead. "More than you know."

Too quickly he pulled away, turning his back on me and practically sprinting down the sidewalk. I stared after his loping shadow until he disappeared, feeling more alone than ever. All of my hopes and dreams disintegrated into the dark.

28

The days were colder now, the crisp scent of snow tingeing the air. A lingering chill hovered in the distance Bryan put between us, as the month changed from November into December. I huddled into my soft comforter on my favorite window-perch. No matter how hard I tried to push him out of my mind, he lingered in the corners, waiting for me in my most vulnerable moments. I thought it would be enough to know I meant something more to him than friends, but I couldn't take it any more.

On a cold Sunday night, I knew I had to call him. We just had to work out some other arrangement, because this was killing me inside. After months of trying not to like this guy and failing, I needed to admit defeat. I couldn't deny my feelings any more. And I deserved some kind of resolution—relationship or no.

I dug my cell out of my new winter purse, a peace offering from Mom. Four rings later it went to voicemail, so I worked up the nerve to text him. *Whatcha up to tonight? Maybe we could hang out somewhere that no one knows us.* Yep, I was getting more than a little desperate.

Tempting, but I'm busy tonight. Maybe another time if I can swing it.

"How could he be busy tonight?" I punched the end button, chucking my cell phone onto the bed. It bounced and floated back to the bedspread with a happy little thud. The nerve of this guy. "He's just determined to keep this stupid distance pact. Pathetic."

"Enough of this, you've got to snap out of it, girl." Shanda switched off her desk lamp and grabbed her purse. "Let's get out of here so maybe you'll stop moping."

"I'm not moping, I'm thinking." I rolled over, only to catch her rolling her eyes. I grabbed my purse, too. "Fine, you're right. I'm starting to annoy myself now. What'd you have in mind?"

She dabbed on some berry lip gloss. "I'm in the mood for a good mocha. Let's go to the coffee shop."

"Coffee sounds good." I stared at my phone, as if sheer will could make it ring, then dumped it in my purse. "Anything to get me out of this dorm room."

We bundled up and scuttled downstairs to the lobby where Monica, Laura, and a few other girls played a game of Mafia. I waved to Laura, opening my mouth to invite her, but Shanda clamped a hand on my shoulder.

"Don't," she whispered in my ear. "I don't want Monica tagging along."

I shut my trap in an instant.

As if she had dog ears, Monica flipped her blonde hair over her shoulder. "You girls headed out?"

I glanced at Shanda, whose lips clenched in a straight line. "Yep, just wanted to get out of the dorm for a little while."

Monica nodded at me, a strange shadow creeping around her shoulders. Her lips curled up, twitching in an odd little half-smile. "Have fun at the coffeehouse, just be back by curfew."

"No prob." I scurried after Shanda.

"Thanks, Mom," she muttered under her breath.

At the front door I turned around for one last glance. The dark cloud had congealed into a serpentine mist hovering behind Monica, contrasting against her blonde hair. Almost like the shadows I'd seen around Will.

"Did I accidentally say where we were going?"

Shanda shook her head at me.

"Weird." A chill crept up my spine. Maybe Bryan was wrong, and Nexis had no plans to leave us alone. "I think you're right about that girl."

Cold night air blasted me as I opened the door. I zipped my black coat all the way up to the scarf at my neck and followed Shanda to her cute little red Fiat.

240

"Duh, you don't have to tell me that." She hopped in, barely waiting for me to close the door before she zipped out of the parking lot. With a flourish she zigzagged her way in and out of Riverdale traffic so fast it swirled my stomach into mush. The lights of the city blurred past, a twinkle of dots and sparks. She veered into the coffee shop parking lot in record time.

A familiar shape emerged from the shadows, and there he was, walking out of the coffee shop—with a brassy blonde.

"Is that Bryan?" Shanda gasped. Her arm flew to the door handle.

"Don't." I clawed at her hand, my nails clutching her leather gloves. I had to see it with my own eyes, exactly why he blew me off.

She turned to me and her eyes softened. "Don't you want to know what he's doing here, who the girl is?"

"I'm pretty sure I already know, but I want to see it for myself." I slumped forward in the front seat, sticking my nose as close to the windshield as humanly possible. "Because that girl isn't his sister, it's Colleen."

I watched the scene play out in front of me like a movie. Before he got to his car, she tugged on his coat. He stopped and said something to her she didn't look too happy about.

"What the—?" Shanda screeched, then clapped her hand over her mouth. He flinched, turning in our direction, and we slid down in our seats. "Sorry."

It didn't matter, her words barely registered, all my energy fixated on one thing.

Colleen tugged on his coat again, and the blood pumped through my veins faster and faster with each inch she got closer to him. Then she threw her arms around his neck and pressed her lips to his. He pulled away, but not fast enough.

Tears beat against my eyelids so hard I didn't know what hurt worse.

"Was that on the cheek, or did that girl actually kiss your man?" Shanda's snarl was indignant. "I have half a mind to go up there and punch that floozy."

Then in a matter of seconds, Bryan tucked Colleen into his car and they drove off.

"Now she's leaving with him?" Shanda's eyes were wide in the darkness.

The dam burst and water gushed down my cheeks. "Let's just go home." My words sobbed out shaky and hoarse. "Before I lose it big time."

"Whatever you need." Shanda squeezed my hand, turned the car on, and spun out of the parking space. "I could ram his car if you want."

"Thanks, but I've tried that before." I just shook my head, as if I could shake out the vision of him kissing her. But it was still there, clear as if I saw it five seconds ago.

Just like before.

I couldn't believe it, apparently nine months and a thousand miles of distance meant nothing. It'd happened all over again, my guy kissing someone else—and I had to watch.

Bryan wasn't even my guy, officially. Deep down, it hurt like he was. No technicality like a distance pact could get him out of this one.

Riverdale's lights were different at slower speeds, like a twinkle of hope in the blackness. Just not enough light to prick its way through the shroud of my present darkness.

Shanda's hushed tone shattered the silence. "Maybe it's not what you think."

"Maybe it is, maybe he's just like Jake." I spit the words out like they were infected.

"This isn't like him, did you think about that? Maybe it's all her, maybe she's the one who wants to get back together with him." Shanda stopped at a red light and turned to face me.

Streetlights cast wavy shadows on her cheekbones. When I finally looked her in the eye, she had her serious face on.

"It is possible, you know. Maybe *she's* just like Jake."

"Maybe." As we got closer to campus, I flipped down the mirror. Splotches covered my face, but I wiped away the teary remnants. Good thing I hadn't bothered with mascara.

Still, none of it made any sense. "I don't know what's going on any more."

"Don't say that." Shanda clucked her tongue at me. "It could all be a misunderstanding. It's possible, you know it is. Maybe you should trust him, at least give him the benefit of the doubt."

"Out of all of my friends, I never figured you'd be the one to stick up for Bryan." I flipped up the mirror as we passed the Montrose Academy sign.

How could two schools a thousand miles apart be so similar? I had hoped this place would be my escape, my sanctuary, but now I was worse off than before. A hollow ache crawled from my throat to my stomach, settling deep inside me.

"That's before I got to know him." Shanda swung her tiny car into a parking space. "We should've gotten out of the car and asked what was going on. He's a good guy, Lucy, there has to be an explanation for what just happened."

"People do stupid things sometimes." I reached for the door handle, but Shanda stopped me.

"Do you trust him?"

I peered back at her, an expectant expression on her face. Slowly, her words sank in. "I thought I did."

"Then maybe you should trust that this is all a misunderstanding. I bet if we just asked him right now, he'd clear the whole thing up."

I exhaled enough air to fog up the windshield. "With everything I've been through, I just don't know. I need to think for awhile. I'm going for a walk."

"Fine." With a huff Shanda let go of my hand and hopped out of the car. "Don't stay out too long. It's getting colder."

My arms felt like barbells as I opened the door. With every movement my body hung heavier, like it was weighed down. We trudged in silence back to the dorm.

At the edge of the sidewalk, Shanda hugged me. "You know where I'll be if you need me." Then she jogged to the door.

I kept marching, not knowing were my feet would lead me. They trampled a path on the dry grass until I reached the quad. The cold bit into me and I wrapped the scarf tighter around my neck. Out of the corner of my eye, a shadow flitted past. I turned in its direction, and saw him.

Not some kind of strange shadow-vision, but the real thing.

I blinked, but my eyes weren't playing tricks on me, it was Jake. The last person I wanted to run into on a dark campus with no one around.

The library's lights were still on, so I picked up the pace, booking it across the quad. *Please let me get there first. Please don't let him catch me.*

The warmth of the library covered me like a blanket as soon as I opened the door. I gulped in breathfuls of musty air, but calm escaped me. My heartbeat thudded in my ears, louder than ever.

Quiet filled the room, not a whisper anywhere. I turned and peeked out the glass door. A shadowy figure lurked outside, but I couldn't see his face. Had Jake spotted me, followed me? I ducked into the ladies' room just in case.

With shaky fingers I dug my cell phone out of my pocket. I dialed Shanda's number and it went straight to voicemail. She must've turned it off. Who else could I call? My fingers did the work for me, dialing Bryan—my last resort. It rang four times, then voicemail picked up. Immediately, I hit the end button as hard as I could.

Bet he was still with Colleen right when I needed him. Besides, what kind of strange message would I leave? Hey Bryan, I think my ex is stalking me, but I'm not sure. Oh yeah, and I saw you with yours so you better explain yourself. Probably wouldn't go over well.

What alternative did I have? If Jake really followed me across campus, I couldn't go back out there by myself. So I did the only thing I could think of, I sent a text to Shanda and Bryan. *Stuck in the library, Jake's outside. Please help.*

As soon as I sent the text, I stared at my phone. No one responded. I paced back and forth across the bathroom tiles, each bootstep clomping back at me. One minute went by, two minutes, five minutes, still no response.

Could I face Jake on my own? Maybe I could sneak past him if I stayed in the shadows, but the idea of it sent a shudder through my body. Maybe it was time to stand up to him, once and for all.

I poked my head out the door and saw no one around. My mind flashed back to the initiation, that horrible night that Nexis made us break into the library.

Then it dawned on me.

When I discovered the book, Shanda dragged me out the back door. If I was lucky, maybe I could sneak out that way again.

I zigzagged among the maze of tables until I reached the back row of stacks. When I rounded the corner, I stopped dead in my tracks. A pair of familiar eyes stared back at me, gray flecked with gold in the shadowy library light.

"What are you doing here?"

He held an old book in his hands, a greenish hardcover, not the Nexis book this time. "Just doing some research for a paper. You okay? You look as white as one of those Twilight vampires."

His hand grazed mine, but it held no warmth. At least there weren't any shadows around him this time.

"You're as cold as one of them." I met his gaze as his lips curled.

Those platinum eye softened, like maybe he really did care about me. "You must be okay after all."

His concern pricked something inside, like a dead flower bursting from the pile of ash Bryan left in my heart. If I had any shot at getting out of this, I had to trust this guy.

"I'm not okay, I saw Jake on campus and now he's right outside. I don't know if I can get out of here without him noticing. Maybe if I sneak out the back ..." As I trailed off my knees started wobbling. I couldn't look at him, what must he think of me? First I shun him and now I expect him to help me? I just stared down at my black boots, not knowing what else to do, what else to say.

"No wonder you look so scared. And I thought it was me." He slung his arm over my shoulder, pulling me into the crook of his elbow. "Don't worry, I'll take care of it. I'll call campus security." In an instant he pulled out his cell, dialed the number, and related the situation to them.

"Why didn't I think of that?" He almost reminded me of Dad coming to my rescue at Thanksgiving. I crumpled into his arms. His strong hands held me steady, stroking my hair.

For the first time in a long time, I actually felt safe. Maybe I was wrong about Will. What if he was the good guy, and all this time it was Bryan trying to reel me in? The overhead lights flickered as the traitor thought crossed my mind.

Could everything I assumed was true actually be false? It would flip my whole world upside down. Seeing Bryan with Colleen had already turned the tables.

"They'll be over as soon as they break up a mob at the stadium. Someone tried to start a fight in the middle of the championship game. Can you believe it?" Right now his gray eyes were warm and inviting, something I'd never noticed before.

"Of course, that's why the quad was deserted. Thanks for calling security." I chewed on my lip, staring up at him.

No shadows surrounded him this time. Had I made them up before, or had he changed since then? Words bounced around in my brain, the right words mixed with all the wrong words I'd said to him over the past few months. How could I have been so heartless?

Somehow, I had to fix this, I had to make it right. "I know I haven't exactly been nice to you these last few weeks. I'm sorry. I wish things had worked out differently. You have no idea."

"Me, too, Lucy. Me, too." He pressed his lips to my cheek, murmuring against my face. "For the record, you have nothing to be sorry about."

Easing back to look at me, his eyes softened. "Maybe I should check and see if the coast is clear, the library's about to close. Who knows how long it'll take to break up a football fight."

"I don't know if that's such a good idea. He's dangerous." Something gnawed at my gut, something akin to dread, but I pushed it back. Instead, I squeezed his hand. "What would I do without you?"

"You have no idea how long I've waited to hear that." His face lit up, then he nodded his he-man head bob. "I got this, you stay right here. I'll be back in a sec."

His fingers brushed my cheek, then he disappeared out the back door.

I stared at the bookshelf in front of me. The titles blurred together until it made my head hurt. Now it looked like Will was on my side, and Bryan abandoned my team—like black had suddenly become white.

Ten minutes passed as I waited, checked my cell, and waited some more. Not a word from anyone, Will, Bryan, or Shanda. A vortex of nothing.

I paced back and forth until I reached the last aisle, racking my brain for some kind of plan.

That's when the lights shut off, an announcement blaring over the loudspeaker. The words sounded like a Charlie Brown cartoon, but one word stuck out, *closed*.

Where was Will? Had he abandoned me, or worse, what if Jake had gotten ahold of him?

I tiptoed to the back door, pressing my face against the glass. Nothing but darkness and more darkness outside. If I didn't leave now, I'd be stuck in the library.

Maybe I could sneak into the woods and skirt the edges of the brush back to my dorm. It was worth a shot. I opened the back door just wide enough to slip out sideways.

Cold air whipped around me, still smelling like snow. I had to make it back to my dorm, fast—without getting caught.

I hugged the bricks with my back and darted across the darkest part of the open lawn until I reached the woods. I made it! I almost jumped for joy. I crunched into the dry grass, staying in the shadows of the treeline.

A familiar melody sang through the night air, *Lucy in the Sky with Diamonds*, like a siren. A stalker siren.

Behind me, footsteps rustled in the underbrush. Was he waiting for me in the woods? I couldn't let him sneak up behind me, so I raced back to the library and banged on the doors. They rattled, but wouldn't open. Why did they have to lock everything?

And there he was, dead ahead, face shadowed in the lamppost light. The ex I'd moved a thousand miles to escape was staring me in the face. So who was crunching through the woods behind me?

29

I stared at Jake coming toward me across the dead lawn, not knowing what to feel first. All those memories swirled inside me, the shock and horror of watching him kiss Becca, the sheer hatred seething inside me when they spread those rumors.

I tried so hard to let it go, to move on, but it happened all over again with someone I really cared about. It was all Jake's fault, and I couldn't let it go this time.

"What are you doing here?" I narrowed my eyes and jutted out my chin, balling up my fists, fight face on. I wouldn't slink back into the shadows this time.

Nebulous specters hovered near him, their murky tendrils hovering over his sandy head. "It's good to see you, Lucy. I just want to talk."

He took two steps toward me, I took two steps back.

"No." I locked my gaze on his, shaking my head so hard my neck cracked. "You know, Jake, I've had enough of you just showing up and demanding things from me. I don't want to talk to you. What I said at Thanksgiving is still true, I don't ever want to see you again. Why can't you get that through your head?"

Adrenaline coursed through my veins. It felt good to finally stand up to him.

"I just wanted you to hear my side of the story, Luce." His voice came out gruff, especially when he said Luce—way more creepy than sweet. "If you just listen to what I have to say, maybe you'll come back with me. I really miss you."

He flashed me that almost-innocent smolder he'd used on me so many times before. Now he looked more like a snake charmer. He lunged forward, his hand grabbing mine.

All of my emotions surged with adrenaline, congealing in a power I'd never felt before.

"Don't call me Luce." I shook off his grip, stepping back again. "What's your side of the story? You cheated on me with my best friend, turned the whole school against me, made my sophomore year hell, and for what?"

In the light of the lamppost his eyes were different, changed somehow. He looked haunted, not like himself. "That was all Becca, she was always jealous of you. I don't know what I was thinking. She wasn't right for me, but you are."

Smoke practically fumed from my nostrils. "Yeah, right, what really happened with Becca? She probably dumped you when she got into Princeton."

His face fell and I had my answer. "This isn't about Becca. Will you just listen to what I have to say? I've changed, really I have. I miss you." He turned those ghostly eyes on me, edging closer.

"Save it." Couldn't he take a hint? I backed up again, my shoulders jamming into something solid.

Rough tree bark snagged my hair. It was the same tree, the tree that marked the start of my new life at Montrose. Funny, now it might see the end of it.

I probed my fingers into the bark, my arms stretching as far as they could. Nothing within reach, not even a branch to swing at him. Fear pricked at my newfound courage, but if I didn't lay into this guy now, I might never have another chance.

"I don't care what you have to say. If you really wanted to tell me your stupid side of the story, why didn't you write me a letter, or call me on the phone? You haven't changed, you've gotten worse. You've turned into a stalker now." And then it hit me. It was true, he was a stalker now—and I was his prey.

"If I wrote you a letter you would've torn it up. I texted, but you wouldn't answer." He edged closer now, like he knew he almost had me.

I glanced around the quad, not a soul in sight. What ever happened to Will, was that him in the woods? Whatever I heard in the brush didn't show itself.

I was trapped like a caged animal with only one thing left to do, claw my way out. "Why don't you get it? I don't want to hear what you have to say, it won't change my mind. If you hadn't cheated on me I would've broken up with you anyway. You're a controlling, selfish, overbearing jerk. If you were a good guy, someone I actually wanted to be with, you would've figured that out by now. Instead you go around stalking me in the city and now on campus—"

"You know what? I'm getting really tired of you insulting me and calling me a stalker." He edged close enough to smell his disgusting aftershave. Strong fingers clamped around my arm. The once hovering wraiths swirled around him now, picking up speed.

"Ouch, let me go." I tore at his hand, digging my nails into him, but he grabbed my other wrist. I squirmed against his iron fists.

He tightened his grip, shadowy tentacles snaking from his fingers up my forearms. Unless campus security showed up out of nowhere, I didn't have a prayer.

Maybe that was all I had left. Why didn't I think of that sooner? *God help me, please. If I'm really the Seer, just send your angel or something, please.*

A pillar of light shot straight down through the black sky, wraiths screaming in its wake. Tendrils of lightning flashed out, sending the shadows screeching away. The lightning materialized in a vaguely human shape, unsheathing a sword of equally brilliant light, poised for battle. An impossible peace bloomed in my chest.

"Don't you see how much I need you?" Jake's low voice sent a shiver down my spine.

"I do see. It's clearer than ever now." I stared at the angel, mouth hanging open. I formed the words with my lips, but the sound didn't come out. *I am the Seer, aren't I?*

My angel nodded with his blinding halo of light, raising his sword toward Jake.

Finally, I knew the truth. But it only brought on more questions. If I really was the Seer, did it also mean I could command my angel?

"If you won't listen to me, I'll make you listen." He pinned my fists against the tree. The back of my head smacked into the bark as his breath steamed my face, eyes glowing with anger.

A shadow man morphed into being beside him, a pillar of dark mist taunting the lightning man who stood still as an ivory chess piece, sword lifted to the sky.

I blinked and blinked, but the scenery didn't change. Angel, demon, and Jake. I could only stare in shock for a few heartbeats.

I'd never seen Jake like this, it must be the demon-wraith. I had to get away, but he held me too tight.

"Please, do something." I whispered to the angel.

He nodded once and those eyes blazed golden and warm as the sun. He punched his lightning sword heavenward. A bright bolt crackled over my head.

I snapped my neck straight up to see purple electricity split open the sky above me. With a zap, it struck the great tree at my back. I whirled around as the huge trunk quivered.

The little hairs on my arms stood straight up, the static tingling as I put some space between me and the tree.

Shadows swirled and shrieked as a jagged line sliced straight down the middle of the giant oak. A rush of air and debris propelled me past Jake, into the empty expanse of lawn.

Freedom, at last.

I turned back to the angel.

Somehow his golden eyes twinkled at me as if he knew exactly what I was thinking. The slate was wiped clean, the past split in two. Like that dead tree, my regrets lay disintegrated behind me now.

Except Jake still lunged at me, his hand gripping my wrist, eyes wide. "What was that? There wasn't even a storm. Did you do that?"

"Sort of." A grin curled up my lips.

His other hand clamped around my free arm.

Desperately I combed the dark sky for the golden-eyed angel.

A clap of thunder rumbled from his light. Suddenly, as if the idea came with the thunder, I remembered the self defense lesson from *Miss Congeniality*, S.I.N.G.

Shackled by Jake's iron grip, I couldn't elbow him in the solar-plexus, but my feet were free. I lifted my boot and slammed my heel down on his instep as hard as I could. His grip loosened.

I wriggled free and started to run away from the library.

A dark specter screeched to a halt in front of me as Jake lunged for my foot. I smacked into the sidewalk, first my knee, then my cheek scraping the pavement. Warm stickiness pooled on my face, on the sidewalk. I couldn't think about that now. I had to get up.

Gingerly, I rolled on my back and kick-boxed his wrist with a vengeance until he let go of my ankle.

Above me the angel thrust his sword into the shadow. It split in two, just like the tree, sparking and screeching into a high-pitched inferno. With a low scream of wind and air, the flames sizzled and morphed back into one wraith-like form, tentacles hovering behind Jake.

The angel planted his fury behind me.

I scrambled to my feet, racing to the open lawn as fast as I could, footsteps pounding behind me. I picked up the pace, shifting into a new gear as I sprinted across the quad, lungs heaving.

Something yanked my right wrist, pulling me back so hard my shoulder cracked.

Pain ripped through my shoulder like a scalpel and I screamed in complete agony. I blinked as stars clouded my vision, matching the ripples of pain that shockwaved from my shoulder blade.

He spun me around to face him, clutching my other arm in his iron grip.

"Don't you see how much I love you?" His eyes read anything but love, more like a cocktail of anger and jealousy, with a dash of something darker. Something twisted, so twisted the shadows paled into innocence.

"You don't love me." I hissed through the blinding pain, my shoulder throbbing with its own piercing heartbeat. "You just want to control me."

"Don't say things like that." He shook me like a rag doll. The pain was so unbearable that I couldn't do a thing to stop him. "I do love you."

His lips puckered as he leaned in for a kiss. I turned my head and he slobbered on my cheek.

"Please, don't." My voice trembled, knees about ready to crumple to the ground. "Someone will come for me soon."

"That's why I'm going to have to take you somewhere else." His white teeth flashed, and then before I could blink he was dragging me down the path. "We've got to hurry, or someone might see us."

"I'm not going anywhere with you." With my good shoulder I crashed my whole body weight against him, thrashing and kicking like a wild dog. I couldn't let him take me somewhere, but it didn't do any good. "Someone, help!" I wailed as loud as I could.

He slapped his hand over my mouth. I twisted my head around the quad for a glimpse of my lightning angel.

Behind me, I gasped at the biggest light show I'd ever seen.

The sky flashed purple and white as lightning sparked across the darkness, shadows lashing at the lightning man with orange sparks. He swung his sword and cut straight through one wraith. It exploded in a puff of smoke.

He lanced the blade to his left, twisting it into a large swirl of shadow. It burst into flames, fireballs screeching from the epicenter in every direction like fireworks.

The angel swung his sword in a wide arc of silvery white across the sky. Then he pointed the tip at me and bobbed his head once. In an instant the searing pain in my shoulder eased, enough for me to at least see straight.

"What do you think you're doing?" Jake snarled, craning his neck to see behind me.

With a renewed burst of energy, I wriggled against his hold and screamed for dear life, only to be stifled by his hand.

"We've got to get out of here." He forced me down the path. With his hand over my mouth and me fighting him every step, we didn't get far.

Streaks of purple and silver lightning crackled above my head as my angel followed me.

A surge of hope welled up in my gut.

I bit into Jake's palm as hard as I could. He flinched and let go for an instant, all I needed.

I bolted as fast as I could across the lawn, then hit sidewalk. Fingertips tugged my hair, but my legs found a new speed. I turned around to see how far back he was. My cheek smashed into something firm, the muscle of a guy's chest.

I lifted my face, expecting to see the angel man. The eyes I stared into weren't golden, they were blue.

"Bryan!" I wrapped one arm around his neck, the other hung limp and sore at my side. He didn't look at me, just stared straight ahead and shoved me behind his back.

The streaks of lightning descended into a pillar beside him. I was right all along, this was one of the good guys.

"Just what do you think you're doing?" He clenched his jaw, fists balling up tight. I arched on tiptoes, peeking between his shoulder and the solid wall of light next to him.

"This is between me and Lucy." Jake sneered, drawing his arm back. "I don't want to hurt you."

Bryan inhaled jagged breaths, cocking his arm for an uppercut. The angel tapped his shoulder with a finger of light, and his uppercut sagged. "Like you hurt Lucy? I saw what you did to her."

"What is she, your girlfriend?" He cackled out a crazy laugh, one I'd never heard before. Bryan said nothing, his body rigid. "That's what I thought. She's mine, and you can't have her. There's nothing you can do about it."

"Yes, there is." Sirens blared in the distance. "I've already called campus security, they'll be here any minute. There's nowhere you can run."

"Uh-oh, not campus security. I'm real scared." He rolled his eyes. "What are they going to do to me?"

"They're going to take you to jail." Bryan's tone boomed with a deep note of strength.

"For what?" Jake raised his hands like he was innocent, such a dog.

"For assault. See for yourself, just look at what you did to Lucy." His rough hand grasped mine, squeezing softly. He turned to me, those aqua eyes full of pain, and nudged my good shoulder.

I inched forward, resting my one smooth cheek on his chest. The other cheek throbbed, probably still bleeding. I dabbed at the scrape with my fingertips and they came back sticky. My drooping arm started throbbing again, pain racking through my shoulder. I winced as tears stung my eyes, burying my forehead into Bryan's bomber jacket.

His hand stroked my hair, lips pressed against my temple. "How could you do that to her, don't you care about her at all?"

Blue and red lights flashed like strobe rays in the blackness. Footsteps clomped on the sidewalk behind us. I shuddered at the sound, and he wrapped his arms around me.

The angel extended his lightning hand, waving at me, his golden eyes closing. With a great rush of wind, his pillar of pure white shot up to the stars, sparkling like glitter in the sky until I lost his light-trail among the constellations. The pain in my shoulder turned blinding again, until I just wanted to skyrocket into the heavens right along with him.

The footsteps pounded closer, splitting in two. Campus security guards surrounded Jake.

I inhaled a full breath. "I know it now, I am the Seer." I whispered into Bryan's neck.

"You're going to be okay, honey." His hand grazed my hair, bumping against my scar. He didn't flinch, instead he pressed me in closer. "It's your destiny, and I'll protect you as long as you'll let me."

30

Jake stared at me, his dark eyes wide, shock etched into his freckled face. "I'm sorry, Luce. I don't know what I was thinking."

The bigger guy yelled at him. "Down on the ground."

He swiveled from the guy to the girl security guard, both in full uniform. Each had some kind of weapon trained on him, a taser, maybe. He shook his head in slow motion.

"Down on the ground. Now." The guard repeated, louder this time.

He lifted up his hands and slid to his knees. The officer planted a foot on his back, smushing his face into the dead grass.

"Put your hands behind you." Red and blue lights reflected off the silver cuffs as the guard snapped them around his wrists. He yanked him up by his biceps, shoving him forward. As he dragged Jake to the car, the female officer turned to Bryan.

"We're driving him to the police station in town. Take her to the security office so we can get her statement, then we can charge him. Know where it is?" Bryan nodded. She turned to me, wisps of black hair sticking out of her cap. "You think you can walk there miss, or should I call for another car?"

"I can make it." I glanced around the empty quad. How did I not know where campus security was? When I shifted to my right, pain sliced across my shoulder and seared through my brain. "Unless it's really far away."

256

"Young man, get her to the road, I'll call for backup. It should only take a few minutes. I better get back and help Dan." She jogged away, barking orders into her walkie-talkie.

Bryan turned to me, arms sliding around my waist, lines creasing his face. "I'm sorry I didn't answer sooner. I feel so terrible."

The images of him and Colleen zoomed into focus, but I let them fade away. It didn't matter now, none of it mattered. He'd come to my rescue. Even my angel trusted him.

I met his eyes, pressing my finger into his soft lips. "I'm just glad you came when you did. I don't know what would've happened if you hadn't shown up. My angel fought off so many shadows, but still Jake wanted to take me somewhere. I don't even want to think ..."

My own pulse pounded in my ears, but even the throbbing in my shoulder couldn't drown out the scary what-ifs. God knows what could've happened, what Jake the evil ex would've done to me. That's why my angel came. My lips curled at that thought—my angel.

"Shush, honey." He cupped his hand around my waist, steadying me. "Let's not think about it, okay? Everything's all right now. Everything's fine."

"Okay." I rested against his chest, slowing my breath to match his.

Heels clicked behind me. "Lucy, what happened?" Shanda gasped, her jaw dropping to the pavement as she checked out my right cheek.

I lifted my chin to show her my good side. "I'm fine now. Can you guys help me to the road? I think he dislocated my right shoulder."

Another set of red and blue lights streaked across the dark sky.

"He did what?" Shanda screeched. "Here, let me help you."

She put my left arm around her neck while Bryan braced his forearm against my back. But every movement, each little jostle, inflamed the fire in my shoulder. I couldn't help but wince with every step.

He paused. "Let's take it slow."

"This isn't working." Shanda's words jumbled together. She ran out of breath and bent over. "You should just carry her."

I turned to Bryan, lifting my good arm to his neck. With one fluid motion, he scooped me up without a word. I muffled a moan into his jacket, but his strong arms told me one sure thing. It was over now, I was finally safe.

He marched with slow and gentle strides to the security car as Shanda's stilettos clacked on the pavement behind us.

Students decked out in full Montrose colors milled around the car, as if they'd just come from the game. Lights flashed, illuminating their faces with blue and red. Maybe they assumed I started the fight, or something. Let them think what they wanted, it was better than the truth.

For a second I glimpsed a set of familiar gray eyes, a dimpled frown. Wasn't he the one who was supposed to call campus security? But then I saw his swollen eye. "What happened?" I called to him over the sirens, but no one heard me.

The female officer opened the back door for me and Bryan, pointing at Shanda. "You get in front."

Bryan lowered me into the backseat.

The officer shut her door and put the car in gear. "We'll stop at the nurse's office first, then take you back to the station."

"Wait, officer." My voice sounded shakier than I thought it would. "There was someone else with me, I think he's hurt, too."

She turned to look at me and I pointed out the window at Will. He mouthed something that looked like, *I'm sorry, I tried.*

"I see." She spoke some kind of code into her walkie and started driving again. "Another officer will come pick him up and get his statement. He might have to come to the infirmary, too. But he doesn't look as bad as you."

"Thanks," I muttered under my breath. She either didn't hear me or ignored me as she rolled the car through the crowd a slow as a parade.

"Will was there?" Bryan stared me down, but I just shot him a look. "No, first things first. I'm so sorry about Colleen. Shanda chewed me out good for that one." He inched his hand along the backseat until he found mine. "Monica told me she had something on you, something she was going to post on Instagram. But it was all a lie. Instead, Colleen showed up drunk."

"She what? I'm going to kill that girl," Shanda hissed. "Both of them."

My head throbbed with beats of pain and I rubbed my good hand into the back of my neck. "Why doesn't that surprise me?"

"I'm sorry. I never should've gone." Those blue eyes lost their light, filling up with such sadness. How could I still be mad?

"You could've told me first, but I'm glad Shanda was right about you." I tried to force a smile, but he still stared me down. "What? Will was in the library when I couldn't get ahold of you guys. He called campus security, then when they didn't come he said he was going to take care of it. I guess Jake got to him first."

"Likely story," Bryan muttered. Shanda snorted in the front seat.

"I don't know what happened to Will, honestly. He didn't come back." I leaned my aching head against the seat. "So I tried to sneak out on my own and it backfired. Big time."

And then it came to me in a whisper, delicate as butterfly wings. Maybe that's why this happened, because I tried to do it on my own. I should've asked for help sooner. Because that's when my angel came. Would he come again when I called?

"Hey, honey, don't worry. You're safe now, and that's all that matters." He squeezed my hand, a pained look on his face like he'd been beat-up right along with me.

The car stopped in front of a tiny gray shack behind the gym. The lady guard opened the door and Bryan carried me to the front.

A nurse in scrubs rushed out with a wheelchair and he cradled me into it. I squeezed his hand, smiling my thanks.

His lips twitched, his face disappearing as the nurse wheeled me away.

When I closed my eyes all I saw was that face, full of heartache. And I finally knew how I really felt about him.

The next time I opened my eyes, I was in a white room, another flashback to nine months ago. Would I ever stop repeating history?

A kind woman smiled down at me. "Let's see if we can get that shoulder back in place."

I nodded, grinding my teeth together as she stuck a needle full of something in my shoulder. She waited for my arm to relax and yanked it with one swift motion. Pain sliced through me like a scalpel at first, then disappeared in an instant. I laid back against the crumpled paper of the doctor's bed. Finally, I could to breathe easy.

With one great exhale, I fogged up the glass of my favorite perch. Flakes of pure white snow floated from the gray sky, trickling down the window pane.

So beautiful, so vulnerable, here one minute then melted away in an instant.

That could've been me, but it wasn't. Thanks to Bryan, and the angel who came when I asked. Especially thanks to whoever sent him. Would my golden-eyed angel always come when I asked, or just when I needed him?

A speck of red bobbed in the field of white, that silly hat his sister made. Bryan looked so small from up here.

I pressed my fingers against the cool glass. If only I could just tell him, if only those three little words would actually change anything. Yet I knew they wouldn't.

"You ready, Rapunzel?" Shanda wheeled a giant suitcase toward the door.

"Wasn't Rapunzel blonde?" I curled my lips, answering her question with another question. It didn't bother me like it used to. Hoisting my duffel bag over my good shoulder, I dragged my suitcase behind me.

My parents agreed I couldn't come back to Indiana for Christmas. Jake was out on bail, he even got special permission to leave the state because he was a minor. So much for the justice system. Still, they hadn't been happy about me staying with Shanda, especially Mom. But I couldn't face my mother and pretend everything was okay. Not with a crazy man running loose in my hometown. It was too much to ask, even for me.

"You're the new Rapunzel." She cackled as we lugged our bags down the hall and stuffed ourselves into the elevator. When the doors, closed she turned to me. "Besides, all the blondes at this school are crazy. It's time for a new reign."

"Hear, hear." I raised my right fist to the ceiling, happy to have full movement again, only a slight twitch of pain. "To the reign of Shanda and Lucy."

"I second that." She clapped as the bell dinged. We both cracked up all the way to the lobby.

Bryan rested against the Fiat, that red ski hat covering most of his dark hair. When he looked at me with those aqua eyes, I wanted to melt away with the snowflakes. Instead, I just let him load my luggage into the tiny car.

"I guess I'll see you girls in January." He closed the trunk, shaking Shanda's hand. "Take good care of her."

"Don't worry, I will." She punched his shoulder, ducking around to the driver's door. "I'll give you two a minute."

As the engine roared to life, I huddled next to Bryan. "I'll miss you."

Biggest understatement of the year. A trio of words waltzed into my head, but I held them in check. I couldn't take it if he didn't say them back.

His arms wrapped around me, holding me close. "I wish I could take you home with me. Promise you'll be careful."

"I will." Squeezing his hand, I forced myself to get in the car.

As we drove off, I stared at the mirror until I couldn't see that red ski hat any more. When I closed my eyes, even Shanda's swerving and sudden braking couldn't distract me. All I could think about was that stupid red hat and all the things I should've said.

31

We drove through the white city frosted with gray-edged streets. Shanda slushed to the curb in front of her condo. Snowflakes landed on the windshield, slowly melting as they slid down. In the distance, a speck of red dotted the white landscape of Central Park. It couldn't be.

"How on earth did he beat us here?" I turned to Shanda.

She had a huge grin all over her face. "What? I took the long way. So sue me." She nodded out the window. "Go on, I'll be inside."

As I opened the door, she nudged me into the cold wind, toward Bryan. I crunched through the snow until I reached him. His face lit up like a Christmas tree as I approached.

"What are you doing here?"

He pulled a bouquet of fresh-cut red roses from behind his back, holding them out. "These are for you."

I lifted the soft petals to my lips, inhaling the sweet scent. "They're beautiful, but I still don't understand."

His gloved hand took mine, drawing me close. "I couldn't let you leave without telling you the truth ... about how I really feel. It wouldn't be fair."

The air froze in my lungs, I couldn't move, couldn't breathe. I just stared into those eyes, biting my tongue. He pressed his forehead into mine, his breath warming the air between us.

"Lucy, I love you."

My heart soared as if it suddenly grew wings. I couldn't believe it, he said those words I'd longed to hear so badly. I parted my lips and I threw my arms around his neck.

"I love you, too." Finally, I told him the truth. It felt good, like a heaviness sloughing off my back.

"You do?" He inched back, then wrapped his arms around my waist. "I thought I was all alone here."

"How could you possibly think that?" Butterflies did a little jig in my stomach as he lifted me off my feet with the lightest touch, spinning me around like a china doll.

He lifted his head toward the sky. "She loves me!"

Chaos, confusion, emotions fluttered around me with the snowflakes. He loved me, so why couldn't I be happier about it? He stopped and set me down on the snow-packed sidewalk.

Something inside me snapped and I knew I wanted more. "What does this mean? We can be together, now, bring down Nexis together, right? I can't do it without you."

His gloves brushed my face, smoothing my hair back. "I know, honey. Someday you'll have to do it on your own."

I jutted out my chin at him. Sometimes I wished I could smack some sense into this boy. "You always tell me to believe in myself. Well I believe in you, I just wish you would, too."

A muscle in his jaw twitched even as those icebergs sizzled. "It's not me you have to worry about. You can't rely on me like a crutch."

Cold air slapped my face as I jerked back, yanking my hand away from his. "You don't really think that's what I'm doing. How can you say that to me?"

"I'm sorry, I didn't mean it like that." His eyes softened, but stayed on me. "I just don't think you see how much I distract you."

I arched forward, inches from his face. "And you just don't see how much you help me."

"That's exactly what I'm saying." His exasperated half-smile wasn't going to calm me down, not in the least.

"No it's not." I shook my head so hard my nose grazed his. "I'm talking about something completely different. Without you, I wouldn't know how to trust people again, and know I can't do it all on my own. After all, it's all about teamwork, right? Why don't you get that?"

He planted his hands on my shoulders. "But you *can* do it on your own, you'll see. My parents want to train you."

His lips were bright red from the cold. Maybe he was right about distractions, but not in the way he imagined. Not to me.

I couldn't think about that now. I had to get to the bottom of this. "What are you talking about?"

Those lips curved into his adorable little-boy smile. "I want you to come back to Pennsylvania with me to start your training." He searched my face.

"You mean like Seer training?" That had a really cool ring to it.

The idea rolled around in my brain, the workings of a brilliant scheme forming in the corners of my mind.

I could meet his parents, his sister, get closer to him. Maybe they could even help me control the visions, or at the very least help me figure out what to do when they came. I could learn how to protect myself. Only one question remained.

"What about us?"

He enveloped me in his arms. "I don't know. I'll talk to my parents, see if we can work something out as long as you don't become a Guardian. But there's no guarantee the council will go for it."

"Fine," I stamped my boot in the snow, "we'll figure it out at the end of break. Before we go back to Montrose."

"Tell me something, do you wish I hadn't told you I loved you?" His Adam's apple bobbed against my forehead. He was silent for a long time. Then he cleared his throat. "If we can't be together."

"No way." I arched on my tiptoes to get a good eyeful of him. A spark of hope danced in those baby blues. For the first time since Jake returned, I finally felt safe, and loved. "I've been thinking about it for too long now. I'm glad it's out there, it's the truth after all."

"And the truth shall set you free." His face lit up, making the whole world brighter.

"I'm tired of hiding, so let's be honest. Right now."

"I can handle that." His mouth smashed into mine. Then he murmured against my lips. "This is a much better way to study your visions."

"Quiet, you." I kissed him back. Those candy-cane lips made me feel alive, like I was exactly where I needed to be. When he pulled back, I stared up at him. "I can't wait to meet your parents."

Puffs of laughter blew into my face. "Not exactly what I wanted to hear right now. Does that mean you'll come with me?"

I met his eyes and nodded. "Absolutely."

His hands clamped on my waist and he hoisted me into the air again. We spun around and around, snowflakes dancing along with us. "She wants to meet my parents. You hear that, New York?"

"Yeah, yeah, get over it," a cabbie yelled out the window as he passed.

Bryan lowered me back to the snow. "I don't think so, buddy. Not ever going to get over this one," he yelled at the yellow car as it zoomed past.

My plan was already working out beautifully. Pennsylvania would be even better.

An hour later, the cold wind bit at my cheeks as a bus sped past. Shanda didn't notice, her arms squeezing around me. "I can't believe you won't be here for Christmas. What am I going to do without you?"

I patted her dark braids and squeezed back. "Plot some grand scheme to get back at the blondes."

Her shoulders bobbed as her breath puffed in my face. "Ha, intriguing idea, diabolical even. I must be rubbing off on you. What would your parents say?"

She pulled back, a huge grin plastered on her face. We looked at each other and busted out laughing.

Curtis loomed large over her shoulder. "Don't worry about your parents. I called them and took care of everything."

His hand clamped down on Shanda's shoulder and she hugged him, such a Kodak moment. They looked like the perfect family.

"Really? Thanks, Mr. Jones, I'm surprised they caved so easily. Who did you talk to?" I watched Bryan stuff my luggage into his tiny trunk, hoping Shanda's dad wouldn't read too much into my question.

"Your dad." His low voice rumbled over the traffic noises. "He sounded okay with the change of plans, but you're supposed to call him as soon as you get to Pennsylvania."

"Of course." I exhaled, my breath steaming out in a cloud in front of me.

"Go on, get out of here." Shanda tapped my shoulder, pushing me to the car. "I've got tons of scheming to do. Don't worry, I'll think of something. Believe me, it'll be good."

"Better be." I pulled her in for another hug. Behind me, the trunk banged and we both flinched.

Bryan wiped the snow off his gloves. "All set, you better get back inside. Have a merry Christmas."

She leveled her gaze at him, hands on her hips. "Now it's my turn to tell you to take good care of her."

"Don't worry, I will." He opened my door as if to prove it. She nodded back at him, grabbing her father's hand.

"You kids drive safe. Call if you need anything." Curtis waved as they crunched back to the condo.

"Goodbye." I cupped my hands around my mouth. "And thanks for everything."

Shanda turned and waved, eyes glistening. Couldn't be, was it the cold wind, or did I imagine it? My tough roomie disappeared through the front door. Tears welled up in my eyes as I climbed into the car.

Bryan shut the door, and I reached for a tissue. I hated goodbyes. Hard to believe I'd made such great friends like Shanda in only a few months.

The engine sputtered, roaring to life after a few seconds. "You ready for an adventure?"

"You sure this old girl is going to make it all the way to Pennsylvania?" I patted the tan dashboard.

"You betcha." He smacked the steering wheel. "I think it's my sisters you'll have to worry about. They'll want to know every little detail, about everything, especially Abby."

"I think I can handle it. I can't wait to meet her." I swatted the cardboard cutout of Betty Boop. "Speaking of sisters, where's Brooke?"

"Abby picked her up on her way in, thought we could use the time alone." He reached across the gearshift, clutching my hand.

"What an angel." That expression took on a whole new meaning now.

My mind flashed back to that night. The lightning man was no sweet little cherub. He was pure strength, pure power, fending off hundreds of shadows, all after me. What if I hadn't called for help? A shiver ran up my spine. I didn't even want to think about it.

"Speaking of angels, I've been meaning to ask you something." As the car slowed to a stop, he turned to me. "What happened that night on the quad? Did you see any angels, or anything else?"

"You didn't see it the last time we kissed?"

"Nope, just what happened at the Hard Rock." His head snapped forward when the light changed to green. The piles of white outside the window outlined his jaw, more relaxed than I would've guessed. "Looks like I've got some catching up to do."

Maybe my visions weren't such a big deal any more. Maybe he could help me make sense of what I'd seen, if that was even possible.

"After Will abandoned me, I ran into Jake." I clamped my lips together.

"I almost forgot about Will." His low growl filled the tiny car. He punched the steering wheel, swerving into the other lane. A car horn blared next to us.

"Watch the road." I snapped on my seatbelt, staring at him across the bucket seat. If I had to do this now, might as well get it over with. "He said he'd check and see if the coast was clear. He never came back. At first I assumed Jake got to him, especially after I saw him all beat-up. Come to think of it, I never heard from him or campus security about what really went down."

His knuckles went white against the steering wheel. "I can't believe that guy. I bet he had something to do with it."

"I don't know." I hunched my shoulders. Tension seeped around the car, even Betty Boop looked mad at me. My head ached until I couldn't take it any more. "Enough about Will, forget him. You'll like the next part. I asked for my angel, and he came. Like lightning, he lit up the sky and fought off tons of shadows. It was awesome, dazzling, really."

"Wow, the angel actually came when you asked? I can't wait to see that." His mouth curved as he looked at me. Warmth flushed my cheeks. "That can mean only one thing." He grasped my hand across the seat.

I squeezed back. "What?"

For a split second, his eyes met mine. "You're ready." Then he turned back to the road, hand over mine.

"Ready for what?" I studied our fingers, entwined together like one, exactly how it should be.

"Ready for training, ready to become all that you were meant to be." He eased the car onto the George Washington bridge, the waters of the Hudson glistening below us. "Ready to be the next Seer."

His words washed over me as I watched the river whiz by.

Was I really ready? It would be hard, even dangerous.

I'd come to Montrose to find myself. Somehow that meant seeing angels, demons, and prophets like they were straight from the Bible. But I couldn't turn my back on it, this was my destiny, who I was called to be. Somewhere, in the back of my mind, I settled into my new corner of reality.

"You're right." I squeezed his fingers. "I'm ready."

I watched the New York skyline disappear as we crossed the bridge and drove away from the city, a city I'd come to love.

He brought my hand to his lips and kissed the back of it. "You'll be the best Seer yet. You already have a headstart."

Was it a headstart or a disadvantage?

If we could keep Nexis in the dark long enough, we could wield it to our advantage.

So many mind games, so much to lose. Yet I knew it was my destiny, fighting Nexis. We would win this thing, we had to—for James, for the Guardians, even for myself.

Finally, I was ready. Let the training begin.

ACKNOWLEDGMENTS

No writer is an island, and I am no exception. For you, my faithful reader, thank you so much for taking the time to live alongside my characters in this story. It truly blesses me to know you're out there, reading my words. Many thanks to my husband Sam who encouraged me to keep going even when I couldn't see the light of day. I'm so grateful you understand how an artist works, that when inspiration strikes at one in the morning you just rub my shoulders and tell me to do what I need to do. Your love and constant support buoyed me up more than you'll ever know.

Thanks to my editor, Grace Bridges of Splashdown Books, who believed in me and my story enough to put it out there. After a year of struggling to find the right home for my book, I'm so glad I finally found the perfect place to spread my wings. Special thanks to Liberty Speidel for her brilliant notes in the proofreading stage. Also for Deb Raney, who encouraged me when I was down and was excited enough about my writing to show an excerpt to her editor. You have no idea how much that meant to me, so thank you.

Stephanie Morrill, thanks for being my sounding board when I was struggling through all the ups and downs of publishing. Your advice and encouragement meant more than you know. To all of my fabulous ACFW KC West writer friends who critiqued my work and brainstormed with me, Lora Young, Susan Hollaway, Donna Geesey, Sally Bradley, Christina Rich, Dan Schwabauer, Susan Mires, Holly Michael, and Bob Johnson. Thanks for being my writing support system.

Much love to my first readers, Kelly Irwin, Darci Webster, Whitney Potter, Jr. and Mary Potter. I cringe when I remember the rough drafts you

269

had to read. Your ideas and encouragement ultimately made this story into a novel. Thanks also to Allison Jones Choate for being my character psychologist and plotting czar.

For my family, without whose support I may have given up long ago. My mom, who provided me with the resources I needed to keep writing and is now as excited as I am that I finally got published. My dad, who always believed in me, even in the early days. My in-laws, Lloyd and Bunny Hartzler who love me like their own and encourage all my creative endeavors. Nick and especially Lindsay Hartzler, I love having another YA reader in the family to discuss books with. Brett and Joan Nelson, for understanding the writing process and taking beautiful author photos. Thanks for making me look good.

I'm blessed with such fabulous forever friends like Allison Jones Choate, Kelly Irwin, Allie Peak, Sarah Atkinson, and Tena Redenbaugh. Walking alongside you in this journey has been a joy. Thanks so much to my CBC buds who got excited about my early work and inspired some of my characters. A big shout-out to Rachel Pyles Worley, who read the early chick-lit short story and was the first to beg for more. To Michael "Boston" Brown, for lending me his sister's name for one of my favorite characters, and to his sister Shanda, who unwittingly is the coolest girl in this book. For my drama teacher, Glenda Mohr, thanks for believing in my writing from the get-go. The tortoise girl is finally in the zone. Also to my Called to Write crew, Corrie Lawrence and Carol Sharp, for taking the time to encourage me right when I needed it.

Many thanks to ACFW for being a place that nurtures budding writers. If I hadn't finally joined, I know it would've taken me a lot longer to get here. Finally and above all, my heart belongs to the light of my life, my Father God, my Lord and Savior Jesus Christ. I am humbled by the call you've placed on my life, and pray every day that I will live it out in a way that pleases you.

ABOUT THE AUTHOR:

Barbara Hartzler is the debut author of *The Nexis Secret*, a paranormal novel about a teen girl with a supernatural power to see the unseen world of angels. She has always wanted to write, not necessarily about angels, but the idea was too good to pass up. She's a born and raised Missouri native living in Kansas City with her husband and dog, Herbie. As a former barista and graphic designer, she loves all things sparkly and purple and is always jonesing for a good cup of joe.

The Nexis Secret is inspired by Barbara's college experiences and peppered with anecdotes from a New York City missions trip. She earned her Bachelor's degree in Church Communication Arts from Central Bible College with an emphasis on drama and media. In college she won a National Religious Broadcasters/Focus on the Family essay scholarship and wrote and directed a successful one act play. A Genesis Semi Finalist in the Young Adult category, she's an active member of her local American Christian Fiction Writers chapter. You can find her on Facebook, Twitter, Pinterest, and Goodreads, and her website where she sometimes blogs at barbarahartzler.com.

Look for her devotional *Waiting on the Lord: 30 Reflections* on Amazon and check out her playlists on YouTube.

MORE BOOKS BY BARBARA HARTZLER
THE NEXIS SERIES
Book 1: *The Nexis Secret*
Book 2: *Crossing Nexis* (November 2015)
Book 3: *The Nexis Conspiracy* (2016)
Book 4: *The Nexis Crusade* (2016)
www.barbarahartzler.com

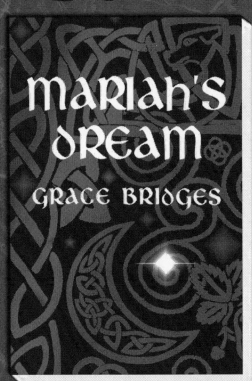

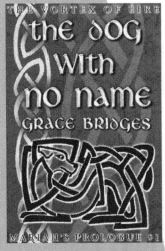 
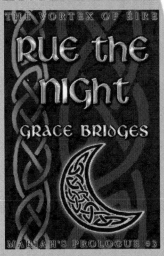 

Printed in Great Britain
by Amazon